PARTING SHOT

The Specialists stood at the rail and watched the boat pull farther from the ship. When it was about a half mile off, it turned and raced at what looked like full speed toward the luxury liner.

"He's making a torpedo run," Roger yelled.

They watched in horror as the small craft came closer. Then there was a billow of white smoke from the Boghammar and a torpedo jolted away from it and headed directly for the luxury liner.

An instant later the Boghammar exploded in a searing fireball that blossomed on the sea seven hundred yards from the luxury liner. Just then an F-18 fighter aircraft slammed over the scene at less than a hundred feet off the water.

"F-Eighteen," Roger said. "Their missiles hit that boat a few seconds too late. That torpedo is slanting right at us."

They watched the white trail of the torpedo as it homed in on the liner.

By Chet Cunningham

THE SPECIALISTS: PLUNDER
THE SPECIALISTS: NUKE DOWN
THE SPECIALISTS: DEADLY STRIKE

THE
SPECIALISTS

★★★★★★★

DEADLY STRIKE

Chet Cunningham

BANTAM BOOKS
New York   Toronto   London   Sydney   Auckland

THE SPECIALISTS: DEADLY STRIKE

A Bantam Book / September 2001

ISBN 0-553-58080-9

Published simultaneously in the United States and Canada

Bantam Books are published by Bantam Books, a division
of Random House, Inc. Its trademark, consisting of the
words "Bantam Books" and the portrayal of a rooster, is
Registered in U.S. Patent and Trademark Office and in other
countries. Marca Registrada. Bantam Books, 1540 Broadway,
New York, New York 10036.

PRINTED IN THE UNITED STATES OF AMERICA
OPM   10 9 8 7 6 5 4 3 2 1

This book is dedicated to all those who help hold the "ship" together, who do the necessary work that allows me time to write. To the real Kat, Kathleen, who smooths the way. My thanks to my coconspirators and wordsmiths: Peggy, Tom U., Ellen, Ken, Mark, Lynn, Judith, Marian, Beverly, Cyndy, Toni, Tom T., and Lee and most of all, to Rosie. My thanks, and thanks again.

★ THE PLAYERS ★

WADE THORNE, thirty-eight, the Specialists' team leader. He's six-two, 195 pounds, ex-CIA who quit to raise horses in Idaho. Eight years as a CIA field agent. He left the Agency when a Russian agent killed his wife and daughters. He can fly anything with wings or rotors. He's a master with weapons of all types, in hand-to-hand fighting, stalking, silent movement, camouflage, and surprise attacks. He's also a class-four chess player, Formula One licensed race-car driver, skier, loves to cook Italian food. Interested in Egyptology and has spent time there. Speaks Arabic, Italian, and French.

KATHERINE "KAT" KILLINGER, thirty-two, five-eight, slender, half Hawaiian and half English. She is second-in-command. A triathlon winner in Hawaii, a lawyer who has passed the bar in seven states, and an ex-FBI field agent. She has long, dark hair, a delicious golden coloring. She's gorgeous. Married at eighteen, divorced at nineteen, no children. Good with weapons, especially an automatic pistol. She has a sharp lawyer's mind, thinks well on her feet, uses karate, and has a historic Barbie doll collection. She's an expert on fifteenth-century Flemish painters, and speaks German, Polish, Spanish, and Russian. She volunteers at a school in London tutoring students in reading.

ICHI YAMAGATA, twenty-four, six feet, 175 pounds. A Japanese-American from Seattle. He's the arms expert for the team. He can repair, rebuild, customize, or create almost any small arm. He's a serious student of the Japanese Samurai warriors and a fantastic knife and short sword fighter. He is the silent killing expert for the Specialists. Had been a weapons expert for the FBI before being recruited for the team. Single, two years of college. A martial-arts expert. To relax he flies exotic kites. He speaks Japanese and Mandarin Chinese.

ROGER JOHNSON, twenty-four, six-three, 210 pounds. An African-American from the projects of New York. Kept out of trouble by playing basketball. Not quite good enough to be college-recruited, so he joined the Navy. Made it into the SEALs. Caught Mister Marshall's attention and received a "special circumstances" discharge from the Navy by order of the Chief of Naval Operations so he could join the Specialists. Knows various African languages such as Chichewa, Swahili, and Akan. Top demolitions expert for the team. Handles all explosives, timers, and bombs. He's the team's underwater expert.

HERSHEL LEVINE, thirty-one, five-nine, 145 pounds. Former Israeli Mossad agent who knew Mister Marshall from the CIA. He's a computer whiz. Can program, hack into almost any system, rebuild, and repair computer hardware. Fantastic touch in researching on the World Wide Web. His young wife was killed in an Arab attack in Israel six years ago. Still has strong ties to Israel. Keeps some contacts with former coworkers on the Internet. Quietly efficient, an expert on all small arms. Speaks Hebrew, English, Arabic, Kurdish, and Persian (Farsi).

DUNCAN BANCROFT, thirty-four, six-two, 165 pounds, blond, clean-shaven, soft-spoken, former English MI-6 agent who used to work with Mister Marshall through the CIA. A team player. Top intelligence man. Knows everyone, has contacts and friends in most nations. Can help procure weapons in countries where they can't take in their own. A bit of a loner off duty. Has a Ph.D. in English literature from Cambridge. Loves to sail his boat. Is a competition pistol marksman. Is divorced with two girls in Scotland. Speaks Danish, French, and German.

✸ FOREWORD ✸

Have you ever heard of working "in a vacuum"? That's what happens to many writers. They get so wound up and wrapped up in their subject and characters that they sometimes lose contact with the real world out there.

I don't want to do that. That's why I'm asking you to let me know what's going on in the latest technology in weapons, spying, black operations, clandestine groups, terrorists, and always covert operations that the U.S. is making that we're not supposed to know about.

Hey, let me hear from you. You can always contact me in seconds on the Internet. I'm at: chetbook@AOL.com. Yell at me anytime about what you like or don't like about THE SPECIALISTS. You'll hear back from me. Thanks.
—CHET CUNNINGHAM

★ **THE SPECIALISTS** ★
DEADLY STRIKE

✭ ONE ✭

Katherine "Kat" Killinger couldn't remember a colder day in Cairo. An unusual chilling fog and misty rain slithered around the old buildings, whipped through this out-of-the-way narrow street, and sliced through the tan cotton slacks, thin white blouse, and casual jacket she wore. The coat completely hid the Walther P88 9mm automatic pistol in her belt holster. She shivered a moment in the damp chill, then concentrated on staring through the thinning fog and mist at the two-story white-and-yellow office building that was the target of her stakeout.

Kat watched for a bomber. She and Specialist partner Duncan Bancroft were here at the invitation of the Cairo police to help them find the terrorists who were targeting American-owned businesses. Six blasts had taken place in Cairo in the past six weeks.

Kat pursed full lips. Her brown eyes wavered a moment and she closed them. She'd been watching this well-painted white-and-yellow office building for hours now and it was beginning to tell. This was the third day of the stakeout and she was starting to question their logic and their plan. She steeled herself for more waiting. The triathlons were more like this for pure energy sapping. Kat let out a long-held breath and leaned against the building just out of the misty rain. This whole street smelled of age and dirt and stale Egyptian tobacco.

The Geological American Oil Survey office she watched

stood just across the street and one building to the right. In spite of the rain, the street was peppered with people. An outdoor market a block down drew shoppers even in the wet. A pair of young girls with backpacks hurried past, chattering and laughing. People came and went from the small offices on both sides of the street. A dozen men and women walked past the survey office every few minutes. Kat studied them all. She tensed as a trio came toward the office on the far sidewalk.

A woman in full chador carried a parcel under one arm and a shopping bag that looked heavy. Close behind her a student with a backpack idled along in no rush to get anywhere.

The third person was a large man with a full black beard and a low-riding hat that hid most of his face. She tensed when she saw that the man carried a black suitcase. Two of the other bombings had involved suitcases. Her right hand hovered over the butt of the Walther.

Kat scrutinized the veiled woman. She was still one office away from the survey firm. As the matron angled closer to the building, Kat watched the man. He had moved to the outside of the sidewalk to pass the woman. He walked quickly and didn't even glance toward the oil firm.

The boy with the backpack couldn't be more than ten. She looked away from him and at the woman near the glass windows of the oil-company office.

A moment later Kat relaxed as the big man strode quickly past the target office and vanished up the street in the mists. The veiled woman hesitated in front of the oil firm, looked around, then continued past it. Two men dressed all in black hurried along the sidewalk blocking out Kat's view of the student with the backpack.

Then she found him. He was only four feet tall, slender with a tumbled mass of wet, black hair. He had stopped in front of the oil-survey office. He shrugged out of his pack. He reached inside it for a moment, then placed the pack against the façade of the store.

At once Kat pulled her Walther and charged away from the empty building she had been hiding beside and sprinted into the misty rain. She was still thirty yards from the youth.

The kid could have reached inside the pack to activate a bomb's timer. She ran flat out toward the office and saw the boy turn and rush away from the building, coming directly at her. He saw her in his way but kept running forward. The boy screamed something at Kat in Arabic. She didn't understand the words but felt his anger.

Kat charged straight at the boy. The youth glared at her, and screeched something else in Arabic. The Arab boy dodged to the left, and Kat stayed with him. He feinted to the right, then changed directions in a flash and jolted again to the right to go around Kat. She had played too much soccer to let him fake her out. She matched his moves and they slammed into each other.

Kat kicked out strongly with her right foot, hitting the boy's left leg and driving it into the other one, sending him into a stumbling roll on the wet pavement.

Kat loomed over him, the Walther put away, her small shoulder purse hanging at her back. "Get up," she barked. He looked wet and forlorn where he lay crumpled on the wet pavement. He couldn't be more than ten.

The kid looked up and yelled at her in Arabic. She had never seen such stark hatred in a face so young. It startled and pained her. How could one this young learn to hate that way? In an instant he rolled away from her on the slippery street.

Kat jolted forward and dived on top of the boy. He fought like a trapped wolverine. Before Kat could subdue him, the backpack bomb went off fifty feet down the street where the boy had left it in front of the American firm's office. The explosion created a raw force thundering through the street with a numbing roar that sucked the breath out of Kat. She automatically closed her eyes and ducked against the coming blast of hot air. The explosion shut off her hearing like a master switch had been thrown and she felt the surging mass of air that tore at her clothes and battered everything in front of it. The hot air seared past her where she lay on the street, then shards of glass, splinters of wood, and jagged metal fragments rained down on both of them like the spawn of a Missouri tornado.

In a few seconds it was over. The boy must have felt Kat relax because at once he pushed at her and screamed. He ripped one hand free and pulled something hard and black from his pocket.

A hand grenade.

Kat stabbed at it with clawing fingers. The boy humped against her hard and pushed her a foot to one side, then he jerked out the safety pin in the lethal bomb.

"I will gladly die for Islam," the boy shouted in Arabic. Kat only heard whispers of his voice. She surged forward on top of him, trapped his right hand, and tore the grenade out of his grasp. Her face felt tight, strained with terror, and her heart stammered, missing a beat, as she realized the grenade's arming handle had already sprung off. The bomb was ready to detonate. Dammit, she wasn't going to die on some rain-slick Cairo street. She had 4.2 seconds before it exploded.

Kat looked around and saw the empty building she had hidden near. She should throw the grenade through the window. But what if she missed getting it inside the vacant office and it bounced back into the street? It could kill half a dozen people. Her mind raced, picking and discarding options. Ten feet ahead Kat saw a storm-drain opening. Without another thought she threw the grenade toward the two-foot-wide hole, saw it roll into the darkness, and moments later the deadly explosive went off with a muffled roar.

The kid wilted. Kat caught both his hands and bound them behind his back with plastic riot cuffs. "Be good and I won't kill you," she rasped in English at him, not able to hear her own words yet, not caring if he heard her or not. She shook her head, trying to rattle her ears back into action.

The youth looked at her, his face mottled with hatred and fury. "If you don't kill me, then I will kill you," he brayed in English. Kat heard part of it and watched him closer. The unbounded hatred. How had he learned it? Who had sent him with the bomb? She had a dozen unanswered questions. He tried to jerk away from her grasp, but she held him down as she cinched another plastic riot cuff around his ankles.

The boy screamed in pain. "Wait until Uncle Abdul hears about this," he bellowed in English. "He'll cut you into little pieces and feed you to the vultures. We are the Sword of Allah!"

"Sure you are but your sword is a bit rusty. For a long time, little wild dog, you won't swing your sword at anyone." Kat grinned as she realized she had heard some of her words. Her ears were starting to work again. Her left arm hurt and when she looked down, she saw a jagged three-inch piece of window glass sticking out of the sleeve of her jacket. It had produced a stain of blood on the fabric. Delicately she pulled the glass out and dropped it. Sirens wailed in the distance. Dozens of people poured out of surrounding buildings to see what had happened.

A Cairo police car with red lights flashing hooted its way down the street, parting the growing crowd. It rolled past Kat and the boy and stopped near the blasted white-and-yellow office. An ambulance whined in from the other direction. More police cars arrived and before Kat could move the boy, Duncan Bancroft came running up.

Duncan was her partner on this mission, and a former member of Her Majesty's MI-6 Secret Service. He was two inches over six feet and a little thin at 165 pounds.

"Kat, what have you here? I think you outweigh him. Let's throw him back and look for the real bomber."

"This one will have to do," Kat said. She noticed how shaggy Duncan had let his blond hair grow. His nose was too large for his otherwise handsome face and his blue eyes glistened. Now his high-cheekboned face frowned as he looked down at the trussed-up youth.

"You mean this is our bomber? He hit your stakeout." Duncan knelt beside the boy. "Son, you should be in about the fifth grade. What the hell you doing carrying around bombs?"

"The little darling looks like he loves it. He's a tough cookie."

"I will kill you both," the boy shouted in English. "I am

the Sword of Allah, the vengeful wrath of Islam. I will kill all Americans. It is my duty." His eyes blazed with a white-hot fury.

Duncan turned the boy over on his stomach where he lay on the wet blacktop, and frisked him. He found a four-inch switchblade, another hand grenade, and a .22 caliber revolver.

"Well, you're a walking arsenal, little man," Duncan said. "Why didn't you bring along a missile or two and an RPG?"

Kat put the weapons in her shoulder purse.

"We better get this one down there to the cops," Duncan said. He hoisted the boy over his shoulder like a sack of wheat, and they walked fifty feet to the yellow tape the police had put around the blast scene. The misty rain had stopped.

Kat stared at the total ruin of the oil-company office. The second floor leaned precariously forward, slanting halfway to the ground. The rubble of smashed furniture, glass, and business machines littered the sidewalk. A pair of medics carried a woman on a stretcher from inside the shattered building and put her in a red-and-white ambulance.

They found the blue-uniformed senior Cairo police officer on the scene, a captain who stood two inches shorter than Kat. He had a gloriously thick mustache and a tired expression indicating he had seen all of this before. They showed him their special ID badges issued by the Cairo police chief. The captain grunted, asked another officer to translate. He made no effort to understand their English.

The translating officer was short and heavy. He smiled at them. "My name is Lieutenant Hosni. Our captain doesn't do English. He understands your special status with the chief. You captured the boy?"

Lieutenant Hosni smiled at them again. His English was British-tinged and perfect. He was shorter than Duncan. He looked at Kat with trusting brown eyes. The misty rain began again, and he let the wetness drip unnoticed from his garrison uniform hat onto his shoulders. Lieutenant Hosni motioned at the boy bomber, who had been stood up and was now flanked by two uniformed Cairo officers.

Kat went through the scenario quickly, explaining what she and Duncan had done.

Hosni repeated the facts to the captain who responded.

"My captain says you did a good job. Now you need to come to police headquarters and swear a deposition of what you saw and did, so it can be used in court. We also have found two other witnesses who saw this boy leave the bomb and run away. We should be able to convict him easily. We will go downtown now, yes?"

It took the rest of the afternoon and until after eight that evening before the Cairo police were satisfied with the statements. Kat's deposition was given before a judge, and taken down by video camera, tape recorder, and a court reporter.

Kat and Duncan were finishing coffee in the police cafeteria when Lieutenant Hosni came and sat beside them.

"Small fry," Hosni said. "Our chief and two detectives say this kid you caught is only a delivery boy. You say, small potatoes."

"Do you know who he worked for?" Kat asked.

"Yes, now we have proof. The boy talked after some persuasion. Unfortunately, he suffered a broken right arm in a fall. Then his memory improved. We have a name and address if you wish to come with us on the raid."

"Yes," Kat said at once. "We need to see this through. When do we go?"

"Right now," Hosni said.

The two Specialists had checked their bag of weapons, containing everything but their pistols, at police headquarters when they arrived two days before. Now they were allowed to take with them their H & K MP-5 9mm submachine guns. The eight Egyptian plainclothes detectives all carried new model Uzis. They went in two cars. The drive lasted a half hour and wound at last into an outlying section of Cairo, a city of almost ten million people.

The street was not paved. Streetlights showed only every quarter of a mile and the houses were older and not well maintained. There was a lingering smell of raw sewage and decay in the air. They stopped the cars half a block from the target. It was one story, with a falling-down wooden fence in front. There were no houses close on either side. The Egyptian detectives carried small radios. Four men went to the rear of the house without causing any alarm. Four detectives covered the front. Kat and Duncan each watched one side of the structure.

On a radio signal, flash-bang grenades crashed through windows and exploded inside the front and back rooms. At the same time the Cairo detectives kicked in the front and back doors and stormed inside as Kat and Duncan kept watch on the sides of the house.

Only a few seconds after the Egyptians surged into the place, two men jumped out a ground-floor window on Kat's side. She lifted the MP-5 and chattered three rounds at the first man. He took the rounds in his thighs and legs and went down screaming. The second man hesitated, then lifted a submachine gun just as Kat targeted him with three more rounds. They blasted into his chest and slammed him back against the broken window he had come through. The weapon fell from his hands and he slid to the ground dead before he landed.

Kat ran up and kicked a submachine gun out of the wounded man's hands before he could fire. Kat stared at the shot-up terrorist. He screamed something at her in Arabic. She ignored him. Both his legs could be shattered. She bound his hands behind his back with a riot cuff.

Kat looked at the dead man. She took a deep breath. For just a second she wanted to cry and scream and bellow out her anger because sometimes there was no other way, she had to kill. She fought down the urge to break into small pieces, and held all of her deep emotions inside. In a minute it swept past. She was a professional and had done this work before. The killing never came easy and she knew it would always bother her. But when it had to be done, it had to be done.

Kat heard several shots inside the target house, then all quieted. Lights came on in the place. Before Kat could move toward the back of the structure, the whole rear half of the house exploded in a horrendous blast that made the bomb detonation she had felt earlier that day on the street seem like a firecracker. The thundering, billowing roar slammed past, then the powerful surge of hot air and debris knocked her down. A moment later the reverse sucking gush of air storming back into the vacuum of the blast made her gasp for breath just before she passed out.

Kat came back to consciousness slowly a few minutes later. She felt someone patting her cheek. She caught the hand. It was Duncan.

"Well, thunderchick, you seem to be drawn to large explosions today. How do you feel?"

At first her mouth wouldn't work. Her tongue was twice normal size and as dry as a desert yucca. She tried to swallow, then licked her lips. At last she could croak out some words. "Feel like somebody sandpapered my mouth. That was their whole supply of bangers?"

"True. They had it booby-trapped, and one of the detectives hit the trigger. Cairo PD lost three men in the blast. Lieutenant Hosni is fine."

"This was their GHQ?"

"Hosni says it was. They grabbed two live ones, along with a notebook of newspaper clippings of the first six blasts and a list of new alphabetical targets from *H* through the letter *M*."

"So, we were right about the first six blasts. They were all American firms that began with one of the first six letters of the alphabet."

"Indeed. We were lucky. The three G stores we staked out included the right one."

Lieutenant Hosni hurried up and knelt beside Kat where she sat in the wet dirt and rocks. The area still smelled of cordite and dusty smoke. "Lady Kat, how are you feeling?"

"I'm fine, just a bit woozy and my tongue doesn't work right."

"An ambulance will be here shortly. They will take you to the hospital to be checked. I see blood on your arm."

"That's not needed."

"Yes, it is needed. We must be sure you are not seriously injured from the blast. You have served us well by stopping the two men who came out the window. One is dead, but we will get much information from the wounded one, who we believe is the leader of this group."

"I really don't think—"

Duncan put his hand on Kat's shoulder, stopping her. She looked up at him and Duncan nodded.

It was nearly midnight when Kat and Duncan boarded the Marshall Industries business jet at the Cairo International Airport. It was standard transportation for members of the Specialists to and from assignments.

"The little bomber told the captain his purpose in life was to kill as many Americans as possible. He said Americans had killed his father in a strike against the Great Evil the day he was born. His family had been in Iran then and his father was with a group trying to blow up an American oil-company office. After that his mother raised him to hate every American."

Duncan took a cup of coffee from the attendant in the company jet and sipped it. "He'll probably have a long time in an Egyptian jail to think over his future."

He turned to Kat. "Sometimes I wonder about terrorists these days. They have no real agendas or glorious causes to fight for. Today there are only a few of the old terrorists left, retired no doubt. They are the smart ones. The dumb ones were killed or blew themselves up early in life. Now there seems to be a whole new generation of extremists. They're indifferent and erratic. Maybe eventually they'll all die out for lack of good causes and no financial support."

"Yeah, like Osama bin Laden is going to go broke soon," Kat said with a grin.

"That's to be hoped for. What was on that fax the pilot gave you just before we took off?"

"Mister Marshall says something ugly is brewing. He isn't sure what it involves but it has something to do with biological or chemical agents and their use by terrorists. A truly frightening prospect."

"Anything solid to go on?"

"Not yet, but he says it's number one on our agenda. He wants us back in London as soon as we can get there."

✴ TWO ✴

It was scheduled as study time for the six Specialists. They sat in the office section of the huge Baldermare Castle a dozen miles outside the village of Kettering, well north of London. Kat and Duncan had come in the night before and had made their after-action report to J. August Marshall, who directed and funded the Specialists team.

Each one had a copy of the twenty-page, monthly Interpol Terrorist Assessment report. They also had the weekly United Nations terrorism survey, and the current CIA briefing on the same subject. It was eight-fifteen and the Specialists had reported for the daily briefing fifteen minutes before. They had only started reading the terrorist reports when J. August Marshall came into the room. Mister Marshall didn't look his seventy-two years. He was five feet nine inches tall, slender, and in good physical shape. He was dressed impeccably in a soft brown pin-striped Savile Row suit, and always wore a white carnation in his buttonhole. He had a tight, wrinkle-free face under a generous shock of pure white hair. His solid jaw dominated his face. Now his green eyes stared at the team with a hint of anger.

It was all Roger Johnson could do to stay seated. The six-foot-three-inch ex–Navy SEAL wanted to jump to attention as soon as Mister Marshall came into the room. It was the way his stringent military training had taught him whenever a ranking officer came into the room. Now he grabbed his desk, hung on, and remained seated.

"Good morning, team," Mister Marshall said. He stood in front of them like a schoolmaster might, a slight frown on his cleanly shaven face. "I've told some of you that there has been serious activity lately in the biological weapons field. Back in 1974 the Russians signed the Biological Weapons Convention treaty along with us to stop developing such materials. Now we know the Soviet Union used the convention as a screen. They went right ahead with a full-blown program, and produced many kinds of biological weapons, nerve-gas weapons, and other agents. We obeyed the treaty and stopped all such work in 1974.

"We know that some of those Soviet weapons were in sites that are now not a part of Russia. Our intelligence reports show that there is a frighteningly large supply of them near Odessa, the capital of Ukraine. We're trying to find out specifics about the bio, chemical, and nuclear weapons stored there, and who controls them.

"A week ago some Pakistani agents were in Odessa sniffing around, trying to buy some of these weapons of mass destruction. Our reports indicate they went away empty-handed. We don't know why. The fact they were trying to buy such material is profoundly disturbing. The CIA has people on-site investigating. If the weapons are there, we want the Ukraine government to admit it, and allow an inspection team to catalog and then destroy them under UN supervision."

Mister Marshall watched the Specialists, then continued. "Biological terror attacks are the worst possible scenario. We know that the Russians developed several types of biologicals: anthrax, black plague, smallpox, tularemia, and the Marburg virus. They produced the viruses, freeze-dried them in a powder form, and stored them.

"Our experts say the life of such viruses is well over a hundred years. So we have to assume that all of the Soviet viral agents are active and deadly.

"Think what one pound of anthrax powder could do if released in London or New York. Smallpox is just as deadly since it is also highly contagious, can multiply rapidly, and sweep across a whole nation. Maybe 10 percent of the world's people have been inoculated against smallpox. Western nations, including the U.S., have about a 50 percent inoculation rate. That means it could still kill a hundred and fifty million people in the United States alone."

Mister Marshall walked the width of the room, his hands behind his back. "Until this Odessa threat is cleared, I want you to concentrate on biological terrorism. Dig out everything we have on it. Jump onto the Internet and the Web. You'll have your regular physical training and weapons work as scheduled. However, I want a real push on this bio terror threat." Mister Marshall paused and looked over at Kat.

"My congratulations to Kat and Duncan, who took care of the bombing problem in Cairo. They brought down the bomber who turned out to be a mule, and from him the Cairo police found the home base and wiped it out."

Kat nodded. "We had excellent cooperation from the Cairo police. But we didn't think it would take a three-day stakeout."

Mister Marshall acknowledged her, then looked at the Specialists' team leader. "Wade, do you have anything to bring up?"

Wade Thorne stood and grinned. "Hey yes, I have a great new weapon I'm really interested in." His brown hair was in a conservative business cut and his long face lent itself more to frowns than smiles.

"This rifle I'm really excited about. It could change the way we run some of our operations. It came to us from the U.S. Defense Department for evaluation. It's still under development, but what they have given us is truly remarkable. Briefly it's a twin-barreled rifle no heavier than an M-16 that can fire 5.56mm rounds as well as 20mm rounds that can explode on impact or as an airburst. It will reach out a thousand yards with pinpoint accuracy. It's a dramatic breakthrough in a ground soldier's weaponry."

"Twenty mike-mike?" Roger Johnson asked. "You shuckin' me? If you ain't, hope they send us a cart to pack along the ammo."

They all laughed. Roger was six-three and 210 pounds and came out of the black projects in New York City.

"I'll leave you to your work," Mister Marshall said. "I have some items to catch up on myself."

J. August Marshall waved to the five men and Kat and left the room. He returned by the elevator to his third-floor office, where he spent most of his time when he was at the castle.

It had been almost a year now since he and Wade Thorne had put together this terrorist-fighting team he called the Specialists. The six were highly trained in various fields, and all working together to fight against terrorism wherever they found it.

Mister Marshall sat behind his big desk and thought about his team. Wade had worked out well as the field leader. He had pulled Wade out of early retirement from the CIA to help him form his group. Kat came from the FBI and was also a lawyer. She was second-in-command and well capable of leading any mission they might mount. Duncan Bancroft had been with the British MI-6 for years and came over to the Specialists with his worldwide contacts and his knowledge of the international terrorist scene.

Hershel Levine had been a top field agent with the Israeli Mossad and still had hundreds of contacts in dozens of countries and a vivid understanding of terrorists.

Ichi Yamagata from the FBI was a top armorer. Roger Johnson was their last man, a huge ex–Navy SEAL African-American who was competent in three African languages.

Yes, he had a good team. They had performed well on several missions now, and had taken only minor wounds except for Ichi. He had suffered a serious chest wound in Alaska and now after two months he still wasn't back to top form. Three other team members had been wounded in the Nuke Down operation as well. Kat's in-and-out

wound on her arm had healed. The bullet they had to dig
out of Hershel's leg had created a problem. He had healed
in the two months, but there was some stiffness and he
sometimes had to drop out of the longer training runs.

Ichi was marginal. He needed another month to fully
recover. He had been in the hospital for a week. Wade's hit
in the right leg by a bullet on the Alaskan ice fields had
been an in-and-out type, and cut up some leg muscle, but
now he was back to one hundred percent. Roger and
Duncan had come through without a scratch.

Mister Marshall had put the group together when he
stepped down after ten years as the United States' CIA director. He felt there was a niche that needed filling that the
U.S. could not do officially. The no-assassination policy
was one of the CIA problems. Sometimes bad men needed
to be killed.

Mister Marshall was a billionaire several times over
from his early-life business operations and could afford to
put millions into this operation. He had bought the old
Baldermare Castle four years ago and spent a fortune re-
furbishing and reconstructing it. On the outside it had
been rebuilt with rock and stone from the same quarry
that the first John Baldermare had used back in 1130
when he built the castle.

The structure had been sacked and looted five times
since then, and took a major rebuilding this time. From
the outside it looked much like it must have back in the
twelfth century.

Inside it was as modern and up-to-date as possible. The
interior had been designed and built to resemble a country
estate. He had hired a top decorator to turn the interior
into a blaze of color and fabric that was a delight to the
eye. There were richly warm brown carpeted floors, historic wall hangings, a scattering of old master original oils,
a remarkable chandelier, furniture from twelfth-century
massive to ultramodern. New plumbing and electrical
wiring were only a start. There were two fine kitchens,
workrooms, a dozen bedrooms with baths, central heat-
ing, and his own den on the third floor loaded with the latest in communications equipment: faxes, big-screen TV,

Internet access, wireless phones, and instant radio-satellite communication with anyplace on earth. The great hall was intact and could seat one hundred guests for dinner.

He looked over the last coded E-mail he had received from H.J. Jansen, the current director of the CIA.

> J.A. I don't like the smell of things in Odessa. We have three men trying to figure it out. Best bet: There are some missiles there with bio, nuke, or chemical payloads in their nose cones, waiting to be sold to the highest bidder. There must be enough biomaterial there to wipe out all of Odessa in a week and then erase half of Europe. What in hell can we do?

Mister Marshall took a long breath and rubbed his face with both hands. What could they do? Ukraine was an independent nation. The UN couldn't waltz into Odessa and tell them to neutralize all of the nuclear, biological, and chemical weapons that were stored in those up-to-now-secret caverns. Many in the Ukraine government probably didn't know about the missiles or their deadly viral components. He shook his head. All he could do was watch and wait.

That afternoon Ichi went to his regular physical therapy in the castle clinic. The rest of the Specialists went on a fifteen-mile run, and when they came to the halfway turnaround point Wade stopped them. Early in their training it had been a spot for a ten-minute break, but not now. Wade waved Hershel to the electric cart that waited there for him. He was still on limited physical training. Then Wade turned the team back toward the castle. He knew there would be some comment.

"Damn, Wade, only fifteen?" Roger said. "Figured we'd do at least twenty today."

"He planned to, but the SEAL couldn't keep his big fat ass up with the rest of us," Hershel cracked. They all laughed.

Roger only grinned, pulled the soaked black T-shirt away from his chest, then wiped sweat out of his eyes and raced ahead, jolting past all of them by twenty yards.

The others picked up the pace to keep up with Roger but nobody tried to catch him. He led the pack for a mile, then Wade kicked into a higher gear, overtook Roger, and passed him. Both men were pumping arms, working too hard for top running form. Wade held the lead for a mile, then Kat put on a kick and caught both the leaders easily and with a smooth even stride passed them and stretched her lead.

Roger groaned as she steamed past. "Damn women's lib. Knew we should have kept them pregnant, barefoot, and in the kitchen."

"Hoooyah!" the Specialists shouted, and watched Kat stretch her lead out to three hundred yards. The rest of the Specialists had to pick up the pace again so they wouldn't be totally embarrassed.

Wade grinned and kept up. Yeah, it was good to have a little competition in the Specialists.

They wore black British-length army shorts, black T-shirts, and berets. On their backs were twenty-pound packs of ammo, water, and MREs. Each one carried a favorite long gun or submachine gun. Wade had set a medium pace of seven minutes to a mile. They were close to five and a half minutes the last two. Fifteen miles were only a warm-up for triathlon winner Kat. She still ran marathons for fun whenever she could fit one in.

They stopped at the firing range on the Baldermare Estate. When Mister Marshall bought the castle, he found that twenty-five hundred acres of rolling hills and farmland were also in the package. It was ideal. They had their shooting ranges in the middle of the estate so not even their machine-gun firing could be heard by neighbors.

Wade took a weapon out of a plastic-wrapped cocoon and held it up. It looked like an M-16 chopped off, twice as thick and with a strange sight on top. A 20mm barrel rested on top and a smaller diameter barrel on the bottom. It had two magazines.

"Looks a little strange, but it's no heavier than an M-16 and it will outshoot the Sixteen from here to Thursday morning," Wade said. "The 5.56 barrel is nothing new. We know what it can do. The new part is this 20mm round. That's just a little over three-quarters of an inch in diameter. Fighter and attack aircraft use twenties in their guns. Now we have them.

"In other words a twenty is one hell of a big chunk of lead. On top of that, the round comes in armor-piercing explosive, and can be made into an airburst round.

"How? See this gadget on top? It's a video camera, a six-power scope, and a laser range finder. To fire around corners or over reverse slopes up to a thousand yards, all you do is laser sight on your target on the ground, say the corner of a building, and pull the trigger. The laser gives the fire-control system the range; it sets the fuse on the twenty mike-mike for the number of turns the bullet needs to make to get to the target. It does this in a nanosecond. When the right number of turns are made by the spinning bullet, it detonates in an airburst right over your target.

"To repeat, this system works up to a thousand yards, more than half a mile. The weapon will hold six rounds in the magazine. One small point here. Each of the twenty-mike-mike rounds prices out at thirty dollars."

"That one work?" Roger asked.

"Try it out and see," Wade said. "I tested it yesterday with three rounds. I love this weapon."

Roger took the gun and hefted it. He checked the loaded magazine, rammed it home, cranked a round into the chamber, and sighted in on a known target five hundred yards downrange. The ancient oak tree snag had been used as a target many times before.

Wade showed him where the laser button was, the sight, and the single trigger and Roger sighted in again, and fired. They all stared at the old oak snag that shook when the explosive shell detonated twenty feet over it.

"Oh, yeah!" Roger said. "This little honey is mine. I'll do the long work. It's like having an M-16 with a grenade launcher that will reach out a thousand yards instead of only two hundred. Yeah, I want one of these."

They spent an hour working with the new weapon.

Each one had a turn with a lasered airburst, and they all fired the 5.56.

"Don't get too excited," Wade said. "We're not allowed to take this weapon on any missions. It's for demonstration only. But, if we like it, we can put in an order. The regular issue to the armed forces won't be until 2005. But we can get three weapons within ninety days. Shall I put in an order?"

Everyone shouted that he should.

Ichi was the last one to fire the weapon. He wouldn't let go of it. "Oh, yeah, get the three," he said. "Get a dozen. They'll come in handy in lots of situations. The rounds are also explosive when they hit without the airburst fusing, right?"

"Right," Wade said. "They can tear up equipment, cars, trucks, antennas, ground-control equipment, or a car filled with terrorists."

Wade led the Specialists to the western range a short distance away in a wooded area. Electronics popped targets up as the shooter walked down a given path through the trees and past a mock-up house, and the computer-selected targets never came up the same way twice.

Kat went through with her MP-5. She walked slowly, watching both sides of a woodsy trail. A terrorist popped up on the right with a grenade. She riddled the target with a three-round burst. Ten feet ahead three forms jolted upward on the left. Two terrorists held a woman captive between them with a bag over her head. Kat drilled the first terrorist with two rounds, aimed past the hostage, and cut down the second terr.

Three seconds later terrorists popped up on both sides of the trail at once. Kat missed one, but nailed the other two.

She continued through the course and came out with a computer printout record of 85 percent. Kat smiled. Yeah, a good score. She was still in competition with these guys on everything. It felt good to shoot well.

They went through the course one at a time, and each had a computer printout.

"Hey, Kat, I nailed you on that one," Hershel said. "Shot me an eighty-eight."

"No way," Duncan rasped. "Must have read it wrong. Maybe it was a thirty-three."

The Specialists laughed.

Wade answered his call on the individual radio that fastened to his belt and had an ear speaker.

"Yes, Mister Marshall. Wade here."

"Bring the team back. Something just came in on the secure line that we need to talk about. It's the Odessa problem."

Wade worried it on the two-mile run back to the castle. He had time to think about it and it scared him. Terrorists were totally amoral. This threat reminded Wade of Siegfried, the former East German agent he had tangled with several times. Wade thought he had killed the vicious and sadistic hit man in Germany.

Then one day he discovered Siegfried was alive and in the U.S. The Agency had warned him not to get married years earlier. He and Vivian had two wonderful daughters. Sighting Siegfried in security videotapes at Kennedy Airport had alerted him. He told Vivian not to open any packages that arrived by mail or delivery firm. One package had been a bomb he had dealt with safely. After that he moved his family and told no one his address.

Somehow Siegfried had found him. One day he went home and the lights were not on in the house. He rushed inside to find the house silent and cold. He searched frantically and found his two daughters in their bedroom, both naked and strangled with a large S carved in each small chest. He screamed in protest as he wrapped his arms around the small forms as tears streamed down his cheeks. Then he stormed out of the room to find Vivian.

He screamed her name, knowing that she couldn't hear him. He tore into their bedroom, but she wasn't there. He stormed into the living room, the family room, the kitchen, but she wasn't in any of the rooms. He was sweating and panting now in fury. It had to be Siegfried. How had he found them? How could he know? He was East German Intelligence but still, how had he done it?

Slowly now, he considered where Vivian could be. He checked the closets, the garage, then moved into the laundry room off the kitchen. A small room with washer, dryer, furnace, hot-water heater, and a small table. The washer door was open. He hesitated then pulled open the front-loading dryer door.

His head pounded and bile rose in his throat as the door came down. One of Vivian's hands flopped out and Wade exploded in agonized fury such as he had never known. He collapsed on the floor. It took him ten minutes before he could lean back against the wall. He continued to sob. He couldn't move. He huddled there for an hour before he had the strength to even lift his head. Then he crawled to the dryer and touched her hand.

"Why didn't you kill me, you bastard!" he screamed. It took him several minutes before he could start to unwind her from the hot slow death container.

Her arms and legs had been folded and wrapped around in the cylinder. When he had her free she was naked and burned red from the heat. Her face was swollen and distorted. He laid her down gently on the floor and covered her with a blanket, then crawled into the kitchen.

He phoned a special number at CIA headquarters. They had an unmarked van and two men at his home within a half hour. They took care of everything. Two days later a small item appeared in the newspaper. Three dead in a tragic car crash on the Beltway.

Wade sat on the couch and held his head. He didn't know if he would ever be able to function as a normal human being again. Then slowly he began to plan. To plan how he would find Siegfried and what he would do to him. It was the only splinter of sanity that he could cling to.

Wade felt a new kind of anger as he ran with the other Specialists back toward the castle. The death of his family had been the end of his work for the CIA as well. He retreated to his ranch in Idaho. Last year he had found Siegfried in Berlin and evened the score. But at one for three it still wasn't right. Wade shook his head. Too many memories. This was a new day, new times, new problems, and he had to help find new solutions.

They made it back to the castle in record time.

★ THREE ★

THE ARABIAN SEA

The forty-one-foot, black-painted, Boghammar patrol boat slid through the dark waters of the Arabian Sea, fifty miles south of the Tropic of Cancer and twenty miles off point al Hadd of Oman. There was no moon as the ex-navy coastal patrol craft edged closer to the huge Norwegian luxury cruise ship, *The Royal Princess,* proceeding south at twenty knots.

Abdul al Ganzouri squinted into night as his craft gained on the brightly lighted luxury liner. He was coming up on the starboard side as arranged. The time was slightly after three in the morning. Most of the passengers and most of the crew would be sleeping. The night watch and operating crew should be little challenge.

Abdul stood five feet nine and always wished he was taller. He had a full black beard trimmed to a conservative two inches. Smoldering black eyes hid under bushy brows. His twice-broken nose showed two bends. He had been a loyal fighter for Allah for fourteen of his thirty-one years. Now he had launched his most ambitious project ever.

The Boghammar edged closer. Tangy sea spray washed Abdul's face, the sudden salty smell new in his nostrils. He watched the huge ship tower over his small craft, which now fought into the bow swell and surged through it into the calmer water near the side of the white-painted luxury liner. It was a serious juggling act to keep the Boghammar moving close to the mountain of steel plowing through the water at twenty knots when the bow wave tried to push it away. Abdul checked the glowing dial of his watch. They were three minutes early, but one of his men on the luxury liner's aft deck would radio their arrival.

Just ahead the dark side of the ship blossomed with bright lights as the dock-level boarding hatch opened, revealing the interior of the liner. Four men stood there with lines and hooks ready to make the Boghammar fast.

Abdul sent three quick beams from a flashlight at the men inside the hatch, then delicately powered the little boat against the steel skin of the liner. The patrol craft slid ahead ten feet, with rubber tire bumpers on the small boat rubbing along the ship's hull before the grappling hooks caught on the forward and aft rails and bound her fast to the liner. The thirty men who had been jammed onto the small boat stepped up to the hatch and boarded. Each of the men carried an Uzi submachine gun, a pistol, and a backpack loaded with ammunition.

Two minutes later the thirty men were on board *The Royal Princess*. Smiles and handshakes from their terrorist allies who had been on board welcomed the visitors. Then Abdul took command.

"So far, so good. You all know the primary control areas we need. Your squads have assignments. Check in by radio when those targets are captured. Work as quietly as possible. No shooting unless absolutely necessary. Deal with any resistance harshly. Continued resistance means death."

Abdul paused and checked over his men. Besides the thirty he had brought with him, there were ten more Arab loyalists in his pay who had taken jobs on the ship three months ago, waiting for this night. He gave the ship workers arms and ammunition and waved the teams away. Each squad had a ship employee who knew the vessel and guided the men to their objectives.

Abdul and four men headed for the bridge. Their ship-steward guide was efficient taking them through crew areas that were vacant this time of morning. Around one corridor they met two bakers coming off duty. Both were Filipinos.

"What is this?" the shorter of the two shouted when he saw the five men with submachine guns. Abdul walked toward him smiling. "Just a drill, don't get alarmed," he said in English. The man relaxed. When Abdul came up to the baker, Abdul smashed the heavy side of his Uzi against the Filipino's head and he fell unconscious. The other Filipino surged past them and ran down the corridor but one of Abdul's men caught him. Four minutes later, both Filipinos had been bound and gagged and stashed in a storage room.

They met no one else until they opened the outer door of the bridge. It was thirty feet wide with another area to the far side. This was home base for the three men who guided the ship and watched all of the video screens and report monitors showing readouts and pictures from twenty-five vital centers in the huge liner.

The senior Norwegian officer scowled and jolted to his feet. "Who are you men? What are you doing here?" He spoke in Norwegian. At once he saw that none of the attackers understood him. He switched to French, then to English. By that time each of the officers had been stood up and a weapon pushed into his stomach.

"We're taking over your ship," Abdul said in English. "You'll be changing course. Faisal here will give you directions. You are to follow his orders precisely."

"Sir, absolutely not. I am Oram Gaston, first officer in command of this watch. I will not allow you to do this. Put down your weapons at once and consider yourselves under arrest." Gaston said it with force and determination, but there was a haunting fear behind his soft blue eyes. He shuddered for just a moment, then frowned. "You must put down your weapons."

Abdul smiled through sudden anger. "You are the second-in-command?"

"That's right."

Abdul lifted the Uzi and fired two rounds into the startled officer's heart. One of the slugs went through his body and thudded into the rear wall. Gaston jolted backward; the nerve centers in his brain went down fast. His legs gave way and he dropped to his knees, then pitched forward, his head grazing Abdul's legs as the first officer sprawled in death on the bridge deck.

"My God!" one of the Norwegians screamed as his eyes went wide and he put one hand to his mouth and stepped backward. The other crewman closed his eyes and slowly shook his head, whispering something in Norwegian.

Abdul didn't even look at the dead man. His expression never changed. He had killed close-up before. It simply had to be done. It was a part of his plan, his great plan to strike at the heart of the hated Great Evil. Abdul remained grim and deadly efficient. "Now that we have that small detail out of the way, you two officers will move this ship on its new course at once," Abdul thundered in English. "Do you understand?"

"Yes sir," both men said almost in unison. They sat down at their controls, removed them from automatic operation, and put in the changes Faisal gave them. At once the big ship began making a gentle turn to the left. Abdul nodded.

"Faisal could run this ship by himself. He knows all of the equipment and controls. Do not try to fool him. Do as you are told and you will stay alive. Is that totally clear?"

"Yes sir," the two ship officers said.

Faisal smiled. He was a head shorter than Abdul, and had been working with his leader for three years. He was slow to anger and careful in his actions. A good counterbalance for the more flamboyant and reckless Abdul. He wore a full beard and the all-black uniform they had adopted. His eyes were sunburn brown, with wrinkles at the corners, and he had a stiff, firm nose. His lips were a thin line, usually tightly held as if he didn't want any of his emotions to seep out.

Abdul turned to one of his men. "Get this body out of here and hide it."

Abdul's small radio beeped twice. He pushed a button. "Yes?"

"Our ship man is having trouble finding the radio and communications center. Will report in later."

"Right. Be sure the radio operator continues to send his

usual reports that all is well and that the ship is on course."

"Yes sir."

Abdul smiled and stroked his beard. He had to enjoy it while he could. He would have to shave it off soon. One down, four more vital areas to control, then the ship would be theirs.

Below in the engine room, Saeed leveled his Uzi at the two engine men on duty in the spotless control room. A huge steam plant worked away in the background.

"I told you to lift your hands, we're taking over your ship," Saeed said again in Arabic. He spoke no other language. The two Norwegian men laughed at him. Saeed swore and lowered the Uzi and fired one round into the largest man's thigh. The sailor bellowed in pain and fell over backwards. Saeed knew the danger of shooting the Uzi in the engine room. This bullet shouldn't even leave the man's thigh. The other crewman shouted in terror, and knelt beside the wounded man.

Quickly two of Saeed's team tied up the crewmen and gagged them, then carried them into a cleaning locker. A third man came out from the big engine, saw the weapons, and held up his hands.

Saeed took out his radio and turned it on. He thumbed the send button twice and listened.

"Yes, Abdul here."

"Saeed. We have control of the engine room. Small problem but it's solved. We have one crewman who will help us when orders come down from the bridge."

"Keep one of our men down there, the others come topside."

"Yes sir."

Several decks above, the radio-room operator gave the terrorist team no trouble. He had never seen a gun that large and it scared him just to look at it.

"Jeeze, point that thing the other way," Sogne Thorbjorn said. "You want the radio, you can have it." By the blank looks on the men's faces he realized they didn't speak Norwegian. He switched to German and one of the men looked up. Thorbjorn said the same thing he had before and the Arab nodded. He motioned him to go to the corner of the room while he and three other men talked. Then they put him back in his operator's chair.

"You must do exactly what I tell you," the German-speaking Arab attacker said. "You will send normal messages that all is fine here and that you are moving on course and on time. You have a set routine to do this, yes?"

"Yes, a regular report schedule to the home office."

"You will do this or I will shoot you dead. Understand?"

"Yes. You don't want anyone to know we've been hijacked?"

"Ya," the Arab said.

In the security office, Bergen Buskerud frowned at his log sheet. He motioned to his buddy across the desk where they watched twenty-four television monitors covering the most important parts of the passenger areas.

"Hey, they missed the regular check-in from the bridge by twenty minutes," Buskerud said. "Should I give them a call?"

His partner looked up from a magazine and shrugged.

Buskerud called. On the bridge, the phone rang four times before anyone answered.

"Bridge."

Buskerud didn't recognize the voice.

"Hey, you all right up there, sir? We haven't had your regular safety check. You're twenty-two minutes late."

There was the slightest pause and Buskerud frowned.

"Yes, yes, we're fine here, just got involved in something and forgot the time. Mark us down as checked on time. Contact you again at the next period."

"Yes, sir. Thank you, sir." The senior security officer scowled. He glanced at the door into the office. Locked, yes, as usual. He couldn't remember the bridge missing a check call by twenty minutes before. Bergen Buskerud tried to relax. The bridge goof bothered him. Was it important? He'd been a cop for thirty years in Oslo. It felt like something was wrong up there. A hunch that cops have. Or was he getting too old for the job? This was his fifth year as head of security on *The Royal Princess*. He was getting tired and his feet hurt. He'd about decided this would be his last cruise before he retired.

He checked the bank of monitors again. He went past it, then looked back. Strange. A man in an all-black outfit. It looked like he had a weapon of some kind. The man turned and looked behind, then moved around the corner off the monitor. Buskerud stood up, knocking over his chair.

"You see that? Monitor twenty-four. Swear I saw a man in black pants and shirt with a weapon, looked like a sub-machine gun."

The other security man, Storen, yawned. "Damn, you're seeing things. I didn't catch a thing. Just a leg going around the corner. Your stomach giving you a bad time again?"

"No dammit, Storen, I saw a man with a submachine gun."

"Yeah, sure."

The bell rang at the security office's locked front door. Buskerud looked at the monitor covering the outside door. He saw an employee, one of the darker ones. They had a regular UN of races on board. Then he recognized him as an Arab who had been hired three months ago. Management said they didn't have any Arabs in the crew. They hired ten. Buskerud had them for two hours of in-struction about security

"I still saw something." Buskerud said, and hit the mike switch to the intercom on the door. "Yes, I hear you. What do you want?"

"A disturbance on the C deck cabin C four-fourteen," the man said in passable Norwegian. "Domestic dispute I think. Wanted to keep it low-key. Should I have phoned it in?"

"I'll send our roving patrol."

"Sir, you better take a look. It could be a killing. There's lots of blood."

Buskerud swore. "Blood? You sure. Can't be. We haven't had any real trouble in five years. Damn, I better take a look." He stepped toward the door and glanced at Storen. "I saw a damned submachine gun, plain as day.

Keep the door locked. Storen, get two of our day-shift men up and head them to room C four-fourteen." He looked away from the monitor, grabbed his side arm, and slipped it into the holster under his right arm. Frowning, Buskerud hurried to the door. He had taken his first step outside when he sensed someone behind him. The side of an Uzi slammed down hard on the top of his head and drove him to the deck. He rolled over and let out a long sigh. The blow crushed his skull and drove the life out of him.

The ship employee in uniform stepped around the door and waved the Uzi at Sergeant Storen in the security office.

"Do not move," the Arab said slowly in Norwegian. Sergeant Storen started to lift his hands, then he pivoted in his chair and clawed at his revolver where it lay on top of his desk.

Three shots from the Uzi ripped into Sergeant Storen's body, two in his chest and one under his chin. The head-shot slanted upward into his skull, chopping up vital nerve centers in his brain and slamming him off his chair to die as he hit the floor behind his desk.

Three more terrorists ran into security. One dragged Lieutenant Buskerud's body into the room, closed and locked the heavy steel door.

A moment later the terrorist pushed the send button on his handheld radio. "Security office captured. I believe there are only four security men on board. They don't wear uniforms."

"Good," Abdul said. "Leave one of our men there, lock the door, and go to your second objective."

On the bridge, the two Norwegian officers looked at Faisal in surprise.

"You have turned us around so we are heading north up the coast toward the Gulf of Oman," the older officer said.

"Exactly," Faisal said. "We will go through the gulf and into the Strait of Hormuz."

"The strait? But why? No cruise ship I know of goes through there. It's a narrow way and always tricky."

"Yes, precisely our point. As to why, you have no need to know. Just do your job and stay alive. Your families will appreciate it." Faisal shook his head. He would never understand the Western mind. Why did they always ask so many questions? Their job now was to do what they were told, so they could stay alive.

Faisal checked the charts again and looked up. "We are now four hundred and twenty-five miles from the strait. We will maintain a speed of twenty knots and arrive at our destination in twenty-one hours and fifteen minutes. It is now 3:20 A.M. We should be on station about thirty minutes after midnight tomorrow."

The Norwegian officers looked puzzled. "We're going to anchor *The Royal Princess* in the Strait of Hormuz?"

"Precisely," Faisal said. "We are ablaze with five thousand lights, so no tanker will run into us." He held up his hand. "No, do not ask why. Simply do your job of running the ship along the course I have laid out and you will survive. When does your relief crew come on duty?"

"Eight o'clock," the older officer said. "We work an eight-hour shift."

Faisal nodded and went back to talk with Abdul, who sat in the softly cushioned captain's chair.

Abdul shouted into the hand radio. "What do you mean shots have been fired? Who shot them? How many times? Are any of our men down? Engineering, right? I'm bringing down reinforcements now." He looked at the crewman holding an Uzi, who had guided them to the bridge.

"Get us down to Engineering fast before this whole damn operation blows up," Abdul shouted, the first traces of doubt starting to cloud his face.

★ FOUR ★

The four men from the bridge stopped at the corner of the corridor.

"Engineering is just around there," the Arab guide said. "I saw two of our men this side of the door."

Abdul took a look. He saw a bright yellow sign that read: AUTHORIZED PERSONNEL ONLY. "Yes, two of our men." He stepped out into the hall and waved at the men, motioning one of them to come to him. One of the black-clad men ran up, his long beard swaying.

"We tried the door, then the boat worker talked to them, but they wouldn't open up," Nabil said. "They told him to come back in the morning. I tried to shoot the door lock off, but that didn't work. The rounds ricocheted down the corridor."

"Nobody shot back at you?"

The man shook his head. "No sir. I didn't mean to let you think that."

"Good. I thought we had a gun battle. So, we have to get in there, Nabil. They can countermand any orders we give from the bridge to change course or to even make the ship stop or move. Do you have the plastique?"

"Yes sir."

"Use it, just enough to blow off the lock. About an inch off a quarter-pound block. Get all of your men back and set the fuse for fifteen seconds."

Nabil took the explosive from his backpack and carefully cut off an inch of the pure white plastique. It looked like an inch cube. He ran to the door and pressed the pliable doughlike explosive fast against the locking area, then pushed in a detonator timer, set it, and ran back around the corner of the corridor. The terrorists put their hands hard over their ears before the charge went off.

It was like an explosion in a tunnel. The white-painted steel corridor channeled the billowing blast, amplifying it as it went, slamming down both ways along the fourth-deck corridor. Abdul looked around the corner once the wave of hot air with its smoky, greasy smell slashed past him. The door hung by the upper hinge. He realized he couldn't hear anything. He shook his head, then touched Nabil on the shoulder and the two charged through the acrid smoke to the opening, their Uzis ready.

There was no need for gunfire. Two crewmen in the engineering department had been blown off their chairs and slammed against the far wall, where they slid down and now were moaning, gasping for air in the yellowish smoke that clogged their lungs.

The Arabs bound the Norwegians' hands and feet, then checked the instruments. All looked in good operating condition. Abdul tried talking and found his hearing had mostly returned. He used the telephone he picked up from the floor and dialed the number on the instrument for the bridge. Faisal answered.

"Any problems with the ship? Any change of course or speed?"

"No sir, all is as directed. We did hear a blast. Was that on the ship?"

"Yes, in Engineering," Abdul said. "Now we have this whole luxury liner under our command. The kitchen will work as usual. All of the other Norwegians and the international crew should report to work normally. We have complete control. Now all we have to do is steam to our anchorage."

He knew it wouldn't be that simple. There would be the passengers and the crew to consider, to dominate, to control. But it all would be worth it. He had waited so long for a chance like this. Now it was here. He had to make it work for him. Such an opportunity might never come again in his lifetime.

He found his man who spoke good Norwegian and English and had him prepare statements to be read over the ship's public address system every half hour after 7:00 A.M. until noon.

"Good morning vacationers. During the night there have been some changes made. *The Royal Princess* is now under control of the Sword of Allah. All ship's officers and crew will maintain their usual functions and will obey without question any order given to them by any of the Sword of Allah men. We are running *The Royal Princess*. We have no plans to disrupt your vacation, although it may last a little longer than you anticipated.

"We are sailing north, heading for the Strait of Hormuz. We will anchor there for a few days. Our advice to all passengers and crew is to stay calm, and enjoy your vacation or your work. The crew must attend to its duties as usual. By doing this, no one will be hurt."

Abdul and his top four men manned the bridge when the first message was sent over the PA system at seven o'clock. Abdul had guessed correctly. At 7:05 two men burst into the bridge. One was older and must have dressed quickly. His white shirt with the blue-and-gold captain's insignia on the shoulder bars hung outside his pants. His hair was uncombed, his face splotchy from sleep. The younger man was dressed in the standard officer's white uniform and his face showed his rage.

The older Norwegian looked around a moment. "Who is in charge here?" he bellowed. He was the captain and this was his ship and no rotten foreigners were going to steal his command away from him. He hadn't put in forty years at sea for this line to have it all explode in flames and gunfire.

Abdul stood from the captain's chair. "I am, Captain. I am Abdul al Ganzouri, and I now control *The Royal Princess*."

"By what authority?" the captain's face bloated red, his eyes bulged, and he took a step forward as he thundered out his question.

Abdul lifted his Glock 19 pistol. "This weapon, Captain, gave me control. My men and our submachine guns have all the authority we need."

"By God, no. I won't stand for this outrageous action. Hand me your weapon at once and you will be treated fairly by police authorities at the first port."

"Not hardly, old man. You may retire to your quarters, where you will remain under guard. I want to hear nothing more from you."

"By God, sir, you shall. You are a scoundrel, a pirate, and I will capture or kill you if I can. I'll spit in your face if you come close enough."

At that moment the young officer beside the Norwegian captain drew a knife from his belt and threw it at Abdul, who sidestepped the poor throw and fired twice with the Glock. Both rounds hit the young officer in the chest and he leaned backwards, surprise flooding his face; then shock hit him and, at the last moment before he fell, his face showed a deadly calm. He died a second later. The acrid stench of cordite flooded the bridge. The roar of the shots in the closed room pounded at the men's ears. No one could hear for several seconds.

The captain roared in rage and charged Abdul. The Arab shot the captain four times in the chest and he stumbled just as he reached the terrorist, clutching at his killer's legs as he slumped to the deck, dying. The roar of the four shots in the closed bridge was four times as loud as before. No one could hear anything for almost a minute.

Abdul took a step backward. No emotion flickered on his face. His dark eyes took on a harder glint as he stared at the two bodies. Slowly his hearing returned.

"Stupid men. You both had the chance to live. By your actions, you chose to die." He turned to one of his men and pointed at the bodies and then at the door. Both dead men were quickly taken away.

Abdul called the kitchen and talked to the executive chef.

"Everything is to remain the same. Your regular first and second seating. Everything is to be normal. You understand?"

The Norwegian chef rattled off a wild chatter of Norwegian.

"In English, stupid," Abdul snapped. "Speak in English so I know what you're saying."

"Yes, I'm sorry, this is so unusual. The passengers must be served. All meals will be as planned. The crew too must eat. Everything is normal here. I don't understand, but I will continue to do my duty to my passengers."

"Good, then you and I will have no trouble. Some of the other officers have not been so cooperative. Carry on." Abdul smiled as he hung up the phone. This way there would be no passenger revolt because they missed their five meals a day. He decided it was going well. He had expected more resistance; perhaps an execution or two to create fear and order. This made it easier and should be productive.

Abdul left the bridge and had his guide take him to the purser's office. The purser, dressed in his white shirt and pants, and shoulder boards but no tie, put down a blue phone and stood when Abdul came into his office. Abdul now carried an Uzi on a strap over his chest. The short, broad-shouldered Norwegian's eyes widened as he looked at the weapon. Sweat beaded on his high forehead and ran down into his eyes and black mustache.

"I am Martin Anderson, the purser," he said, his voice shaky.

Abdul watched the shorter man a moment. He didn't like his eyes, too bland, shifty, never looking him in the eye. "You are having questions from the passengers?"

The purser nodded. He wanted to turn and run and get out of this firestorm of ringing phones and shocked, screeching passengers. They were worried about making connections, about the rest of the planned cruise, about a hundred things. Hijacking a passenger liner? It was outrageous.

The telephone rang on his desk. The purser looked at it. A second phone on another desk rang as well.

"Leave them be," Abdul rasped.

"Yes sir, the phone has been ringing constantly. Questions."

"Tell them they are in no danger if they do as they are told. They will get no answers to their questions until I'm ready to give them some. I am Abdul, your new captain. I need your ship. When that need has been met, you can have it back. Caution your people to cooperate with my men and all will go as usual. Suggest to the passengers that they forget that new management has taken over and tell them to go about their vacation as usual."

Anderson frowned. He wished he was back in Bergen with his wife, watching his garden grow and the new green of leaves burst out on the trees. His wife had almost come on the voyage. He cleared his throat. "With all respect, sir, it's hard for the passengers to feel safe and normal with your men carrying around submachine guns."

Abdul's temper flared for just a moment. Then he relaxed. He needed this man. No one on his team could keep the passengers calm. He squinted at the purser and lifted one hand. "True, but the weapons are needed, they are a fact of life. Your first mate and captain did not agree. They attacked me and both died. The same thing could happen to any crewman or passenger who opposes us in any way. Remind your callers of that. There will be more announcements to all hands and passengers. I'll remind them of their conduct, as well."

At the door Abdul paused. "Mr. Purser Anderson, do you understand me fully? I am on a mission for Allah. I will not hesitate to kill anyone who gets in my way."

Purser Anderson's voice quavered. "Understood," he said.

By noon the bridge reported to Abdul that they had progressed up the coast and edged into the Gulf of Oman. In another twelve hours they would be nearly at the strait.

The first trouble developed on the Lido deck. The passengers were mostly Americans, and many of those senior citizens. One man, Norman Eckert, a retired master sergeant from the Marines, had a few midday drinks and his military training came out strong.

"No sonofabitch foreigner gonna push me around. Where is the bastard? Him and his A-Rab friends? I'm gonna get my goddamned forty-five out of the case and blow a couple holes in that asshole." Sergeant Eckert looked around at the collection of balding men and their fat wives at the bar. "Hey, who's with me here? Need a squad to go and get them fuckers. Can't be more than twenty of them."

Sergeant Eckert's wife, Madelyn, tried to calm him down but he snorted. "Woman, this is man's work. Marine work. Get back to your kitchen. Who's with me?"

Two men walked over and looked at the Marine. One was over seventy and used a cane. "Hey, Marine, I can help. Sergeant Petresky from the big one, WWII. Blasted me a few Japs with my old M-1 there near the end of things. Damn right I can help."

The other man was younger. He snorted. "In my day we'd wipe them snotnoses off the face of the globe. Chase them down and run them through with cold steel. Yes sir. Did my time in Korea. That's the first one we never won. We can win this one. What do you want me to do?"

"Good men, that's three of us," Sergeant Eckert said. He paused. The Marine looked at the dozen or so men round the outdoor bar and its green, brown, and pink decor. "Hey you jarheads, I said I need volunteers. This is Sergeant Eckert talking and I need about ten more good men."

Four of the males in their sixties looked up from their beers and mixed drinks. One of them in a bright red-and-blue Hawaiian shirt scowled. "Sure, what the hell we gonna do? You saw them guys with submachine guns? We going up against them with a damned forty-five and eight rounds?"

"Hey, no sweat," Sergeant Eckert said. "Hell, we use Marine tactics. We jump them one at a time and hit them over the head with a bottle or something. Ten or fifteen of us can rush one and he'd be down and out before he knew it. That way we pick up a sub gun from each one we way-lay. Pretty soon we have as much firepower as they do."

"So we start mowing down them and the passengers at the same time?" the man in the red-and-blue shirt asked. "You're nuts, Eckert."

The group quieted as one of the Arabs, dressed in black

pants and shirt and holding an Uzi walked down the deck and stared at them unsmiling before he went to the elevator.

Sergeant Eckert pointed at the hijacker. "See, see. We could have had him the second he turned his back. Ten of us swarmed him and he'd be down and a goner."

"Yeah, son, I'm with you all the way," Sergeant Petresky said. "Say, Sarge, you kill any Japs?"

"Huh, what? Japs? Oh, hell no. That was before my time. Got my share of slopes over in 'Nam, though. Oh, yes, more than my share. Wish to hell I had me a Sixteen. After they got the bugs out of them and put in the right kind of chamber, that was a shooting sonofabitch. Yeah, just one M-16 and I'd take down all the damn-looking A-Rabs."

Two more men came up. Both said they had done some Navy time and as long as nobody got hurt, they would help.

Sergeant Eckert nodded. "Yeah, we got five stouthearted men here. In another hour we should have six more. Talk to your friends, maybe they'll help. We'll meet here at five this afternoon. You all come back. Oh, any of you have a piece, even a thirty-two, bring it along. Out of sight, of course. Give me your names before you leave and your phone numbers so we can get together quick like. Remember, five o'clock. We'll get a little action going."

In the radio room, Sogne Thorbjorn looked at the ugly submachine gun and then up at the man who held it. "It's time for our regular morning report on the radio to the home office in Oslo. Should I make it?"

The Arab guard nodded. They were speaking in German. "Do it as you would normally, in Norwegian."

"Right."

"Go ahead. No tricks or you're dead."

Sogne swallowed hard and looked again at the gun. He could tell the home operator exactly what had happened, but the Arabs on board would find out and he would be shot for sure, or thrown overboard. He thought about his wife and two small girls in Bergen and decided to give the usual report. He keyed the radio that bounced its signal off a satellite and directly to Bergen.

"Bergen, this is *The Royal Princess*. Respond."

There were a few moments of silence, then the speakers overhead sounded.

"Yes, *Royal Princess* you're right on time."

"All is well here. On schedule, average speed 20.05 knots, no bad weather. No special messages not sent before."

"That's received and noted, *Royal Princess*. What's your ETA on your next port of call?"

"All the way to Adan in Yemen, long cruising stretch."

"Keep us informed. Out."

Sogne wiped sweat off his forehead and looked up at the German-speaking Arab.

"Everything by the book. No hint that we are in trouble."

"Your life depends on it, small Norwegian man. Now, we play cards. You know poker?"

Back on the bridge, Abdul watched the two new Norwegian crewmen. They had been carefully briefed by the outgoing ship drivers and looked just frightened enough to do the job correctly. Neither seemed to be a threat. Abdul watched the screen that showed the exact location of the ship from its GPS. They had turned into the Gulf of Oman. Now it was a straight shot into the Strait of Hormuz. He left Faisal in charge, with one other man to relieve him, and went down to check on the Boghammar. The patrol craft had been a gift and came with its firepower intact. It had one 12.2mm machine gun, and one rocket-propelled grenade launcher. It had originally cost someone over a hundred thousand dollars. Abdul had one torpedo tube jury-rigged to each side of the deck of the Boghammar facing forward. He had both tubes loaded and two more torpedoes in the hold of the forty-one-foot patrol boat. They were not the latest torpedoes but did have search ability. They were set to be fired on command from the little boat. He figured he would have to use one or two and then everyone would cooperate. The fifty-caliber machine gun would be useful in many ways when they needed it.

Less than an hour later, when Abdul had just finished a delicious lunch brought to him on the bridge, the phone rang. The lead Norwegian officer took the call and pointed to Abdul.

"Sir, I am Hayma, one of your men, a steward who got a job on board. I have been listening to the passengers. I have the fair English. There is a group of men on the Lido deck at the Capri bar. The men are talking about revolting against us. I can't be sure how serious they are, but I thought you would want to check it out."

"Thanks, Hayma. I've been waiting for something like this to develop. Now we can make examples of this group and no others will have the nerve to try it again. I'll get right down there."

★ FIVE ★

GULF OF OMAN

Abdul found his man Hayma on the Lido deck down from the Capri bar. Hayma was one of the Arab terrorists/workers on the liner who had been placed there earlier.

"The one causing the big talk isn't there now," Hayma said. Only two women and three men stood at the bar. "He and some others went to play shuffleboard."

"What's the big talker wearing?" Abdul asked.

"White T-shirt, red shorts, and a brown cap that says 'Nam—Yeah' on it."

"Let's go find him." Abdul still wore the all-black outfit in which he had stormed on board. He liked the effect on the passengers. Instant recognition. The Uzi didn't hurt any either. He had to stop this kind of big talk before it led to action. He didn't have time or men to take care of that. He wanted the passengers and the crew all calm and peaceful.

They walked down the Lido deck, the open one over the top deck of cabins, and around the pool. The shuffleboard courts were at the fantail.

Abdul saw the man a few moments later. He was maybe sixty, thirty pounds overweight with a belly and sagging jowls. The brown baseball cap had the right lettering and probably covered up a balding head. The two black-clad men walked ahead as if to go past the players to the stairs, then turned and covered the twenty feet to the three players quickly.

Sergeant Eckert looked up, surprise tainting his face. He hadn't shaved that morning. "Woman, I'm on vacation and I'm gonna do what I want to do. Drink and shoot trap off the fantail and stare at any pretty girls I see."

He frowned when he saw the Uzis. He knew what they were. Fully automatic submachine guns. High rate of fire. He held the pusher stick and leaned on it as he turned toward the men.

"You the guys who hijacked the ship, huh? Yeah probably don't understand English. A-Rabs, for sure. Why the hell you messing up our vacation plans?"

"For some excellent reasons," Abdul said in perfect English. "And your name is?"

Sergeant Eckert snorted and took a step backward. "You do talk English. Yeah. I'm just a passenger. Who are you?"

"My name is Abdul and I am the new captain of this ship. As captain, I have absolute power." He patted the Uzi. "Now, who are you?"

"Norman Eckert, I'm an American. I don't like what you've done."

"That's too bad, Norman. It's done. You do what you're told and don't mess with my people and you could live to see your grandchildren."

"Hey, how you know I have—" Eckert stopped.

Abdul laughed. He turned his back on the American and walked away.

Sergeant Norman Eckert scowled at the two black-clad men. When they were out of hearing, Eckert threw his push stick on the deck and marched to a green chaise lounge and flopped on it.

The older man with the cane, Sergeant Petresky, sat down opposite him. Petresky wore a red T-shirt with lettering on the front that said: "Been there, done that twice."

"Petresky, you hear what that bastard said to me? You hear that sucker spouting about his absolute power? I've got some power I'd like to shove up him."

"Yeah, Sarge, but he's got them Uzis. I hear there are more than twenty of them black-shirt guys. Maybe thirty. They're all over the damn ship."

"He even knew I got grandkids."

Petresky chuckled. "Hell, Sarge, most men our age have grandkids. No big surprise."

Sergeant Eckert sat there getting madder and madder. The nerve of that damn A-Rab. He felt sweat on his forehead. This was just like that big German tourist in the bar in Tokyo who thought he knew everything. He had a few surprises before he spit out three teeth.

"Damn that asshole. We can't throw him off the boat, but we can put a dent in his plans. Yeah. Tonight we'll get five or six guys and we'll trap one of the terrorists, grab his Uzi before he can use it or that pistol they all carry, and pitch the bastard overboard."

"Kill him?"

"Damn right. I done it before. You done it before. We're back in a shit-hole war here, Petresky, and I know you'll do your duty."

"Yeah, but throwing a man overboard?"

"You don't think that Abdul guy would do the same thing to us if he catches us? Fucking right he would. We nail one before they nail us."

"Then when it gets light he comes right for us," Petresky said. "He'll know who to look for."

"Maybe he won't find us." Sergeant Eckert said. "Hell, we just hide out in your cabin for a while. He doesn't know your name. We dress different, wear big shades. How he gonna find us out of fifteen hundred eaters on this boat?"

"Sarge, I don't know. Hell, I'm seventy-two. I'm too old for this kind of action."

"Short action, Petresky. Deadly serious. Goddammit, it's them or us, just like in 'Nam. Shoot them slopes before they shoot you. Yeah a couple of slant-eyes shot me. Took three slugs from the slants. Still have some damn gook shrapnel in my ass. I want you there when I call you tonight, Petresky. We'll go right before the midnight supper. Not a hell of a lot of people around the Lido deck then. Wear some dark clothes and a cap. You got a piece with you?"

Petresky rubbed his right hand over his face. "Ha, no

way. Martha wouldn't let me bring my .38 Colt. I told her in this part of the world there could be trouble."

"So show up and we'll get the job done. If it works out that we can get one of them without a shot being fired, we'll do it. Otherwise we'll wait for the next night. My bet is these jaspers gonna be around for four or five days."

"Oh, damn. Don't tell Martha. To get away from her, I'll say I want to gamble on the slots some more. That she'll understand."

Sergeant Eckert whacked the older man on the back. "You're okay, Petresky. Now I want to catch me a quick nap. We could be up half the night."

On the bridge, Abdul watched the Norwegian officers doing their work. The computer did most of it, guided the big ship through the water at the right speed and on the course. No human hand could do the job so precisely.

He checked his watch. Seven o'clock. Another three and a half hours and they would be on station, right in the middle of the Strait of Hormuz, with over five thousand lightbulbs burning brightly. Then the fun would begin. He nodded as he went over the plan again. There wasn't much that could go wrong. He would have the big powers with a noose around their balls. They had to cooperate or sing soprano in the choir forever. Oh, yes, it would be glorious. And this was just the start. Once he had the cash in hand . . .

"Sir."

Abdul looked over at the black-shirted man who stood near him. He was aware that his man had said the word before.

"Yes?"

"Some trouble on the Sun deck, sir."

"What happened?"

"One of our men clubbed a passenger with his Uzi. They took the bleeding American to the medical unit."

"Why did this happen?"

"The way I understand it is that the passenger became incensed when one of our men touched his wife. Evidently he kissed her on the mouth."

"Bastard of a camel-dung eater," Abdul bellowed. "Bring our man to me here at once. He forfeits his stake in this venture and is lucky if I don't throw him overboard. All of you had strict instructions about how to behave around their women. Isn't that true?"

"Yes, sir. It's true."

"Bring him here."

"He's right outside," the man said, and pointed to one of the doors off the bridge.

Abdul tightened his grip on the Uzi and marched toward the door, his steely eyes sparking with anger. He held his Uzi in both hands chest high.

Abdul went out the door and stared at one of the thirty men who had come on board with him. He had forgotten his name. A recent recruit.

"Did you do it?"

"A quick kiss, that was all. Her man went crazy. I disciplined him as you said we should."

"I told all of you to stay away from their women. Their culture is different. They mistakenly revere and honor their women." Abdul stepped closer to the man.

"I'm sorry, Abdul. It won't happen again. I'll be—" The side of the Uzi slammed against his forehead, driving the man backward two steps until he jolted against the bulkhead. His eyes glazed for a moment. Then he shook his head. "I don't understand."

"You certainly don't. I should shoot you right now. You are through with this mission. You will be locked in a room and left there when we move away from the ship. You could compromise our work here. We have a divine purpose. No actions by our people can detract in any way from it."

Abdul turned to the man who had spoken to him first. "Take this stupid one away and lock him up. I never want to see his face again."

"But Abdul, surely—"

The Arab leader lifted the muzzle of the Uzi and pressed it against his man's lips.

"One more word and it will be the last one you ever

speak, the last thought you ever have, and you will not be a martyr for Allah. Take him away."

Abdul stood there a moment, watching them push the man down the corridor and to the steps. He had come so close to shooting one of his own men. If he had, it all would have filtered back to the passengers. There must be no hint of any differences among the men in control. He had to use a steel-hard fist with his men and in dealing with the infidels. It was his destiny. He had been selected by Allah for this mission. He could not fail. His family was precious to him, but they knew his work. Now he had to strive to carry it out in every way that he could. Praise Allah.

Sergeant Norman Eckert sat on the Lido deck, drink in hand, and watched the night people moving around him. He hadn't seen the assault by the black-costumed Arab on the American, but he had heard about it in detail.

His nostrils flared as he began to breathe hard just thinking about it. The damned A-Rab had slugged the guy with his Uzi. Took off a strip of skin down his forehead and cheek. Blood all over the place and the guy down and out cold on the deck. Everybody screaming and the A-Rab waving the damn Uzi. The hurt guy would be lucky if he didn't lose an eye.

Eckert doubled up his fists and relaxed them. At first he wasn't aware he was doing it, and when he saw it, he kept right on. There had to be a way. He didn't drag himself out of the Great Depression and the dust bowl in Nebraska to let something like this pass. He had been steeped in the tradition of helping your neighbor in the tough times.

Now was another tough time. *Damned if I'll let the fucking A-Rabs get away with it.* Tonight was going to be the night. He told the four men whose phone numbers he had, and they would meet on the Lido deck at eleven o'clock. There were places they could hide out of the lights and still give them a short charge to get to one of the patrolling A-Rabs.

He figured that the terrorists would have some kind of roving patrol just to be sure nothing got out of hand. Sergeant Eckert snorted. At least one thing was going to be way out of hand before morning, if they had any luck at all.

Only a sliver of the crescent moon showed in the darkness. Stars winked and faded. It was a good night for retribution. Yes, the damn A-Rabs were killers. They had shot down the captain, the first mate, and at least four more officers of the ship. In cold blood. A life for a life. They owed this bunch six dead.

Sergeant Eckert worked on his beer slowly. It was still fifteen minutes until eleven o'clock, 2300. Just a few more minutes to wait, and then they would meet on deck and move to their spots carefully, one at a time. It would work. He wondered if all four of the others would show up.

Sergeant Eckert felt the heavy, .45 automatic in his pocket. He had a second magazine loaded with eight rounds and ready to go. If all went well, there would be no shooting.

Petresky used his cane more than he needed to as he walked into the Capri bar and bought a beer. He sat at a table and didn't look at Eckert. Yes. Good.

Five minutes later, two more of their five came and stood at the bar waiting. Not talking with the others, nursing beers and watching.

A half hour ago, Sergeant Eckert had seen a black-clad figure walk past the bar. He was on the outside on the Lido deck ambling along, evidently watching everything without seeming to. Yes, the man had his Uzi, but it was slung over his chest. Would that make it quick to swing up and fire? Eckert decided it could be a sudden and simple move. He'd have to watch that.

Just after 11 P.M., the fifth man hadn't shown up. Even so, it was time. Sergeant Eckert stood and walked slowly to the door. He didn't look at the others. On the deck he found the shadowed place they had agreed to meet. The other three men drifted into the dark, meeting a few minutes later. Eckert knew the other two as Bill and Larry. Both had been military. Both agreed on what they had to do.

Sergeant Eckert whispered greetings to the men. "You know what we're here for. I figure the roaming sentry will be past here every half hour. So we could have a short wait. Get to your spots and keep cool. When we see the guy walk past us, we charge him flat out and roust him off the port side before he knows he's in trouble. In twenty seconds he'll be in the water and swimming for his life.

"My job is to grab the Uzi away from him so he can't fire it. Bill, you get the pistol off his belt. As we do this, we drive him over the rail. Larry, if you get a chance, clamp your hand over his mouth so he can't yell." Eckert looked at the three men in the darkness. "You all ready?"

Heads nodded. "Okay, get to your assigned spots and we wait."

The men drifted off, then vanished into the deep shadows they had carefully selected.

Now was when time dragged like molasses at the North Pole. Wait and watch.

Sergeant Eckert checked the layout, the killing ground. This slice of the Lido deck was no more than twenty feet from the rail. From there it was a straight drop down to the water. If the four of them did it the way they planned, there should be one fewer terrorist on board by morning.

He waited. After what he figured was a half hour, Sergeant Eckert checked his watch. Only fifteen minutes had passed. He looked at the hiding spots again. He couldn't see any of the men. Good.

Footsteps sounded away from them, then slowly came closer, and gradually a form materialized out of the half-light. A man dressed all in black ambled forward. He glanced around but without much enthusiasm. Sergeant Eckert tensed. He felt his heart racing. Sweat popped out on his forehead. He wanted to cough, but held it in. The Arab terrorist walked forward on the same route Eckert had seen him take earlier that night.

Yes, yes, keep coming. Eckert breathed through his mouth to cut out any sound. He drew the .45 and pushed off the safety. Earlier that day he had charged a round into the firing chamber.

The Arab terrorist was halfway across their target area. Another thirty feet and his back would be to all four of them. Sergeant Eckert lifted the .45 automatic and slid his finger onto the trigger. He counted down the steps. Ten more was all they needed. Ten more steps, and then it would happen.

Five, four, three, two, one.

Sergeant Norman Eckert pushed away from the cold steel of the ship and charged forward on his soft-soled shoes toward the terrorist.

✴ SIX ✴

GULF OF OMAN

Sergeant Eckert had positioned himself so he would be the first man to reach the Arab. Ten running steps that Eckert took didn't alert the guard, but the last two did and he turned just as the sergeant hit him with a shoulder block in the side. The two crashed to the deck and the Uzi skittered away. Bill dropped on the sentry and clawed the pistol out of his holster.

Larry thudded on top of the Arab's legs and clamped a hand over the black-shirted guard's mouth. Petresky came in late, grabbed the Uzi, and knelt in front of them.

"Pick him up," Eckert whispered. The three men got to their knees, then lifted the small Arab and moved toward the rail. In the soft light from the Lido deck, Eckert could see the Arab's frightened eyes.

"Tough luck, little man," Eckert whispered. "Little boys like you shouldn't play with guns. You're in the major leagues here, asshole."

Bill held the man's legs in an iron grasp with both arms. Eckert had one arm pinned to the Arab's body, and Larry had the other one grasped firmly as they shuffled toward the rail.

It seemed to Eckert that it was taking forever. He hurried the pace and stumbled. They slowed and soon were at the rail.

"We really going to do this?" Petresky asked.

"Damn right," Eckert said. "You saw what they did to that poor slob trying to protect his wife."

"Yeah, we all saw, so let's do it now," Bill said. The three men pushed the Arab terrorist over the rail and dropped him. They watched him vanish into the darkness below. Eckert never heard a splash. Petresky threw the Uzi submachine gun over the rail.

"We can't keep it," he said. "It would lead them right to us."

The four men stood there a moment, Eckert not really believing what they had done. It had been a long time since he'd killed. He relived how he felt when they had pushed the small man over the rail and let him drop. Elation? Pride? And just a little bit of fear of discovery. Hell, it was done, now they lived on. He recovered in a moment.

"Back to your rooms, do everything normal," Eckert said. "No sweat. We just hit a home run." The four men went singly by different routes off the Lido deck and headed to their cabins.

Eckert frowned, suddenly aware that his pants felt funny. He stopped outside the elevator and looked down. His dark pants had a large black, wet stain from the crotch halfway down his right leg. "Dammit no!" Eckert whispered. He hurried to his cabin, avoiding everyone he saw.

On the bridge, the time was 11:21 P.M. Abdul and Faisal watched the controls and readouts carefully.

"Gentlemen, there will be no mistakes, no slipups," Abdul said. "The chart shows that we are less than three miles from our target point. You will bring the ship to anchor in the middle of the Strait of Hormuz."

"We can't do that, Captain," the lead man on the Norwegian bridge crew said. "Our charts show the channel is three hundred feet deep at that point. We don't have that much chain or cable to anchor there."

"How close can we get to the center of the channel and still anchor securely?" Faisal asked.

"We've checked that. The channel runs roughly north–south. If we move a half mile west, we can anchor safely."

Faisal looked at Abdul, who nodded.

"Do it," Abdul snapped, and went to stare out the forward windows. He could see almost nothing but blackness. Tomorrow morning would be his finest hour. He had worked over the wording for weeks. Faisal had helped him as well as two others, and he had the wording exactly the way he wanted it. Strong, unyielding, absolute. He nodded at Faisal to see to the anchoring and went to the captain's cabin. It was like a shoreside apartment. Three rooms and a large bath. Earlier in the day he had had three stewards clean it thoroughly and throw out what he didn't like. Now he settled down in the king-size bed and within ten seconds was asleep. He had left word to be called on the phone promptly at 6 A.M.

Faisal took the phone call on the bridge just after 4 A.M. There had been trouble anchoring and they had to move in another quarter mile toward the Iranian shore to find the bottom where their hook would hold. Now he picked up the phone, his voice harsh with weariness.

"Yes?"

"Faisal, this is Hayma at the security office. I've been monitoring our six men on watch and I've lost track of one man. He was to patrol the Lido deck where we had the problem. I haven't heard from him over the past two time checks."

Faisal twisted his mouth as he sometimes did when he was tired and unhappy. "You may have missed it, or he may have forgotten to call in. Don't worry about it. Double-check with him in the morning and let me know what happened."

"Yes sir."

Faisal told the Norwegians not to move a control without his approval, and went to sleep in the soft captain's chair. He wanted to be on hand for the 6 A.M. announcement.

Abdul awoke at 5:30 A.M. He couldn't get back to sleep. He got up and put on the captain's shirt, the white one with the gold bars on the shoulder boards. The white pants were far too large so he wore his black ones. He took the prepared statement from his pocket and read it over four times out loud, so he could get the correct emphasis on the words, and still maintain the right steely tone.

He hurried to the radio room and prodded his man there awake. The ship's radio operator was sleeping as well on a built-in bunk. Abdul roused him with a kick in the side. When he was sure the Norwegian was awake he pointed at him.

"You, set up the radio to broadcast to all hailing channels. I want as widespread coverage as I can get with this radio message. Do you understand?"

"Yes sir. But I'm not sure—"

"Just do it. Tell me when you're ready and give me a microphone."

The operator turned on several buttons, switched some frequencies, and then handed him a mike.

"Just push that switch to the on position when you're ready, Captain."

"Radioman. I want you to record this so you can broadcast it every hour on the hour until 6 P.M. Do you understand?"

"Yes sir."

Abdul saw Faisal come to the door. He waved him inside and turned the mike on. He would read slowly and forcefully just the way he had practiced.

"Attention. Attention all shippers in the Persian Gulf. Six hours from now, at exactly twelve o'clock noon, there will be a special exit tax applied to all loaded tankers preparing to leave the Persian Gulf through the Strait of Hormuz. This tax will apply to all nations and all shippers of petroleum.

"The tax is one hundred thousand U.S. dollars per tanker, to be paid only with U.S. one-hundred-dollar bills. Empty tankers are free to pass through the strait going into the Persian Gulf.

"Any outbound tanker not stopping to make payment at or near the large luxury ocean liner in the strait will be torpedoed and raked with fifty-caliber machine-gun fire.

"I am Abdul al Ganzouri, the Sword of Allah. I now control the Norwegian luxury liner *Royal Princess*, and its fifteen hundred passengers and seven hundred crewmen. You may consider these men and women as hostages, my security, to ensure your payment of the tax.

"Any military involvement against my ships or my men will result in the immediate execution of twenty passengers. There will be no overflights by military aircraft, no movement of naval vessels toward my position, or in the immediate area or the execution of twenty passengers will be made for each infraction.

"Ships now in transit from your ports have until noon to pass through the strait free of charge. You see, I'm a reasonable man. If you can't make it past me by noon, be sure a helicopter brings out the one hundred thousand U.S. dollars to you so you can pay the exit fee to the Sword of Allah. This ultimatum will be broadcast every hour on the hour until 6 P.M. I thank you for your cooperation."

Abdul switched off the mike.

"Well?" he asked.

Faisal laughed softly, his eyes glowed, and he nodded several times. "Yes, perfect. Just the way you practiced it. Perfect. It will bring immediate results."

Faisal and Abdul had argued about the method of payment for weeks as they assembled their cash and strike force. Faisal said that the ships would have no way to get a hundred thousand dollars on short notice.

"Not so," Abdul said. "These ships are gold mines for the owners. They haul massive amounts of oil, up to a half million barrels of raw petroleum on one of the supertankers. At thirty dollars a barrel on the market, that cargo in one huge tanker is worth fifteen million dollars."

"That much?" Faisal said amazed.

"Yes, absolutely. Even a medium-sized tanker with a quarter of a million barrels of oil has a cargo worth eight million dollars. People with that much money can get their hands on a hundred thousand with little trouble, and quickly. They must have money available for all sorts of problems and helicopters are a dime a dozen around oil fields."

"Beats ransoming the passengers, I guess," Faisal said.

"Beats them dead. We'd have to dicker with twenty nations. The U.S. says it won't bargain with hijackers. Cuts down the list. We'd get maybe fifty thousand for some and five thousand for some. It could take a month. We need to be in and out quickly."

Back on the ship, Faisal nodded. "Yes, I think we decided right to go for the exit fee of a hundred thousand. Cleaner, works better, and we should be able to do it and be gone before any real opposition can be launched."

The radio began to talk as several calls came in different languages. The radio operator looked at Abdul.

"Turn off the receivers. Don't take any calls from anyone. Leave on the transmitter and send this same message every hour. I'll be monitoring you."

BALDERMARE CASTLE

When J. August Marshall entered his study shortly after 7 A.M. he saw the flashing red light on his telephone and computer. He had E-mail and someone wanted to talk to him. He grabbed the phone first and listened to the frantic message.

"Some terrorist, sir, has hijacked a luxury passenger liner and is blockading the Strait of Hormuz and demanding a hundred thousand U.S. dollars exit tax for each tanker. We have four Marshall oil tankers in the gulf now; two are loaded ready to leave. Should we take the cash to pay the tax? It's now 6:12 A.M. Waiting your response."

Mister Marshall called his man in London. "Do not sail. Keep the ships in the gulf. We don't pay terrorists. More instructions later."

He phoned MI-6 in London and identified himself.

"Could I hear a recording of the terrorist's message from the Strait of Hormuz? You must have it there on tape. My group is vitally interested."

MI-6 played the message for him, which he recorded. He thanked them and hung up. His next call went to the CIA director H.J. Jansen in Virginia. He was at home where it was after one in the morning Eastern Standard Time. The director hadn't heard of the blockade. He thanked Marshall and said he would get his people on it at once.

J. August Marshall sat at his desk, peaking his fingers and tapping the tips together gently. There had to be a response. What? Any military action could mean civilian executions. It could be a bluff, but the militant Arabs were not known for their bluffing. The military card was canceled out. That left only civilians. By the time the President was awake the Specialists had to have a plan to offer him.

Fifteen minutes later the Specialists left their early-morning workout and jogged back to the castle. They were in dirty cammies with uncleaned weapons, sweat and grime on their faces.

"Good to have you here. Please sit down. We have a problem and I need the best counsel you can give me. We need an absolutely brilliant and foolproof plan in six hours. This is the problem."

THE ROYAL PRINCESS

"What do you mean one of our men is missing?" Abdul snapped at Faisal shortly after they left the radio room on their way back to the bridge.

"Our man in security reported it about 4 A.M. I told him to check again with daylight. Mohammad might be sleeping somewhere. He isn't. Nobody has seen Mohammad since just before eleven o'clock when he talked with the sentry on the Aloha deck. He isn't in the quarters assigned him, and nobody has seen him this morning."

Abdul slammed the flat of his palm against the bulkhead wall and swore in Arabic. Faisal grinned in spite of himself at the colorful language.

"So what does this mean?"

"That some act of violence may have been done to Mohammad. He may have been captured and held in a stateroom bound and gagged. He may have been shot and dumped overboard by a band of Americans trying to over-throw us or at least harass us."

"I agree," Abdul said. "Which means we need to make an example of someone. It doesn't have to be the one who made the attack on our man. First we make an announcement. We give the American passengers and the Norwegian crew an hour to produce Mohammad. If he isn't found, two passengers will be selected randomly and thrown overboard."

"That threat should produce some results."

"Make the announcement at once over the entire ship's PA system, Faisal. Do it now."

Abdul noticed that it wasn't yet 8 A.M. The first seating at the dining room wasn't ready. This announcement should shake up a lot of people. What he hoped was that Mohammad would come crawling out of some empty cabin where he had been sleeping when he was supposed to be on watch.

Abdul stayed on the Promenade deck while the announcement came over the PA system. He watched the shock and surprise show in the faces of the passengers heading for breakfast. Good. It might rattle somebody enough to come forward.

By nine-thirty Mohammad had not been found. Abdul stood outside the doors of the dining room and watched the people coming out. He had called up two of his men by radio. One stood on each side of him. He pointed to a man coming on the deck. He was about forty, looked in good shape, and had a pretty wife by his side.

"You," Abdul said. "Over here." One of the Arabs caught him by the arm and pulled him toward the leader. His wife screamed.

"What the hell? What you doing?" the husband yelled.

"Quiet," Abdul said. "You have a distinct honor." He waited a few minutes and selected a tall woman with blond hair and a good figure for the second victim. He pointed and the other guard grabbed her arm and pulled her with him. A man behind her protested and he was knocked to the deck.

Abdul walked the pair to the rail. "Hold them here," he

told his two men in Arabic. He looked at the frightened pair. "You heard that Mohammad is missing. You two will pay the price for his disappearance. Two for one. I could make it twenty for one."

The woman began to cry. Huge tears rolled down her cheeks and her chest heaved but no sound came from her throat. The man's eyes went wide for a moment, then turned angry.

"You can't do this. There are international laws. Our air force will blow you out of the water."

"What, and kill a thousand U.S. citizens? I don't think so." He lifted a bullhorn he had brought from the bridge and aimed it at the passengers still coming out from breakfast.

"Now listen to this. I want all of you who can hear me to come on the Promenade deck for a little lesson in behavior. You have five minutes to get here. Move quickly. This is not a request. Move now to the port side of the Promenade deck."

He knew they would come. Most out of curiosity. Some from fear. But they would come.

Five minutes later there were what he guessed to be five or six hundred people crowding the side of the Promenade deck. He lifted the bullhorn.

"Good, you have come for your lesson. I am Abdul, and I control this ship. Your lives are in my hands. Last night one of my men vanished. We believe that some of you hurt him, perhaps bound and gagged him, maybe even threw him off the ship. Now you will pay. These two at the rail behind me will give their lives for the sins of the rest of you.

"They will die because a few of you tried to strike back at us, and did so as cowards under cover of darkness, then sneaked back to your cabins. These two are walking dead right now. The woman will be the first overboard so we can see if she can swim to Iran. It's only thirty miles."

He then spoke softly in Arabic to his two men six feet away at the rail. "Don't throw her over, but pretend to."

"It's time to pay the piper. Throw her overboard."

There was a gasp from hundreds of throats. Then one voice came out clear from the center of the people.

"Noooooooooooooo. Don't kill her. I'll take her place. I'll go over the rail in her place."

The crowd gasped again as a man struggled through the crowd and ran across the opening toward Abdul. "Take me, Abdul, you fucking bastard. I'm Master Sergeant Eckert, U.S. Marine Corps. Throw me overboard instead of her."

★ SEVEN ★

BALDERMARE CASTLE

Wade Thorne took the lead. He looked around the conference table loaded with pads, pens, and reference books. "So, we know the problem. What can we do about it?"

"Military is definitely out?" Roger asked. "Why couldn't they send the SEALs in covertly and take over the ship?"

"Covert would be the problem," Mister Marshall said. "If for any reason they failed, and were identified by their gear, it could mean a hundred United States citizen-hostages shot or thrown off the ship."

"Theoretically, Mister Marshall," Roger said. "But we both know that the SEALs never fail."

"Sometimes they need to initiate a retrograde movement under overwhelming odds," Kat said, and they all chuckled.

"So, no military, that grinds down the chances of beating this ragtag Sword of Allah," Wade said.

Kat snapped her fingers. "Hey, that's what that little kid said we tackled in Cairo. He said 'Wait until Uncle Abdul hears about this.' Then he said he was the Sword of Allah."

"*Uncle* can have a lot of meanings in Arab countries," Duncan Bancroft said. "Many times it means a friend of a friend, or just an older friend."

"But what about the problem?" Hershel Levine said. "What kind of a plan can we come up with to take care of this little matter?"

"He said ships, plural in the broadcast," Ichi said. That must mean he has some kind of a torpedo boat to use to threaten any tanker trying to run his blockade. If we take out the torpedo boat, we pull his fangs and he can't sink any ship trying to run the strait."

Kat turned to Roger. "How big are torpedo boats?"

"Most countries don't use the old PT boats anymore. My guess is that this could be a naval patrol boat anywhere from forty to a hundred feet. A terrorist could buy a small one and jury-rig it to fire torpedoes, and it could have a fifty-caliber on it."

"So his weak spot is the torpedo boat," Wade said. "Strip that off and he's bluffing. Most luxury liners don't carry much in the way of offensive weapons."

"But he still has over two thousand hostages," Mister Marshall said. "He could threaten to drop a dozen U.S. citizens into the Strait of Hormuz for every tanker that passed without paying."

"I'm sure the CIA and State would consider that an even more potent threat than the torpedo boat," Kat said. "So looks like we have two objectives, the torpedo boat and the luxury liner hijackers."

"How good is the radar on a ship like that?" Roger asked.

"Probably the best money can buy," Ichi said. "But it wouldn't have high-resolution stuff that could pick up a Rubber Duck in the dark. We could play like SEALs, drop out of a chopper about six or seven miles off the strait, then motor in at fifteen miles an hour until we get close to the liner. Then creep up and take out the torpedo boat, which must be tied up alongside."

"Sounds good so far," Roger Johnson said. "How do we get on board the big boat?" He looked around. Nobody said a word. "Yeah, my turf. The tough way is to come up on her in a Rubber Duck about 2 A.M. Use grappling hooks over the rail on the Promenade deck. That should be thirty to forty feet off the water. We climb up the ropes to the deck. Only problem, not all of us are rope ready. Ichi is out of that plan. The other way is to use hand and foot magnets and literally crawl up the metal side of the ship hand over hand to the rail. Not an easy job either."

"Neither option sounds all that good," Wade said. "How else can you attack a luxury liner like that?" He looked around the table.

"Maybe we should wonder how the terrorists got on board," Hershel said. "They didn't tell us. I've been on a few luxury liners and most of them I remember had dockside hatches that are no more than four feet off the water. They open them in port sometimes if the tide is right for boarding and taking on supplies. Now if this one has a hatch down that low, and if we could get that door open . . ."

"Could be that's how the hostiles got on board," Roger said. "One or two confederates on board could open that low-level hatch and let the bad guys in."

"How would they tow a torpedo boat?" Kat asked. They looked at Roger.

"I'd do it by lashing it to the big ship alongside that low-opening hatch. Which means it wouldn't be closed all the way, probably with a couple of men there covering to be sure the small boat didn't get slammed to pieces by the bow wave."

The Specialists looked at each other. "So that dockside hatch could be our salvation here, if this ship has one," Mister Marshall said.

"Could our satellite get a shot of the sides of that ship to show us if there is a boat tied up there?" Wade asked Mister Marshall.

"Yes, if there's an orbit anywhere near there," Mister Marshall said. "It takes a while to switch an orbit on these sky pirates. But when it's overhead, it can read a deck of cards on the table. Finding a boat tied to the side would be easy. If it's there."

Heads began to nod. Duncan spoke first. "So it looks like it's a go if we can find that door open. First we capture the patrol boat at that dockside hatch. Then get inside and the six of us hunt down the bad guys and take them out as quietly as possible."

Mister Marshall stood. "Let me see who I can wake up

in the CIA to get some information for us about orbits. If we don't have one in the right spot, which is probable, I'll see how long it will take to change one."

"A fifty-thousand-foot flying spy plane with a good lens could do the same job," Wade said. "At that altitude nobody on the liner could possibly know that the plane was up there."

"A good backup," Mister Marshall said. "If we don't have the right orbit, I'll ask for the spy plane to do the job today before dark." He turned and headed for his communications center.

"How is our swimming?" Roger asked. "We don't get in the water often enough. There's that lake we use about ten miles over. My guess is we should get in a couple of miles of swimming just in case we need it."

Wade pointed his finger at the former SEAL. He would check with Mister Marshall to get an okay to use the neighbor's private lake. They had taken long swims there before.

"Weapons?" Ichi asked. "My suggestion would be silenced MP-5 submachine guns, the fourteen-round auto pistol of your choice, and explosive primer cord and timer-detonators in case we find some barricaded terrs. We could have a spare Colt M-4-A1 for longer stuff. Shouldn't be much need for long shots on a luxury liner. Motorolas for commo and jungle cammies, and our usual vests and harness."

"So how do we get within ten miles of the place?" Roger asked. "I bet the Navy would loan us a CH-46 Sea Knight and a Rubber Duck," Roger said. "Know damn well they would if the President tells the CNO to do it. Officially it's an IBS, Inflatable Boat Small with an outboard motor that can push six of us and our gear along at fifteen knots."

"How do we get close enough to use the CH-46?" Kat asked. "Don't we have friends in the United Arab Emirates, right there on the horn of Oman? We could fly to Kuwait and then on to Dubayy by fixed wing. Roger, what's the range on a CH-46?"

"Plenty, over three hundred and fifty miles. From Dubayy

on out to the strait couldn't be more than a hundred miles. Out and back, no sweat."

"Timing," Wade said. If that orbit or spy plane can confirm a side-loading hatch on that liner, we should be ready to hit that ship at first dark. Take some fancy footwork but Mister Marshall can arrange it if we get a go from the President. With so many U.S. hostages involved, the President will want to be positive this is the best attack plan.

"Let's get our gear ready just in case," Ichi said. Wade looked at Ichi.

"How are you feeling? Have you been walking the two miles?" Ichi nodded. "Any problems breathing? Has the doctor checked you out lately?"

"Not for two weeks, but I'm feeling good. Don't think I could swim very far, but anything else."

"I'll want a doctor's okay before I sign you on for this, Ichi. I know it sucks, but we don't want to lose you for good. You might get to play hooky on this one. See about that doctor check. Have the doctor drive out here and work you over." Ichi frowned, nodded, and went for a telephone.

The rest of them trooped into the equipment room. They had duplicate gear to what they kept in the London office.

Mister Marshall came into the area ten minutes later.

"No orbit over that area, but I shook up Washington and most of the top people are awake and working. CIA chief Jansen has ordered a spy plane to do a flyover and take pictures of both sides of that luxury liner. It should be taking off from England about now. They'll have the films back, developed, and evaluated in three hours."

"What does the President say about our plan?" Wade asked.

"He's with his advisors now. Middle of the night back there but they're working on it. I figure they'll come up dry on any military move and that leaves us."

"Mister Marshall, can you check with the CNO to see if he can have a CH-46 and a Rubber Duck for us to use at Dubayy, in the United Arab Emirates, at first dark today?"

Wade asked. "That bird can fly all of us to within ten miles and we use the IBS to motor to the liner."

Kat asked him how they planned to get to Dubayy. He said they could fly all the way in the small corporate jet and wouldn't have to risk a foul-up making connections with the Air Force.

"Good, I'll see if I can roust out the CNO. We won't know anything for certain for another three and a half hours."

"What happens if there isn't a hatch we can get into?" Kat asked.

Roger shrugged. "We take grappling hooks and go up the side of that liner to the Promenade deck, where the life rafts can swing out for deployment. Anybody who can't climb a rope we can pull up with a rope harness. It's only maybe forty feet at the outside. First we send two men up to secure the area. Watch for roving patrols. Then we get the rest up when we're safe."

"All of our people aren't rope ready," Wade said. "Let's hope that there's a hatch we can get in. Until we find out, let's get suited up and ready. Take any combat goodies you think you might need. The MP-5s for everyone. Two long guns. This will be combat in and around more than two thousand civilians. So we'll have to make every shot count and not let them use their fast guns, whatever they have. We want to be combat ready when we leave here so we can drive directly to the airport."

"What about grappling hooks and ropes?" Kat asked.

"Should be some small ones here," Roger said. "Remember last year we used them on an exercise climbing up the side of the castle."

"What kind of weapons will the terrs have?" Kat asked.

"My guess is they'll have some kind of submachine guns," Ichi said. "Ingrams, maybe a model twelve Beretta or a Mat forty-nine from France. Pistols, too, I'd suspect, and an ankle hide-out so pat any live ones down carefully."

"We better be ready," Wade said. "A sub gun and a pistol. Let's get our gear together."

Ichi went to Wade. "Talked with the doctor. He gave

me an okay for this mission if we don't have to use the ropes. And if we don't have to swim, which we shouldn't. If that dockside hatch shows up in the pictures, I'm on the team."

Wade slapped him gently on the shoulder. "Great. We'll need you."

ON BOARD *THE ROYAL PRINCESS*

Abdul stared at the pudgy man who ran across the deck toward him. One terrorist stopped the Marine, holding him back with an Uzi across his chest.

"Hey, you A-Rab asshole," Sergeant Eckert bellowed. "Throw me overboard instead of her."

Abdul stared at the man's red face and snorted. "Yes, the man on the Lido deck yesterday. The big mouth U.S. Marine, I remember you. Good idea. We'll pitch you over the side too. Three is better than two."

Shouts came from the crowd, then a roar of anger. Some men started forward. One of the black-clad men fired his Uzi on full automatic, slamming ten rounds into the air. The people on the deck stopped moving.

"How many of you want to die right here?" Abdul screamed at the crowd. He glared at them, then looked back at the three hostages by the rail. Another terrorist had come up to hold Eckert.

"Master Sergeant, you must be an interesting man to throw yourself on my sword this way. You have a death wish? Are you just a little crazy? I wish I had time to talk with you, discuss the world situation. I don't have that time." He turned to the guards.

"Throw both of the hostages overboard, now," he said in Arabic. "For real," he continued in Arabic. "Pick the woman up and throw her over the rail, then the man. Do it now. Right now."

The crowd shrilled in anger when the two black-dressed terrorists picked up the woman. Screams came from the crowd. A dozen men ran forward but three bursts of automatic Uzi fire in the air stopped them.

The woman bleated in terror as she dropped over the rail. The two men at once grabbed the man. He fought them. They struggled. A third terrorist hit the captive on the head with the Uzi and he sagged, unconscious. The terrorists pitched him over the side.

The crowd stood in shock and horror. Many of the women cried. The men swore and some advanced straight at the guns, then stopped. There were fifteen of the black-dressed terrorists all with their weapons pointed at the crowd.

Abdul used the bullhorn again, speaking in English. "So, you thought I was bluffing. I don't bluff. This Marine, I have some special treatment for him."

He spoke rapidly in Arabic. Two guards grabbed Master Sergeant Eckert and cut off his clothes with their knives until he was naked.

In English again, Abdul talked to the crowd through the speaker. "He will be tied to a pole near the swimming pool to cook in the sun for three days and nights. If anyone touches him, talks to him, or gives him anything to eat or drink, they will be shot on the spot. Take him away."

A black-dressed terrorist ran up to Abdul and grabbed his arm and towed him toward the pool.

A short time later, Abdul walked into the bridge and looked at the radar screen one of his men pointed to.

"It shows twelve tankers heading for the strait. All of them are making about eighteen knots and should pass through well before the twelve noon deadline. In back of those are more tankers but we can't get good sightings or distances on them."

"So, it's beginning. Take the torpedo crew down to the boat and wait for action. Have the radio keep in contact with the bridge. We'll probably have to torpedo one or maybe two of them before they believe that we're serious. Get the torpedo crew to check out the tubes to be sure they are ready to fire. We'll have them push off at eleven-thirty and be sure they keep in radio contact. Go."

Two men left the bridge and two more took their places watching the officers of the ship.

"Now we wait and see what happens," Abdul said.

Master Sergeant Eckert went from mortification to anger and then on to a stoic sense of doom. He had made the charge to save the woman out of common decency and a sense of duty. He had failed to save her. He was a Marine, dammit. Then it became more personal with the sonofabitch who had hijacked the boat.

He stood ramrod straight against the pole they had tied him to. His hands were fastened behind his back, his legs bound to the pole as well. No one was in the pool that early. No one stared at him. The few people who had been near the pool when he was marched in yelled insults at the guards, then promptly left. One woman screamed at the guard, ran up, and slapped him hard on the face. He didn't retaliate. She left sobbing.

Eckert saw his wife sitting by herself at the far corner of the pool in the warm sunshine. She watched him, sending him her love and support. It was all she could do. She knew where his .45 automatic was. God, he hoped that she didn't get it and go crazy and start shooting the hijackers. He stared at her, sending her stern messages not to do anything crazy.

He would endure. This wasn't nearly as tough as the training he'd done in the Corps for years. Hell, this was nothing. Naked was nothing. The sun might turn him bright red, but he could live with that.

Three hours later, the last of the twelve tankers had passed through the strait and headed into the Gulf of Oman.

"Our radar shows ten more tankers moving up," Faisal said. "None of them will make it through before the noon deadline. The torpedo crew boat is ready and in position. The first two tankers coming are of the smaller type. We don't know what flag they're flying. We'll know what they are going to do in fifteen minutes."

"Good. Where's my lunch?"

It had been set up on a separate table for him with silverware, cloth napkins, and a steward to pour wine if he wanted it and to bring him anything else he desired. He didn't want the wine. He marveled at the array of foods and had only started eating when Faisal's voice cut into his pleasure.

"It's a Panamanian flag tanker and it's not stopping," Faisal said.

"Give the order to fire," Abdul said. He took another bite of the crab salad and went to the forward windows to watch. The long tanker plowed ahead at eighteen knots. The Boghammar did a slow dance toward it, held up two hundred yards off, and angled slightly toward the tanker's path of travel.

A gush of white smoke foamed around the small craft and Abdul and Faisal could see the torpedo launched off the Boghammar. The small craft scuttered backward twenty feet as the fish dived for the water. It was set for a surface run and at once made a bubbly trail as the lethal torpedo slashed through the water at thirty-five miles an hour, homing in on the nearby tanker. The Panamanian ship was on this side of the channel less than a quarter of a mile from the passenger liner.

Abdul and his men saw the explosion before the sound came to them. The flash of a direct hit, then the gushing white-and-black smoke, followed by another bright flash.

"Got him," Faisal yelled. He pounded one fist into the air. "Hit the damned blockade runner."

Inside the bridge, they barely heard the explosion. But they saw the immediate effect. The tanker slowed. Fire gushed from the ragged hole twenty feet high in the side plates. Oil streamed out of the punctured hold, spreading crude into the Strait of Hormuz. The tanker lumbered to a stop. They could see frantic efforts on board the ship to contain and put out the fire.

"The other oil transporters coming toward the strait have stopped," Faisal said. "They must be rethinking their next move."

A half hour later the fire on the tanker was out. The big ship began a slow turn and headed back up the Persian Gulf.

"Going back to port for repairs, I'd guess," Faisal said.

"Another tanker approaching the strait," a lookout said who held binoculars. "It has a Kuwaiti flag and someone is waving a pure white flag. It's slowing."

The Boghammar's radio spoke. "We have a winner. The second tanker has called on our frequency saying they will lower payment to us on a line. We'll check it and let you know if it's right."

"That's understood, Boghammar," Abdul said, taking the handheld radio. "I think the other captains have seen the light. Repairs on that Panamanian boat are going to run more than a million dollars."

Abdul went back to his crab salad. It was followed by a stuffed-chicken entrée and his choice of three deserts. He took all three. All the time he ate, Abdul was working his calculator. They had heard that more than twenty tankers went through the strait on some days. If they had twenty from now until dark, that would bring in two million dollars. That would be enough to finance his new project. Yes! Two years of planning and working were about to pay off.

Another tanker slowed to produce the packet of payment to the small boat next to it. Abdul counted at least another dozen tankers up the gulf. Abdul didn't try to contain his smile. This indeed was his day.

★ EIGHT ★

Master Sergeant Norman Eckert tried to lick his lips. There
was little moisture for his tongue to work with. He had never
dried out this fast in his life, not even on a twenty-mile hike
with a bunch of boots. He tried to swallow. There was no
saliva left. How long? He'd been cooking here in the hot sun
for almost seven hours. He still had his watch on but
couldn't read it behind him. He'd heard an explosion off the
ship somewhere but he had no idea what it was. Damn sure
it wasn't the U.S. Navy coming to his rescue. He remembered
what Abdul said about any military action. He'd kill twenty
people without a second thought or a touch of conscience.
Abdul was a cold bastard. The ropes around his ankles were
chafing. He tried to remember all of the training he'd had
about what to do if you were captured. Hell, name, rank,
and serial number. A few kids were swimming in the pool.
None of them ever looked in his direction. Three women
with red-and-blue straw hats on, sat watching the kids but
had their backs turned to him. Damn thoughtful of them.

What now? Yeah, those years in Hawaii. What a kick
that had been. The flowers, the girls, the sun, and that wonderful surf. It had been one little bit of heaven. Best years of
his life. Yes, he'd remember the best times, the best girls, the
best of everything. He'd been young and single, the girls
were young and in a party mood all of the time.

Just out of sight of Master Sergeant Eckert, Sergeant
Petresky hovered near a railing. He had been watching

Eckert for the past three hours. Eckert had sagged against the ropes quite a bit in the last hour. He was getting weaker. How long could a man stand that way before he died? Something could go wrong. Hell he could have a heart attack and die before anyone could help him. Damn that Abdul and his gang. At least the four of them had nailed one of the murderers last night. Petresky closed his eyes, remembering, and a shiver slanted through him. He shook his head. He had slept only an hour last night, re-membering. It had been a long, long time since he had killed another human being.

Yeah, slobber all over yourself Petresky. You ain't standing out there in the sun. What could they do to help him? Petresky decided he could get his two buddies from the other night. As soon as it was dark, they could charge the one sentry, knock him out or kill him, and whisk the master sergeant off to one of their rooms. It would take the A-Rabs a whole ship search to find him. Yeah, an idea. He'd go find the other guys and see what they thought. Now he just prayed that Eckert lived until dark.

On the bridge, it was getting routine. Twelve tankers had slowed and paid the price of exiting. They showed a white flag on the bow, cut power coming up to the Boghammar, lowered a packet with the money in it, then steamed away, picking up speed.

Abdul could see half a dozen more ships up the channel. Yes, it would be a good day. He had decided to make it a two-day strike. The second day should be just as produc-tive. He might be able to close up shop here with almost five million dollars.

He wasn't sure if the ships went through the strait at night. He would find out. He was the Sword of Allah.

DUBAYY, UNITED ARAB EMIRATES

Kat sat in a VIP waiting room at the airport at Dubayy. It had been a long flight in the Marshall Gulfstream II business jet. They had jolted away from London, grabbed the maximum cruising speed of 581 mph, and headed for Cairo, where they took on fuel and food, and flew on to Dubayy, something over five-thousand miles total.

They had been on the move for over nine hours and their workday was about to begin. It was dark; they had lost three hours, as she remembered, to the time-zone monster. The Navy CH-46 was fueled and ready, the IBS and motor were on board, and Roger had checked them out. The Specialists would take off in five minutes.

She had not worn her combat vest or harness during the long flight, but now Kat put them on to get used to them. She wasn't looking forward to the drop out of the chopper into the cold Persian Gulf, but they had to. It would be a new experience. She loved the water, that was no problem, getting out the door, jumping the eight feet into the dark, cold water was new. Then trying to find the small rubber boat.

"Time to move," Roger said at the door. He had made one last check on the boat and motor, and zipped up his radio in a watertight bag on his harness. The set could contact the chopper if they had any trouble.

"The pilot will give me a compass reading just as he drops us, so we know how to find that big ship," Roger said, as they walked toward the helicopter. "This should be a piece of cake. We'll ask whoever we see first if the bad guys are wearing any kind of uniform so we can ID them. First we take over the torpedo boat.

"Oh, the locals just had word that one tanker was torpedoed this noon trying to run the blockade. She's limping into port here for repairs. After that all the tankers slowed and paid the ransom to get past."

"Do tankers move through there at night?" Duncan asked.

"Couldn't tell you. It's a rather wide area. I don't see why they couldn't. We'll find out."

"What if the torpedo boat is out collecting fees when we get there?" Wade asked.

"We wait for it to come back and dock at the liner, or I go up the side," Roger said. "I've done it before. I have rope, grappling hook, and magnetic plates. Either way, we get on board. Hell, I can help Ichi go up if he can't climb the rope."

They filed on board the big chopper and settled on the floor. Roger shouted so they could hear. "Flight time about forty minutes. We'll get a red light ten minutes before we drop."

Ichi wasn't worried about jumping into the water. He loved the water. The chopper would hover about eight to ten feet off the water and they would push out the IBS, then jump out themselves. They had float bags holding their weapons and ammo with buoyancy devices. Water wings.

Wade had decided at the last minute to take Ichi along. The doctor had said he would be all right if he didn't have to swim more than a few yards. He wouldn't be good on a rope climb. Wade would stay right beside Ichi until they were both on the luxury liner's deck.

"You guys grab me if I go under more than twice," he had told them at Dubayy.

"Piece of cake," Roger said. "I've done this water drop a thousand, two hundred and forty-eight times, and we've never lost a jumper. You'll be fine."

"If I drown, I'm going back for new water wings," Ichi chided. But he was worried. He figured he wouldn't have to swim far. The damn wound wouldn't let him get to one hundred percent. He hated that. He scowled in the darkness. Hell, it would all work out. It had to. He'd get the job done. Yeah, it might hurt a little, but he'd hurt before. Just another challenge. Better by far than being stuck in some little room in the basement of the FBI building.

Wade wasn't concerned. He wished there had been a chance to practice run, but this would have to do. This time there just wasn't time for the best possible training. They would go on gut instinct and experience.

The big rotors and motors made a continual blast of noise that killed most conversation. Roger looked up and saw the red light.

"Ten minutes," he shouted, and all understood. They

got to their feet and checked each other, including the float bags that were tied securely to their right wrists.

They moved to the rear of the helicopter where they would jump. Wade tied a thin nylon line on Ichi's harness and the other end of the ten-foot line on his own wrist. They would jump together and Wade would make sure Ichi got on board the IBS.

A moment later the green light came on and the rear hatch swung downward. Roger pushed the inflated IBS out the hatch, then stepped off the edge of the chopper into midair. Kat was next in line. She took a deep breath and jumped. Almost at once she hit the water and went under. The cord on her right wrist attached to the float bag helped her pop up quickly. She could barely make out a dark shape directly ahead of her.

The blast of the chopper rotors had pushed the boat ahead of her twenty feet. She swam to it and saw Roger already on board. He grabbed her arms and dragged her and her float bag over the rubber side of the craft. Wade and Ichi swam up to the small boat, and they pulled Ichi in the same way they had her. Wade powered on board by himself.

A minute later Duncan and Hershel crawled on board and pulled in their float bags. The chopper had left the moment the last man had dropped out of it. Now it receded into the night and a few minutes later they couldn't even hear it.

"Everyone all right?" Roger asked. He got a chorus of grunts and ayes, and moved to the motor. He made some adjustments, removed some waterproof elements, and pulled the cord. The 35-hp engine started on the second try. The muffled sound seemed louder than it really was.

Roger grinned. "Hey, it works. Good. Hell of a long way to row. Now we take a reading with my handy-dandy wrist compass and we're off to Disneyland."

"Damn cold," Hershel said, trying to squeeze some of the salt water out of his cammies.

"It'll dry in our first firefight," Wade said, grinning.

Roger took over. "First we take down the bridge. That's the key. Then we capture Engineering where the bridge commands get processed. These ships are mostly run by computers. Now it's on hold just sitting there, but all of the other systems must work, air-conditioning, electricity, cooking, everything. If we can, we grab a steward or two who know the ship and can lead us where we need to go. Should be no trouble getting their cooperation."

Ahead they saw trouble.

"Heavy fog," Roger said. "That should stop all traffic through the strait even if they wanted to go at night. Which means our little torpedo boat should be safely tucked up to mother ship at that open hatch. We hope.

"I figure about a thirty-minute ride in this IBS at fifteen knots. We'll slow down when we can see the lights of the ship. These turkeys have thousands of lights on them for advertising. No trouble finding her even in pea soup like this. Fog is thinning out a little but it will stop all tanker traffic dead in their wakes."

Kat's teeth chattered. "I've never been so cold in my life," she said. "Not even in the Channel swim I tried once."

They rode in silence. Hershel stared at the dark water. It made him think of his computer and he couldn't figure out why. He hadn't had much time for it lately. Amazing what a good computer could do. He had learned to program and create web sites and even did a bit of hacking just for fun. Maybe when they got back from this bit of action he'd have more time for it. Hell, he'd make more time.

"Better get out our weapons and clear and charge them," Roger said. "I show another four minutes to the target. We should see the lady of the seas pretty soon."

They took out the silenced MP-5s and pistols, checked them, loaded in magazines, and put their pistols in shape as well. Then they waited.

"Put everything you want to take with you on your harness," Wade said. "We drop the float bags just inside the lower hatch. Roger, you guaranteeing that it's open?"

"Hell yes. If it ain't, sue me."

Ichi saw the glow ahead first. He pointed it out and Roger grinned. He'd never missed a ship yet on one of these drops. He cut the throttle by half and they crawled forward.

"Which side?" Roger asked.

"Try whichever one we come up on," Hershel said.

Four minutes later they were a hundred yards from the stern of the huge luxury liner. The fog had lifted slightly.

Ichi shook his head. "No boat, no hatch on this side."

Roger moved the IBS forward and around the rear of the big ship. They all saw it about the same time. Less than fifty yards ahead of them a small boat with all running lights and work lights on the deck, gunned its motor and angled in toward the side of the liner.

"Bingo," Roger said. "We're a little early for the ball. We'll let them tie up and get lost, then we go in and take over."

They edged closer. "It's a Boghammar for sure," Roger said. "Some country in Europe bought too many of them for its patrol craft navy and sold them cheap."

"Do we cut it loose or keep it tied up there?" Wade asked.

"No chance we cut it loose," Roger said. "We might need it to make a fast getaway. We secure it and take out anyone in the door hatch."

It was almost ten minutes before the last terrorist left the Boghammar and stepped inside the big ship. Two lines went inside the partly closed hatch door tying the patrol craft on tightly. The hatch door dropped again, but was still two feet off the deck.

"We move in now," Roger said. "Wade and I go on board and into the ship first and clear any sentries. Then we give you the word to follow."

Kat still shivered. Partly it was nerves. She'd never been on a seagoing operation like this. She felt the rubber boat bump the stern of the Boghammar and watched Roger jump on board, then Wade. Duncan held the rubber boat to the larger one, then used some line and tied it fast.

All was silent on board the luxury liner. Kat saw Roger crawl under the partly open door, then Wade went in. Less than a minute later the big door came open and Roger waved them inside.

One terrorist wearing black shirt and pants lay on the floor; blood had gushed from his throat and now puddled on the floor.

"Only one terr here," Wade said. "Looks like our boys wear all black. Watch for them. Take them prisoner if possible. If not, waste them and be sure you're silent." Roger pulled the dead terrorist to the hatch and dropped him into the water.

They were on the Emerald deck, the lowest one that held passenger cabins. Two corridors led off the small lobby area near stairs and an elevator just ahead. Wade checked his watch. It was almost midnight.

He looked up to see the elevator open and two couples come out. The men jumped in front of the women when they saw the military-type uniforms. All four passengers were in their sixties.

Kat hurried forward.

"No, don't be afraid. We're the good guys. We're going to take the ship back. Are all the terrorists dressed in black shirts and pants?"

"Yes," the shorter man said. "We're glad you're here."

A steward came around the corridor corner pushing a small cart. He stopped, frowned then came forward.

"Young man, do you speak English?" Wade asked.

He nodded. "Some."

"Can you show us where the bridge is and the captain's cabin? We're here to rescue you and take back your ship."

The steward's face broke into a delighted smile and he nodded. "Yes, yes, this way. I take you where no bad guys are patrolling. Come, come."

"Wait. Where are the patrols?"

"On each deck. Men walking, with machine guns."

"Two of you take this deck, two the one above," Wade said. "Watch for the black outfits. How many terrorists on board?"

"Maybe thirty. Come quickly."

Wade pointed to Hershel and they sprinted down the corridor. Wade was lost within five minutes. They had been in elevators, through doors marked CREW ONLY, and down past supplies, and now they came out on a deck high over the others.

Wade and their guide peered around a corner. Clear. The three stepped out and headed for a door marked OFF LIMITS TO PASSENGERS. BRIDGE. At the same time a man carrying an Uzi and wearing black pants and shirt came around a corner not twenty feet away. The terrorist shouted something in Arabic and pulled up his submachine gun.

★ NINE ★

A fraction of a second after Wade saw the terrorist, he slammed the steward out of the way with his left hand, lifted the MP-5 with his right, and jolted off a three-round silenced burst. The three slugs made a line upward from the terrorist's chest to his throat and the third one punched into his forehead.

He stumbled backwards from the force of the rounds, slanting off the bulkhead and pivoting onto his back and side, dead in half a heartbeat. The Uzi dropped soundlessly against his chest.

Wade jerked the steward back and pointed to Hershel and they darted back around the corner. After ten seconds, Wade looked around the wall from the deck level. Nothing had changed. The door to the bridge was still closed.

Wade and Hershel ran down to the dead terr and pushed him into a nearby storage room. They closed the door. Hershel put the Uzi over his back on the sling and they hurried to the bridge door.

"I've got the right," Wade said. They tensed, then the two Specialists pushed open the door and surged inside. They were in a section of the bridge to one side of the operation center. No one was there, only two desks and some readout screens. They continued across ten feet of open space and jolted through the next door and found only one terr and two ship's officers on the bridge. The terrorist scowled as he stared at the two MP-5 sub guns aimed at his body. He slowly lowered his Uzi.

"Don't kill me," he shouted in Arabic. Hershel knew the language and ordered him to lie facedown on the floor. They tied him with plastic riot cuffs.

"Ask him where the head man, Abdul is," Wade said.

The Arab shrugged. Hershel kicked him hard in the side just above his kidney and tears came to the terrorist's eyes. He spat out a dozen words. Hershel kicked him again, this time upside the head just hard enough to knock him out but not to kill him.

"The little bastard called us some nasty names."

The two Norwegians in the bridge talked excitedly a moment. Then one looked at Wade. "You are help us?" he said in accented English.

"Yes. We need to find Abdul. Is he in the captain's cabin?"

"He was," the same man said. "I take you."

He pointed to the door on the other side of the bridge. They went out it and down a corridor and then down one flight of steps to a pair of double doors with a crest over them.

"Here," the Norwegian said.

Wade tried the doorknob. Open.

"Right," he said.

"Left," Hershel said.

Wade kicked the door open and charged inside, his MP-5 sweeping the right-hand side of the room. One man lifted off a couch and clawed for an Uzi beside him. Wade shot him with three quiet rounds in the chest and he collapsed back on the couch.

Hershel had one target but he dived off the bed, hiding behind it. Hershel sent three hushed rounds under the bed then jumped forward onto the bed and fired twice more at a figure on the floor behind the bed bringing up an Uzi. He sagged to the floor out of the fight.

"Abdul?" Wade asked the Norwegian.

"No. Both no."

"Where is he?"

"Radio maybe?" Hershel asked.

"Take us to the radio room. Communications?"

The Norwegian nodded and led the way down one flight of steps and then on an elevator to the communications center. Wade looked around a corner in the companionway at the windows on the room to see if there was any activity. Nothing moved. He heard someone coming. Two men evidently talking and laughing. Both wore black pants and shirts and carried Uzis.

"Tell them to surrender," Wade said.

Both Specialists pushed their MP-5 muzzles around the corner and Hershel shouted to the two terrorists in Arabic to put down their weapons.

One went flat on the deck and fired. The other one stood, with his mouth open, frowning. Hershel slanted three silent rounds into the terr on the floor, ripping two into his skull, and spraying the wall with blood and bone fragments.

The second man lowered his weapon, shock sliding across his face, leaving it hollow, dark, and lost. He dropped the Uzi and put both hands over his head.

Wade grabbed him and pushed him toward the commo room. The door was not locked. Wade opened it and shoved the terr inside. One man in a white shirt looked up from a desk filled with radio, cable TV screens, and switches. He pointed to a terrorist who snored softly in a chair nearby, his Uzi propped up on his lap so the muzzle aimed at the radioman.

Hershel drew his pistol, reversed it, and slammed the butt down hard on the terr's head. He slumped in the chair.

"Great, who are you guys?" the operator asked.

"Some friends helping you take back the ship. You know where there are any more of the terrorists?"

"No. They've had me boxed in here. Even brought in my meals. Want me to tell the home office what's going on?"

"Yes. We have the bridge, but not Engineering. Our friend here needs to show us where that is."

•   •   •

Kat and Duncan took the Emerald deck. They were about amidships at the hatch. Both moved cautiously along the narrow passageway. They met two couples heading for their cabins. The people seemed frightened and didn't make any conversation.

They had moved up a hundred feet when they came to another lobby with two elevators. Just as they came into the lobby, a black-shirted terr sent two rounds at them from his Uzi, jumped into an elevator, and closed the door before they could get off a shot. His shots missed but Kat frowned.

She took the Motorola radio out of the waterproof pouch and turned it on.

"Wade, Kat here. Trouble."

The speaker in her ear came alive at once. "What trouble, Kat?"

"We just flushed one terr out but he got on an elevator going up before we could nail him. Surprised both of us. So Abdul will know soon that somebody is on board with weapons coming after him."

"No sweat. We have the bridge and communications. Heading for Engineering. Keep clearing decks. There are ten decks if I count right. My Norwegian guide tells me the terrs killed at least six of the officers on the ship and two passengers. Down and dead is the play of the day."

"That's a roger. We'll finish this deck. Corridors on both sides of the ship to patrol. When it's clear, we'll move up a deck or two."

Kat and Duncan found another lobby near the stern of the ship, made the crossover, and began moving back the other way. They approached the elevator lobby, and Kat bent low and looked around the bend in the corridor.

Four terrorists stood talking. It looked to her like they had just come off the elevator. They grouped for a moment, then they split up, two heading for Kat's side of the ship. Six passengers came off the second elevator and flowed through and past the terrorists, trying to ignore them.

"I've got the left," Duncan said. The Specialists brought

up their weapons and waited for a clear shot past the civilians.

On the sundeck ten stories above, Sergeant Petresky and the three men who had thrown the terrorist overboard the night before crouched in the shadows down from the pool.

"Sergeant Eckert is still there, the bastards," Petresky said.

Bill scowled in the darkness. "Yeah and the damn guard hasn't even nodded off in the last fifteen minutes."

"Diversion," Larry said. "I'll play a drunk and wander out there and almost fall into the pool. He'll be watching me and the two of you come up behind him and coldcock him with the butt of Eckert's forty-five. Clip him damn good so he's out cold."

"Might work," Petresky said.

"Hell, let's give it a try," Bill said. "He'll take the bait, I bet."

The guard stirred then, moved from where he had been sitting. He walked around a little and went back to sit in the same spot.

Larry slid through the shadows closer to the pool, and then began a drunken laugh and edged closer. He could see the guard watching him. The guard yelled something.

Larry paid no attention to him. He dipped one shoe into the water, teetered on the edge, recovered, and went another three steps along the edge of the pool.

The guard yelled again. Petresky and Bill had moved through the shadows on the Lido deck until they were behind the guard. He stood and shouted at Larry. The old soldier shook his head as if to clear it and looked at the guard. He pointed at himself.

The guard bellowed something else.

Larry cocked his head. He was still thirty feet from the terrorist. He began talking to the guard and staggering toward him. He saw his buddies move up closer. Then they rushed the guard. Bill brought the .45 up high. They got to the man before he heard them. When he turned, Bill slammed the butt of the .45 into the terrorist's forehead.

The force of it sank the butt plate an inch through his skull. The guard died before he could fall to the deck.

Bill felt sweat stream down his face. He panted. His stomach churned and he stared at the dead man. *Christ, I really killed this man.*

Petresky felt tears on his cheeks. It had been thirty-five years since he'd even watched a man die close-up. The guy over the rail was long distance. Petresky wiped a spot of the dead man's blood off his own forehead.

Bill wiped clean the bloody butt of the .45, and tried to beat down vomit in his throat. He couldn't hold it. He turned and vomited on the deck, still remembering the look on the dead man's face. The second one. He'd done this one all by himself. He shivered, wiped off his mouth, and spat out the last of the foul-tasting stomach juices. Then they all ran to where Master Sergeant Norman Eckert sagged on the pole. Gently they cut the ropes and lifted him away. They carried him to the steps and went down the back way to Bill's cabin, which was closest. They didn't dare use the elevators. All three were worn out by the time they carried Eckert into Bill's cabin, 434C. Gently they stretched him on the bed and wet his lips. Bill turned up the air conditioner. After ten minutes they let him take a sip of water.

He drifted in and out of consciousness.

As soon as they got in the room, Sergeant Petresky used the phone and called the ship's doctor.

"We have an emergency, Doctor, in 434C. A man has been in the sun all day tied to a pole. Can you get up here right away."

"Is it the same man—" The doctor stopped. "I'll be right there with everything I have that can help. We can't bring him to the medical unit here. Yes, I'll be right there with some help."

The civilians parted on the Emerald deck and Kat got off a single suppressed shot that knocked down a terr. Three more passengers on the floor ran for the corridor. Duncan cut down two terrorists with a three-shot silenced burst. The fourth one darted into the corridor behind some of the passengers. They could hear him running down past the cabins.

Duncan darted out and checked the three downed men. Two were dead, the third one was badly hit in the chest. Duncan saw one passenger staring at him and waved him over.

"You a cop?" Duncan asked.

"No, want to be one."

"Good. Stay with this terrorist and don't let him move. If he doesn't die in ten minutes, put these riot cuffs on his ankles and wrists, binding them together. Then call the ship's doctor. Got that?"

"Yes sir. Who are you guys?"

"Friends. Now take care of this one."

The man bobbed his head and sat cross-legged, watching the man. He picked up the Uzi and laid it across his legs.

Duncan and Kat hurried down the corridor where the other terr had vanished. "We don't stand a chance of finding him," Kat said. Duncan nodded. They had to try.

Wade, Hershel, and the Norwegian officer came up to the Engineering section quietly. They saw the door blown off its hinges.

"The terrorists did that," the Norwegian said.

Wade moved so he could see inside. He saw monitors and instruments and screens. He didn't locate any people.

"Go check it out," Wade told the Norwegian. "If anybody's there, tell them you had some trouble on the bridge and didn't want it to get repeated down here."

The officer nodded and marched forward. He hesitated before he went to the door, then slipped through. He came out quickly.

"One of our officers is dead. One of the terrorists is dead from what looks like a knife wound to the chest. Our man must have stabbed him and then was shot before he could get away."

"Shouldn't somebody be there on the controls?"

"It's almost automatic when we're standing still. I'll get somebody to go in and take over."

"Where are the rest of the terrorists? A steward told us there were about thirty of them."

"I have no idea. I need to get back to the bridge and contact our home office with a report."

"We don't have control of the ship yet. Some ships' officers were killed. Exactly who?"

"The captain and first officer and this engineer. I'm not sure who else. Four more I believe. We're down to our second officer to be in command."

"I understand. Do you have any ideas how we can dig out the rest of the terrorists?"

"Not a one. I'm concerned about the ship."

"I understand."

The Norwegian hesitated. "You might ask them to leave. Make an announcement on the public address system, say at seven-thirty in the morning. Let them have that small boat they came on board from."

"That doesn't sound—"

"The alternative is to do a cabin-by-cabin search, which could take a dozen men probably two days. Remember all of the crew cabins as well as the passengers, and the compartments where the terrorists could hide."

Wade scowled. "Yes, I see what you mean. Then after we let them go, it's a long way to shore, and some of our Navy planes could come in and greet them."

"Precisely, with air-to-ground missiles."

Wade took out his Motorola. "All Specialists, listen up. We have a situation here. We might not be able to dig out all of these terrorists. More than a thousand cubbyholes they could crawl into. I'm thinking of inviting them to leave. Give them back the Boghammar. We have any kind of a kill-and-capture count so far?"

The count came in at twelve. "Still leaves eighteen of them. I'll be making a call to Abdul at 7:30 A.M. on the ship's PA system. In the meantime we get radio contact with the closest F-18s and see if we can get some air cover over this old scow. I'm on my way to communications if anyone wants me. In the meantime, work those decks and let's see if we can flush out a few more. Eighteen is far, far too many to let get away."

★ TEN ★

Wade and Hershel took a detour on the way to the communications office. They stopped by the purser. The door was closed and locked. Wade looked again. A shadow drifted from one dark area to another.

Hershel carried a .45 automatic. Wade knew the hitting power the big round had.

"Somebody's inside who shouldn't be," Wade said. "Blow the lock off." Hershel drew the weapon and fired once at the locking mechanism, then again. After the second round, the door swung softly inward.

Before Hershel could move, three rounds from a submachine gun slanted through the open door. One caught Hershel in the left arm and knocked him down. Six more rounds blasted through the open door and buried themselves in the wall opposite it. Wade dived to the left out of the line of fire and dragged Hershel with him.

They couldn't see anyone to fire at. Wade sent six rounds through the door and waited. There was no response. He rolled and kicked the door open farther with his foot. Three more rounds drilled through the open door down low. They missed.

"Isn't this where they keep the passengers' money and valuables?" Hershel asked through his pain.

"Usually. Maybe Abdul decided to clean out the safe as well as his loot from the tankers. How is that arm?"

"Hurts, but I'll live. Wonder who's inside?"

They didn't hear anything for two or three minutes. Then a door slammed from somewhere deep inside the office.

Wade snorted. "Must be a back door to this place. Let's take a look." He ran through the opening and dived to the far right. Hershel ran in and eased to the floor on the left. No shots came at them.

In the back room, they found one safe that had been blown open and ransacked. The passengers' lockboxes were intact. Evidently it took two keys to open them as with a safety-deposit box in a bank.

"Too damn late here," Hershel said. "Where else could that coward be hiding?"

Wade checked Hershel's right arm. The bullet went in and out his upper arm midway to the shoulder. Wade used a white roller bandage from his med kit and wrapped the wound tightly to stop the bleeding. Hershel winced at the wrapping but didn't complain.

"That will hold you until we get to the ship's doctor. Looks like it's a little after four now. Not much we can do until daylight. Hershel, I need you to go down and guard the Boghammar. We don't want them to take it for their getaway until we want them to. I'm going to communications and see if I can get to Navy air. We could use a couple of F-18s overhead."

Wade talked with the radioman. It took them a half hour to find a channel where they could talk to the U. S. Navy. They contacted a carrier in the gulf about two hundred miles north. Then it was another hour before the carrier people roused the CAG out of his bunk for a chat.

"You know what time it is?" Captain Boniface asked. He was the Commander of Aircraft Group, the boss of all aircraft on the carrier.

"Yes sir, Captain, I do. I'm working on direct orders of the CNO and the President. You know about the hijacking in the gulf. I'm on the luxury liner *The Royal Princess* now and have it halfway under control. What I need is a pair of F-18s with full combat loads to fly cover on us here at daylight. You may want to check with the CNO for clearance. We'll need weapons free on my command.

The hijackers may be leaving the liner in a forty-foot Boghammar patrol craft and I want it shot out of the water."

"You're asking a lot. Who the hell are you?"

"I'm Wade Thorne, ex–CIA field agent. The CNO and the President authorized us to take back this luxury liner last night. I really do need those two F-18s at daylight."

"Yes, I know about the hijacked liner. We have orders to stay fifty miles away from her."

"That's changed. By daylight we should have complete control of the ship. Then I'm inviting the terrorists to leave in their Boghammar."

"Okay, Thorne, I'll take a chance and call the CNO. If he burns me, I burn you, understand?"

"Yes sir, Captain. I understand. May I call you on this frequency in two hours to see if I get the cover?"

"You may. Out."

Wade gave the mike back to the radioman and lifted his brows. Now it was up to Captain Boniface to get to the CNO. Wade hoped that the man wasn't out playing golf. He frowned. What time was it in Washington, DC, anyway? He didn't even try to figure it out.

Wade took out his Motorola and pushed the send button. "Team, have you noticed personal radios on any of the terrs? If so, we need one to see what the bad guys are doing. Check the bodies we have and any new guys we take down. Continue the sweep of the decks for guards and patrols. Any comments?"

"Yeah, Wade. Ichi and Roger on Baja deck. We've been on two decks now and found no terrs. They must be goofing off someplace. Baja has more suites, fewer cabins. Hold it, just spotted three of them taking a break. Later."

Ichi and Roger flattened against the side of the corridor leading to the lobby area around the stairway and elevators on the Baja deck. Three terrs had flaked out on the carpeted steps. One looked as if he was sleeping. The other two talked and drank from a flask.

"Move up as far as we can," Roger whispered. "They might surrender."

The Specialists left the wall and leveled their MP-5s at

the terrs and began a slow walk forward. They were still thirty feet away when one of the terrs saw them and grabbed his Uzi.

He was on Roger's side and the ex-SEAL blasted him with three rounds of 9mm. The small Arab blinked in surprise that he was dying and crumpled backwards on the stairs. The second terr watched his friend die and slowly lifted his hands. The third one slept through it all until he found his hands and ankles bound with riot cuffs.

"Either of you boys have a radio?" Roger asked. Both of them stared at him, not understanding. He took out his Motorola and showed them. One nodded and fished out a handheld radio about twice as large as Roger's. He tossed it to Ichi. "Your baby, monitor it and see what they're doing."

"We better clean up the trash," Roger said. They made the two terrs carry their dead buddy to the elevator. Roger punched the bottom button on the display and they got off on the last deck nonstaff guests could use. Halfway down a corridor they found an open door that led to a steward's room. They stashed the terrs there and rebound their ankles.

"Back to the Baja deck for more fun and games," Roger said. The terr radio had been silent during the move.

By seven o'clock the Specialists had swept all the decks, found three more terrs, and captured them without a shot. Wade called the CAG on the aircraft carrier in the Persian Gulf. Yes, he had confirmation. The CNO said give Wade Thorne anything he wanted. The aircraft would have guns free on Wade's command.

At seven-thirty, Wade made his announcement over the ship's PA system.

"Your attention please. During the night there has been a change in command of the ship. The terrorists who seized it have been beaten and are in hiding on board. We give them this chance. They may retreat to the lower deck and take their patrol boat and leave the ship. We give them this chance to get away with no strings attached. The prisoners we have will remain on board to be dealt with by the proper authorities. Abdul, you have thirty minutes to get your people to the boat and cast off. After that time we will hunt you down.

"Now, if there are any active military personnel on board or any police officers, we would ask that you come to the Lido deck at 8 A.M. so we can set up a posse for a search of the ship if that is required. We expect that Abdul and his hijackers will have exited the ship before then. Thank you. This message will be repeated again in a half hour."

Wade nodded to the radio operator, who had just called the home office with a report.

Hershel had been brought up from his duty of watching the Boghammar. The Specialists gathered near the communications center and waited.

Kat went to the rail where she could see the Boghammar. Ten minutes after the PA announcement went out, Kat reported on the Motorola.

"Yes, activity at the Boghammar. I can see six, now eight men with black shirts and pants getting on board. All have their Uzis and the terrs look mad as hell. Yes, six more just jumped on the boat. That's fourteen."

By the end of her report there were twenty men on the small boat.

Roger looked at Wade. "We did disable that other torpedo in the tube, didn't we?"

Wade shook his head. "Didn't even think about it. Let's hope they don't try to use it."

Thorne made contact with the two aircraft overhead through one of the ship's radio channels.

"Luxury, this is Red Dog One over *The Royal Princess*. Do we have any action?"

"Red Dog One, Luxury here. The terrorists are now boarding a Boghammar patrol boat. About forty feet. Should be pushing off at any moment. We believe they still have one available torpedo on board. Once they are away from *The Royal Princess*, you have been given guns free by the CNO. Blow the bastards out of the water."

"Will do, Luxury. We confirm guns free with our CAG. We're at six thousand feet and watching."

The Motorola cut in. "Hey, guys, you should see this," Kat cut in. "Abdul himself must have come on board. He has two suitcases. You suppose they are full of U.S. cash money?"

The Specialists all hurried to the rail, where they could see the Boghammar. It cast off and eased away, then the motor started and it pulled forward. Without warning the gunmen on the small boat fired their Uzis at the big ship. The Specialists all surged away from the rail. The firing lasted only a minute, but hundreds of rounds slammed into the ship, broke windows and made holes in the walls. They heard screams. Just down the deck a woman was down, with blood pouring from a neck wound. When the final count was made, eighteen passengers had bullet wounds, and three had died from the gunfire.

Moments after the firing, the Arabs were out of range of the Specialists' MP-5 weapons. They went back to the rail and watched the boat pull farther from the ship. When it was about a half mile off, it turned and raced at what looked like full speed toward the luxury liner.

"He's making a torpedo run," Roger yelled.

They watched in horror as the small craft came closer. Then there was a billow of white smoke from the Boghammar and a torpedo jolted away from it and headed directly for the luxury liner.

An instant later the Boghammar exploded in a searing fireball that blossomed on the sea seven hundred yards from the luxury liner. Just then one F-18 fighter aircraft slammed over the scene at less than a hundred feet off the water.

"An Eighteen," Roger said. "Their missiles hit that boat a few seconds too late. Look at that torpedo slanting right at us."

They watched the white trail of the torpedo as it homed in on the luxury liner. It was still three hundred yards away when a large explosion erupted in the sea, turning it into a froth of smoke and spray and angry water.

"Oh, yes," Roger said. The second F-18 screamed past them not thirty feet directly over the smoking spot on the water.

"Thank God that second Eighteen stayed in reserve," Roger said. "Those boys just saved our skinny little necks."

When the smoke blew away there was only a small wash of debris at the site. Five minutes later two small power boats left the side of *The Royal Princess* and their crews searched the area for survivors.

The second mate, Helgstrom Norblad, now in command of the luxury liner, found the Specialists. He shook their hands. There were tears in his eyes.

"We owe our lives to you," Norblad said. "I'm not sure who you are or who you represent, but you have done a tremendous service to the owners of our ship and to our crew and passengers."

Wade shook his hand. "You'll get an explanation later, I'm sure. Have the searchers out on the water found anyone alive?"

"No. They have found four bodies. There are some body parts but we instructed them not to bring anything back. There is no sign of anyone alive."

"Just as well," Wade said. He was thinking about how they would do the pickup to a Navy helicopter. He looked down and saw the IBS floating fifty yards off the bow. The terrorists must have cut it free when they left.

"Captain, could your crewmen bring back to the side the rubber boat drifting out there? We may need it."

Ten minutes later the IBS had been tied to the side of the big ship as its crew began making preparations to get under way and back to its regular travel route. Stewards rushed around. The first seating at breakfast took place. Slowly, activities on board the big ship were returning to normal.

Wade called the F-18s again. "Hey guys up there. Thanks for the timely action. Nice work on that torpedo shot."

"Figured they might try that. Not a chance we could miss. Any other small duties needed?"

"Not that we know about. Thanks, you're released from duty. Talk to your CAG. Thanks again." The F-18s did a flyby on each side of the big ship a hundred feet off the water and a hundred yards on each side. The passengers cheered. Then the fighters did a roll and angled to the north.

Wade sent Hershel to the doctor to get his arm treated. Then he called the carrier and asked the CAG there to arrange for a CH-46 Sea Knight to come out from Dubayy to pick up the Specialists.

"It'll be a rope-ladder pickup from the IBS," the CAG said. "Can your people do that?"

"Yes sir, Captain. Our crew can do it. Thanks for your help. Especially thanks for that pair of Eighteens."

"That's what we're here for, Mr. Thorne. You take care. Out."

Down in the hospital ward of the huge ship, Master Sergeant Norman Eckert felt better. He'd been fussed over and pampered and treated and given tender care for almost eight hours. His sunburn had been medicated, he had been dehydrated but brought back with IVs of saline solution, and he endured the well-wishes of his three other conspirators. The two doctors had found no serious or lasting damage from the ordeal in the sun.

When the doctor and nurse were out of his small room, Sergeant Petresky confided in the patient. "Hey, we took care of another one of them damned hijackers. Yeah, he came in contact with the butt of your forty-five that sank a half inch into his cranium. That's when we snatched you off that pole and got you down to Bill's cabin and called the doc."

Bill grinned. "I hear you're a hero for trying to stop that man and woman from being thrown overboard. You tried your damnedest. The company is giving you and your wife a lifetime pass on their line. Any of their fifteen ships, to cruise anywhere in the world. Hell, you can cruise year-round with their blessings."

"Yeah, sure," Eckert said. The words came out slurred and hard to understand. His lips were still swollen nearly double their size.

"True, and the captain is making you the guest of honor

at a big hairy banquet as soon as you're able to sit up," Larry said.

Master Sergeant Norman Eckert, United States Marine Corps, retired, turned away. Tears seeped out of his swollen eyes and ran a jagged path down his red blistered cheeks. Dammit, he couldn't let them see this. What the hell, Marines don't cry.

Later, as the Specialists lounged in the sun on the Lido deck, Roger briefed them on the pickup. "Nothing to it. We're in the Rubber Duck. The chopper comes in and hovers. He drops the rope ladder out the back hatch. We hold the bottom and our people simply climb up the rope ladder and into the chopper."

"What if I fall off?" Ichi asked.

"Easy, we let you drown," Hershel cracked.

"Then I pick your dead body out of the wet, sling you over my shoulder, and climb up the ladder and dump you inside," Roger said. They kept looking at Roger.

"You've done this before," Wade said.

"One thousand four hundred . . ." Roger stopped and they laughed. "Hey, it isn't that hard. Best part is nobody is shooting at us. We have all the time we need. I'll help anybody up who has trouble. I'll be the last one up. That's the only hard part, with nobody holding the bottom of the ladder."

"The IBS?" Kat asked.

"We donate that to *The Royal Princess*," Roger said.

Two hours later, the Specialists were in the IBS a hundred yards off the luxury liner. The big chopper came in and hovered while a crewman lowered a rope. Quickly all the floatation bags with weapons, ammo, and vests were pulled up into the bird.

Kat was the first one to go up the ladder. She made it up three rungs, then missed a foothold and almost toppled off, but caught herself and surged on up and into the big bird.

Ichi started up, grabbed his chest, and stepped back into the IBS. Wade and Hershel and Duncan went up without a problem. Then Roger put Ichi on his back, told him to hold on, and Roger climbed one rung at a time up the swaying ladder until those in the bird grabbed both of them and pulled them the last three feet inside. The crew chief retrieved the ladder and closed the hatch.

"Next stop the picturesque village of Dubayy," the crew chief shouted over the chopper noise. The Specialists relaxed. This part was over. They had been up more than thirty hours. All were sleeping when they touched down in Dubayy forty minutes later.

✷ ELEVEN ✷

THE STRAIT OF HORMUZ

The water washed over him again.

Darkness, then light.

He remembered a huge fireball.

An explosion that had shut down his ears, blinded his eyes, catapulted him thirty yards through the air and into the sea.

The salt water sloshed over him.

His head went under again. He snorted and blew water from his nose and mouth.

So this was what it was like to be dead.

No.

He hurt too much to be dead. The water again, washing over his face, making him blubber and gag, then spit out water and suck in air.

Blackness.

Everything black and silent.

His arms hurt as if they were on fire.

A shaft of light glared past his eyelids. Then more light and a second later his eyes snapped open.

He was alive.

A current dragged him along through the tepid water. He saw the two suitcases that he had tied to his wrists so none of his men would steal them. Had they saved him?

They must have air in them. Far off he could see part of the wrecked Boghammar where it burned and smoked. The current had drifted him three hundred yards away.

He kept moving. Gently, he tried to kick his legs. Yes, they worked. His arms were not broken. He brushed one hand over his head and realized that most of his hair had burned off.

Explosion.

He had seen two jet fighters high in the sky. They must have attacked. Missiles. No warning. They travel at the speed of sound.

Others must be alive. There had to be some of his men alive. Were all of them dead in the explosion and fire? He looked around at the choppy water. Nowhere could he see any survivors. The strait was angry today. He saw white-caps where the wind whipped the water into a froth.

Abdul heard the motorboats before he saw them. They came from the same hatch on the luxury liner he had just departed. Two of them. They powered straight for him, then stopped at the wreckage. He was farther away now. Out of sight in the troughs of the waves. They wouldn't see him. Where was the current taking him? South. How far to any land? He tried to remember the charts on the bridge. Thirty miles, maybe fifty.

How long would the suitcases filled with two million dollars keep him afloat? Wouldn't the suitcases leak? Then he remembered that the bills had been sealed in plastic, straight from the mint.

They might hold him up for thirty miles. Land? Could he see land? Not thirty miles away. The sun still rose and set in the same place. He could use the sun as his compass. Yes, he had to swim to the left, toward Iran. They would help him. With the money he had anyone would help him.

Or rob him.

Probably kill him.

He had to think. For a moment he nearly passed out. No. No. He had to stay awake and conscious and swim gently to the left. There were some islands to the left. He had no idea how close they were to the mainland. Closer there than all the way to Iran.

He swam, kicking his feet gently, then with more force. The current was moving him to the left as well as south.

Iran swept around to the south here, following the

waters of the strait, which were to the east. He had left the liner at a little before eight o'clock. He had all day to drift and swim.

An hour later he saw a fishing boat, but it was only a mast over the tops of the waves. The sound of the motor was faint. No chance anyone on board could see him. The craft continued on its way and soon the tips of the masts and the motor sound disappeared behind the swells.

Abdul had no doubt that he would get to shore. He was Allah's servant. Allah would not let him die here in the Strait of Hormuz. He clung to the suitcases now, one under each arm as he rested. The current moved him faster. A gentle breeze had freshened and blew stronger.

After another hour he thought he saw a spit of land through the trough of a wave. When he was lifted on the next swell, he stared hard to the left, but it had only been a cloud hugging the water. Land seemed a thousand miles away. He had lost sight of the tall luxury liner. It was somewhere behind him. If it returned to course, it would come down this way to get into the Gulf of Oman. He prayed to Allah that no one on board would spot him.

Without his floats he could swim a mile. No more. He prayed again to Allah to keep the American dollars safe in their plastic seals with their trapped air that would help him stay afloat, and alive.

A dozen birds circled him for a moment, probably wondering if he would make a meal. They came close, then wheeled and flew away when he shouted at them. Just what he needed, to be lunch for some seabirds.

Wait. Some alert fishermen might see the birds and investigate. Might. The birds came back. He lay still. Maybe if the birds stayed. He knew that a school of large feeding fish often drove small bait fish upward until the smaller fish jumped out of the water to escape the hungry jaws. The birds saw the bait fish boiling on the surface and pounced on them from above. If only . . .

He didn't move. A bird landed on one of the suitcases.

He remained motionless. The bird pecked at his hand. It hurt like fire, but he remained frozen in place.

He heard a low moan of a boat engine far off. Was it

coming closer? Yes. He lay there without moving. Another bird landed on him and pecked at his arm where his shirt had been burned away. It hurt like a needle piercing his flesh. He heard the flapping wings of another bird, then a dozen more came in and landed. He opened his eyes. A bird on his shoulder aimed a peck at his eye but he brushed the beak away. Half the birds squawked and scattered, then settled again near him.

The sound of the boat came closer. He went limp and covered his face with one hand. A bird pecked at his ear. He yelped in pain and saw six birds take off, wheel in a circle, then come back and land.

He could hear the sound of the motor on the boat moving closer. How far off was it? The birds. He had to let them draw some blood. One pecked at his arm. He tried to relax. The piercing pain came as a beak tore through skin into flesh. He yelped in pain as the bill came down again and again.

Then the sound of the motor was so close he should be able to see a mast. He turned his head. A dozen birds flapped away. When he looked back a mast and three long outriggers showed in front of him, and then he saw the side of a fishing boat. He flapped his arms and shouted.

The birds rose in a cloud and he realized there must have been a hundred of the seabirds around him. They were smaller than he had guessed. He lifted up in the water and bellowed.

A head on the ship turned.

Abdul waved one arm as high as he could.

The man had turned away; now he looked back at Abdul and watched, then shouted something and the boat slowed and turned toward him.

Two hours later, Abdul felt strange in the borrowed clothes that were too large for him but warm and dry. He rested, ate the fishermen's food, and drank their water. They drove a hard bargain, but he had hired them to take him to Bandar-e Abbas in Iran. It was the closest town of any size. He said they could keep the fish and sell them. He offered them three hundred American dollars for the trip. They couldn't believe their good fortune when he gave them the three one-hundred-dollar bills.

He didn't let them know what else was in the suitcases. Early on he stole one of the filleting knives to keep with him for protection. He knew there would be no sleep for him until he was safely onshore, and could get away from these two fishermen.

Allah be praised. He had lifted Abdul from the very edge of a watery grave and provided him with the money he needed to make a telling and deadly strike at the Great Evil. Now he was ready.

ODESSA, UKRAINE

Four days later, Abdul met with three men in Odessa. He had drawn the men from his pool of Muslim activists who knew what they were doing and how to get a job done. Now he cast about for the best way to contact the people in this former Russian country to whom he must talk.

He had two names, one a former commissar in the old Soviet Union from Odessa. He knew everyone, had more power than any of the Ukraine people knew, and was approachable. Abdul started there.

Abdul knew all about *biopreparat*, the system, and how it had functioned in the old Soviet Union. Back in 1974 the Russians had signed an agreement with the U.S. called the Biological Weapons Convention treaty, which banned the development, stockpiling, and use of biological weapons. Even as they signed the document, the Soviet Union charged full speed ahead on a clandestine bioweapons program devoted to the creation and production of sophisticated biological powders to be used as weapons. These included powdered black plague, anthrax, smallpox, tularemia, the Marburg virus, and certain other brain viruses.

Abdul had followed the secret project over the past few years. He knew that in the 1980s the Russians had thirty-two thousand scientists and staff working the program in fifteen major facilities scattered across the Soviet Union. Control was by the Soviet Ministry of Defense.

Soon after they perfected the powder base to carry the virus, the material was loaded into special ICBM missile warheads. His reports were that each warhead had from one hundred to four hundred pounds of the freeze-dried virus in a powder base. His best information showed that hundreds of these missiles carried the virus warheads and had been dispersed to several spots around the old Soviet Union for top security.

The strategy would be to direct the missiles at selected targets, where the warhead would explode at a given altitude, maybe twenty thousand feet. Each warhead would release thousands of canisters over a wide area. When they reached a certain altitude, they would explode, scattering the powdered virus over a huge area. The powder, which was heavier than air, would drift into the atmosphere and settle onto the buildings and people below in the city, where it could not be seen or sensed. Inhaling even a few of the powder particles would be enough to infect the victim with the disease. The powder was extremely fine, from one to five microns across. Fifty of the powder grains laid side by side would extend to the width of a human hair.

Abdul was not sure why Russia had chosen the small-pox virus as the one it mass-produced. His only reasoning was that since it was extremely infectious, one person being exposed could then go on and expose a dozen or a hundred, and they could expose another thousand and it would accelerate to the square of the number involved. In a few weeks the virus could sweep across a whole nation. With air travel the way it is, the smallpox plague could be in every nation in the world within weeks.

Abdul's first meeting with Commissar Petroff was at a luncheon in a highly public restaurant in Odessa. Abdul had arranged the luncheon through a mutual friend. As soon as they sat down, Abdul slid a letter-sized envelope across the table to Commissar Petroff.

The Commissar moved the envelope off the table to his lap, where he opened it. Inside was a new ten-thousand-dollar Rolex watch.

"I didn't want you to be late to any of your many appointments, Commissar," Abdul said.

"Please, it is just Petroff now." He smiled, showing a gold tooth and heavy jowls under his nearly bald head. "I am sure now that I will always be on time, at least for my meetings with you. You hinted at a highly dangerous subject."

"I am vitally interested in it. My defense program for an unnamed country will rely heavily on such potent weapons."

"Understood. Does this country have unlimited resources to facilitate the transfer of this product?" The commissar used his best smile but it came out tainted with greed.

"Limited resources, Commissar. Extremely limited. But we do not need a great deal of the material. We understand there is not at the present time a large demand for this product."

"Unfortunately, you are correct. You do understand the dangers?"

"Absolutely."

"How much do you need?"

"I'm not sure how big these canisters are."

"They are a third of a meter long, about fourteen inches."

"And inside, how much material?"

"It is extremely light, but there's almost a pound, enough to saturate a square mile from a thousand feet."

"I'll need twenty of the canisters."

"That will cost you twenty million American dollars."

Abdul smiled. It was bargaining time. "Since there is no real market for this material, the buyer should set the price as they do in a fine Iranian market."

"I may have to bend a little," Petroff said. Their lunch vodka drinks came and Petroff downed his in two huge gulps.

"All right, five million, not a cent less."

An hour and a good lunch later, Abdul left with an agreement to pay a million U.S. dollars to Petroff for the twenty canisters. They would be sealed airtight in heavy plastic, packaged in Styrofoam, and enclosed in a sturdy wooden box. They would be shipped by air to Abdul in

Kuwait the following day. Abdul returned to the restaurant that evening, met Petroff in the bar, and gave him a new suitcase that held one million U.S. dollars in uncirculated one-hundred-dollar bills.

MANISHA, IRAN

Four days later, Abdul brought his rented car to a stop in the small Iranian village of Manisha far out on the Iranian Plateau and well over six thousand feet in elevation. The village consisted of four houses and a barn. The only road in the entire area dead-ended in the settlement. There was nothing beyond it but the windswept upper plateau and sand, rocks, stark forbidding wilderness, and several small goatherds. The little town had only twenty-four inhabitants, all goatherders and their families, all related.

Abdul had brought one man to help him. He had selected the area carefully. Little notice would be taken about what happened in this out-of-the-way place. It was over four hundred miles south of Tehran.

Abdul stopped the car near the first house and sent Hakim up to the second house to ask directions. Hakim started to rap on the weathered doorframe when the panel opened and a small, shriveled-up old woman stared up at him.

"Yes? You're lost, right? Nobody ever comes here unless they are lost. Where were you going?"

"Woman, I am not lost. Hunting a man I know. Jacoped. Do you know him?"

"Strange name. Nobody lives here by that name. We are all of the Sahar-e clan."

"You sure he isn't working for the clan?"

"Nobody but us works here."

Behind the woman he saw four children. Three of them looked retarded, with heads too large for their bodies. Two of those seemed to be blind.

"You sick or something? Out of your head? You best turn around and drive away before our men come back. They will slice you into small pieces and feed you to the he-goats."

"Just trying to find my friend."

The old woman drew a six-inch curved-blade knife from her dress and waved it at him. "Out, you scum. Out and be gone."

Hakim had always been afraid of knives. He backed away slowly, then ran for the car.

Hakim was Iranian, and not the smartest man Abdul had worked with. The best thing about Hakim was that he was expendable. When Hakim left the car, Abdul took out one of the canisters he had bought in Odessa. It was still sealed airtight in heavy plastic. He cut the plastic free and shivered as he held the fourteen-inch-long aluminum cylinder in his bare hands. He taped a timer-detonator on the side and checked it. Yes. He had set the timer for ten minutes. He left the car and put the canister on the ground near the first house, then pushed the activating lever on the detonator and hurried back to the car.

Hakim was already in the vehicle and they drove away.

"Is it set?" Hakim asked.

"Yes, ten minutes. We drive out a half mile and wait."

"Sure that's far enough?" Hakim asked. "Praises to Allah, but I don't want to be anywhere near when that bastard explodes."

"We're upwind, stupid," Abdul snapped. "We'll be fine."

Abdul stopped the car a short time later. "We're a half mile off, now relax." They waited.

Precisely ten minutes after Abdul activated the timer, the detonator exploded with a sharp crack like a dynamite cap going off.

"That's it?" Hakim asked.

"All it has to do is blow the aluminum container apart and spray the dust into the air," Abdul said. "I told you how it would work. Now we drive."

"Yeah, but I figured at least a big explosion."

"We don't want to blow them up," Abdul said.

Hakim kept watching Abdul as they drove. "You never told me what this is all about. What's in that container? You said some bad camel shit."

"You don't need to know. Do the job I hired you for and you get paid."

"I want to know, now. Tell me right now or I just might blow a big hole in your chest and on through your heart."

Abdul looked over at the short-barreled .38 caliber revolver Hakim held. The black hole of the muzzle almost nudged his side.

Abdul chuckled. "Yeah, Hakim. I knew you were a good one when we first talked. You're on the team, I had to test you. Now put the revolver away and I'll explain the whole project to you, exactly how we're going to take the Holy Muslim War to the Great Evil."

Hakim frowned. He stared at Abdul. "Why should I believe you? You wouldn't tell me before."

"You are a fellow fighter for Allah. A soldier in our holy war. You would give your life for Allah and his wonders. That's why I trust you."

Hakim lifted his brows. "What you say is true." He frowned, then shrugged. "All right, I know you will tell me everything." He pocketed the revolver, careful to let the hammer down gently first.

"So, what is the great battle we're going to fight?" Hakim asked.

He looked up as he said it. His nostrils flared and his eyes went wild with raw, unbridled fear as he tried to grab his revolver. Abdul's 9mm Glock 19 blasted three times, the parabellums digging through ribs and flesh, tearing a large hole in Hakim's heart and lungs. The force of the rounds jolted Hakim against the far door. Abdul slowed on the dirt road and stopped. He got out and looked around. He couldn't see a person, a building, or a vehicle in any direction.

He opened the door and dragged Hakim out of the car and dumped him in a shallow ditch at the edge of the road. It might be months before anyone found him. Now there was no one who could tell what happened to the small village of Manisha and the twenty-four pathetic, barely-human idiots who lived there.

★ TWELVE ★

BALDERMARE CASTLE, ENGLAND

It had been a week since the Specialists returned from the luxury liner *Royal Princess*. Kat's arm slice taken in Cairo was healing nicely, and Hershel's bullet wound was improving. Neither one of them did any training that involved heavy work with their arms.

Every day that week they had a fifteen-minute critique of the operation at sea to figure out where they could have improved.

"We never should have left the bridge unprotected once we captured it," Roger said. "That's the heart of the operation. We did take Engineering and keep it as we should, so I guess we could have countermanded any orders coming from the bridge by Abdul's people."

"Can we believe that report from the search boats that there were no survivors?" Wade asked.

"They did say they found four bodies," Kat said. "None of them was Abdul."

"So what about Abdul?" Wade asked. "We can't say for sure that he's dead, can we?"

"Not without a body," Ichi said. "But we can figure at least a 95 percent chance that his time ran out."

Hershel shook his head. "Hey, explosions are weird things. I've seen a man standing near a hand grenade that goes off almost at his feet and he doesn't get a scratch. Depends how the body of the grenade fragments and which parts go where. Same thing with big explosions.

The Sidewinder air-to-air missile jolts along at around fifteen hundred miles an hour. The big Phoenix air-to-air will hit Mach five. All I'm saying is that with missiles strange things can happen when they hit the ground or water."

"So let's not worry about the Ghost of Abdul until we see him," Duncan said. "We've got some real potential problems. Venezuela for instance. Chavez there has refused to submit his budget to congress for approval. He turned to a special assembly that he set up to adopt a draft constitution vastly increasing his powers."

"Pakistan is a real mess," Ichi said. "The new government there arrested hundreds of industrialists and politicians and charged them with graft. They face fourteen years in prison on trumped-up political charges for non-payment of loans. It's getting ugly."

"Even Armenia is having problems," Mister Marshall said. "The parliament was seized by gunmen who killed Prime Minister Sarkisian and six other high government officials. They took hostages and demanded to meet with the President. They claimed they had staged a coup."

"So, Mister Marshall," Wade said. "Is anything in the pot boiling over? Are we anywhere near to an assignment?"

"Nothing on my alert board is on fire yet. We haven't had any more news about the bio-chemical-nuclear problem in Odessa. Maybe it's cooled off. We've only had a week since the ship. We need some more time to get everyone healed up and ready to go. Oh, Roger suggested that we should do some work on rope climbing and practice on rope ladders. I agree. We can suspend some from oak trees. I'll have the carpenter build a platform on top for a landing spot."

"That wraps us up here, then," Wade said. "We have fifteen minutes to get on our cammies and boots, and fall out for our regular physical and weapons training. The SAS and a few other outfits like to go for head-shots. They say it gives a better kill ratio despite the smaller target. Arguments both ways. This afternoon we'll do one whole session on head-shots only. We'll do at least two hundred rounds today so bring that much ammo from the supply room. See you outside in fifteen."

Mister Marshall motioned for Wade and they went up to his office/den. The big-screen TV was on a newscast. The screen came on automatically whenever anyone entered the den. The newscast caught their attention.

"The Iraqi jet passenger liner went down over Iraq less than twenty minutes after it took off. Witnesses report that the plane exploded in midair and fell some thirty thousand feet into a desert area in northern Iraq. Word of this tragedy is accented by a yet unconfirmed report that another passenger liner, this one out of Indonesia, crashed into the sea after the pilot said he felt a bomb blast in the tail of the aircraft cutting all pilot controls to the elevators and rudder. He kept transmitting until the radio suddenly cut off, evidently on impact with the water. So far there is no hint that there could be any connection between these two incidents."

Mister Marshall turned off the set. "We'll get a report on those crashes later. I have something that's been bothering me and I wanted your slant on it. You know we get information from time to time about militia groups in the U.S. Some of them are looking dangerous. One outfit in Utah has actually set up its own country and refuses to let anyone inside who isn't a member. This is fine for a hunt club, but this group controls an area of more than fifty square miles that is cut through by two U.S. highways. Something we need to keep our eye on. I have a report I want you to digest and give me your eval on it."

"Right. I'll do it tonight. I better get down with the troops."

Mister Marshall gave Wade a wave, and Wade hurried to his quarters to change into his training cammies. They would start with a ten-mile run, then work the woodsy obstacle course.

Wade sat for a moment as he put on his boots. Eval time. How was this whole Specialists operation going? So far, it was good. They had been on several missions now and had done what they were supposed to do. They went in where individual nations couldn't or wouldn't for a variety of reasons, and took out the bad guys.

It was satisfying, fulfilling, worthwhile. Better than

raising quarter horses on that ranch in Idaho's outback? Well, on that one he'd have to think for a while. He still had the ranch, bought and paid for, and a good man to run it. He wished he could be there for the foaling season. Maybe next year. For just a moment he wondered where he would have to go to do some really good skiing. Sure, Austria or Switzerland. Where closer? He'd have to find out. He hadn't been skiing for two years.

The ten-mile run was not a pleasure jaunt. It was Kat's turn to lead and she pushed them just past the six-minutes-a-mile pace. Ichi went along for the first time since his bad chest wound. He hung in there for four miles and then slowed to a walk. When he left the pack, Kat picked up the pace.

"Hey, Kat, you ran this fast in a triathlon?" Roger asked, wheezing outrageously.

"Not a chance. This is too slow. Shall we speed up to the five-and-a-half-minute pace?"

A loud chorus of No's came to her and Kat grinned. "You big strong hunks gonna let a mere girl beat you?"

"Any day," Duncan said. "I've never even tried to run a marathon."

"Except after those luscious English rich widows," Wade shouted. They all laughed. Duncan was the ladies' man of the group.

"We British are reserved and have definite standards when it comes to lovely women," Duncan said.

"Sure, they have to be breathing," Hershel shouted.

They ran the last two miles at a slightly faster pace. All the Specialists but Kat were panting and wheezing when they finished. Most had bent over with hands on their knees.

"For the next ten miles . . ." Kat began.

All the men threw their soft hats at her and Kat laughed.

After they recovered, Wade led them down a hundred yards to the Close Combat House. It was a real building, created for the sole purpose of simulating a firefight inside a house. The walls were filled with bullet-absorbing material. Electronic signals lifted targets from behind beds and tables, from darkened corners, often providing four terrorists to one of the good guys.

Wade and Kat took the first run. Before they moved inside, which would automatically trigger the randomly selected series of targets by the computer, Wade reminded them about the purpose of the practice round.

"We're talking about head-shots only this time. It will slow you down, and we might think about single shot vs. the three-round burst. Let's try it. We're not shooting for records here. I've set the computer to count only head-shots. Kat, let's go."

Wade kicked in the door. Kat darted inside to the left, Wade took the right. At once, before their eyes could become accustomed to the semidarkness, two terrorists popped up on each side with submachine guns.

Wade recovered in time to hit one terrorist in the head, the other vanished. He heard Kat swear as both her targets dropped out of sight before she could fire.

"Glad they don't shoot back," Wade said. They moved forward slowly toward the door into the next room. In an instant two terrs stood there in the open door with guns firing. Wade shot the one on the right, Kat got the one on the left. Both head-shots.

In the next room four terrorists jolted upward. The MP-5s stuttered and the targets pulled down. Two more rooms with terrorists, this time holding innocents with sacks over their heads.

Kat pushed the selector lever to three rounds and fired at them, cutting both of hers down but hitting both in the chest area as they had trained for so long to do. There were two more rooms and half a dozen more surprise terrorist targets.

"We did rotten," Kat said, frowning, letting her anger at herself come through. "How did we do so bad?"

They looked at the box next to the door where the scores were printed out. Roger went for the scores.

"You don't want to know," Wade said after he read them. Kat held out her hand. She groaned when she read the marks. "We haven't had low scores like this since we first started. I blew away two innocents, which deducted twenty points."

The two other teams ran the course and came up with equally miserable scores. They sat under the big oak trees reloading magazines. Wade used his Motorola talking with the castle.

Five minutes later an electric cart pulled up at the shooting range. One of the regular drivers waved at the Specialists and waited as a man dressed in jungle green-and-black cammies, and a matching soft hat eased out of the rig. Wade stood and went to meet him. They talked a moment, then walked over to where the Specialists sat in the shade.

"We knew it wouldn't be easy, this head-shot technique," Wade said. "That's why I anticipated our lousy scores and sent for a man to help us. Please meet Lieutenant Morris Lester-Smythe, one of the top hands in the SAS. This man knows more about marksmanship of all types than most of us will ever hope to learn. He has two hours to give us some basic techniques of fast-targeting terrorist heads, and how we can build up our scores, and our success rate when we need this technique. Lieutenant Morris Lester-Smythe."

For the next two hours Wade watched and learned from the crack British Special Air Service veteran. It came down to finding and recognizing the target quicker, then taking a second longer to aim before firing. Two simple steps that should bring results.

The lieutenant took the Specialists individually through the Close Combat House, guiding, correcting, teaching. At the end of the two hours the same pairs went through the course again and scores were much higher. When they came out, the SAS trooper was gone.

For the next week, Wade kept the Specialists working hard on the physical end of the job and doing from two hundred to five hundred rounds of practice with all of their weapons, including the new Bull Pup with the 20mm rounds. They limited practice with the 20mm rounds because of the cost. All became proficient with the new weapon for airbursts. Ichi improved each day on his wind and stamina. By the end of the week he could do the ten-mile run, but faded on the fifteen-miler. Wade was pleased with his progress.

Twice during the week Kat had been excused from training to go to London, where she went to her regular tutoring sessions with fourth-graders. She had four whom she worked with as a group and then individually. It was one of the lowest-income areas of London and the school reflected that. The students were far behind their grade level in reading, and each time Kat came she brought an armload of books that she gave out to the ones in her class and others in the same grade.

She made the trip chauffeured in one of the smaller Mercedes-Benz sedans, stopping to buy books on the way.

Today little Elizabeth couldn't quite grasp the idea of stopping at the end of a sentence. She looked up with big blue eyes and shook her head.

"Why should I stop? There are more words right there."

Kat gave her a tight hug and then drew in the book to make the period look like a wall between the end of the sentence and the beginning of the next.

"What's that, Elizabeth?"

"Boards."

"Yes, boards, and they are nailed up high in a wall. What do you do when you come to a wall?"

"I go around it."

"But first you have to stop. Right?"

Elizabeth frowned, looked at the picture, and nodded.

"A period in a book is like a wall, Elizabeth. You have to stop before you go on."

Elizabeth's brows shot up, a smile lighted her face, and she squealed. "Like a wall. Yes. I stop at a wall."

The session went smoothly after that and Kat hated to leave. They had another long hike and target practice that afternoon. She and the driver stopped for fish and chips wrapped in the *London Times*. Then the drive continued from the London school back to the castle.

When she arrived at the estate, she found the hike had been called off for the day. The Specialists and Mister

Marshall were in the situation room clustered around an atlas and listening to a TV broadcast.

"That brings you up to date on the situation. The Iranian minister of health says he can't explain the sudden outbreak of the disease in the small southern Iranian village. The curious part is that all twenty-four members of the town have contracted smallpox. Already eight are dead, mostly the babies and young children unable to fight off the early effects.

"One Iranian medical official who visited the site said that it's too late to save any of the victims. All will surely die within two or three days. The village is isolated at the end of a road high on the Central Plateau. It's possible that no one has visited the area since the outbreak when the disease would have been highly contagious.

"Roadblocks have been set up around the village. No one is allowed to enter or leave. Relatives of the afflicted must remain away until the disease has run its course and the area is determined not to be contagious.

"The Iranian minister of health reported that there were only six cases of smallpox reported in his nation last year and all of those had been contracted outside of Iran on trips and vacations. He has no possible explanation for this sudden onslaught of one of the modern time's most contagious diseases, which has been all but wiped out in most of the world."

The newscast ended and Wade shut off the TV.

"Remember that report we read a few weeks ago on the potential for bio terror and the biologicals that Russia developed in the eighties?" Wade asked. "I wonder if this sudden outbreak of smallpox in that Iranian village has any connection with the Odessa stockpile of smallpox virus?"

✳ THIRTEEN ✳

SIRJAN, IRAN

Abdul rested in the hotel in Sirjan, a good-sized town on the edge of the Central Plateau, and waited. He had heard the television reports from the Iranian Ministry of Health. He hoped they were true, but he had to make sure himself. Abdul had relaxed in the hotel for two weeks. The trip to Odessa and then to Kuwait and on here to Iran had sapped his strength. He had been burned worse than he realized at first and had to have a doctor treat him in Kuwait.

Now he was healing and his strength was coming back. He knew he was lucky to be alive after that missile attack on the Boghammar in the gulf.

He evaluated the reports from the Iranian state health agency. They would make the matter look as benign as possible. So far there had been no hint that this might have been a biological attack. That was good. The ministry said that smallpox vaccine was in short supply in Iran as in the rest of the world.

"We shall attempt to obtain more vaccine to have on hand in case this outbreak spreads," the minister said. Abdul had taken the shortage of vaccine into his plans. Some could be sent by jet plane from one area or country to another. However, there would not be time enough to produce any large amount of new vaccine, say enough to inoculate a city of a hundred thousand. Even though reports said that half the world's population in the advanced nations had been immunized against smallpox, the other half had not. He would settle for killing 150 million Americans.

Abdul groaned as he moved, putting pressure on his right leg. It had been damaged the most in the blast in the Strait of Hormuz. His pant leg had been charred and a second-degree burn blistered into his flesh. He shook his head in wonder about his miraculous escape from the explosion. The missile itself must have detonated on the boat, setting off the two torpedoes they had belowdecks, making one huge fireball and thunderous blast. Allah had been watching over him that day.

Abdul stood from the bed and began to do his daily routine of exercises. He was slender, well muscled, and in good shape. He wanted to stay that way. He could do his arm and upper-body workout with no pain, but the exercises involving his legs hurt like fire. He put off doing those for another few days. Now he needed a good night's sleep. Tomorrow was an important day. He would decide then if the virus was potent enough to continue with his mission against the Great Evil. He desperately hoped that he could go forward. Without intending to, he thought of his wife and family in Tehran. He had not seen them for three months. They were used to his being away for periods of time. They were well cared for. Abdul had sent his wife a package last week with twenty thousand U.S. dollars. His wife was good with money. He sighed. When this was over he would stay at home for a solid month and play with his small boys.

The next day he drove a rented car as close as he could get to the small village of Manisha, where he had left the smallpox virus. An army unit had the road blocked off five miles from the tiny settlement.

"Quarantined," the Iranian Army corporal said, holding his automatic rifle in front of him and glaring. "Turn around and leave. No one is permitted in there. Haven't you heard about the smallpox these people have?"

"Smallpox?" Abdul said. "Nobody gets that anymore."

"Tell the dead and dying in that village. Every man, woman, and child in there is dead or soon will be. Now turn around and get moving."

Abdul drove back the way he had come until the road went through a small wadi and dropped out of sight of the roadblock. He pulled off the highway and parked. He would have a six-mile hike, but that he could do even on his hurting leg. He took a bottle of water and his ten-power binoculars and began to walk.

He followed the wadi half the way, then had to climb the sides and go directly toward the village. He was over a mile from the road now so the soldiers there couldn't see him. Twice he drank from the water bottle. The sun penetrated the hat he wore and made his healing scalp itch.

After more than an hour and a half, he came up the side of a deep wadi and saw the village two hundred yards away. He eased back down so only his head and shoulders were over the top of the dirt. Then he took out his field glasses and focused on the first house.

He saw nothing but the boards and windows. He moved his view to the next and then the next. At the third house he saw a man edge out the door, throw out a bucket of waste. When he threw, the easy movement made him lose his balance and he fell. He couldn't stand. He crawled back inside, the bucket abandoned.

Near the last house, Abdul saw what appeared to be bodies wrapped in blankets and laid out under the only tree in town. He counted fourteen silent forms.

He felt a moment of glorious frisson. The virus was alive and well in its freeze-dried state, waiting only for moisture of any kind to bring it back to full life and to get into action.

Watch out, Great Evil. I'm coming to get you, to make you suffer, to make you die. You will be devastated, terrorized, and all because of the anguish and death you Americans have brought to the nations of Islam over the past forty years.

Abdul hurried back to his car. His pains and burns were forgotten in the rush of total joy he felt when he knew for certain that the virus was alive and potent. He would use it carefully, and the Great Evil would suffer a monstrous sickness and death unlike anything the world had known since the horrendous black plague that killed half of Europe's population in 1348.

He had work to do. First settle on the four men he wanted to be in his action group. They had to be old hands at this business, hard and tough and willing to take orders and work as a team. He had three picked out and needed a fourth. He would pay each man $25,000 up front for unquestioned loyalty.

Abdul knew he could hire more men in America if he needed them. With money you could buy anything in the United States, even traitors to their own kind. Abdul smiled as he reached his car and sped away from his experiment in death.

He had taken a precautionary step last week. One of his longtime friends and trusted fighters for Islam went to Odessa to cover the back trail. Anyone trying to tie Odessa to him and any shipment out of Odessa during the last three weeks would be dealt with harshly and permanently by Zahir. He was a mountain of a man, with a short beard, small, dark eyes, and a huge head. He had the patience of a stalking tiger and the strength of a gorilla. He would keep the trail covered.

BALDERMARE CASTLE

For the past two days the Specialists had been following the news reports from Iran concerning the village of Manisha. Last word was that a flyover by Iranian helicopters showed no life, no movement in the village. The bodies of two large dogs were spotted, but two cats were seen wandering around. A medical team would go into the area after the last incubation period of the virus was over, fourteen days from now.

Duncan looked up. "The incubation period for smallpox is ten to fourteen days. Which means people can infect others long before they know they have the disease themselves. With airline travel the way it is, the disease could jump from nation to nation within hours."

Duncan frowned for a moment, then went on. "Isn't it

odd that everyone in the village seemed to get the small-pox at the same time. The usual pattern is that one person gets exposed, gets the disease, then infects several others, but they don't come down with it for up to two weeks. By that time the one who brought the sickness into the village would be terribly ill or dead. But the progress of spreading the disease would be in increments as one infected another. How did all twenty-four people in that village become infected at once?"

Duncan stood and walked around the situation room. "There can be only one answer. They were all exposed at one time. How could that happen? A joint love fest and kissing contest, which is doubtful for the Iranians. The other method would be with a biological weapon. Someone could have planted a bomb there with the smallpox virus in it and exploded it, flooding the whole area with the air-borne virus that settled in every lung in town."

"Which means somebody dropped a bomb on that town that contained the smallpox virus," Roger said. "Or they fired in an artillery shell loaded with the virus or maybe somebody simply planted a container of the virus then exploded it when he was well away from the area."

"But why would anyone want to do such a terrible thing?" Kat asked.

"A test, an evaluation of the virus," Wade said. "I know everyone is thinking about the Russians and their development of the biological agents. That with the activity around Odessa lately makes me think that maybe some of the Russian viruses were stolen or sold. Maybe some nut tested the merchandise to see if the twenty-seven-year-old virus is still alive and ready to kill."

"You're right, Wade, but I don't want to think about it," Hershel said. "I've seen the Arabs do some mighty dirty things in our continuing war with them, but nothing as low as this. A little chlorine gas here and there, but this—it's monstrous."

"That, Kat and gentlemen, is precisely why it's so appealing to the nut fringe we call terrorists," Mister Marshall said. He had been sitting in with them the last two days. "A nuclear weapon would be better, but they are almost impossible to get these days. Next most potent are biologicals or nerve gas. I had a signal from the Company late this morning. The CIA has three experienced field agents in Odessa now checking on the report that some items were sold, paid for, and delivered recently from the Odessa munitions depot, the huge cave near Odessa where the ICBMs and other munitions have been stored for forty years.

"One of the agents reported he had a good lead, a hot one he called it. That was last night. This morning he was found dead in an alley under garbage some thirty miles from the munitions caves.

"I told H.J. that we'd send some backup over there to support his agents. I just received confirmation. I want Kat and Duncan to get ready to travel. The small jet will be flying to Odessa this afternoon. I'll have the CIA briefing and all the information we know on Odessa and the problem there ready for you before you leave."

"If somebody is trying to cover his tracks in Odessa, I'd say we have at bay a serious terrorist determined to use whatever weapon he bought from the Ukraine warehouse," Duncan said. "It could be nuclear, nerve gas, or biological. We've got to find out."

Kat and Duncan left the group to put together what they called their travel kits. They were small airline type carry-ons big enough for clothes and personal essentials, but no weapons. They would be supplied with arms in Odessa.

"When we find out, gentlemen, we run this terrorist to ground, we make him permanently dead, and we incinerate any biological agents that he might have," Mister Marshall said.

He watched the four men left around the table in the situation room. "Yes, gentlemen, it looks like we have found our next project. It might be that it has found us. In any event we have a sniff at something that smells most foul. Let's see what we can do about it."

✱ FOURTEEN ✱

ODESSA, UKRAINE

Kat and Duncan arrived just after 10 A.M. the day after they left London. They carried their luggage to the terminal clock near the information stand and looked around. At once two CIA men came up and gave the correct greeting.

"Sorry to be late," Duncan said. "We were hung up in Budapest over some air clearances. At least we got through."

They introduced themselves, then crawled into a small Russian-made car. Their briefing on the situation began as they drove to a safe house in the higher-priced side of town.

Clark Davis was slender, thirty-eight, with a small hook in his nose and piercing green eyes. His face was Mr. Average. He could melt into a crowd and pass for anyone. That was the best insurance any agent could have. He had a fine grin and he turned it on now.

"We have good contacts here. So far we have narrowed the top suspects who actually could swing a deal like this down to three men. One a former officer in the old USSR, the second the present top political figure, who is mayor of Odessa and pulls a thousand strings. The third man is a shadow really, who is here and there and doesn't seem to have any office or platform and no visible means of support. His base of operations is the waterfront."

The other agent, Emery Chase took over. He was larger,

roughly built on a six-foot-two-inch frame. He could have been a college linebacker and had a reputation for having that kind of a personality. His face was rugged, chiseled, with heavy brows, high cheekbones, a twice-broken nose, and dark brown eyes that could bore through granite.

"We haven't touched these three yet. It's taken us a week just to work our way through the mire and chaff to get this far. Infuriating that it's taking so much time. You heard about Scotty. We know he was damn close to something. Now we want some blood and the top dog as well. We hope you two can help us."

"We hope so, too," Kat said. "We believe there was a shipment made from here about three weeks ago. You heard about the village in Iran that was wiped out by a sudden smallpox epidemic?" Kat told them about it and their theories.

Clark nodded. "Yes, sounds like somebody bought some of the smallpox virus. We know Russia made it, and we suspect that it's in the munitions depot outside of Odessa. They call it the Cave."

"Is there any way to get inside the Cave?" Duncan asked.

"Nobody officially will admit that it even exists," Emery said. "They are embarrassed by it. The good people wish it would go away. The corrupt see it as a huge piggy bank for them to draw on when they can make a discreet sale. We believe that the current mayor of Odessa wants to come clean and turn over everything to the United Nations for destruction. But he knows that he can't do it. Politically it would kill him."

"Who was Scotty working on?" Duncan asked.

"We're not sure. It came up suddenly. He phoned and said he would have big news for us in the morning."

"Three top guns, didn't you divvy them up?" Kat asked.

"We were getting ready to. I was going to take the guy they call the Commissar, Clark would go for the mayor and top politico, and Scotty would try to find the shadow guy known only as Opteba."

"The Razor?" Kat asked.

"Afraid so," Emery said. "All the people we've talked to so far are even afraid to admit that they know him, let alone tell us where we can contact him."

"I want him," Kat said.

The CIA agents both said no at the same time. Clark waved one hand emphatically. "Not a chance. Not after what happened to Scotty. My boss would keelhaul me through the Potomac for a year if anything happened to one of Mister Marshall's people. Absolutely not."

"Fine. So you have no starting place to get a handle on the Razor. I'll just have to freelance. You said his power base was in the port and shipping."

"Can't help you with anything else," Emery said.

"You won't stop her," Duncan said, grinning. "You might as well give her anything you have."

Clark wilted. "Be careful. All we know is that he has powerful friends in shipping and the port and airport areas."

They came to the safe house and the hosts carried the travel cases inside. It was an apartment on the third floor of six and on the inside away from the street.

"We move our safe house every two months," Clark said. "We figure if they are bugging us, it will take them that long to find us and get their microphones installed."

The furnished apartment had three bedrooms, a kitchen, and a tiny living room with a TV set.

Kat went into the bedroom where Clark had put her case. She closed the door and came out five minutes later dressed for the grubby streets. She wore old jeans, scruffy boots, a black turtleneck sweater, and a light jacket that held a stained area and one tear in the right sleeve. She even had a dark smudge of something on one cheek.

"I'm heading for the docks to see what I can dig up," Kat said in Russian.

Clark laughed. "You are good with the Russian," he said in English. "Mine isn't quite that colloquial." He gave her a phone. "Digital, satellite. Good reception here. You can get any of us at any time. I have one for Duncan, too. There are three numbers pasted on the back." He went up to her and touched her shoulder. "Hey, take it easy. Do you have enough of the hryvnya notes? They go about five to a U.S. dollar."

"Yes, we brought plenty with us." She patted his cheek. "Now, don't you worry. If I get in over my galoshes, I'll yell for help." She held out her hand. "May I use the car?"

Emery gave her the keys and chuckled. As soon as the door closed he laughed. "Yes, I think Kat is going to do all right here in Odessa." He looked at Duncan. "Danish French, and German. None of those will help you here. The main language is Ukrainian, but 90 percent of the people also speak Russian. So we get by. I'll work with you, if it's all right." Emery frowned. "You're tall enough but a little light. You play ball in college?"

"No football, but I did three years on the soccer team," Duncan said.

"The running game, yeah. Well, let's get at it. I'll go over with you everything we know about this guy they call the Commissar. Not much to go on. No political office, but a tremendous power base."

Clark called from the kitchen. "They fed you on the plane, but you must still be hungry. So, it's flapjack time in Odessa."

Kat drove carefully, working her way to the waterfront on the Black Sea. She had never been there before. She drove around watching the people, the work on ships, the nearby bars and eateries. She picked one of the grubbier bars and parked near it.

Inside there were only three customers at the bar. She took an end stool and asked for a dark beer touted by a sign in the window. An unshaven man in his thirties wearing seaman's clothes moved up the bar and sat beside her.

"You're new in here."

"Do I need a license? That makes you an old-timer."

"Not that old."

"Do you remember the days when we were in the USSR?"

"A little. Lots of years ago."

She sipped the dark beer. It was surprisingly good. "Who knows everything that goes on down here?"

"You a spy?"

"Absolutely. I'm spying on civilian ships that haul bat shit to Poland."

They both laughed.

"You're lucky, I'm an expert on bat shit."

"You don't smell the part."

"Good showers."

"I'm Katherine. I'm writing a long story about the Odessa docks and the drug smuggling that goes on around here. Who can help me?"

His knee nudged against hers. She eased away from him. His knee came back, pressing harder.

"I can help you, but it will cost you something."

"Money?"

"Not exactly. Come, I'll show you how to find him. His name is Vanya and he's an old bear, rough and gruff and vulgar. Sometimes he stays in a back room here. He knows everything that goes on around the docks and the airport."

"The back room here?"

"Right. I'm not sure he's there now, but we can look."

Kat weighed the chances. A good source would be unbeatable. But it could be a con. She had to go. She couldn't pass up a chance it was the man. The seaman's knee pushed against hers again. This time she didn't move it.

"I'm Umenya, just a sailor. I can help you." His smile was broad, but she couldn't read any more into it. She shrugged.

"Let's give it a try. Which way?"

He led her through a side door into a hall and down three doors to a fourth.

"In here if he's on board. He might be with a woman. I'll take a quick look."

He edged the door open a crack, then closed it, nodding. "Yes, he's here, resting and reading. Vanya looks more agreeable than usual." He opened the door and waited for her to start inside.

She took one step past the door, then sensed a problem, but Umenya pushed her from behind and she stumbled on into the room. There was one light on and a bed to one side, but no one else was in the room.

He slammed the door, snapped a lock, and turned toward her.

"Such a beautiful little Russian flower must be picked before it wilts. That would be a tragic waste. No, don't try to fight me. I'm bigger than you and stronger. You lose either way. Why get beat up for nothing?"

Kat turned slowly to face him. He moved toward her and before he knew she would fight him, her booted foot lashed out aimed for his crotch. He turned just in time so it was only a partial blow, but she heard him groan and grab for his privates. Kat followed up with a flat upward palm thrust with her right hand, catching him under the chin and blasting his head upward. His eyes went wide and he backed away.

"Bitch, bastard of a bitch."

He charged her. Kat waited until the last possible second and dodged but he stayed with her, caught her around the waist, and powered her backwards until they both fell on the bed. His weight was only half on top of her. She drove her right knee up into his crotch, jolting his whole body forward six inches. Umenya screeched in pain and tried to curl up. Kat heaved with her whole body and shoved him off the bed. He fell to the floor and lay there moaning. Kat sprang off the bed and watched him a moment. He lunged at her feet but she jumped back. Then she slashed out with her boot, slamming it hard into his side just over his belt where his exposed kidney lay. Her kick hit the kidney and Umenya screeched in agony. He doubled up into a fetal position and whimpered in pain. A moment later he vomited.

"Umenya, stupid sailor. If you ever try this again, don't be so damned confident. I should kill you, but I'll let you live to suffer through the rest of your pain. Was it all a con or is there really a Vanya who knows the waterfront? Tell me or I kick your other kidney."

He looked up at her from the floor. He blinked back tears and slowly nodded. His voice was whispery.

"Yes, there is a Vanya, but I don't know how to find him."

Kat turned and left the room, then the bar without talking to anyone else. At least she had the name of a man to look for.

Kat hit every bar within a mile along the waterfront. She used Vanya's name. She told everyone she was looking for him. She had to see Vanya. He should forget what happened last night and give her another chance. She left her name, Sonja. In situations like this it would be all but impossible for her, an outsider, to find a man, a powerful one like this, who didn't want to be contacted.

But if it were up to the man, he could find her easily. She made return trips to the bars she had already covered, asking if anyone had come in asking for her while she was gone. At the sixth place she returned to, the barkeep nodded and pointed to a man sitting at the end of the bar working on a drink. She ordered a beer and watched the man. He seemed harmless enough.

Short, slender. Thinning gray hair, maybe sixty. Vanya or a messenger? She stood at the bar beside him. He stared straight ahead.

"I need to see Vanya. Can you help me?"

"Who are you?" he asked, still looking ahead.

"A person with a problem that Vanya might be able to solve."

"I am Vanya. I don't like my name thrown about like a piece of old newspaper." He turned and looked at her from soft blue eyes. His face was plain, his eyes set far apart and just the trace of a dark beard showing through his morning shave. Kat felt as if she were being put through a tough evaluation. At last Vanya nodded.

"Very well. The back booth. Follow me."

A few moments later they settled into a booth. No one was near them. They still had their drinks.

"What is your problem?"

Kat told him about a possible shipment from the secret munitions cave.

Vanya shook his head. "Nothing went by boat. I would know about it. Yes, there has been some activity around the caves. It's hard to keep track of, but I know of only one actual sale of goods. I don't know who the buyer was.

He paid in cash, brand-new packets of American hundred-dollar bills still in their plastic wrappings."

"Vanya, you're sure of this? It is tremendously important. You know about the Russian biological weapons stored in the munitions cave?"

"The old Russian weapons? Yes. Now they are Ukrainian property, no? They are ours."

"Yes, your responsibility to the world, Vanya. We think that a quantity of smallpox virus, from the warhead of a missile, was shipped from the caves." She watched him closely. Vanya never twitched a nerve, didn't blink or take a breath or change his face or demeanor in any fashion.

"Yes, a responsibility I have had talks with . . . with certain people. But the munitions remain."

"Was some shipped from there about three weeks ago?" Kat asked.

Vanya looked away. Now his face worked, his breath came in short gasps, then he sighed and nodded.

"Yes, yes. There was a shipment. I tried to stop it. One of my men was killed. The shipment went out by British Air Freight. But I'm not sure where it went. It was a large wooden box stenciled with words meaning farm machinery. But not heavy enough for that use."

"Was it one of the biological weapons?"

"My man there says he thinks so, but he isn't sure. Now I can't ask him again. He was the one shot to death at the airport."

"Do you know the exact date?"

"Yes, the twenty-fourth, the day my friend died."

Kat touched his shoulder. "Vanya, I'm sorry about your friend. We are trying to track what we think is smallpox virus. You have helped us. If we find the man who killed your friend, he will taste your justice." She watched him. He nodded slowly.

"I do this only because of my dead friend. Their man here is powerful, strong. I will find him eventually, but what you do now will be a good help." He looked at her. "Good hunting."

She stood, looked at Vanya a moment, then hurried into the street and to where she had left the car. As soon as she stepped inside and locked the doors, she took out the digital phone and dialed the first number from the back.

"Yes, this is Emery."

"Emery, Kat. A lead. A man who should know says that a shipment from the Cave left by air on March 24 from British Air Freight. He's not sure what it was. Not too large and in a wooden crate. The box had stenciled words on it indicating it contained farm machinery."

"Duncan and I will move out there at once and see what we can find out. Duncan's MI-6 background might help. Will keep in touch."

"I'm on my way as well. See you out there."

Kat put down the phone and sensed something wrong. At the same moment a man lifted up from the backseat and pushed a pistol muzzle against the back of her neck.

"Easy, lady, you ain't going nowhere." The words were in Russian and she understood them perfectly.

"Now hand over the car keys like a nice lady. Then you and me are gonna have a little talk. Friend of mine wants to know why you're so interested in Vanya."

★ FIFTEEN ★

Emery took the lead at the British Air Freight office. It was in a building away from the passenger terminal.

"Is there anyone here who is British?" Emery asked in Russian. The clerk nodded and pointed to a man who had just come from an office toward the back. He called and the man came over.

"I understand that you're British," Emery said as the man in a suit and narrow tie came up.

"Right. I'm the new manager here. Trying to bring a little order to this place. Only been here four months."

Duncan stepped up and introduced himself. "I used to be with MI-6. I was moved into this new position and we have a problem. There was a shipment went out from here on March 24. We believe it contained contraband goods of the most dangerous nature. We're trying to track down exactly where the shipment went so we can follow up on the shippers."

"I say, you know this is frightfully irregular. MI-6 you say. Well, I don't think it will hurt anything to bend the regs a little. Let me check the computer records for the twenty-fourth. I'll have a printout. Would it have been a small package or a large one?"

"Large wooden crate. I'd guess somewhere around three hundred pounds," Duncan said.

"Quite. Just a moment."

They waited, watched the process of a man shipping a

dog in a special carrier. It would be kept in the pressurized section of the plane. Yes, it would be given water during the trip.

The manager came back scowling. "Terribly sorry, but there seems to be a glitch in our computer. We show no shipment of over a hundred pounds for that day. But the total weight of all shipments does not tally with the total in the printout. The difference is over three hundred pounds."

"Could someone have deleted from your computer one or more shipments of over three hundred pounds?" Duncan asked.

The manager scowled. "Could have. I don't know our people here that well yet, or the system. But surely—"

"If someone wanted something hidden, wouldn't this be a good way to make it appear that no such shipment went out?" Emery asked.

The manager agreed. "But why would they want to do that?"

"Because we think that shipment contained some highly dangerous material. Anyone remember a big shipment on that day?"

The manager smiled. "We move two to three hundred items a day through here. You're talking about six thousand items ago. Even a large shipment would be hard to remember."

"Give it a try. We'll talk to you again about this. Right now, we'd like to talk to some of your workers who were on duty on the twenty-fourth." Duncan paused for just a moment and went on before the manager could object.

"No law or rule says you have to let us talk to your people, but you could be saving hundreds of thousands of lives by doing so. This package was unusual enough that we think some of your workers might just remember."

The manager frowned and looked away, then back at them, then away again.

"Do you know a man called only Vanya?" Emery asked. "He's helping us on this project. I'm sure he would react favorably if you could assist us."

"Vanya?" the man's eyes flared for a moment, then he

swallowed and cleared his throat. "Well, yes, I think it would be all right for you to talk to our people. I'll get you a list of those who worked during the day shift on the twenty-fourth."

Two hours later, Duncan and Emery had talked to all but one of the men who worked on the target date. None of them could remember an item of over three hundred pounds.

"A shipment gets that heavy, it costs a fortune to ship it by air," one man said. "Sometimes they drive it or send it by boat. Depends how quickly they need it on the other end."

"This particular one was in a wooden crate and stenciled on it were the Russian words for farm machinery," Emery said.

One of the men frowned, scratched his chin, then nodded. "Yeah, I do remember that one. Couldn't figure out what kind of farm machinery we manufactured here in Odessa, and who would want to buy it anyway? If it was real farm machinery, it would be huge and heavy and would go by boat."

"You remember the crate?" Emery asked.

"Oh, yeah. Big, slat boards around it, and those words meaning farm machinery, all over it."

"Where did it go?"

"Destination? Hell, I don't remember. At the time I thought it seemed unusual. Not a lot of farming done in that little country."

Duncan looked at the CIA man. "Didn't Kat say she was coming right out here? Where is she? That must have been an hour ago."

"True. I'll call her." They had no more workers to question. Emery took out his pocket-sized digital phone and dialed a remembered number.

"No answer. Which could mean she's extremely busy, lost the phone—"

"Or that she's in trouble," Duncan finished the sentence. "Odessa isn't exactly a small town. How do we find her?"

"We can't. We wait for her to call or to show up."

•   •   •

Kat felt the muzzle of the pistol and knew it was the real thing. She hadn't locked the car when she left it. Her goof. She passed the keys to the man in the backseat as he had demanded.

"Now, pretty lady. Remain extremely still and I won't have to shoot you. First. Who are you? We know that you are not CIA. We know who they are."

"I'm Kathryne Krane. I work for a world peace organization. We don't like the idea of the nuke weapons being in the caves here in Odessa. I'm trying to find out how many there are."

"Is that all?"

"What else is in there, nerve gas?"

"I have a man who wants to see you. Slide over to the passenger's side and lace your fingers on top of your head. Do it now. Bullets travel extremely fast, so don't think you can slip away while I come into the front seat. I'd rather shoot you than take you in, but orders are orders."

The man moved to the far door in the backseat, training the pistol on Kat. He eased out the door and Kat expected him to rush into the front seat. Instead, there was only a silence. She looked where the man should be, but saw no one. What had happened?

"Miss, don't be alarmed," the strange voice came from outside the car where the kidnapper should be.

The door unlatched and it opened. A slender man edged into the driver's seat. Kat had never seen him before.

"Your Arab friend is unconscious on the street outside. Vanya invites you to come back and see him in a room behind the bar where you talked before. We'll take our Arab friend along and see what he has to say."

Slowly Kat let her hands down.

"Vanya?"

"Yes. He thinks you're doing a good thing. He has had someone watching you since you first left word about wanting to find him. Please, we should go. I'll put the Arab in the backseat. You drive. It's only two blocks." He handed Kat the car keys. She grinned at him in the morning light and pushed under the wheel.

Five minutes later, Kat had a good look at the man who had kidnapped her. He was definitely Arab, with a full black beard, a hook hose, and black eyes that now sparked off hatred.

"You infidels will all die soon by the hand of Allah," the man shouted. The slender man who had carried the Arab into the back room slapped him hard on one cheek then the other where he sat tied in a sturdy chair. He was stripped to the waist, showing a slender frame and no chest hair.

"I have some questions to ask you," Vanya said to the Arab. "You will answer quickly and with a civil tongue or you will lose one eye. Do I make myself clear?"

"I will die for Allah."

"Yes, but how much pain can you stand?" Vanya asked. He took out a knife with a slender blade six inches long that gleamed in the bright lights.

"Now, who do you work for?"

The Arab said nothing, stared straight ahead. Vanya motioned to the Ukrainian helper, who put his right hand on the Arab's head with his thumb touching the inside edge of the right eye socket.

"I'll ask you once more and perhaps save your right eye. Who do you work for?"

The Arab gasped, then let out a long-held breath. He started to say something, then stopped.

The blade flashed in the light and a thin blood line sprang red and glistening across the Arab's chest. Small blood rivulets crept down his skin and across his belly.

The Arab screamed.

The third time the question came, the Arab answered.

"He is called the Great One, the leader of all Arabs in Ukraine. He told me to watch anyone interested in the port or the airport, and to watch Vanya."

"Where were you taking her?"

"To see the Great One."

"Fine," Vanya said. "You may do that, only we will go with you. We'll have ten armed men and this young lady."

Another blood line developed on the Arab's chest and he gasped, then screamed.

"You have an extremely low threshold of pain, my small Arab friend."

Kat moved up. "Vanya, let me try. I have an idea, hypnotism."

"He's unwilling."

"He's also frightened, weak, and bleeding. Let me try."

Vanya's eyes hooded, then he lifted his brows. "Try," he said.

"Do you have a first name?" she asked the Arab.

"Yakim."

"Yakim, I won't hurt you. I'm trying to help you. Listen to my voice. Close your eyes and think of a pleasant place, where you are safe and no one can hurt you. Think of it. Yes, close your eyes."

Yakim strained against the ropes that held him. "No, I won't do that. You're trying to fool me."

"I'm trying to help you, to save your life. Now, relax, close your eyes. No one will hurt you. Think of a pleasant place. Yes, that's right. Relax. Your eyes are getting heavy, heavier."

Yakim snapped open his eyes. "You're trying to hypnotize me. I've seen it done. I won't let you."

"Yakim, you're tired, it's been a long day. Those other men will kill you, if you don't let me talk to you. Come on. You have nothing to fear from me. Just relax. That's it. Now close your eyes and think of a pleasant place. Yes, good. Your eyes are heavier. Relax. Yes, Yakim, you're totally sleepy. Go to sleep, Yakim. Good. Go to sleep."

Yakim's head fell to one side. His eyes remained closed.

"Yes, Yakim, you are sleeping, but when I snap my fingers you will come partly awake and answer the questions I ask you. Do you understand? If so, nod once."

Yakim nodded.

"Who is the Great One helping?"

"I . . . I don't know."

"What Arab country did the men come from he helps?"

"Iran."

"What did they buy from the munitions cave?"

"I don't know."

"What country was it shipped to?"

"Arab country."

"Which Arab country?"

"I don't know."

Kat frowned and shook her head at Vanya. "He doesn't know. He can't be faking."

"Yakim, when I snap my fingers twice, you will be fully awake and remember nothing of the questions I asked." She snapped her fingers twice and Yakim opened his eyes.

"I told you that you couldn't hypnotize me," Yakim said.

After that they drove around for an hour, but Yakim couldn't find the place where the Great One lived. At last Kat stopped the car. The thin man who had rescued Kat pushed the Arab out of the car and kicked him. A moment later the Arab screamed.

"You broke my arm," he wailed. The thin man stepped into the car and Kat drove away.

"Thought I'd give him something to remember us by," the thin man said.

Kat dug the phone from her purse and dialed the number on the back.

"Emery here."

"Kat. You do any good at the airport?"

"Not much. Something went out but we don't know where. I've been working with an Arab agent of some kind. He finally admitted that the package was sent to an Arab country, but he didn't know which one. Vanya has been helping me."

"Come to the airport, British Air Freight. We have one last shot at one of the workers. Duncan said you can hypnotize. We might use it on this man. Get out here quickly. He's about to go off shift."

Kat dropped the Vanya man off, and then it took a half hour to drive in the CIA car to the Odessa airport. She found the air-freight office and Duncan and Emery.

She gave them a three-sentence summary of her work that morning, then they went to find the employee who had recognized the farm-machinery shipment. He squirmed under the attention.

"I still can't remember."

"It was an Arab country," Kat said.

He blinked. "Arab? Yes there were three Arabs who delivered the big box on the back of a small truck. Yes, Arabs, I remember that now. But which country? There must be ten or fifteen."

"What's your name?" Kat asked.

"Yalin."

"Have you ever been hypnotized?"

"No."

"If I hypnotize you, you might remember that day and where the shipment went to."

Yalin nodded. "Yes, yes, let's try."

Kat had to say only a dozen words to put him into a hypnotic trance.

"Yalin, I want you to think back to the day that big crate of farm machinery came in. Move up close and look at the manifest that shows where the big box goes. Can you see it?"

"Yes."

"Where does it go, Yalin?"

"Twenty-five, twenty-five Old Quarry Road, Kuwait City, Kuwait."

Kat heard Duncan say something softly. Emery let out a held-in breath.

"Are you sure, Yalin? Read it again to me."

The Ukrainian gave the address and city again exactly the same.

"Does it say anything else? A name?"

"Yes, Kuwait Farm Machinery, Ltd."

Kat looked at the others. "Time we call London." She brought Yalin out of the trance. They thanked him and Kat gave him five thousand hryvnya in large bills. It was over $1,100. More than he made in six months. Yalin thanked her, kissed her hand, and held it so long she wondered if he would let go.

Outside in the CIA car, Kat looked at Duncan. "Like I said, I think it's time that you call London with the news so Mister Marshall can jet somebody down to Kuwait and see if we can track this shipment any farther."

☆ SIXTEEN ☆

KUWAIT CITY, KUWAIT

Abdul al Ganzouri sat in a hotel suite watching television and fine-tuning his plans. In two more days he would have the shipment ready to go to New York. All was on schedule. He still had to select the last man he would take to New York with him. His team was the best and most reliable in the Arab world. They came from the hard core of dedicated men who fought the Great Evil.

Right now, it was time to relax and enjoy a few moments of the good life. A fine hotel, dining as he had never known it, money to spend without worrying about the price. He motioned to the woman who stood in the bedroom door. She wore only black lace panties. Her bare breasts with dark red nipples jiggled when she walked toward him.

"Now?" she asked, sitting on the edge of the large chair and pushing against him.

Abdul watched her for a moment. She reached in, pressed her breasts against his chest, and nibbled at his ear. He leaned away and caught her breasts with his hands.

"Now is always a good time," he said.

It had never been like this before. He told everyone he was from Iran, but actually he began life in Syria. He was the second son of a small shopkeeper. He remembered dozens of times when his older brother was pushed forward by his parents to show how bright he was, how popular, how smart, how goddamned everything.

Abdul slinked around in the background, hating his father more than his brother. More than once he had asked his father for a pair of shoes, only to be slapped and told to get back to work. His brother had six pair of new shoes. Abdul only had his hand-me-downs and they always were too big.

By the time Abdul was ten he was so angry that he ran away from home. He was caught and brought back. His father beat him with a thick leather belt so badly that he couldn't lie down for a week. He slept huddled in a sitting position with pillows around him. He refused to cry, but late at night he couldn't help but whimper. He kept it soft so no one else could hear.

After that his father didn't trust him to go to school. They kept him home and he worked in the shop from opening to closing late into the evening. When he was twelve his father first molested him. Then a month later he did so again. Then it was a once-a-week ritual.

When Abdul was thirteen he caught his father bone weary after a hard day at the shop. Abdul hit him with a heavy stick and broke his right leg.

His father bellowed in pain and screamed at him. "You worthless camel's dung. You goatherder's spawn. I should have sold you when I could. Now call the doctor."

Abdul ignored him and swung the heavy club again. His father pushed out his left arm and the club snapped both wristbones. His father slumped in a chair and keened in pain and terror. When his screaming stopped he stared hard at Abdul.

"You're going to kill me, right? And leave your mother and brother and sisters with no income. So they will wither and die."

Abdul tried not to listen. Then, deliberately, he broke his father's other leg. He locked the front door, took all of the money from the box under the counter, and from the small open safe in the back room. He didn't bother saying good-bye to his father. He simply left. That same day he vanished into the slums of Damascus and never saw any of his family again.

The money he took from his father vanished quickly. Some of it spent, most of it stolen by those who had even less than he did. He found friends who helped him learn to live in the slums and not be ground down by the hard-scruff life of a street beggar and small-time thief. He stole food so he wouldn't starve.

One day he darted across a street getting away from a fruit vendor where he stole two bananas. He didn't look in the street and collided with a car. He wasn't hurt but had the breath knocked out of him and couldn't move. The driver of the car picked him up and said he'd take Abdul to a hospital. A few minutes later when Abdul recovered, he jumped out of the car at the first traffic light. The man ran after him, caught him, and took him back to the car.

"Young man, I'm going to get you checked over if I have to tie you hand and foot. I don't want to be sued for some injury you claim a year from now."

The doctors said Abdul didn't even have a bruise and pronounced him filthy but sturdy and uninjured. The driver was Don Anderson, an official in the American Oil Company.

Anderson liked the boy he had run down. He made him take a shower in the company office, then bought him some new clothes, including fancy running shoes, and fed him three days in a row. After that Anderson hired the boy as a janitor and let him sleep in the building. He made Abdul read all sorts of books and educate himself as much as possible.

Abdul learned a lot about America, about how U.S. companies function, and about the people who live in the United States. Mostly he envied the residents their wealth and luxuries. Why did they have so much and he so little? It wasn't fair. Even Mr. Anderson was rich. Abdul was paid only enough to live on. Every day he hated the Americans more. Anderson was the root of it; he hated his benefactor the most. Why were all Americans rich and living in luxury? It wasn't fair. Someday he would strike back at them.

Abdul worked for the oil company for two years until he was seventeen. Every day he planned how he could get even with the Americans and Anderson. Then one Friday night, he stole everything he could from the office and sold it over the weekend before his boss came back to work on Monday. With the wad of money, he vanished into the slums of Damascus again, but this time on a slightly better economic level. He was full-grown now and much smarter. He knew what he wanted to do.

Abdul soon met two men who felt the way he did about America. It was the Great Evil as Muslims said. Before long he contacted more men of the same bent, and after a careful investigation of Abdul, they took him into their "action group" and taught him how to make simple bombs.

One night he graduated to placing the bomb he had just made at a British oil firm. He planted it at the front door and raced away, then peered around a building from fifty feet and watched the explosion. It solidified his deep hatred for all Westerners, especially Americans. Here was a way that he could start to pay them back. He was never the same again. From then on he was totally dedicated to killing as many Americans as he could, any way that he could.

When Abdul was nineteen a man talked to him. The man said he worked for Osama bin Laden. Abdul had heard much about the man who provided money and weapons to terrorists. The contact invited Abdul to join his bin Laden–financed group on several projects attacking the Great Evil. Abdul was delighted and signed on. From bin Laden and his men, Abdul learned how to make better bombs, how to sway mobs into action, how to set up protests as a diversion for a deadly strike at an important target. He had his advanced lessons in terrorism.

Abdul made several strikes with the bin Laden group, but he soon became restless. They weren't doing enough. America was getting stronger and the Arab nations were weakening.

For two years he worked with bin Laden. Abdul knew he wasn't fighting against America enough. They should be striking America hard at least once a month. The Great Evil must pay for its transgressions.

When he was twenty-one years old, he quit bin Laden and formed his own group of activists. Two came from the bin Laden group, others from friends he had made in the business. Their biggest problem was that they had no money. For a year they robbed Western firms and Western banks and cars and even one train to get enough money to stay in operation. During that time they only made one small bombing in Syria against an American oil company.

Abdul and his number-one man, Faisal, tried to figure it out. There had to be a better way to get money. How? The idea of blockading the strait came after months of talking. Then they had to get enough money to buy a small boat. Instead they stole the boat, and then bought the torpedo tubes, machine-gun ammo, and four torpedoes from an illegal arms smuggler. At last they were ready to take over the luxury liner.

Abdul turned off the TV set and paced to the Kuwait City hotel-room window. Everything had to be perfect. He would bring America to her knees. The timing was critical. It was April 13. In two days the shipment would be on its way to America. But first he had to be sure that everything else on this side of the world went the way he had planned it. No foul-ups. No problems.

Packing the container would be done soon. To move it, all he needed was to hire a truck and deliver the package to the airport. There he would sign the papers, make the payment, and watch them put the virus on a British Air Freight jetliner.

The airtight seals must all be perfect. The packing and cushioning materials must all work exactly the way they were supposed to. Yes, he was coming closer. Nothing could get in the way, nothing could go wrong.

His one regret was that Faisal had not lived through the explosion in the strait. Luck of the draw. How could they know that the U.S. would respond so quickly with fighter aircraft with missiles? He just wished that both he and Faisal had been lucky. Abdul sent the naked woman away to take a bath and changed the TV channel, hunting for a violent war story. As he searched, a grin broke out when he imagined what it would be like to have America groveling and coming to him, begging him to stop the attacks.

BALDERMARE CASTLE

The phone call hit the Specialists like a bomb.

"We have a lead, a destination," Mister Marshall told the assembled four. "I just talked to Kat and she says she knows the shipment left Odessa on March 24. We're just not sure what was in the shipment. It could be nuclear warheads, nerve gas, or biowarfare virus. Wade and Hershel, you both speak Arabic, so you will be flying out first thing in the morning for Kuwait. Better take the big jet for a quicker trip. The rest of us will try to figure out what this group plans to do with the weapon, whatever it is."

"We don't know for sure that it's smallpox virus?" Wade asked.

"No. We know that the Iranian village was wiped out by smallpox. We can check our calendars. Kat says the shipment went out from Odessa on March 24. A little over three weeks ago. The attack on the village could have happened a few days later. The virus has an incubation period of ten to fourteen days. We know the villagers suffered their sickness the tenth of April. That fits in with the incubation of the virus if it actually was the smallpox virus that arrived in Kuwait on the twenty-fourth or twenty-fifth."

"So the men who have the virus could be anywhere by now," Wade said. "It's the sixteenth today."

"But we still can't be positive it was virus in that shipment." Hershel said. "Hopefully we can tie that down tomorrow in Kuwait."

"Now," Mister Marshall said, "no matter which deadly weapon these terrorists have, they need a target. Any ideas about what a target could be for any of the three possibles?"

Ichi scratched an ear and shook his head. "An impossible question, Mister Marshall. They could be going for anything. A nation's capital for pure kill numbers or to hold it for ransom, a population center to kill as many as possible, even a metropolitan water supply to kill off millions."

"Remember the 'Sword of Allah' words that Abdul spouted when he captured the passenger liner," Roger said. "He was yelling about the Great Evil. I'd say we have to limit our targets to the U.S."

"Wait a minute," Wade said. "We don't even know if Abdul is alive. The odds are against it. We can't assume this is his work. What we can figure is that whoever is doing this would go for the biggest and richest nation. If we agree on that, what would his target be in the U.S.?"

"DC," Roger said at once. "Biggest, baddest, worst consequences for the nation if half the Congress and the President and his cabinet get wasted."

"Yeah, any big city," Ichi said. "Smallpox would terrorize a city like Chicago as it multiplied by a hundredfold every day. There wouldn't be time to manufacture enough vaccine to protect half a city like Chicago, New York, or LA."

"No matter what the target is in the U.S. it would be devastating," Hershel said. "Even if a small town of twenty thousand got wiped out, think of the backlash. Every Arab in the country would be rounded up and half of them shot by civilians."

"We can't let this happen," Mister Marshall said. "First we have to be sure what is in that shipment from Odessa to Kuwait. Then, if at all possible, we have to try to capture it in Kuwait. If we can't do that, we must track it. That will be the tough part. What time is it?"

"A little after 2 P.M.," Ichi said.

"Changed my mind," Mister Marshall said. "Hershel, you and Wade get ready now. The car will leave in ten minutes for the airport. I'll have them get the big jet ready. It will take off for Kuwait as soon as you get to Heathrow."

★ SEVENTEEN ★

KUWAIT CITY, KUWAIT

Wade and Hershel arrived in Kuwait early the next morning, dropped their luggage at a hotel where rooms had been reserved for them, and caught a cab. They gave the driver the address of 2525 Old Quarry Road. The driver frowned.

"I don't know that road," the driver said.

"Look it up in your city guide," Wade said.

"No guide."

"Then radio your dispatcher for directions," Hershel snapped.

The driver turned and shrugged. "No radio. I know the city. There is no such place as Old Quarry Road. We don't have a quarry in Kuwait City."

"Figures," Wade said. "Nobody would ship out that cargo with a real address. They would pick it up at the airport."

"The airport," Hershel said. "The British Air Freight terminal. We'd like to get there as quickly as possible."

Their next target was the point of delivery. Wade hoped that they had better luck there.

The clerk at the desk referred them to an office inside, but the manager wasn't there. A secretary said he would be back tomorrow.

The clerk was busy when they went back. After ten minutes of toe tapping and walking back and forth, Wade and Hershel worked up the waiting line to talk to the clerk again.

"A shipment from Ukraine? What confirmation number do you have?"

"None, we didn't ship it. We're trying to find out who did and who picked it up."

"Are you police?"

"No. We work with the police."

"Bring back a policeman and I can tell you more."

"How many shipments do you have coming in from Ukraine every day?" Wade asked.

"Twenty or so a day. Sometimes more. Over a hundred for the average week."

"Anything unusual come in?"

"That would be something I could talk to the police about. Now stop bothering me. I have work to do, people waiting."

"We also have work to do," Hershel said, and they went outside. Near the side entrance to the large warehouse that housed British Air Freight, they saw six men hanging out. Two smoked, two played cards, one slept snoring softly, and the last wrote as fast as he could in a notebook.

Hershel nodded in that direction and Wade walked with him.

"What's happening?" Hershel asked when they came up.

"Just waiting around," one of the card players said. "Sometimes they hire us for day work. Pay not good but better than nothing."

"Sometimes people who pick up goods here hire somebody to help load and unload it," one of the smokers said. "Not often. A good way to starve your family."

"Anybody get hired three weeks ago?" Wade asked in Arabic.

"Maybe yes, maybe no," the card player said. "Who remembers?"

"Anybody hear anything about Odessa?" Wade asked.

"She isn't from around here," the man writing said. "I know all the good women."

The others shouted and laughed at the writer, who grinned and went back to his notebook.

"Who else might know about workers who were hired on March 25 or 26?" Hershel asked.

The other card player looked up. "You should talk to Old Omar. He's not here today. Probably drunk. He's a real drunk, that one. Loafs around here pretending he wants to work. Twice I've seen him turn down day jobs."

"I didn't think Muslims drank," Hershel said. "Where does he get his booze?"

"Strict Muslims don't drink, much," the second smoker said. "But all of us know where to get some whiskey or beer or wine if we really want to. Omar is a master at finding whiskey, his specialty."

"Where can we find Old Omar?" Wade asked.

"Try every tourist trap in Kuwait City," the first card player said. "He likes to talk to tourists and mooch drinks from them."

"We just might do that," Hershel said. "Hey, we'll be back. If any of you hear about anything unusual going on at British Air Freight, we'll pay good money for it. If it's the information we need."

As they walked away, Wade had an idea. "If he spends a lot of time with these guys, he could live nearby. If so, he could haunt the passenger terminal. Lots of tourists in there."

They took a look. No bars or cocktail lounges. This was Arab and Muslim country. British Air had a "Customer Lounge." Wade and Hershel looked it over. A slender woman with flashing black eyes and a fetching smile came up and asked if they needed any help with their tickets. She spoke English, guessing at their nationality.

"Looking for a friend," Wade said. The woman smiled through her dark eyes, long black hair over her shoulders.

"Who is this friend?" she asked.

Hershel read her name badge and sent her back his best smile.

"Well, Elizabeth, we're looking for Old Omar. Have you heard of him? Incidentally, Elizabeth doesn't sound much like a Kuwaiti name."

"Yes, you're right. They give us English names so our many English-speaking passengers can remember us. No, Old Omar isn't a name I'm familiar with."

They looked around, found no one who could possibly be Old Omar, and went out to the car-rental agencies. They rented a Volvo, then tried to decide where to look next. A tourist's guide to Kuwait City with the car's papers decided it for them. They spent the rest of the day working from one visitor attraction to the next. One was the open market, where they were assaulted by the wonderful smells of cooking meat, spices and herbs in open containers, and the flash of hundreds of red-and-green shirts all for sale.

They wound past the camel market, with its own brand of odors, and on to a mosque said to be the most beautiful in all of Kuwait. Everywhere they asked if anyone knew where Old Omar was today. Some had heard of him. One man quickly patted his pocket to be sure his purse was still inside. Then he laughed.

They ate at a small restaurant, but were confused by the menu. They settled for the shrimp dinner, locally caught shrimp, large and the best Wade had ever tasted.

Before they gave up on the day, they drove back to the airport and talked to the two men who remained of the casual labor force.

They were one of the card players and the writer.

"We saw Omar for a few minutes," the writer said. "He said to tell you he would be at the Café Kuwait, inside the passenger terminal. He said he might have the information you're looking for."

Wade gave the man three hundred dinars, about a hundred U.S. dollars. The man leaped up and hugged Wade, then tried to kiss him on the cheek, but Wade pulled away.

Inside they found Old Omar. He sat by himself in a booth near the back. The hostess led them to him. He drank something from a tall glass. He motioned for them to be seated. Quickly a similar tall glass filled with a pale yellowish liquid was set in front of each Specialist.

Wade sipped his. Lemonade he decided, made with highly carbonated water.

"Omar?" Hershel asked.

"Yes, but usually Old Omar, the loafer." Omar was a small man and looked to be in his mid-sixties, with a short, trimmed beard and graying hair that had thinned on top. His head looked smaller than average and jutted abruptly from a short neck. He wore Western clothes, a sport jacket and shirt with open collar. Omar smiled at them. "You're looking for a shipment into British Air Freight?"

"We are, maybe three weeks ago. Something highly dangerous, that's all we know."

"Where did it come from?" Omar asked.

"Odessa."

Omar grinned and sipped his drink. "There are many dangerous things in Odessa. In the caves."

"You know about the caves?" Wade asked.

"To hear many things, a man must keep his mouth shut and his ears open."

Hershel chuckled. "Well said. We think something highly dangerous came from the caves and was flown to Kuwait. We're trying to track it. Can you help us?"

Omar took another drink. It was a delaying tactic that both he and the Specialists understood. When he put down the glass, his eyes sparkled through their dark brown color.

"I am a businessman who sells information. The price depends on the importance to the buyer. Do you represent some government?"

"No," Wade said. "Although we both have worked for our governments in the past."

Omar nodded.

"If your information is good, we can offer you thirty thousand dinars."

Omar waved the offer away. "Let's talk U.S. dollars, then we won't become confused. Ten thousand U.S. dollars."

"Close enough," Wade said. "What do you know?"

Omar took a long pull from the lemonade, then nodded. "Today is the seventeenth of April. On the thirteenth two men from the work group near the side entrance to British Air were hired after almost everyone had left. They were excited. Said they were hired for two days at a better-than-average wage.

"I haven't seen them since. On the radio, I heard that two men had been found at the edge of the city, both shot in the back of the head. Executed. I inquired. The two men were my friends who had talked, and sung, and waited there at the gate for work. Check police records for yesterday morning, or look in the newspaper." Omar picked up a folded paper beside him. A story near the bottom of a page had been circled with a pen.

"Addresses of both men there?" Wade asked.

Hershel read the story. He nodded.

Wade unfastened two buttons on his shirt and opened a money belt inside. He took out a stack of hundred-dinar notes and counted out thirty-three. They vanished into Omar's pocket.

Omar looked at them. "Gentlemen, I won't detain you. I'm sure that you have some work to do. Perhaps talk to the widows."

They drove back to town and parked the car at their hotel, then gave the first widow's address to a cabby. He waved them inside and drove. They worked into the outer rim of the town, where the streets were unpaved, with streetlights only every half mile. The cab came to a stop in front of a house filled with people.

"A celebration of death," the cab driver said.

"They died two days ago," Wade said.

"It is the custom," the driver said.

Wade waved some dinar notes at the cabby. "Wait for us. Yes, we will pay you well. Now wait."

They were greeted as soon as they approached the house.

"Welcome to the celebration of the dead," a man said. "Welcome."

Twice more they were greeted. Inside they asked who the widow was and she was pointed out to them. It took them fifteen minutes to work through the throng to the woman's side. Hershel took the lead.

"Mrs. Sulaiman, we offer our condolences to you over the death of your husband. Could we ask you some questions?"

"You are police?"

"No, but we have important business. Did your husband say who he worked for those last two days?"

"No, only some rich man."

"Do you know what he did for the rich man?"

"He said they loaded some material into a box."

"Did he say what the material was?"

"Not at first. It was light and inside airtight plastic bags."

"Did he describe the material?"

"He said it was all in long cylinders, as wide as both his hands."

"Were there a lot of them?"

"He said twenty."

"Did the material, the cylinders, have any printing on them?"

"Yes, it had Russian printing. He knew some Russian. He said inside was live smallpox virus. He wasn't paid for the first day. He went back to get his money."

Hershel nodded to Wade, who understood that it was smallpox.

"Do you know where he worked? Where did he go to get his money?"

"Yes. He wrote down the address so he wouldn't forget it. I have it somewhere."

"Could you find it? It's tremendously important. If you find the address, we'll be glad to help you pay for the funeral."

She frowned and left. It was five minutes before she came back. She had in her hand a piece of paper.

"I couldn't find it when the police were here. This is it. Forty-one twenty-three Circle Road. I don't know where that is."

Wade had taken money from his pocket. He gave the woman two thousand dinars. She was overwhelmed. She cried and hugged them both. Just before they left she tugged at Hershel's arm.

"He said this Iranian was crazy. They packed the material in a large ornate casket. They strapped it to a wooden platform with steel bands."

The cab driver had waited. They gave him the new address on Circle Road and he drove.

"A casket without a box around it for protection?" Wade asked. "Sounds crazy. Why?"

"Save him time building a box," Hershel said. "A naked casket just might trip somebody's memory at British Air Freight."

"They still open?"

"Man we need should be there in the morning."

At the Circle Road address they found several old warehouses and a few closed businesses. Everything was dark and shut down. The number they wanted was deserted, with a padlock on the door. A side entrance yielded to some hard kicks. Inside they found nothing. They used their pencil flashes and saw a few boards and some tire tracks, but nothing else. The casket had been shipped.

As soon as they left the warehouse and headed for their car a bright flashlight beam nailed them.

"Don't move or I'll shoot," a gruff voice said in Arabic.

★ EIGHTEEN ★

KUWAIT CITY, KUWAIT

Hershel reacted at once. "Hold it yourself. Get that light out of our eyes. We're undercover police. Who the hell are you?"

The light wavered.

"Let's see some identification."

"Don't be stupid. We don't carry any. We get mugged and our ID stolen it would cause all kinds of problems. Turn out the light."

The light wavered again, then snapped off.

"Better," Hershel said. "We had a report of some drug business going on in this old warehouse, but there isn't any now. You a guard in this area?"

"Yes sir. I was paid to guard this building for three nights, but two nights ago everyone was gone. I got paid so I do the work."

"Commendable, but you can go home now. The show is over. Who paid you?"

"No name, just money and a gun to use. He took the gun with him. Now no gun."

"Bluff?"

"Works in the dark."

"Not on us," Hershel said. "Now get out of here."

They watched in the half moonlight as the man shrugged and walked the other way.

"So, we take on the British Airways Freight tonight or in the morning?" Hershel asked.

"We'll need to talk to the day shift. They would be the ones who could have made a shipment of a naked casket."

"So this bastard terrorist executed two casual workers so they couldn't talk," Hershel said. "I'm going to enjoy meeting this guy, whoever he is."

"By the time we find him, you'll probably have to take a number."

The next morning just after nine o'clock, the two Specialists arrived at the British Air Freight office. Instead of going in the front door, they meandered around to the side and went in an employees only door and up to the work area where stacks of boxes and packages waited to be loaded on a huge freight jet standing by.

Wade picked out the foreman of the group and approached him.

"Hi, need to take up some of your time. I'm with a special group investigating airport security and we have some questions we need to ask."

The man frowned a minute, then lifted his brows and finished his notes on a clipboard.

"Right, who's getting nailed this time?"

"We're not sure yet. We've heard that there was an illegal cargo shipped out of here two or three days ago. It was an unprotected coffin. An expensive one painted a soft blue held onto a plank foundation by steel straps. Is this true?"

"Coffin? Oh, yeah, I remember. Didn't seem like a big deal. These two guys brought it in. I pegged them as Iranians, but I couldn't be sure. They said they didn't have time to build a box around it, and why pay the freight on a lot of wood when the coffin was built to last under torture for fifty years."

"So you shipped it?"

"You bet. The customer is almost always right."

"That's what we were afraid of. We'll need to see the manifest or shipping order, whatever you use. We'll need the name of the shipper and the destination."

"Oh, I should talk to Mr. Lindstrom about that. He's British and stiff and formal as camel shit. Damn, I don't think he's here yet."

"We don't want to charge anybody here. But if this went down on your watch, you would be one of the responsible parties."

Wade watched the man frown and think it through.

"If we could get this cleared up quickly, before this Lindstrom shows up, we could misplace the name of the supervisor on duty at the time."

"That sounds good. Yeah, right. Let me take a look in the files. Right over here."

They went into a small office that was lined with five-foot file cabinets. The foreman pulled out three drawers before he found the one he wanted.

"Yeah, here we are. It went out on the fifteenth. Shipper's name is Omar Sharif and the destination is to be picked up at our facility at Kennedy Airport in the U.S.A."

Wade pointed to the name of the shipper. "Isn't that a familiar name to you?"

"No sir. Popular name in many nations."

"Omar Sharif is a famous movie star, who has made dozens of big films. Just my guess but I'd say that Omar Sharif is not the shipper's real name. Thanks."

Wade headed for the front door, saw Hershel, and gave him a thumbs-up. Hershel waved at him and pointed out the way they had entered.

"Just saw the manager come into the front office," Hershel said. "No reason we should tangle with him if you found what we need."

"We have it and it's bad news. Twenty cylinders of smallpox virus flew out to Kennedy Airport in New York City, on the fifteenth. We need to call Mister Marshall."

Two hours later, Wade and Hershel had collected their gear from the hotel room and turned in the rental at the airport. The Marshall jet had been warmed up, preflight-checked, and was ready to go when they came out of the waiting lounge for private jet passengers at the far side of the Kuwait airport.

The pilot had his instructions by digital phone from Mister Marshall. He would fly the most direct route available to London with one stop.

Lunch had been rushed on board from one of Kuwait's

famous restaurants. It began with a delicate chowder soup, followed by a melt-in-your-mouth breakfast steak with sides of baked potato, cauliflower in a heavy tangy cheese sauce, baked beans and corn on the cob. Desert was a flame-baked ice-cream sundae.

When the meal was cleared away by the onboard steward, Wade called Mister Marshall. It had been almost three hours since he had first talked to the billionaire industrialist.

"Wade, yes. Things are in motion. I called New York at once when I heard and Garth Freemont there has contacted British Air Freight. It's 5 A.M. in New York. A night man said he'd seen the outlandish blue casket and he's sure it's gone. He can't check until they open that section at 8 A.M. We want you and Hershel to leave for New York as soon as you hit Heathrow. You have your traveling gear. I'll notify them to have your jet serviced and fueled for a turnaround. Then come on over. The rest of us are on our way in number two. We left London about 8 A.M. Depending on head winds, we should get across the Atlantic in about six hours. That makes us at JFK at around 9 A.M. counting the time-zone changes. I want to be at Kennedy as soon as possible. We could get there about when BA Freight opens for business. We'll land at JFK and so will you. We'll see you then."

Wade extended the Learjet's seat back as far as it would go. "Looks like we'll be busy as soon as we hit New York. We better get some sleep while we can. If we can make our one stop cleanly and get away without a lot of red tape, we should be in London in nine hours. Then an hour for turnaround and another six hours to JFK. I don't even want to know what time we'll get in there. Wake me up when we hit London."

A PRIVATE JET
40,000 FEET OVER THE ATLANTIC

Mister Marshall couldn't contain his fury. Some Arabs had actually flown biowarfare material into Kennedy. Outrageous. Monstrous. It had to be the same maniac who wiped out that Iranian village with smallpox. Mister Marshall had stormed up and down the narrow aisle for a hundred miles, then sat down to eat the breakfast that had been brought on board.

That mollified him a little. Breakfast was French toast made from slabs of specially baked cinnamon roll. He spread the slices with boysenberry syrup and pats of butter and devoted himself to eating all four plus six strips of extra thick bacon. Cholesterol be damned. The doctors said his arteries were in good shape. He had two cups of coffee and began to feel almost human.

How could any sane man do what this Arab did to that village in Iran, and what he evidently was intent on doing to America? Only a crazy person could. Therefore their terrorist was insane. He probably didn't even realize it. Maybe all terrorists were insane with some strange religious psychosis.

But it didn't help a bit about what they could do to stop him. How to stop him was easy. Grab all twenty canisters of virus before the madman could expose anyone in the U.S. The hard part was that first they had to find them. Would he keep them in one spot, or stash them in various places? Mister Marshall knew that if he had the same job, he would plant the canisters in six or eight accessible spots so he couldn't lose it all at one time. He hoped that this Iranian wasn't that smart.

Head winds had their say, and the jet didn't land at Kennedy until almost 10 A.M. Kat, Duncan, Roger, and Ichi had all slept part of the way. They knew they might not have a chance to slumber again for some time.

Ten minutes after landing, the team met their man, Garth Freemont, at the British Airways Freight office. Garth had brought along an FBI man Mister Marshall had suggested. Mister Marshall introduced the FBI man as Oliver Rawlins. They all shook hands. They had the airport police alerted and the head of security at the airport was on hand as well. The whole contingent moved into the freight office like an invading army.

The airport's top security man had told the freight-office people a group would be coming. The manager of the office had three men on tap as the ones who had checked out the off-loading and pickup of the casket.

They were in a room closed off from the airport noise. Only the whine of a jet engine came through now and then.

"Do you have the papers on the shipment?" Mister Marshall asked.

One of the men produced a clipboard with four pages of papers that dealt with the shipment and delivery of the casket. The first was the customs form approving entry of the casket without duty. The second showed the name of the shipper, and the name and address of the man who accepted delivery. It had been prepaid so there was no money collected.

The last form was a waiver acknowledging that there had been scrapes on the sides of the casket during shipment. The men who picked up the casket said they did not want to ask for any settlement on the damage. They accepted it "as is."

Roger looked at the signature at the bottom of the form. There was a place for an address but it was smudged and hard to read.

"Can you decipher the address on that name?" Roger asked.

One of the men looked at the paper, scowled, then spelled it out. "It's Jasper Glenn at 13056 Pearl Drive, in Great Neck. We checked it while we waited for you. There's no Pearl Drive listed in the Great Neck directory or phone book."

"Fake name, fake address," the FBI man said. "Who picked up the casket?"

Another of the freight handlers spoke up. "Two men, both Arabs by the look of them. Both clean-shaven except for full, black mustaches. Lots of black hair, casually dressed except for their shoes, which were expensive black leather. I figured they had dressed down so they wouldn't attract attention."

"How tall were they, how heavy? Any scars?" The FBI man, Rawlins, asked it.

"Short, maybe five-eight, not more than a hundred and

fifty pounds. Dark brown complexion, black eyes. No scars I could see."

Ichi spoke up and the FBI man glared at him. "What were they driving to haul away that heavy casket?"

"A big pickup, a Ford 350, only an older one, six or seven years. It was two shades of green, like the door had been replaced and painted but it didn't quite match."

The oldest of the three freight handlers frowned. "Hey, what's the big deal over a casket? We get them in here all the time. It's routine."

"But aren't the caskets usually picked up by a mortuary or funeral home?" Kat asked.

The FBI man lifted his brows.

"Yeah, true. Most of them. But not all. These guys did seem kind of nervous, come to think of it. Hey and not a tear. I've seen private parties cry up a storm as we load a casket into a station wagon say, or a pickup. These guys were a little on edge, and nervous, but neither of them let loose a tear."

"Hey, on the truck," the smallest of the three company men said. "I remember that it had New Jersey plates and they were out-of-date, you know like a year too old. I figured they might get a ticket for the plates."

"Did you write down the plate number on the release form?" Kat asked.

The worker shook his head. "Hey, no spot for that. We don't need it. Just a release."

One of the cargo handlers chuckled. "You mean there might have been dope in that box instead of a body? Don't remember it being that heavy. I mean if it had a ton of cocaine in there, it would have weighed a lot more on the manifest. What was inside?"

"That's something you don't need to know," Rawlins said. He had been warned not to let slip what they knew had to be in the casket.

"Anything more?" Mister Marshall asked, looking at the three men. They shook their heads.

"We'll need copies of those forms," the FBI man said. He went to the office with the manager to get the copies made. The airport-security man saw the party breaking up.

"If there's nothing more you need me for, Mister Marshall, I should get back to work."

"You are working," Roger said. The uniformed airport-security man smiled and went out the door.

Roger and Ichi looked at the spot where the casket had been delivered and walked through the space, then out to the sidewalk in front. The FBI man and Mister Marshall met his four people there.

The six stood on the parking area. Kat took the floor. "Let's say we know what's in the casket and the Arabs are going to have to get it out. What will they do with an empty casket once the canisters are safely in their control?"

"Dump it," Roger said. "Maybe mash it up somewhere. Make it look like a damaged casket that had to be thrown away."

The FBI man Rawlins chuckled. "Hey, I was unsure of your people, Mister Marshall. I know about you and your record. You have some sharp ones here. Yes, good idea on finding the casket. I'll have the New York City Police and the State Police put out an all points bulletin for that 1993 to '95 green Ford 350 pickup with Jersey plates. The second one will be for any reports of a discarded or broken-up casket. Can't be a lot of them out there."

"What's next?" Ichi asked.

"Not a lot we can do right now," Mister Marshall said. "Let's get down to the office in Manhattan and see what develops. Our best bet is that Ford pickup and the discarded casket. I've talked with the director of the CIA, Jansen. He says I should talk to the President and let him know of the threat. He'll set up a three-way phone call later this afternoon.

"Then my guess is that the CSG will meet. That's the Coordinating Sub Group of the Deputy Secretaries Committee. That's made up of all the government agencies, including the National Security Council, State, Defense, CIA, Justice, and the FBI, that would be involved in a terrorist attack. It also includes the Departments of Energy, Transportation, Treasury, Health and Human Services, Agriculture, as well as FEMA, EPA, and the Nuclear Regulatory Commission."

"What can a committee like that get done?" Duncan asked.

"That's the group that can declare a national emergency, call out the troops, even suggest to the President that he declare war. It can also deploy a DEST," Mister Marshall said. "That's a Domestic Emergency Support Team. It's equipped and staffed by people to help prevent a terrorist attack and to take immediate action through all the agencies involved if an attack takes place."

"So the FBI handles all of the intelligence operation," Duncan said. "Your guys know about the smallpox?"

"Only three of us do, and the President does. But he wants more details."

Mister Marshall looked at Garth Freemont. "You bring a big enough car to take all of us back to town?"

Garth grinned. "Yeah, Mister Marshall, I think I can handle it." The car at the curb was a Lincoln stretch limo. "I always come to pick you up in the limo. Let's go."

★ NINETEEN ★

NEW YORK CITY

On the way into Manhattan, Mister Marshall's phone rang.

"Marshall? This is Jansen."

"Yes, H.J. How can we help?"

"Internally it's the FBI's jurisdiction, but the President wanted you and me to talk with him about the problem. His secretary will get him on the phone as soon as we're both ready."

"Go," Mister Marshall said.

"Phyllis, we're both ready," Jansen said.

"I'll let him know," a woman's voice said. "Please hold."

A moment later a strong voice with a little too much bass boomed over the handset.

"Jansen, Marshall, you both ready to talk?"

"Yes, Mr. President," Jansen said.

"Always ready to talk to you, Mr. President," Mister Marshall said.

"Good, this problem we have. Is it as real as I've been told?"

"More real than I wish it were, Mr. President," Marshall said. "We've tracked this shipment from Odessa to Kuwait City, where it was repacked into a casket and shipped to Kennedy. It's here now and we think in twenty canisters."

"Jansen?"

"We agree with Mr. Marshall. These international terrorists will stop at nothing. Our people are in Odessa. It's been confirmed that former Russian germ-warfare products are stored there. It looks like the Ukrainians, or some of them, at least, have sold off some of these substances to the highest bidder."

"How do we stop these maniacs?" the President asked.

"We continue our effort with the FBI to track the goods once they left Kennedy. That's the program right now. We have to do this as quickly as possible. We fear that they will attack a metropolitan area. We believe that Washington, DC, will be one of their prime targets."

"I've checked with the CDC people in Atlanta," the President said. "They report there isn't enough serum in the nation to inoculate 5 percent of our population. They estimate that probably about 50 percent of our people are immune due to old inoculations and school-required shots. That still leaves over a hundred and sixty million of us at risk."

"Can the Centers for Disease Control accelerate the production of serum for inoculations?" Jansen asked.

"Not in time to do any good if these maniacs strike quickly," the President said. "I've alerted the CSG. The deputy secretaries of the agencies are gathering this morning to be briefed. We haven't told them what bio-agent is involved. I see no reason to let them know which one just yet."

"But aren't those agencies the ones that come in after an attack, sir?" Mister Marshall asked.

"Some are, but the group can set in motion all sorts of defensive and offensive movements. They can move things immediately. We also have regional DEST units that can be at anyplace in the U.S. in two hours after an outbreak, an attack, or a radiation spill."

"Don't we have any other groups or units that can help track these people down?" Mister Marshall asked.

"We've never had this problem before. The FBI is our front line of defense, attack, and investigation. If there is a serious outbreak in one area, that state's National Guard units can be called out if needed. As state units they can work against civilian insurrections, disasters, and in this case a serious outbreak of a deadly disease."

The speaker went silent.

"Which means, Mr. President, that we better get our tails into motion," Mister Marshall said. "We have damned little to work with. Since this is foreign-generated, can't the CIA work with the FBI on that aspect?"

"Marshall, you were CIA director. You know what they can do. They can be backup with information and perhaps lend some people, but that's about all. By law, Marshall."

"I was hoping the law could be circumvented a little to save a few million lives. We need action right now, before these maniacs can use the deadly virus they have."

There was another silent period.

"Any ideas, H.J.?" the President asked.

"We can lend experts on terrorists' tactics, background, on Arab activists. Marshall tells me there may be a link between the recent luxury-liner hijacking in the Strait of Hormuz with this Odessa buy. One name came up, Abdul. We have chapter and verse on him. We've given it to the director of the FBI.

"We can make what we call unrecorded assignment of agents expert in this field and send them to FBI units on request. They function in tandem with the FBI agents, but have no official capacity."

"Call Vincent and tell him I've authorized you to make all the unrecorded assignments that he wants to ask for. Better get on the horn right away."

"Yes, Mr. President. I'll sign off."

"Good-bye, H.J. Stay in close touch with me."

"I will, Mr. President. Good-bye."

The air was silent for a moment.

"So, Marshall. What more can we do?"

"I have my people here. We are following up on every lead we can find. The New York State Police and the NYPD are hard on it as well. It's their jurisdiction. Agent Rawlins, head of the New York office, has it for the FBI. I have two more men coming in soon. We'll do everything we can. I would appreciate a word from you to the FBI so they don't cut us out. Can you give us temporary status so we can function as law enforcement officers in the U.S?"

"Yes, the FBI could shut you out. I'll call Vincent and tell him that the seven of you must be sworn in as deputy FBI agents and have total and complete privileges and responsibilities as other FBI agents."

"Good, that's great, Mr. President. Now we have clearance. I need to contact my Manhattan office."

"Call me anytime I can help, Marshall. Good to be working with you again, in spite of the deadly threat."

"Thank you, Mr. President. It's good to talk with you again."

Mister Marshall closed the digital phone and put it back in his inside black suit pocket. He outlined briefly what he and the President had said in the conversation.

Later, just as the limo swung off Grand Central Parkway onto the Long Island Expressway heading for the Queens Midtown Tunnel, Mister Marshall's phone rang again.

"Yes?"

"Mister Marshall. Rawlins, FBI. Wanted to tell you that the Great Neck police responded to our APB on the casket. They have a blue one that was reported yesterday. It's been broken up and looks like it tumbled off a roadway and down an embankment. We have people on the way there now to check for fingerprints, and any sign of the virus. We understand this is to be considered a top-secret operation, with no mention of the material in question. No press, no leaks."

"Thanks, Rawlins. Our guess is that there will be no prints except those of some Kuwaiti workers and New York British Airways Freight handlers. Be interested if you find any residue of the material. Our information was that the goods were all packaged in airtight containers before leaving Odessa."

"We'll check it out. I'm about halfway up there now. Will keep you informed. Our people have been up-to-date on shots on smallpox so no worry there. Will be in contact. Out."

Mister Marshall told the rest of the Specialists about the talk with the FBI man.

"For sure they won't find any prints of the Arabs,"

Duncan said. "They would have wiped it clean of any possible prints before they dumped it."

"The pickup might be the best lead we have," Kat said. "If we could get some input on that from the cops in the area. They dumped the casket where?"

"Great Neck," Ichi said. "That's east of Kennedy by about ten or twelve miles. Outside New York City, so it's a different police department."

"So maybe the pickup is in that general area," Kat said. "They probably used the pickup to dump the casket after unloading it. Wish we had a license plate on it."

"Maybe the New York State Police will find it," Roger said. "This should be a top-priority task for these cops."

"Not unless we tell them about the virus," Mister Marshall said. "We can't risk that. We could have a panic."

"It'll be worse than a panic if those terrorists start dumping those canisters onto our cities," Kat said. "There has to be a way to stop them."

They rode in silence through the Midtown Tunnel. Kat wondered if the digital phone would work so far underground and underwater. It didn't ring.

The Specialists' headquarters in New York weren't located with the other Marshall complex of offices and buildings. It had its own structure in a lower-rent district not far from the East River, way downtown on Houghton Street. It wasn't far from City Hall and they could see the Brooklyn Bridge. It had a ground-level loading dock, an inside garage, and four floors above, for apartments, offices, weapons room, communications room, and a private office for Mister Marshall and his secretary. She worked full-time although his use of the facility was intermittent.

The apartments were two rooms each, with bedroom, bath, and small kitchen. There were eight of them and the Specialists settled into their usual rooms.

Kat paced the hallway. She couldn't get it out of her mind that there must be more they could be doing. Did they have simply to wait for the terrorists to attack and then react? That was a sure formula for failure. Kat didn't like to fail, or even come in second place. What if they exploded a canister over New York City? Thousands would be infected, then tens of thousands. How can you quarantine a place the size of New York City?

The Specialists met in the situation room. The secretary, Rachel, had put up on the board the location of the casket, Kennedy, and New Jersey.

Below all was a note about an older Ford 350 pickup with New Jersey license plates.

Rachel was small and a little chubby, with dark eyes and long black hair. She hurried around making sure the Specialists had what they needed at their desks. When she was satisfied about that she looked up.

"Beer or sodas?" she asked.

She took the orders and hurried out.

"I don't think Rachel ever slows down," Duncan said.

They looked at the board.

"Dammit to hell, there's absolutely nothing productive that we can do," Roger said.

"Afraid so," Duncan said. "Must be what, twenty, twenty-five million people within a hundred miles of here. These jaspers can melt into the woodwork and we'll never find them until they do something."

"Unless we get a tip on that damn pickup," Kat said. "Why couldn't those guys just have written down the number of that plate?"

Nobody answered.

The communications speaker in the situation room came on.

"Yes, Mister Marshall. This is Rawlins with the FBI. We've been over that casket a dozen times. Looks like somebody did a complete job of wiping it clean. We couldn't find a single print on it. Like everyone down the line from Kuwait used gloves."

"About what we expected," Mister Marshall said.

"We've been pressuring the State Police up here to put out a dragnet for that pickup, but so far nothing. Some of these small police departments have computers that can sort out arrests by category. We've put out another APB for them to search for speeding tickets and DUI arrests for pickup drivers. Hoping we get something back from that."

"That could be promising."

"Anything developing on your end?"

"Nothing. We're blind here until we get some ray of light from somewhere. We're frustrated."

"We're pushing everyone we can without telling them why. We'll be in touch."

"Thanks, Rawlins. We appreciate it."

The Specialists sat at the big table, doodled on pads, or called local contacts. Duncan tried to make a solid crossword puzzle with nine squares on each side. He gave up.

An hour later another call came through that Mister Marshall put on the speaker.

"Marshall, glad I caught you in. Vincent here, FBI. We've been working another angle. I've had twenty people looking into our files to dig out known Arab terrorists and their contacts in New York. So far we're doing some good. We've nailed down three hot contacts and have men in the field running them down. If these imports need any help in their projects, they might turn to some locals who are sympathetic.

"We're checking out six different Arab friendship groups in the New York area. Some of these are legitimate, but we think that one or two might be subversive."

"If you need any people to run down some leads, we have four here now and two more expected soon."

"Thanks, Marshall, right now we're in good shape. If we develop a whole passel of Arabs who might be worthwhile, we'll give you a call. Right now the pickings are slim. I received the word from the President about making you deputies to the FBI. Good. We might need you."

"Mr. Director, have you checked with Jansen yet at CIA? He might be able to give you some Arab hotheads that they have been keeping tabs on overseas. I'm sure he has a few files that might be helpful."

"Good, Marshall. I'll give him a call right now. Yes, good idea. Do you know if he's in Washington?"

"Not sure."

"Thanks for the tip. We'll call you if we get anything hot."

They said good-bye and the speaker went silent.

A short time later, Wade and Hershel came in, still groggy from their long double flight.

"We're here, you can start now," Hershel said.

"We're dead in the water but grab a paddle," Kat said.

"Nothing?" Wade asked.

Duncan brought the two up to date on what had happened that morning.

"So we wait?" Wade asked.

"We not only wait, we go to lunch," Ichi said. "Anybody interested in that little Greek café we used to go to over a couple of blocks?"

They all were interested. They tested their digital phones for battery power and checked out with Rachel. She manned the office and the phone and worked on a deli sandwich Mister Marshall had had sent in for her.

During lunch they decided to get in a workout before anything popped.

"Where?" Kat asked.

Ichi, who had spent time in the New York office of the FBI, reacted. "Hey, the only good spot in town is Central Park. That's about an hour's ride by car all the way up to Fifty-ninth street. This time of day the traffic is brutal."

"How about the subway," Wade asked. "Sounds a little funky to get out of a stretch limo and go running around the park."

Mister Marshall gave them leave and they charged the subway, found an express uptown, and rattled through the tunnels and up to the closest station. Ichi led the parade.

They ran up to the reservoir and then went around it eight times before they collapsed and headed back to the subway.

"How far?" Duncan asked.

"A hundred and twenty-seven miles," Hershel said.

"Maybe ten to twelve," Wade said. "Not sure how far the loop around the reservoir is."

They made it back to the Houghton Street building just before four o'clock. Mister Marshall paced the inside reception area waiting for them.

"We have a job," he said. "The FBI has a pair of Arab groups they want us to check out. Probably low on the scale, but Rawlins wants them covered. Seems like the FBI guys have their hands full trying to double-check all of the Arabs they had on their monitoring list."

"Who and where?" Wade asked.

"I'll let you know right after your showers. New York clothes and side arms will be enough. I'll see you in the situation room in thirty minutes."

✳ TWENTY ✳

As she showered, Kat thought back over what she had done so far. Was this really what she wanted to do? Chase terrorists who threatened and killed innocent people?

She nodded. Yes, it was exactly what she had been pointing to all of her life. She wanted to get married and have two children, but not until after she was thirty-five. Sometimes she had to batter down the motherhood instincts, but so far she had managed to keep her mothering urges under control.

Kat realized now that she had been spoiled when she was eighteen. She had won the Miss Honolulu contest but then in quick succession she had been defeated in the Miss Hawaii finals and married on the fly. An elopement for which neither of them was ready. Lon Hascal had been a news anchor on Honolulu's best TV station and ten years her senior. He was a celebrity himself. He was an actor as well as an anchor and he often took leaves to appear in feature roles in motion pictures and TV series. The station management loved it and encouraged his acting. He was vain and self-centered, and now she had no idea why he wanted to get married. He was gorgeous, a real handsome man. He also attracted women like flies to curdled milk. She soon heard from friends that her husband was fooling around but she didn't want to believe it.

Then one day she walked in on him and a good friend of hers in bed in their new apartment. She packed him up and moved him into the hall before he could get his pants on. She never spoke to him again. She had a divorce after a little less than a year of marriage.

Then she charged into college. She studied two years at the University of Hawaii, then transferred to Stanford in California. In high school she had been a good student. In college she was outstanding, with straight A's. Law school came next and after she had passed seven state bar exams, the bid came from the FBI. School again in the FBI Academy and then working up to special agent. It all had been thrilling, worthwhile, invigorating. She had felt a physical rush when she had participated in the triathlon in Hawaii. She barely finished the first one. The next year she trained every day and won the race then called the Ironman triathlon. She was best in the swimming leg, and outdistanced her nearest woman rival by three hundred yards. Then came the grueling bike race of 120 miles. She had maintained her lead there and moved away again from the second-place finisher on the twenty-six-mile marathon run. She still enjoyed the adrenaline rush of competition.

Her mother, a full-blooded Hawaiian, loved the old days, and never completely understood her up-front, competitive, pushing, lawyer daughter who soon was an FBI agent. Her mother often dressed in traditional Hawaiian style, had authentic luaus for her friends and for family gatherings, and was a dedicated worker in the traditional Hawaiian exhibits and events around the Islands. One of her concerns was that full-blooded Hawaiians were becoming fewer and fewer with interracial marriages like her own. Kat had no brothers or sisters, and as she became older, realized that her mother was also her best friend. They talked on the phone every week when Kat was not on a mission.

Kat and her mother planned traditional Hawaiian events in Honolulu that Kat would fly out to whenever possible. Someone asked her mother if she worked and she snapped back that of course she did, usually about twelve hours a day.

Kat's father, an Englishman who excelled at the import/

export business from Hawaii, encouraged Kat every step of the way. He was well-off from his business dealings. He often told her he worried about her being in this dangerous terrorist-hunting business. She told him not to fret. She hadn't worked this hard to get where she was only to be cut down by some undereducated, overangered, underinformed, underfed, foreign sociopath who carried a submachine gun.

Her father had gladly paid for her studies all the way through law school and often talked with her when she phoned her mother. Twice he had called her from London when he was at trade shows and on selling trips.

While stationed in New York Kat fell in love with eighteenth-century Flemish paintings. She couldn't afford any originals but did have three finely mounted prints that she reveled in. Modern music left her totally indifferent. Rock and roll was never her choice, and the advent of rap made her angry. To think that these people could get up and chatter away a batch of nonsense, and sometimes seditious prattle, infuriated her sense of law and order, moderation, and personal responsibility. What angered her most was that these so-called artists could become rich spouting their vindictive trash. So, she was old-fashioned, she admitted it, and tried to appreciate some of the lighter operas.

Her personal creed was that every person had an obligation to leave this earth a better place for his or her being here. In her case that meant tracking down as many terrorists as possible before they could kill more innocent people. It might mean tutoring at a small London school helping students from low-income families learn to read. It all came down to what a person thought was right and proper, and from which mankind as a whole would benefit.

Kat shook her dry hair out of the large plastic cap and stepped out of the shower. She was going to be late. It had happened before. She dressed quickly and hurried to the situation room. She was the second one there.

She had appraised each of the Specialists when she signed on. None of them had appeared to be suitable husband material, so she could function with them on a person-to-person basis. No subtle meanings, no hidden ploys, no innuendo, everything right up front and in the open. Over the past two years it had worked well. But the more she saw of him, the more she was impressed by Wade Thorne. Eventually he might be a marriage candidate, if and when she decided to retire from the terrorist-fighting business to settle down and raise her family. That was at least four or five years down the pike. Wade was still a candidate in testing.

The other four Specialists straggled into the situation room, and Mister Marshall came right after them. All but their leader wore sport outfits loose fitting enough to hide weapons. Duncan had on a tie, as he usually did on these kinds of occasions.

"Good, let's get moving," Mister Marshall said. "I'm going to work closely with you on this mission. I don't like it. It is too outrageous to consider, but we have to. Wade will go with two others, and I'll take three with me. We have two Lincolns at the side entrance ready with drivers who have the addresses. They're in different areas, so we'll use our digital phones to communicate. Let's go."

Wade took Kat and Roger with him.

"We're heading way up north into the Bronx," Wade said. "It's out near Van Cortlandt Park. The driver said he knew the way. He's using the West Side Elevated until it hooks up with the Henry Hudson Parkway. That will shoot us all the way upstream beside the Hudson River to Van Cortlandt Park in the Bronx."

Once in the Bronx, the driver turned off the high-speed road into the city streets. After two more turns he found Spencer Avenue and slowed.

"Right along here somewhere," the driver said. Then he pulled to the curb. They were in a section of small business and a few houses. The number was two doors down, an older house that needed a coat of paint.

"Kat and I'll go up to the front door; Roger, cover the rear. Not that big a place. Keep it quiet and easy."

Roger left the car and walked toward the house, then vanished into the side yard toward the back of the old house. Kat and Wade took the sidewalk right up to the front door. There was no doorbell showing. Wade rapped firmly four times on the wooden door.

"Nearly six o'clock," Wade whispered. "Might not be anyone here until later."

As he said it, they heard movement inside. Both shifted so they had an easy reach for their concealed handguns. The door opened a crack.

"Yeah, whadda ya want?" The voice came low and accented.

"Looking for the Arab Friendship League," Wade said. "I have an Arab friend who wants to find some people who can at least speak his language."

The door remained open only an inch. "Yeah, well, we used to have a group here. Kinda evaporated, know what I mean? Nobody came after a while. So we shut it down. Never done much, just talked mostly in Arabic. Never had more than four or five, mostly men."

"You have any visitors from Iran during the last few days?"

"Iran? Not a chance. Me, I'm from Saudi Arabia. We don't even cut bait with them Iran guys."

"Sure you haven't had any visitors?"

"Hell, I know who's in my house."

They heard a door close toward the rear of the place.

"What was that?" Wade asked.

"My wife putting out the garbage. Got to have it out by six in the morning or they drive right by. Damn garbage guys make way too much money and they get downright nasty."

Kat eased away from the door and hurried to the side of the house so she could see toward the back of the building. Roger walked up, pushing a man in front of him.

"This son tried to make a run out the back door," Roger said.

Wade heard him. He hit the front door with his shoulder blasting it open and pushing the man standing there three feet backward.

"What the hell?"

"Yeah, what we'd like to know," Wade said, rushing

into the room and grabbing the man. He pushed him against the wall and frisked him. No weapon. Wade turned him around. Lights on in the room showed the man to be dark with Arab features. Roger brought his prisoner inside. He also looked like an Arab.

"Don't say a word," Roger's man said in Arabic.

Wade understood him but didn't let on. "Who is this man?" Wade asked. The man leaning against the wall took a deep breath. "I told him not to stay here. The cops are all over this area. He's my brother-in-law and he's wanted for three armed robberies."

Roger shook the man he still held. "That right, Buster?"

"Yeah, maybe. You guys ain't cops."

Wade stared at the house owner. "What's his name?"

"George Ali Rajai."

"Kat, call 911 and tell them about our buddy Ali."

Twenty minutes later the Specialists were back in their black Lincoln heading for their Manhattan headquarters.

The first two New York City cops who reported to the house in a squad car had been surprised.

"Hey, thanks," the younger cop said. "We been tracking this weasel for two weeks. He's got more relatives than a rabbit."

Wade had shown the NYPD men his temporary ID as an FBI deputy. A minute later the Specialists slid into the Lincoln. Wade called in his report to Marshall. His team had come up empty as well.

"What is there to do now?" Kat asked. "I'd like a list, a schedule, a project, something. Are we going to have to sit around and wait for these maniacs to kill a few people so we'll know where they are?"

"Seems likely," Roger said. "Not a chance in Hades that we can find two or three men out of twenty million when we don't have anything to go on. They could be in Texas or California by now. Maybe they rented a truck and are driving to Washington, DC."

"Whichever way you count it, we're dead in the water for a while," Wade said. "You all know the waiting game. Looks like that could be in the works for a while."

"Maybe our FBI buddy Rawlins will give us something else to check out," Ichi said.

"Now that would be a stretch," Roger said. "If there's anything in this jurisdiction to be found, old Rawlins wants to have his men find it. Pride and promotion go hand in hand."

"When I talked to Mister Marshall," Wade said, "he indicated there might be something more for us to do. We're to report back to headquarters as soon as possible."

✶ TWENTY-ONE ✶

SEATTLE, WASHINGTON

Abdul loved Puget Sound. He looked out from the pier-front luxury hotel and marveled at how much water there was around Seattle. Coming from Syria and Iran, he could never see enough water. He relaxed for the moment in the sunshine and sipped his drink. He was becoming too fond of Scotch whiskey. He knew that. Abdul laughed softly. He could forget the hard-line fundamentalists. He could make his own rules. He always had.

He remembered the hectic two days he and his two men had spent in New York. They had driven north from the airport in the borrowed pickup and stopped in a small town. There they found a curious firm called Personal Mailboxes. The sign said they did packaging. He told them that he had some highly important material that must be packaged in medium-sized cardboard boxes and then filled with the plastic peanuts.

They understood, asked no questions. He brought the canisters in four at a time in a box, and they padded them and packed them in boxes about two feet square. Perfect. He had nineteen canisters. That made five boxes.

Later they dumped the casket down an embankment. He made a phone call to the pickup owner and told him where he could come and get his rig. Then he checked out local airports. Great Neck had one, and after haggling for a half hour, he hired a pilot to fly him, his five cartons, and three men to a large airport in New Jersey.

There he could hire a larger plane. They landed just before dark.

The firm in New Jersey that had a plane he could use was closed for the night, which meant staying at a hotel.

The next morning Abdul at last made the arrangements. It would cost him $20,000 to make the flight with a stop in Omaha. Abdul called ahead to Omaha on his digital phone and made the connection he needed. His man was there, had rented a house, and would be glad to see them. One of his men would stay there.

Two days later in Seattle, they rented a car, kept the two-foot-square-box with one canister in it, and tried to relax. He had selected the site, and the next morning they drove out of Seattle on U.S. Highway 90 heading east and south for Wenatchee. They drove rather than flew because Abdul wanted to become lost in the woodwork, only a shadow in the crowd.

At Wenatchee, they rented a motel room. Abdul left his two men in the motel and drove to the Pangborn Memorial Airport and hired a small aircraft. He showed a U.S. private pilot's license he had hired a forger in New York to make for him, and paid the deposit of a thousand dollars in cash. He showed his real Visa card in the same name of Andre Marktow, that was on his pilot's license. He had applied for the card months ago when he was in Kuwait.

Abdul could fly several types of planes up to four motors. Now he settled in behind the controls of the high-wing Cessna. He had checked the flying speed and his time in the air. It would take half an hour to fly from Wenatchee to Kettle Rapids, the small town that had the honor of being the first U.S. test. He had brought with him timer/detonators that were vital to this operation. They had been deep inside some padded gloves that the customs inspectors had missed. Later he would tape a half stick of dynamite to the canister. Then he would make a hole in the top of the dynamite with a sharp pencil and push the explosive end of the timer/detonator in the hole until it was tight. Then his smallpox-virus bomb would be ready.

At a tiny airport like this there would be little notice of

a plane taking off after dark. There were no runway lights
here. It would be much easier to take off in the dark than
to land blind. He took the plane up for a test run. It handled a little sluggish, but was true and firm in most re-
sponses. It would do. He came back to the airport and
landed. There was no tower, it was every pilot for himself,
which took a lot of neck stretching and looking on all
sides of the small plane as he made his approach and came
in to land.

At the motel, they had food brought in, then he took a
nap. He told his men to awaken him at 2 A.M. They did.

One of the men he brought from Syria was Bani-Sadrd,
an old hand who had been in the business of blowing up
things for twenty years. The other one was younger, with
fire in his blood. He was Abolhassan. Either one would
gladly die for the cause, for Allah, for this mission. He had
explained to them in detail what was involved and what
they would do. They were both volunteers.

Abdul drove to the airport at 3:30 A.M., had his preflight check done in twenty minutes, and waited until four
before he took off. The canister with the half stick of dynamite and timer/detonator rested on the seat beside him.
Abdul shivered for just a second, thinking of the terror, the
death that lay inside that thin aluminum skin. It would be
total. He knew that half of the U.S. population could have
some form of inoculation against smallpox. But much of it
was twenty years or older. It might not be effective. If he
scored with half of the population of Kettle Rapids, he
would be pleased. And America would be put on notice.

He had no trouble taking off in the blackness. He had
done a lot of night flying and landing. Now he concentrated on his compass, following the route he had laid out
on the map. If that didn't work, he could simply track the
shine of the moon in the turbulent Columbia River, which
came surging from the north right past Kettle Rapids, and
on down past Wenatchee as well.

The wind. He would determine the wind drift over the
site. Then he would get upwind of the small town, set the
timer for ten seconds, and toss the canister out the window. He would drop it from three thousand feet. It should

fall 1750 feet in ten seconds. That should put it a little
over a thousand feet when it exploded. He would be well
away and upwind of the spot when the detonator went
off, spewing the fine powdery particles over the whole
town.

There were 564 residents of the village. Half would be
plenty. Yes, he hoped for half. The streak of the river
showed below him as he powered forward, then he saw
the village coming up. It was exactly where it should be,
with the rapids visible on the river in the moonlight.

Wind.

He had noticed little drift as he flew up the river. Now
he checked again, dropping lower over the land so he
could determine the direction and possible wind speed.
There was almost no wind blowing, a virtual calm. He
climbed back to three thousand feet, made sure the timer
was set for ten seconds, and patted the canister.

A few minutes later he turned the Cessna and flew toward the town from the north, figuring any possible wind
would come from that direction. He kept the plane at
three thousand feet and when he was one block from the
edge of the town, he opened the side window, activated the
timer, and dropped the canister. It was one minute after
4:30 A.M. on April 21. He would remember this date forever. At once he pushed the throttle to maximum, turned
180 degrees, heading directly north, and away from the
village below. He watched behind as he counted down the
seconds.

Seven, eight, nine. The flash seemed unusually bright in
the totally dark sky, the sound rippled through to him over
the hum of the Cessna's engine. He smiled with grim satis-
faction. *Take that, Great Evil. Take that, America, who
has pushed the Arab states around for more than a century. Take that, you 564 residents of Kettle Rapids, a tiny
village that will be a wasteland in only a few months*. He
made a wide sweeping turn to the south after he had flown
for ten minutes north. He should be well out of any chance
for contamination from the virus. He kept twenty miles
away from the area as he headed back toward Wenatchee.
It wouldn't be light for another hour. He used the hour to

enjoy flying, heading back toward the airport, and overfly-
ing it when it was still too dark for a landing.

He would fly around until daylight. He wanted no
crash, no trouble at the airport that might link him in
some way with the tragedy at Kettle Rapids.

That same morning they would go by commercial air to
Yakima and then to Omaha, Nebraska. It would be a good
spot to wait for developments at the small Washington village. The incubation period for the smallpox virus was ten
to fourteen days. He figured that the ten-day figure would
be more likely at Kettle Rapids. With the massive amount
of virus invading the lungs, most of the unprotected people
would fall sick quickly after exposure.

Even before the bombshell hit the American press and
TV networks, he would have a second town ready. He
would time it so the second town would erupt with smallpox four or five days after Kettle Rapids exploded. He had
work to do during the next few days.

KETTLE RAPIDS, WASHINGTON

Chief of Police Lawford Irwin didn't like the night shift, but
in a town this small, and with only two cops the total force,
he had to trade off with his patrolman on a regular basis. It
gave him time to think. It let him expand his mind. Tonight
he was sitting in his pickup patrol car at the edge of town
watching the lights begin to come on, as the early risers
punched off alarms and kicked warm feet out onto cold
floors. He'd be off at eight; those sods would just be starting to sweat and slave. At least shortly after eight he would
get home, have some dinner, then get ten hours of sleep.
Unless Martha was feeling particularly horny. She got that
way some nights when he was on duty. Martha, now there
was a real piece of work. So she was twenty years younger
than his own forty-five. Hell, she made him feel twenty-five
again. Yeah, he could lose fifteen pounds and never miss it
and his forehead seemed to be creeping higher every year.
Nobody complained about either one. Not even Martha.

He stepped out of the cab and looked toward the river.

It was always there, making that subtle hissing, roiling sound that he had come to love without even realizing he heard it anymore.

A sound broke into his reverie and he frowned, then looked up. Some kind of an aircraft. Not a passenger jet, they weren't routed this way. Anyhow they would be at thirty thousand feet and he'd never hear them.

This was a small plane. He'd done some flying when he was in Wenatchee. Never did get his license but he had twenty hours and had soloed in a Piper Cub. He listened to the sound as it came closer, then right overhead. It wasn't high, under two thousand feet he figured. Law said light planes had to stay a thousand feet above any settlement or city. This jasper wasn't much more than that. Chief Irwin watched but couldn't make out the shadow above as the sound whipped overhead, then faded as it went north. The sound almost faded away, then came back louder and louder.

By the engine sound, he knew the plane was lower. What the hell? Was this jasper lost or something? There was no spot to land in town or nearby, that was for damn sure. Chief Irwin squinted but could see nothing in the dark sky. The plane was coming directly overhead again. Maybe somebody's boyfriend showing off? No, he'd do that in daylight.

The plane was almost at the edge of town.

Then it turned and headed north at a faster speed. Chief Irwin had only time to reset his uniform cap when a brilliant flash splintered the darkness, outlining the buildings for a frozen second, then it was gone. A moment later a cracking roar of an explosion bored holes in the silence and erupted through the small town.

"Be damned," Chief Irwin said. "That was a stick of dynamite, or at least half a stick." The dumb ass in that small plane had to be the idiot who threw it out, then hightailed it to the north. He'd make a report on that. He checked his watch: 0432. The date was April 21. He made a note on his pad in the headlights of the pickup. Chief Irwin put down everything about the incident. The plane's two trips over the town, the second one lower, the abrupt turn, then seconds later the explosion. He read the notes, snorted, and put away his book. He still had to finish his patrol around town. He didn't want anything bad to happen on his shift.

Half a mile away, Dr. Patricia "Patty" Olson had just come through the Dawsons' front door when she saw the flash of light in the sky and heard the explosion.

She was so tired that she could only stare upward, her mouth dropping open and her eyes trying to focus on the light that vanished in a second. It had been a hard labor for Tricia Dawson, but it had been worth it when a fine baby boy had entered this world slightly before 3:40 A.M.

Dr. Olson had taken her time cleaning up the infant, making sure its eyes were clear and its nose and throat working. The kid screamed like a frightened eagle for five minutes, then quieted and slept against his mother's breasts. She told the father what to do and that the next day he should take his wife and new son to Wenatchee for a checkup at the hospital. The boy had arrived a week early as a surprise disrupting the family's plans to go to the hospital.

Just at four-thirty she headed for her car when the bomb went off. It took her weary mind a few moments to think what had happened.

"A bomb, over Kettle Rapids?" she asked out loud. Patty took out her digital phone and dialed the town police. The phone rang four times before someone answered.

"Yes, police, Chief Irwin."

"Chief, you been outside? Did you see that explosion in the sky? What in the world is going on?"

"This you, Doc?"

"Yes, Chief. Just delivered a baby. Was that a bomb?"

"Doc, I don't have the foggiest idea what it was. I heard a light plane go over, kind of low, then poweeee. Some nut or some kid trying to impress a girl, or scare somebody. We'll find out soon as we can. Nearest airport is Bridgeport to the north. I'll call them up later today and see if they had any rentals. Got to be some local boy."

"Well, glad you're on it, Chief. I should have known. Now I'm out on my feet and I have clinic tomorrow at nine. I better grab at least four hours of sleep. Makes me think I'm a resident again on a forty-eight."

"You get some sleep, Doc. And don't open your office until ten. Them folks can wait a bit. We waited ten years for a doctor to come to town. We want to keep you here."

"Is that a police order, Chief?"

"Damn right, Doc. Now drive safe and get some sleep."

"Thanks, Chief."

Doctor Patricia Olson wore a tired smile as she drove. The town had offered to pay forty thousand dollars on her student loan and give her $70,000 a year guaranteed salary if she'd come be their doctor. They needed a doctor bad for emergencies and for general practice. She had been fascinated with the country and one visit had sold her. Now, after a year here, she was glad she had come.

Five minutes later she parked outside her apartment the town furnished and made it inside, where she promptly fell on her bed without undressing. She closed her eyes, then lifted up, set the alarm for nine o'clock, and collapsed on her bed.

★ TWENTY-TWO ★

NEW YORK CITY

The third day the Specialists were in the city the on-call medical doctor invited them all up to the fourth-floor med-aid room.

"Please roll up your left sleeve for a vaccination," Dr. Vernon Walton said. Wade figured the medic was under thirty and had just finished his residency. A real doctor.

"Yes, it's for smallpox. All of you must have the vaccine no matter how short a time it's been since you had a vaccination before."

"Mine was three years ago," Roger said.

"For best results the vaccination should be done at three-year intervals for high-risk individuals," Dr. Walton said.

"This the usual stuff or do they have a new vaccine out?" Kat asked.

"It's the standard vaccine that's made from the vesicles of vaccinated calves. It's closely related to cowpox but not the same."

"You know why we're getting this, Doc?" Ichi asked.

"No, and I'd rather not know. The fact is I have no need to know. I like it that way. No bad dreams." The doctor grinned. "I have some idea what you people do, and even that scares the hell out of me. Who's next?"

That same morning, the President, and the cabinet all had vaccinations as well. No one told the cabinet members why, they knew better than to ask. More than seventy-five members of the FBI were given vaccinations that afternoon. Some of them knew why, most did not.

Twice more the Specialists went to check on Arabs who had expressed anti-U.S. feelings in the past. The first trip was to a town in Pennsylvania. The man and wife no longer lived in the area and neighbors said they were heading back to Iran. They hadn't been seen for three months.

The second wild-goose chase took the Specialists to a town in upper New York State not far from the Canadian border. The three men who lived at the address were all Arab. They said they were from Iraq and Jordan. All were surprised that they had been singled out by the FBI for investigation. They had integrated into the small town, all had jobs and paid taxes, and all said they would never consider going back to their Arab homelands.

The seventh day in New York came and the Specialists were showing the strain of not having anything to do and wondering where the terrorists were with the twenty canisters of smallpox virus.

"Isn't there something we can do?" Kat pleaded with Mister Marshall.

"I wish there were. Right now we're caught in a time trap. Let's say the terrorists had their target and got to it the first day they hit this country. That was probably three days before we did. If they went to the target that first day, dumped the virus on some town, there would be a waiting period before anything happened."

Roger nodded. "Yeah, the incubation period for the virus once it got into somebody's lungs."

"Precisely, Roger. What time period is that?"

Duncan frowned, "Hey, a week?"

"More than that," Mister Marshall said. "I looked it up. It's from ten to fourteen days. Say it happens in ten days in small children and older adults, the most susceptible. That could mean this is the tenth day the terrorists have been in-country."

"Have the Centers for Disease Control in Atlanta been updated on this threat?" Wade asked.

"The FBI has warned them of the potential danger," Mister Marshall said. "They will be on the alert for any reports of smallpox anywhere in the country from today on. I understand they are stockpiling vaccine. Now and then a case comes in via the airlines. People do pick up the virus in some of the lesser-developed nations and import it into this country. But those would be isolated situations, with only one or two being sick."

"So we wait," Wade said. "Let's do some PT. How about a ten-mile walk down to the Battery and back?"

"We did that three days ago," Duncan said.

"Then we can walk uptown for two hours, then turn around and walk home," Wade said.

They did.

It was May 3, thirteen days after the Specialists arrived in New York, when the report came in. It didn't come from CDC in Atlanta, but over CNN.

"Our reporter in Wenatchee, Washington State, has the story. He was as close as State Police would allow cars this morning. Harry Johnson, tell us what happened."

The picture switched to a reporter outside a building. "This morning I drove to Kettle Rapids, a small town about forty miles north of us here in Wenatchee on the Columbia River. The police chief has reported that they have eighty cases of smallpox in the town that has only five hundred forty-six residents. I talked to him by phone. He has sealed off the town and only medical personnel are allowed in or out.

"He said babies and children under three were most heavily affected. The high-school gymnasium has been converted into a hospital for the ill. So far he reports that about a third of the cases are the elderly who haven't had a smallpox shot in forty or fifty years. The town has no hospital.

"A few adults are down, but most who had smallpox shots within the last ten years seem not to be affected. There is only one doctor in town, a GP, who is pleading for help from wherever it can come. She's asking for enough vaccine to inoculate everyone in town who hasn't contracted the disease. This can often prevent the disease even if the person has been exposed, or make the illness much less severe.

"Chief of Police Irvin did not offer any ideas how the virus could have hit his town so hard. He says this kind of total exposure of his town must be a tragic accident. He says it looks like he and the FBI are going to have to do a lot of digging to find out how this happened.

"Medical authorities here say that babies and the elderly are the most susceptible to smallpox, where the death rate can run as high as 80 percent. School-age children should have had a smallpox vaccination as part of the shots required before entering school. Adults in their thirties and forties without recent shots may be also in the danger class. A 60 percent fatality rate is not unusual in smallpox cases.

"I will be going to Kettle Rapids within the hour with a mobile TV truck and bring you continual updates on developments there as they happen."

Wade snapped off the TV set and phoned Mister Marshall. He had not been watching the newscasts.

"Washington State? Peculiar. Send Hershel and Ichi out there. I'll have the small jet warmed up and it will be ready to go by the time the Lincoln can take them out to Kennedy. The pilot will find out if there's a runway at Wenatchee long enough for him to land. This must be the terrorists. This is no test. It may be the first in a series of hits to traumatize and enrage the American people. If this is Abdul, he has made a mistake by starting out small. This will give us a chance to find him. Move them, Wade. Now."

WENATCHEE, WASHINGTON

The Marshall business jet landed at Wenatchee and as soon as Ichi and Hershel walked into the small terminal building an FBI agent from Seattle welcomed them.

"I'm Henderson, FBI Seattle," the slender agent in his thirties said. The Specialists introduced themselves. "Our chief agent is out at the roadblock now. My orders are to drive you out there. We have a motor home on site and will take out two more."

"Any further developments in the town?"

They settled into a Buick at the front of the terminal. The FBI man drove.

"Just a report from the police chief about the number of cases. State Health has sent in a dozen doctors and twenty nurses to help the community. Also a truckload of medical supplies. As of an hour ago they have a hundred and twenty confirmed cases. There may be more in homes of older people who can't get out."

"Any deaths reported yet?" Hershel asked.

"No, typically deaths would come at a later stage and often from some complication to smallpox."

Henderson looked at them. "You both are current on your smallpox shots, I hope."

"We had booster inoculations a few days ago," Ichi said. "Both of us had smallpox vaccinations a year ago."

"Are they letting anyone into the town yet but medical?" Hershel asked.

"Our chief has been in. He says it's ugly in that small town. The gym is almost full of cots and they will need more space. The State Health people estimate that there could be three hundred cases. Anyone with a ten-year-old vaccination could get a mild form of the disease."

They rode in silence for a while. A phone rang. The FBI agent took out his digital and answered.

"Yes, Chief."

He listened for a moment. "The plane was on time and we're on our way. ETA in another thirty minutes. Right." He turned off the set and folded it into his pocket.

"Our chief agent welcomes you. We had some transmissions from the director about your group."

"Good. We'll want to go into town as soon as we arrive," Ichi said.

"We'll work that out."

"Has anyone reported anything unusual happening in town ten to twelve days ago?" Hershel asked.

"Yes, I see what you mean," Henderson said. "How did this happen? The incubation period for smallpox is ten to fourteen days. Yes. I'll give our chief agent a call and see if he's heard anything."

The call was quick and short.

Henderson put the phone away and frowned. "My boss said he hasn't worked up to that yet, and that he will handle it. He didn't sound pleased. He's getting slugged from all sides at once."

"Can you get the chief of police on your digital?" Hershel asked. "Do you have his number?"

"No, afraid not."

"No matter. Oh, what's the area code here?"

"It's five, zero, nine."

"Thanks." Hershel took out his digital phone and dialed 509/555-1212. He had an operator almost at once.

"Operator, I need the number of the police department in Kettle Rapids, Washington."

A moment later the operator dialed the number for him and Hershel waited through three rings.

"Police Department, Chief Irwin."

"Chief. My name is Hershel Levine and I'm working with the FBI. I need to know if you heard or saw anything unusual ten to twelve days ago there in Kettle Rapids."

"Ten or twelve days ago. Damn. I'm so busy right now I haven't had time to think back that far. Let me look at my notebook. Damn, the other line. I'll get right back to you."

Hershel snorted as the air went dead. He waited. It seemed like an hour but was only two or three minutes. At last the chief came back on.

"Sorry, an emergency—one of the doctors who came in to help. Now what was it you wanted?"

"Anything unusual happening ten to twelve days ago there in town. You were going to look at your notebook."

"Oh, hell yes. I don't need to look twelve days ago. I was on night duty. Yeah about four-thirty. Oh, yeah, I remember. But it ain't something I want to talk about on the open air this way. You on a digital phone, right?"

"Yes."

"Then the whole world could tune in. No thanks. Your name was Hershel what?"

"Hershel Levine, Special Agent with the FBI."

"When we let some of you in here, I'll talk to you face-to-face. Not until then. I have a lot of work to get done."

"Right, Chief. I'll see you later."

"So?" Ichi asked.

"Something did happen ten or twelve days ago, but the chief won't talk about it over the air. He's our first order of business as soon as we can get in to see him."

They came to the roadblock a few minutes later. The block itself was a lowboy trailer with a Caterpillar D-12 on board and the diesel tractor and trailer parked across the four lanes of the highway with dump trucks on each end totally blocking the road and the narrow shoulders.

More than two dozen cars were parked there along with three TV mobile-broadcasting units. Half a dozen State Police cars mixed in with the other cars. To one side sat a thirty-foot motor home, complete with antenna. Hershel saw what must be thirty men and a few women milling around.

Agent Henderson led the Specialists up to the motor-home door, where he knocked. Someone opened it and talked for a minute with Henderson, then he waved the pair inside. Six men worked there, some on computers, some on notebooks. One held a radio, another talked on a digital phone. The one on the digital looked up. "You the guys from New York?"

"Yes," Hershel said.

"Which one of you is Hershel Levine?"

"I am. You talking to Chief Irwin?"

"Yes. Aren't you moving a bit fast?"

"No. We're ten days late now. We need to go into town and talk to Chief Irwin. He knows something he won't talk about on the digital."

"That's what he said. I still don't like the idea of a couple of civilians—"

"Hey, we have authorization by the director," Hershel said. "We have carte blanche here, Chief Agent. That means your total cooperation. Or do you want me to call the director direct? I can do that."

Chief Agent Vuylsteke shrugged. "Hell, don't pull rank on me. My job is to keep out everyone possible. You up-to-date on your smallpox shots?"

Hershel told him.

"Hell, okay, I'm going with you. I'll drive. Outside."

A detour of sorts had been fashioned on Highway 87 by sending through traffic down a country lane to an old county road that hooked up with U.S. Highway 97 a mile beyond Kettle Rapids. A State Police car led a dozen or so cars single file north through the detour. Then those waiting on the other end came downstream.

The mile drive into town went quickly. Vuylsteke knew where the small police department headquarters were. He parked in front and a middle-aged man in uniform with a .45 on his hip came out the door.

"Oh, hi Vuylsteke. Thought I said I'd call you."

"Something else, Chief. This is special agent Hershel Levine. You talked to him earlier."

"Yeah, Levine. Didn't get your name at the time. Come in, I'll get my notebook."

Five minutes later the chief had laid it out for the three listeners just as he has seen it happen and as he had written it in his notebook.

"I typed up a report on it for the daily file April twenty-one. Only one other person reported it, our town's only doctor, Patty Olson. She told me the same thing. She's pretty busy right now."

"You're sure it was dynamite?" Ichi asked.

"Not positive, but I've done some blasting. As kids we used to take half sticks and set them against trees and get back with our twenty-two rifles and shoot until we blew them up. I know the sound. It wasn't a hand grenade. I've thrown a few of them and the sound is entirely different."

"Anybody turn in any aluminum that might have been part of a small canister?"

"Oh, God. You're telling me that some sonofabitch flew over town and deliberately dropped a package that blew up and sprayed this whole town with smallpox germs?"

"That's our best bet so far, Chief. It would explain why so many people came down with the disease at the same time. It has been eleven days now since the bomb went off over your town. The incubation period for the smallpox virus is ten to fourteen days."

Chief Irwin slumped in his chair. "I thought it might be some kind of terrible accident, some freakish thing. But deliberate. Oh, damn."

Hershel let the chief consider it all for a minute. "Chief, you said a light plane. Any idea how big or what kind?"

"Been a while since I flew. But nothing bigger than a four-seater light plane. What are around now Pipers, Cessnas? Only ones I can think of. Could have come from Wenatchee or Ephrata or Bridgeport. Not sure about the airfield at Bridgeport."

"Good, Chief. You've been a big help," Ichi said. "Now we really have to talk to Dr. Olson. Can you get her by phone?"

"Can try. She's running the whole operation. More doctors and nurses coming in all the time. They're vaccinating everyone who hasn't shown signs of smallpox yet. I'll try."

It took him two calls ten minutes apart to get an answer.

Ten minutes later, they met the doctor outside the high-school gym. She wore a clean white doctor's coat and a weary expression. She blinked often and at one point held her head with both hands covering her face.

"Dr. Olson. We need you to tell us exactly what you saw that night eleven days ago the morning of April 21 when you saw a light in the sky."

"Oh, yes. I told Chief Irwin." She went through it, confirming what the chief had said.

Hershel looked at her a moment. "Doctor, have you had a vaccination lately for smallpox? You're looking a little gray."

Dr. Patricia Olson frowned. "Well, let's see. I'm not sure. Not in the past year or so for sure."

"You better get a vaccination right now, Doctor," Hershel said.

"Yes, you're right. I'll go over to the vaccination tent right this minute."

"Can we drive you?" Ichi said.

"It's only a block over—"

"We'll drive you," Hershel said. "Step inside."

They let the doctor off at the thirty-foot-long white-walled tent, and waited until she walked inside.

"So?" Ichi said.

"We've done all we can here. Two eyewitnesses say that a bomb came out of a small plane and exploded over the town. Now we head back to Wenatchee and Ephrata and Bridgeport and check out the rentals on small planes for the past two weeks."

"I can have Henderson drive you back," Vuylsteke said.

"That will be helpful, Chief Agent Vuylsteke," Hershel said. "You realize that this information about the plane and the deliberate bombing of this town is top-secret information. This is terrorism, and we want the man flying that plane. We think we know who he is, but we're not certain. Now we have a track on him. We don't want a news story on CCN and NBC to blow it for us."

"Understood. No reporters or TV cameramen will get within a mile of either one of those eyewitnesses."

"Good. Now if we hustle, we should get back to the big town of Wenatchee just after noon."

They made it in plenty of time. They thanked the FBI man and he headed back to Kettle Rapids. This trip they had time to look around the airport area. There was only one place to rent small planes. "Donovan's Flying School. J. Donovan, Prop." Two small planes were ground-tied at one side of the hangar. They tromped up the wooden walk to the door and inside found a desk, two chairs, and a computer in the corner.

A young man looked up.

"Hey, yah. What can I do for you gents?"

"Donovan?"

"Right on the money."

"Can we rent a plane here?"

"If I have what you want. The only planes I rent are ones I'm not instructing in. They have dual controls. What are you looking for?"

"Actually we're looking for a guy you rented a plane to ten or twelve days ago. The date was April 20. You rent a lot of planes around here?"

"Not a lot, but one thing I don't keep are good records.

You keep good records, the IRS will nail your tail to the wall. I do a lot of under-the-counter kind of business. God, hope you two aren't IRS agents."

Hershel took an immediate dislike to the guy. He was too young, too brash, too smart for his own pants.

"So, Donovan, did you rent a plane on April 20?"

"Well, let's see what I did that day. I do keep some records." He thumbed through a book on a table. "Yep, I had three students that day, which is a big workload for me. Don't see how I could have rented a plane. I only have two and one is down for regular inspection and mainte-nance. That I keep track of like a big bird."

He looked on the next page. "Yeah, I guess I did rent the plane, but not until four o'clock that afternoon. Yeah, that explains it. He took her up and did some flying and then came back. Didn't see the plane again until the next morning."

"You remember what he looked like?" Ichi asked.

"Sure, little guy, maybe five-five and skinny. Chinese I'd guess. But he could have been Japanese or Vietnamese. I never can tell them Orientals apart."

"You sure you have the right day?" Ichi asked.

"Yeah. Oh, no offense meant, I just can't tell them apart. Are you Chinese?"

"Japanese," Ichi said. "You sure this was the guy?"

"Right, evidently he took off during the night and came back after daylight on the twenty-first. He paid up and went in to pick up a flight on our puddle jumper airline to Yakima or Spokane."

"You're positive he was Oriental?" Hershel asked.

"Oh, damn sure. I'm not that blind." He paused. "Anything else?"

"No, nothing else," Hershel said.

Donovan watched them as the two men walked toward the small passenger terminal. He snorted and then grinned. Hell, he wasn't about to tell them who really rented that plane. Not when the guy gave him five hun-dred dollars to forget he'd ever seen him. These two were probably some damn cops. He'd had his belly full of cops, enough to last a lifetime. Donovan laughed softly as the two men walked inside the passenger terminal.

Ichi rented a car and Hershel found a map that showed them where Ephrata was. About forty miles south and east on State Highway 28.

Ichi drove. "Another wild-goose jaunt," Ichi said. "This guy could have flown in from anywhere."

"So we check out the other place close to Kettle Rapids," Hershel said. "Has to be done. We might get lucky. An Arab renting a light plane isn't the usual routine in this outback country."

They arrived at Ephrata about three o'clock in the afternoon. The only place to rent a plane was at the edge of the field with three ships tied down out front. The owner said he had no rentals showing for April 20.

"You positive?" Ichi asked the pilot.

"Absolutely. I keep precise records. Have to in this business or somebody will shoot you down."

"Anybody in Bridgeport rent planes?"

"Not sure; the little runway up there changed hands recently. I don't know what they have there now."

Back in the car the Specialists looked at the map.

"What about Bridgeport?" Ichi asked.

"Probably another wild-goose chase. It's up north of Kettle Rapids. Let's try a phone call and see if anyone is there." They did. The phone rang six times before somebody picked it up.

"Hi, you rent planes?" Hershel asked.

"Just to members. We're a small flying club. We don't rent to nonmembers."

"No exceptions?"

"Not if I want to keep my job here."

Hershel thanked him and hung up. They headed for Wenatchee. At the Wenatchee airport they turned in their car and found the best way to fly back to New York. A small airline had flights to Spokane and Richland.

"Spokane would be your best bet to get a flight to New York," the ticket clerk said. She was blond, with glasses and dimples and made Duncan think of his ex-wife. They bought tickets, hurried on board, and settled back for one of several flights they would need to get back to the big city.

They would be on night flights all the way to New York. Ichi tried to sleep, but couldn't. It gave him time to think. Yes, he was pleased with his life. For a while his mother had chided him because he had not married, but she had eased off lately now that she had six grandchildren. He had been happy at the FBI in the weapons department, but this was more exciting than anything he had ever done before. Always on the move, from one important job to the next. And they were important. Usually they were doing a job that had to be done that no one local government could do. It was satisfying.

He was being paid well, but that wasn't his main objective. He had saved a lot of money, and had an honest financial advisor who had helped him invest his money in real estate, and stocks and bonds.

He did have one major vice that he admitted. He loved to fly expensive and exotic kites. For a hundred dollars he could buy a kite that would keep him occupied for months. Lately he had been practicing with dueling kites, one in each hand in mock air battles. The one that stayed up without crashing won. He had seen notices in kite shops about competitions for dueling kites. They even had them in England. He wanted to try his hand at them, just as soon as he could fight with himself a little bit better. It would be a learning process. At least the dueling kites were not that expensive.

Ichi stared at Hershel, who had dropped off to sleep as soon as the snack tray had passed. It was a skill Ichi had yet to learn. Give him time. He moved slightly to ease that pain deep in his chest that hadn't quite gone away. The last doctor he saw said the hurt from the bullet wound would probably always be there when he made certain movements. He had to learn what they were and avoid them. Sure, easy for the doctor to say.

Now he had to keep doing the special exercises and get the rest of his strength back. It was tough keeping up with a marathoner like Kat, and the big SEAL man. But he would do it. Damned if he wouldn't.

He dozed and didn't realize it until he woke up from a

dream that he was leading the daily run and he was a hundred yards ahead of Kat and lengthening his lead. He grinned. *Yeah, that will be the day*. He turned sideways on the lean-back airline seat and at last drifted off to sleep.

✴ TWENTY-THREE ✴

WASHINGTON, DC

Mister Marshall looked around the table in the situation room of the White House. He had been there before. Vice President Vickers led the meeting. The deputy director of the FBI was there, a CIA representative, and the entire CSG. Every federal agency that had anything to do with disasters and terrorism. A DEST man was on hand as well. The feeling was grim as the men and two women assembled.

"Ladies and gentlemen," the Vice President said. "This is not a happy meeting. Most of you know what has happened. A terrorist has dropped an explosive device containing what we are sure now was live and potent smallpox virus on a small town in Washington State.

"At last count there are two hundred and twenty-three confirmed cases of smallpox in the town ranging from week-old babies to a grandmother who is ninety-four. The fatality rate of smallpox for all individuals is over 60 percent. Yes, about half of our entire population has had smallpox vaccinations, but that figure shrinks to 30 percent who have had the inoculation within the past three years, giving almost sure immunity. Beyond three years the protection drops off drastically.

"We have kept this bottled up, but it's going on twenty-four hours and we can't hold the stopper in the bottle any longer. The President will make an announcement about the outbreak of smallpox in Kettle Rapids, Washington.

The town is out in nowhere, on the edge of the mountains with few settlements of any size nearby. There are five hundred and sixty-four souls living in that town where there is one doctor and a two-man police force.

"We will not suggest in any way how this outbreak occurred. For your ears only, it has been confirmed that a small plane dropped a device over the town on April 21. It exploded at about a thousand feet and evidently blanketed the town with smallpox virus. Now twelve days later the virus has incubated and we have over two hundred cases. All of the medical aid and help needed has been flown into the area and trucked into the small town. There is a detour around the village that's located on U.S. Highway 97.

"We think we have the outbreak contained, but some from the town may have traveled after contracting the virus and before they developed the disease. We're watching all over the nation for these cases.

"Our problem, people, is what are we going to do next?"

"Does the FBI know who dropped the device?" the deputy secretary of the Interior asked.

"We do not," the FBI man said. "There is one possible suspect who has been tracked from Ukraine to Iran, through Kuwait to Kennedy Airport in New York. This may be the same man. No one is sure."

"This terrorism of a small town, why?" asked the deputy secretary of Health and Human Services. "Is this a precursor of a larger strike against a metropolitan area? Is it a bid for attention so the perpetrator can launch his demands for millions in tribute if he stops?"

"We simply don't know. We have a man here from the Specialists, a nongovernmental group based in London who make it their full-time business to track and destroy terrorists. They have been watching a man called Abdul for the past month. He may be the one. If he is, he's hiding somewhere in our nation. That makes him almost impossible to find until he makes a mistake."

"What can we do?" two men asked almost in the same breath.

"We must alert all of our groups to be on twenty-four-hour alert," the Vice President said. "The DEST people have sent in the closest team to Kettle Rapids. Other units must be on a ten-minute alert status. This Coordinating Sub Group of the Deputy Secretaries Committee must guarantee interagency cooperation and decision making at the chief operating officer level and to provide coordinated advice to cabinet secretaries and the President.

"The National Security Council was informed of this threat and actual terrorism within minutes after the word came from Kettle Rapids. Unfortunately, the news came by way of CNN. Their reporting operation is faster than our own. Since this is biological terrorism, we also have on board the Environmental Protection Agency and the Federal Emergency Management Agency."

"We know that, Mr. Vice President," the deputy from Treasury said. "What I want to ask this Specialist is does he have any history of this group to show what it might do next? Will they hit a metro area, DC included, or will they make demands?"

The Vice President turned to Mister Marshall, who stood. "Good morning. I know some of you. I ran the CIA for ten years. This is a new player on the international terrorist scene. We think he wiped out a village in Iran. We think he bought the virus from an old storehouse. The virus was made by the USSR and now is in a hiding area near Odessa, Ukraine. Remember the hijacked passenger liner in the Strait of Hormuz? Abdul was the one who did the deed. We thought Navy Air had killed him in his boat when they blew it up when he was escaping. He may have survived. We have no track record to go by on him. Unfortunately, we have to wait for the terrorist's next move."

"Then what the hell can we do?" someone shouted.

"Do?" The Vice President jumped on the word. "We can prepare for a huge tragedy if he strikes a metro area. We can have our troops ready to put into action to make the losses as small as possible. If there is no metro hit, we can be glad and work the small areas that are hit. FEMA is on scene at Kettle Rapids. They were called by the NSC as soon as word came to them. The governor of Washington has called out three infantry units of the Washington State

National Guard, who will put a security ring around the town to prevent ingress or egress.

"We want you to decide what else must be done now, get it into gear, and make our sub group work to protect the rest of the state of Washington and the rest of the U.S. We must be able to react with all of our assets within minutes, not days. Are there any questions?"

"Is there any other vital information?" the man from the Nuclear Regulatory Commission asked.

A man brought a piece of paper to the Vice President, who read it. He looked up. "Yes, we have some new information. The sick report in Kettle Rapids has risen to three hundred and five. The note says the number is tapering off. They are still far short of facilities, personnel, and medical supplies. FEMA is busy on that. Use your regional stores, raid the military posts nearby. Get those people in Washington taken care of. Let's all get to work." The Vice President stood and headed for the door. The twenty people in the room stood at once.

While he was in Washington, DC, Mister Marshall checked in at CIA headquarters at Langley in Virginia. He talked with H.J. Jansen, who figured he would be coming and had the only file the CIA had on Abdul al Ganzouri.

"Not much, August, best we can do. Nobody had heard of him before a year ago. He turned up involved in some small-time bombings and a bank robbery. Then came *The Royal Princess* hijacking and we have a little more. You think he's behind the Iranian wipeout and Kettle Rapids?"

"We can't be sure. He probably is. When we catch him, we'll know."

"What will he do next?"

"No scouting report. He could hit a larger town, put panic into the whole damn country, or he could hit a metro area and get his big kill count. Or he might lie back and make some ransom/payoff demands, like five billion dollars in new one-hundred-dollar bills."

The two CIA men stared at each other.

"Agreed. We don't have a handle on this bastard either." Jansen balled up a sheet of paper and shot it at a small basketball type hoop eight inches across on the nearby wall. He missed.

"Yeah. But we can't afford to miss on this one. Your best bet, Marshall?"

"For Abdul? He'll play it both ways. Pull up now and make his money demands. Five billion seems about right. Then after any payoff, he'll go right ahead and make his big hit on a metro area: the DC beltway, Chicago, or New York, in that order."

"So when we don't pay?"

"He'll hit us as hard as he can."

"If we don't stop him before."

"We're trying, H.J. . . . Dammit, we're trying, but we don't have any handle to grab hold. I hate this waiting. What else can we do?"

Later that same day Mister Marshall went back to the downtown area of Washington and checked in with the FBI. Director Vincent's secretary ushered the guest to the director's inner office. They had never met.

After the introductions, they sat down. "Director Vincent, we thank you for giving us standing along with your agency men. It might be helpful."

"It has been already. Your men on the site in Washington gave us our first solid lead. Our men at the Wenatchee and Ephrata airports found little more than yours did. The ticket sellers at that small airlines couldn't remember any of the individuals who bought tickets on April 21."

"When is the President speaking to the nation?"

"Tonight at eight Eastern. That makes it five on the West Coast."

"I hope he doesn't panic everyone."

"He won't if he follows our suggestions. We wrote the speech for him. It won't be a press conference, just a TV announcement on all five networks simultaneously."

"Dammit, Mr. Director, I hate this waiting. What is that maniac going to do next?"

Before they left Wenatchee and Ephrata, Ichi and Hershel had received manifests of every passenger on board four flights from the small towns of the feeder lines on April

21. The eighteen passenger planes were full four times, almost empty the other four flights for a total of eighty-eight passengers. None had an Arabic-sounding name. The ticket clerks swore that each person had a picture ID and a second printed ID.

Most flights from Wenatchee went to Yakima. A clerk said from there another feeder line with larger planes flew over the mountains directly to the airport at Tacoma-Seattle. From Ephrata flights went to Richland and Spokane. The Specialists had the passenger lists when they flew into La Guardia Airport in New York City.

ROCK SPRINGS, WYOMING
APRIL 23

Abdul left his two helpers at the rented Omaha house this time and flew with the one canister safely padded in a carry-on bag he kept between his feet. He flew on a commercial airliner into Cheyenne and took a feeder airline plane on to Rock Springs. He timed it so he landed at Rock Springs about four in the afternoon. He carried his bag and checked out the airplane-rental firms. There were three at the airport. He chose the smallest one, showed his pilot's ticket and Visa card.

He took the plane, a small Piper Cub, for a test run just before dark, and landed as the runway lights came on. Good. He could get out and back in the dark and not have to see anyone.

The distance to the new target town of Lost Mine was ninety miles. It lay just outside of the Shoshone National Forest on the southeast side. His current map said the town had 3,146 residents. The Rocky Mountains in that area were eight thousand to eighty-five hundred feet. He'd fly around them and slip through South Pass where the highway climbed to seventy-five hundred feet. He'd have to be sure to check his altimeter so he didn't drop the package too low.

He had considered one canister or two, at last deciding that one should be plenty. He had been told that the canister could cover a square mile if exploded at the right altitude and if there was no wind.

This time it seemed routine. He took off from the deserted Rock Springs airport at 3 A.M. and flew directly to the small community of Lost Mine. Abdul checked his altimeter over the town on the first pass. The town of Lander twenty miles away was at fifty-three hundred feet. He'd use that as ground level. So he needed eighty-three hundred feet for his drop pass. This town was much larger than the one in Washington State. It had spread out along the highway. He might not get his 50 percent hit ratio here.

Abdul said a Moslem prayer as he activated the timer and dropped the canister out the plane's window. He did an abrupt turn upwind and pushed the throttle to full. He didn't count this time, simply watched behind for the brilliant flash, then seconds later he heard the crack of the explosion.

"Take that, Great Evil," he chanted. Abdul made a ten-mile detour around the town as he headed back toward Rock Springs. The date was April 23. In ten days there should be a second big outbreak of smallpox. That would be on May 3. He would wait it out in Omaha.

⋆ TWENTY-FOUR ⋆

NEW YORK CITY

The Specialists were going stir-crazy. They had been on four more Arab hunts as they called them. All had been unproductive.

"Damn waste of time," Wade said after the last one yesterday. "There has to be something we can do."

"Finding one Arab in this whole country is like finding a special grain of sand on Waikiki Beach," Kat said.

Mister Marshall had no answers for them. They had their regular meetings, worked on international terrorism threats, and did their daily runs and walks around the reservoir in Central Park.

"Things are settling down in Kettle Rapids," Mister Marshall told them. "FEMA has moved in there with twenty trucks and enough medical supplies to last them a year. The National Guard from Washington State has the town sealed off. Food trucks have been brought in so the one grocery store can restock its shelves."

"What's the sick count?" Ichi asked.

"Three hundred and twelve have had smallpox to some degree," Mister Marshall said. "As of this morning there had been sixty-five deaths. Twenty were under three years, and thirty more over sixty-five. The rest are in the healing process. The National Guard set up a field hospital and four more large hospital tents. One more note here. Ichi and Hershel, I know you met some of the people in that town. One of the fatalities is reported to be the town's lone doctor, Patty Olson."

"No," Ichi bellowed. He jumped up and ran out of the room. Hershel pounded his fist onto the table a dozen times like a bell tolling, measured, strident. "Oh, shit," Hershel said. He stood and walked out.

The room remained quiet.

At last Wade broke the silence. "Yes, we grieve for the dead and sick. Then we shake it off and go on with our job, which is to find and stop this bastard.

"Let's do some math. Ten to fourteen days. I'll never forget that phrase. What if Abdul exploded another canister a day or two after he hit the first town? If it went off on April 26, the sick could begin to show up soon. So far no reports.

"If he hit another town on the twenty-seventh, that would make the incubation period end May 6, and sick could show up quickly. Another thought. The first town was in Washington State, far West. Why? Is he going to move eastward? Is he going to terrorize the population in his line of fire? Possible. Yes, I know. There is nothing we can do right now. Frustrating. Thousands of us are in the same boat. The DEST people, the entire FBI establishment. It's their turf and they can't get a sniff of this guy. Is he that good or is he that lucky?"

"Thought of something," Duncan said. "Hershel said this pilot they talked to at Wenatchee was real flaky. Hershel said it was like he was making up a story just to put them off. What if this guy was lying, protecting the guy who really flew the plane?"

Wade stood. "Let's go find Hershel and Ichi. My guess is they might want to call this guy and tell him exactly what Abdul did from his plane. Tell him he could get fifty years for aiding and abetting and another four hundred years for eighty cases of second-degree murder."

They found Hershel outside, staring at the Brooklyn Bridge. He listened to Wade, then ran inside and found a phone. He got the number from information in Washington and soon dialed the Donovan Flying School's number.

"Yeah, Donovan."

"Mr. Donovan, my name is Hershel Levine. I talked to

you a few days ago. You know what's going on up at Kettle Rapids?"

"Oh, hell yes. A tragedy. How did something like that happen? I mean that's a crapper. Do they know what caused it?"

"We know exactly how it happened. We know who killed those eighty people and all the others who might die."

"What you mean, you know? Some person did that? No way, it's a disease, man."

"Yes, a disease. And one man did it, and another one helped him. Guess who it is who helped? No guess, Donovan. It was you. Yes, you helped."

"Off your rocker, whoever you are. I never been up there for months. I couldn't have done anything."

"You did, Donovan. You're as guilty of all those deaths as the man who was there."

"You some kind of a nut, I'm hanging up."

"Don't do it, Donovan, or the FBI will be on your case within half an hour. These guys are tough. Settle and listen. The fact is a canister was dropped from a small plane and exploded over the town. The canister was filled with live smallpox virus. It's called bacteriological terrorism. That canister was thrown out of that Cessna of yours. You said some Oriental rented the plane. That was a lie, wasn't it?"

"What? Oh shit. Somebody actually threw out a bunch of that shit and it . . . Oh, Chrisinabucket. Hey, you can't nail me for this. Hey, I didn't know what he wanted to do. He just rented my plane. I can't control what anybody does with it. Not my fault."

"The federal judge will listen to you crying, then throw the book at you, Donovan. Your lying to us about who rented the plane is your fault. It's called withholding information in a felony case. That alone can get you ten to fifteen."

"Jesus. Hey, all I did was rent the guy my plane."

"Who was he? What did he look like?"

"Look like? Dark, black hair and heavy mustache. Heavy beard if he didn't shave it. Five o'clock shadow, you know, only it would be there all day."

"Nationality?"

"Hell, maybe an Arab of some kind."

"He had a pilot's license?"

"Yeah, looked good to me. I got the name, and he had a good Visa card. I checked it on the phone."

"You take down the number?"

"Yeah, it's here somewhere."

"Donovan, I'll give you a break. You find that number and we'll get a police sketch artist to you with a computer. You stay put right there and don't run, and maybe you won't go to prison. You stay put. Understand?"

"Yeah, damittohell. How did I get myself into this mess?"

"Stay there, right?"

"Yeah, right."

Mister Marshall had been listening. "I'll call the FBI. They can have a sketch from him this afternoon. Three hours earlier out there." He left to make the call.

Hershel put the phone down and tried to relax. He couldn't. He shook his head. "I need to go on a run, a long damn run. Don't worry, I can find my way back."

"Take Ichi with you?" Wade asked.

Hershel shook his head. "No. Ichi will want to be by himself and meditate. Seen him do it before."

Hershel grabbed his running shoes and hurried out of the office.

Hershel angled off the main streets into the less-traveled ones, where he wouldn't have to dodge as many pedestrians. He was still angry that the lady doctor had died. She had worked so hard and had saved a lot of people. He was also furious at the asshole in Wenatchee who had lied about who rented his plane. They would get him one way or another.

Maybe he should have stayed with the Israeli Mossad. They had simple black-and-white rules. Save friends, kill enemies. And Israel had so many enemies. But he had thrown in with the Specialists with the blessings of his Mossad boss. So far it had worked out well. They had done things no single government could do. They had made a difference. Now they were trying to save the U.S.

from the horrors of a terrorist attack like the world had never known. They had to stop this bastard Abdul.

He had killed that lady doctor. Hershel fought against it but it made him think of his young wife, Sadira. He couldn't bear even to say her name. He had waited for so long to find exactly the right woman. A month after their wedding Sadira had been at the market just down from her apartment to do some shopping.

A terrorist had driven an old sedan to a spot beside the market and walked away. Thirty seconds later the entire car blew up. The authorities couldn't find enough left of his dear wife to bury. They had a service in the blasted market where four others had died.

He brushed wetness from his eyes as he ran. Another block, another mile. It wouldn't be enough. It would never be enough. How could he ever wash away the anguish of Sadira's loss?

He had plunged into his work for Mossad. He asked for the most dangerous assignments, crossing into the Arab territory many times hunting the leaders of the Arafat Fatah movement on the West Bank. At last the surge of hatred burned low and he could get back to normal duties. Slowly reason replaced his fury, a sense of balance returned to his life. He dived into the computer he had begun to use and used it to track Arab terrorists. Then the offer came from Mister Marshall and he had accepted it. Now he was trying to do more for the good of the whole world.

Back in the Specialists' headquarters, Wade tapped his pen on a pad of paper. "What do we have? The FBI or CIA must have some sketches of Abdul from the passenger liner people. Dig them out. Then we get the guys at the loading dock at British Air Freight to do a sketch. Been a while but it could still work. With the three sketches we might come up with something that will help. We post his sketch at every airline ticket window in the country, ten or twelve thousand. Send them out on the Internet and have them downloaded at each airport and distributed. Can be done in an hour. Yeah, now at least we're doing something."

It took three hours for the FBI to contact Donovan and get the sketch faxed to headquarters. They had the one from the loading crew within an hour and compared them. Another sketch artist blended the two. By that time Wade had the name on the pilot's license. "It's fake but he will have to use it if he rents another plane to fly. The Visa number is good with the same name but the address is a fake here in New York City."

Wade tapped his pen again. "We send out the pilot's license number and his description and his Visa card. It's already been canceled but he might try to use it. We get this all on that page for the Web or the Internet."

The sketch, the numbers, and description went out to every airline headquarters in the country. They downloaded and posted the pictures in every major and minor and feeder airline ticket window in the nation.

Wade grinned. "Hell, at least we did something. It might not work but it could be productive. Now we sit back and hope some sharp-eyed airline ticket seller or gate person spots our boy."

By nine o'clock that night, Wade had checked with the FBI twice and no one had called the special 800 number on the notice about Abdul. Nothing. He hung up the phone, yelled at it, then did fifty push-ups. When he was finished he was tired but still mad that the number hadn't produced even one call.

The next morning they put in two hours working on hot spots of international terrorism. There was nothing pressing, but two areas they would keep high on their project board.

The phone rang in their situation room at ten-thirty.

"Yes, this is Wade."

"Wade, this is Rawlins, NY FBI. We've had another outbreak. The sheriff of some county in Wyoming reports ten cases this morning of smallpox. He said he isn't sure it's the same thing as Kettle Rapids, but the local doctor said he'd never seen ten people from different families all get smallpox on the same day. Two of the kids are pretty bad already. This is May third."

"Where is it? I'm on our plane in an hour."

"Little place called Lost Mine, Wyoming. South of Lander about fifteen miles and north of Rock Springs about ninety miles. Rock Springs has a good-sized airport."

Wade hung up and called Marshall.

"That's what the FBI knows. I'll take Kat and get out there. Is the small jet ready to travel?"

"It will be in an hour. Take you that long to get to Kennedy. We should keep one jet at La Guardia, closer in."

"Yes sir. I'll report back as soon as I have anything."

In the Gulfstream II it was a four-hour flight to Rock Springs, Wyoming. They rented a car and drove up U.S. Highway 191 past Edon to Farson, where they turned right on State Highway 28 and charged for the South Pass at 7550 feet. Wade drove and passed everything on the road. He saw one state cop going the other way but didn't even wave.

It took them almost two hours and Wade saw the roadblock ahead well before he reached it. The highway had cut through the edge of Shoshone National Forest, then out of it. The roadblock was two State Police cars sideways across the lanes. Only two other cars were there. So far they had devised no detour around the town for through traffic on the highway.

A policeman came over to their car but before he could speak, Wade held out his FBI card.

"Any more of my people here?" Wade asked.

"No sir. Sheriff asked us to close off the road. Good idea. Talked to him a half hour ago and he says he has almost forty cases so far. Using the gym at the high school, a church, and a little clinic that the two local doctors run."

"How big is the town?"

"Last figures were three thousand one hundred and forty-six."

"As soon as you get enough manpower, you better work out a detour around town. We don't want this end clogged up with tourists. You're keeping anyone from leaving the town, right?"

"Yes sir. Sheriff has his twenty deputies in a loose net

around the town. He's called the governor for the Wyoming National Guard. Sure could use them."

"Take a while. We're going in to see what we can find out. Nobody else gets in except medical personnel and medical supplies. Clear?"

"Yes sir. Oh, you've had your vaccinations?"

"Twice, Officer. Work out that detour even if you have to go cross-country and cut a fence or two."

Wade drove on the shoulder around the patrol car and back on the road. He could see the buildings ahead, less than a mile away. The town had grown up along the highway, half a mile long and no more than three blocks deep on both sides. There were few cars on the street and he saw almost no people. A sign pointed to the Baleen County Sheriff's office and Wade turned toward it.

He parked in front of a two-story concrete-block structure and he and Kat went up to the door. A man came out quickly. He wore a khaki uniform, had a belted pistol and a sleeve patch declaring him a deputy sheriff.

"How in hell you drive in here?" the deputy asked more in surprise than worry.

"FBI, your boss inside?"

"FB . . . yes sir. Right this way. The lady, too?"

Kat held up her FBI temporary ID and marched in behind Wade. Inside the front door Wade saw a counter across the room and a swinging hip-high door that led into the back and several offices.

"Who was it, Virgil?" a booming voice asked.

"FBI," Wade said. A moment later a door swung farther open and a man rolled out. He was heavy, in a too-small khaki uniform with two stars on his collar. His face looked like soft wax and only his eyes had any strength. They were brown and shifted from Wade to Kat. His face melted into a soft smile as he stared at Kat.

"Well, well, well. The FBI in my small jurisdiction. I'm Sheriff Utts. Glad you're here. You taking over?"

"How many victims so far?" Kat asked.

He shifted his eyes along with his shoulders as he looked back at her. "Kat Killinger," she said. "Good to meet you. How many victims?"

Sheriff Utts wilted a little. "Not sure. Doc Jones said he had at least sixty, and more coming in all the time. From both sides of the highway and both ends of town. Can't figure it out."

"You have many aircraft fly over here, Sheriff?" Wade asked.

"Not many. No airports nearby. One down at Rock Springs, another one up at Riverton. A few recreation flyers, I guess."

"You have any reports of any planes on April 23, late at night or early in the morning?"

"Don't figure anyone would report a plane flying over. Why?"

"We think somebody deliberately bombed your town with smallpox virus. That's why everyone is getting sick at the same time. Have you had your smallpox vaccination lately, Sheriff?"

"What? Bombed our town. Now I don't know why—"

"Remember a week ago a town in Washington State came down with over three hundred cases of smallpox?"

"Yes, but I don't see—"

"That town was bombed with the smallpox vaccine. I think the same man did the same thing to you. Call all of your deputies now and ask if anyone on the night shift the twenty-third of April remembers hearing or seeing a plane that night."

"Yes, I can do that."

"Please, Sheriff," Kat said. "We need to know as quickly as possible."

"Mabel, get on the horn to all deputies," the sheriff said.

"Sheriff, Mabel ain't here, remember?" the deputy who met them said. "She came down with the pox this noon and I drove her over to the gymnasium."

"Oh, hell. I forgot. Sly, you make the call. Ask the men if any of them on duty the twenty-third of April heard an airplane over town that night."

"Yes sir."

The deputy put out the radio message. Two minutes

later a response came. "Deputy Price, Sheriff. I told you about it. Put it in my report. We figured some crazy kids. Flew over town low and threw out some kind of a firecracker. Maybe a half stick of dynamite. It went off with quite a roar. It's all in my report."

"Yes, Price. Thanks."

"You need to see the report?" the sheriff asked. He slid into a chair, bulging on both sides of it.

"No, Sheriff Utts, the officer's word is good enough. That firecracker was a half stick of dynamite and you do have a serious problem. Half of your population is going to be sick. Maybe a hundred of them will die. You better work with the doctors to figure out where to put the new cases. Where is the gymnasium you're using for the sick?"

Five minutes later they drove up to the gym. It was flooded with cars and with people. Some sick were being carried in. Others arrived in wheelchairs. The town's only ambulance moved slowly with its backup horn beeping.

A man in a white doctor's coat came out and looked at the cars. He shook his head. Wade and Kat hurried up to him.

"Doctor, how is it?"

"Terrible. Damn bad. I've never seen anything like this."

"We're with the FBI. Want to tell you to plan for at least six hundred patients, maybe more. Start screaming at the governor to have the National Guard bring in two field hospitals. You'll need them."

"Why? What caused this?"

Kat told him. He shook his head in disbelief. "It's monstrous. Who in God's name would do something like this? Something this evil, so diabolical."

"We think we know who, we just don't know where he is."

They drove. Kat looked at a map she had bought at Rock Springs.

"Riverton or Rock Springs airport?"

"Which one is closer?" Wade asked.

"Riverton. It's north about thirty miles."

"Riverton it is. We should be able to get there in half an hour."

"I wonder how many plane-rentals places there will be? The map shows it as a regional airport."

✷ TWENTY-FIVE ✷

RIVERTON, WYOMING

Kat looked around outside the airport terminal and pointed. "Three places to rent planes," she said. "Which one first?"

They tried at the largest and most prosperous-looking. The manager said they didn't rent planes anymore. Too much hassle. Their only business now was flight instruction.

The second place on that side of the field was run-down and needed some paint but the sign said planes for rent. A woman in the office said their planes had been grounded by the FAA until they made certain repairs and had the regular mechanical inspection. At the third place the manager said sure they had planes to rent, but they were mostly crop-dusting rigs and they were usually out of town into the farming areas to the south.

"So, we take another drive?" Kat asked.

"Rock Springs, here we come," Wade said. "Only a hundred and thirty miles. At eighty-five miles an hour, shouldn't take long." On the open stretches he did hold it at ninety-five and slowed down only when the road and traffic demanded. It took twenty minutes to get around Lost Mine on the bumpy cross-country detour.

Kat grinned. "You suggested we go cross-country," she reminded Wade.

They rolled into Rock Springs at sunset and hurried to the airport. There were four firms that handled rentals.

The first two were dry holes. The third one proved to be better.

"Sure, I rent whenever I can," the young man behind a counter inside the small office said. He was about thirty, sandy hair, freckles, a long, thin face with bushy brows. Wade figured he was at least six inches over six feet tall. "How long you need one for?"

They asked him about any rentals on April 23.

"Got it right here in my book," the young man said. He looked up, frowning. "Nobody ever asked me that question before. This have anything to do with that problem up in Lost Mine?"

"It could," Wade said. "Let's see your book."

"Had a couple in searching for dinosaur tracks. They used one of my planes for three days. Nope, they started on the twenty-first."

He pushed his finger at an entry. "Here, this guy took the plane on the afternoon of the twenty-second, brought it back the next morning early. It was parked when I came at 6 A.M."

"Who was that?" Kat asked.

He flashed her a big smile. "Regs say I got to put down the license number. Yeah, here it is, his number and name."

Kat shivered as she looked. "Same name we have and that has to be the same pilot's license number," she said. "What did he look like?"

"Yeah, I remember him. An Arab. Snotty to me, little guy not more than five-eight. Thought he was hot shit. Stuck-up as hell. Paid me in cash but I made him show me a credit card. Had a Visa. I have the number on the rental form. I always put it down in case some jasper tries to steal my plane."

"You said he was about five-eight," Wade said. "What else about him?"

"Let's see. He wore a full beard and heavy mustache. Kept his hat on. I almost didn't rent to him. Then I did. Paid in cash, hundred-dollar bills, new ones."

"Thanks. He say where he was heading next?"

"Not a word. He a crook or something? You guys got to be cops. What did he do?"

"You don't want to know," Kat said. "Was he alone?"

"Was when he came in here. Later at the café I saw him with two men, both dark as he was. More Arabs?"

"Probably." Kat looked at Wade.

"Thanks, you've been a help."

"What did this guy do?"

"Think it through and you can figure it out," Wade said. They walked out the door and stood for a moment.

"The restaurant?" Kat asked.

"Can't hurt."

They had dinner and talked with the waitresses. One of them remembered the three Arabs. She was about thirty, pretty, slender with a good figure.

"The A-Rabs? Hey, be a while before I forget them three. This one seemed to be the boss. He ordered for them and paid the tab, and left me a twenty-dollar tip."

"Is that why you remember him?" Kat said. The woman with the name tag that said she was Wanda, laughed.

"Oh hell no. He kept propositioning me. Then he said he'd give me a present. He kept putting one-hundred-dollar bills on the table. When he had five of them out there I was tempted. Hey, I'm no angel. I've been around the barn a time or two, but five hundred bucks. The boss came by just then to ask the trio how the food was. The bills vanished under the napkin and I got back to the kitchen."

"Did the man look something like this?" Kat asked, and showed Wanda the composite.

"Oh yeah. He had a beard but the eyes are the same. Hey, be a while before I forget those eyes. Then, too, I have a new standard. Five hundred if you want to see me naked." Wanda giggled. *It fit,* Wade thought.

"You remember anything else about him?" Wade asked.

"Well, sweet thing, I just don't. I mean I was getting a little worked up myself when those hundreds kept showing up. Naw, he was Arab, he was smooth as goose grease, and he was dark and mysterious and damned attractive." Wanda paused. She lifted her brows, seemingly closing the memory. "So, how was the roast beef? You good folks want dessert?"

The news of the second massive outbreak of smallpox hit the networks and this time an explanation had to be given. The first time the President made the announcement about Kettle Rapids, he had skirted the issue of how it had happened. This time the Attorney General talked on the networks. She said that the outbreak was the result of a person or persons who had deliberately planted the virus in these two towns.

"This can only be described as an abhorrent crime against humanity, a vicious, wanton mass murder. Officially the United States has labeled these two attacks as acts of terrorism by agents of a foreign power. We are not free yet to say who has perpetrated this massive murder of Americans, but we are getting closer to the culprits and we will bring them to trial and convict them and subject them to the ultimate penalty, paying with their lives."

Outrage erupted from half the nations in the world. The Arab countries were strangely silent. The Pope made a pronouncement condemning the culprits.

News reports now said that ninety-two residents of Kettle Rapids, Washington, had died from smallpox and over two hundred were recuperating; most would have scars on their faces for the rest of their lives.

The first day of the outbreak in Lost Mine, Wyoming, over two hundred had reported to the small clinic and the high-school gymnasium in the first stages of smallpox. The town was still quarantined, with Wyoming National Guard troops arriving to seal in the whole community.

Wade and Kat took off in the Gulfstream at 8 P.M. and would arrive at La Guardia Airport in New York about four hours later.

NEW YORK CITY

The Specialists gathered in the situation room in the downtown headquarters and watched the latest news from CNN. Overnight another two hundred people in Lost Mine had come down with smallpox. The town was sealed off now by three hundred National Guard troops with live ammunition. FEMA, the Red Cross, and dozens of state medical associations were all rushing vaccine and medical supplies to the site. The Army had put on an exercise where they erected three field hospitals on the county fairgrounds and left them there for the people of Lost River. No one had died from the pox yet, but that record would not last long.

"There is high speculation about what group or what nation has stooped to such a horrendous murdering act," the CNN newscaster said. "The prime suspects must be the Arab terrorists who continually spout their hatred for the Great Evil, that being the United States. Many of these fringe terrorist groups have dedicated their lives to hurting the United States. Government sources will not even hint at who they suspect as the culprits. Huge retaliations and perhaps economic sanctions will surely result from these mass murders."

Mister Marshall snapped off the set. "Wade and Kat say that the same man using the same pilot's license rented a plane in Rock Springs. This time he had a full beard. I suggest we send another Web page and E-mail to the airports and airlines, showing our sketch with a two-inch full black beard."

"I'll handle it," Kat said, and hurried out of the room to a phone and the computers.

PIERRE, SOUTH DAKOTA

The three men who came into the town's biggest TV station looked like businessmen. They each carried a briefcase. When they asked to see the station manager, the receptionist showed them to his office. As soon as the door closed, Abdul took a 9mm pistol from his briefcase and leveled it at the manager behind the desk.

"We require the use of your station for an hour. You will cooperate, you will not call the police, or you and some of your workers here will die. Is that perfectly clear?"

The manager stood slowly. He had served in the Gulf War, he knew Arabs. He nodded. "Yes, whatever you want. Don't hurt anyone."

"We won't if you follow orders strictly. First, take us to your studio where you do the news and where you can tape a message I will give. One of my men will be in the lobby. Lock the front door. No one leaves the building or comes in until we are done. Understand?"

"Yes. Up this way to the studio."

Abdul saw it was a typical small station setup, with two cameras and plenty of lights. One cameraman stood by his camera. Abdul told the people what he wanted.

"We both have guns. None of you will be harmed if you do exactly as I say. Now light me and get the camera ready."

The workers did what he asked. The camera moved up and the red light came on as the cameraman tested his coverage and angles.

"One requirement. You will not photograph me above my neck. My head must never appear on camera. Clear?"

"Yes sir," the cameraman said. He smiled. It was too late. For the past four or five minutes while the Arab had been talking with the manager and the floor director, he had been shooting everything the Arab and his friend did, with their guns showing. Now he quickly zoomed in to the Arab's chest, cutting off his head.

The Arab looked at the monitor showing the picture. "Yes, keep the camera there while I speak. Don't show my face or you are a dead man."

"Yes sir," the cameraman said.

"Hold that shot right there," the Arab said.

The cameraman looked at the floor director, who had sweat running down his forehead. He nodded vigorously at the cameraman.

"The rest of you sit on the floor," Abdul shouted. "Nobody leaves the studio. Floor director, make sure this is being taped for later release to all the networks. You have an exclusive here. I want an introduction by someone off camera. You may give the name of your station. Is everyone ready?"

"Ready," the cameraman said.

The floor director looked at the control booth, listened to his earphone a moment, then began counting. "Five, four, three, two." At that time he pointed to the Arab.

"Hello, America. Hello, Great Evil. Hello to all of the people in Kettle Rapids, Washington, and in Lost Mine, Wyoming. You are tasting a small sample of what waits for one of your larger cities, and the attack will come soon.

"A major city in America will be targeted and more than a million Great Evil men, women, and children will die of smallpox. This million dead will be a token payment to the glorious nations of Islam, for the sins of your government leaders and their unspeakable acts against Arabs during the past one hundred years.

"Now, Americans, you will pay. There is no chance you can rush enough vaccine to every large city to protect your citizens. There isn't time. Instead, use your power and throw out the despots, the evildoers, the government vassals who have been kowtowing to the industrial complex for years. Throw them out of office and elect those who will treat Islam and Muslims with the respect and courtesy that they are due.

"This won't be a long announcement. It will be released two hours after I leave this delightful small town of Pierre, South Dakota. Do not attempt to follow me. Only death awaits any who try. I am the Sword of Allah. I will fight his battles forever or to the death, whichever comes first.

"Remember, there is no way you can stop me. Your fate is in my hands; those who survive will have a secure future only if you throw out the criminals now in your seat of government.

"The mighty and unstoppable Sword of Allah is about to take a tremendous slice out of the sins of America. Praise be to Allah."

He looked at the floor director, who nodded. "Cut on the tape. This is done."

Abdul stepped out of the lighting and talked with his friend, who still held his gun on several persons.

"Did the tape show my face?" he asked the other man in Arabic.

"No, not once. I watched the monitor. He did as you said." The reply was in Arabic as well.

Abdul grabbed the first woman he saw in the group. She was an assistant floor director. He jerked the headset away from her.

"This one will go with us. If you release the tape sooner than two hours from now, she will die a most painful death. Do you fully understand me?"

"No reason to take a hostage," the station manager said.

Abdul walked up to the man and slashed the automatic handgun down across his face. Blood spurted from a gash across the manager's forehead and cheek. He bellowed in pain and dropped to the floor.

Abdul, his helper, and the hostage moved to the door and through it. They hurried down the stairs and picked up the Arab guard at the front door, then rushed outside to the rented car they had waiting.

No one followed them. They drove to the outskirts of the state capital and there left the girl bound and gagged in the backseat of the car. They transferred to a second car they had left there and drove directly to the airport, where they boarded a plane waiting for them. They had chartered it and told the pilot to file a flight plan for Chicago. Once in the air they told him they were going instead to a small airfield north of Minneapolis called Johnson Air Park. They ordered him not to change his flight plan.

The three ate meals the pilot had brought on board for them and they all went to sleep. The pilot radioed the Pierre airport, changing his flight plan.

At Pierre the city police and airport police were too late to catch the Arabs. They did not use the terminal but a transient airplane-boarding area. The FBI had called local police to watch for the three Arabs. They checked with each airline ticket counter and loading ramp. No one had seen the three Arabs. The local police thought that the men might have driven out of town. Then they found that the rental car the three Arabs had taken had been abandoned in the airport parking lot. Less than a half hour after the three Arabs left the television station in Pierre, the local anchor went on his network with a news flash that broke into every program on the air on the five major networks.

"This is Art Brachman from Pierre, South Dakota. I have just witnessed the most cold-blooded recitation of terrorism that I have ever experienced. What follows is shocking and outrageous; it also happens to be true. The man who forced us at gunpoint to record this message was an Arab, about thirty to thirty-five years of age, clean-shaven except for a mustache. He would not let us tape his face. This is his mind-boggling threat to the citizens of the United States."

All five networks carried the story live. It was repeated twice before regular newscasts began, then it was the lead story in every newscast in the nation.

Before the tape aired the second time, Roger and Duncan were on their way to La Guardia Airport to board the Gulfstream that would fly at maximum cruising speed to Pierre, South Dakota.

It was dark when Roger and Duncan landed at the Pierre airport. They contacted local police, who reported what they had done for the FBI.

"Did you check the transient planes and charters?" Duncan asked. The cops shook their heads. "Nobody told us to contact them," the cop said. Only two of the charter companies were still open. Both said that they had no charters that afternoon, and certainly didn't see three Arabs looking for a ride.

The transient aircraft were easier. The tower reported that only two transients had been in and out that day. Both were flying to the west.

They checked the doors of the closed charter aircraft firm. It had an emergency number. Duncan dialed it.

"Yeah?"

"This is the FBI. We're looking for three Arab men who chartered a plane today or yesterday and flew out today. Was it at your company?"

"Well, yeah. They paid in cash, had a Visa for ID. Looked okay to us. They in trouble?"

"Yes. Did you file a flight plan for them?"

"Yes, Chicago, some little field outside of town."

"Could they change it once in the air?"

"Could."

"Give me the type of plane and the call letters, I'll check with the tower."

Five minutes later the tower reported that the charter had changed its flight plan. "The pilot radioed about a half hour out to change it from Chicago to Johnson Air Park, north of Minneapolis."

"Thanks. Could they change it again?"

"They could, and they could land anywhere else they wanted to. A flight plan is not a contract or anything like that."

"How fast is that plane they're flying?"

"Cruises at two hundred fifty miles an hour."

Duncan looked at Roger. "With the Gulfstream, we can get there shortly after they do. Let's go for a plane ride."

"First, let's talk to the people at the TV station. There may be something they forgot to put in their video report."

"Will anybody be there?"

"Always people at a TV station."

They found the assistant manager running things. He was still pumped by all the publicity their small station had generated.

"I had an interview for *Good Morning America*," he said.

"What about the people on the floor at the time of the taping the demands?" Duncan asked. "The floor manager, the director, and the cameraman. We'd like to talk to all three."

The director was through with his shift and gone. They found the floor manager and the cameraman in the lunchroom.

"Hey, big day for you guys, right?" Duncan asked.

"Yeah, big day," the cameraman said. "Boy, that guy with the gun was a bad one."

"You shot the videotape on him?" Roger asked.

"Oh, yeah. I get the big jobs."

"Just from the waist up to his chin?" Duncan asked.

"Yeah. Oh, I did some fooling around before the announcement started. Then the floor manager told me to put in a new tape, we might need to shoot the whole thing."

"What?" the floor manager said. "You heard him say not to shoot his face."

"Yeah, but he said that way after I shot about four or five minutes of him and his buddy with the gun and the manager gabbing. I knew that part wasn't any good for the big announcement so I didn't mention it."

The floor manager grabbed the cameraman by the shoulders and shook him. "You could have got us all killed."

"Hey, he'll never know. I still have that tape around my bench somewhere."

"You what?" Duncan said.

"Dropped it in the NG basket in the editing room I think."

Duncan held up both hands. "Hold it. Just hold it. Are you saying that you shot tape of these guys before they told you not to shoot their faces? And that you still have the video on it?"

"Well, yeah. Might be messed up a little."

"Show me," Duncan said. "Show me right the hell now!"

"Okay, okay."

Ten minutes later, Duncan and Roger slipped out of the editing room, a videocassette with four minutes of pictures of the two Arabs clutched in Roger's hands. "There are several close shots on the man I'm sure is Abdul," Roger said.

Duncan bellowed in triumph as soon as they got into their rental car. "We have it now, positive ID on the sonofabitch," Duncan said. "This nails the bastard. Now we jump in our jet and see how fast we can get to Minneapolis."

★ TWENTY-SIX ★

Once the Gulfstream jet was off the ground, Duncan talked to Mister Marshall in New York.

"Yes sir, it's firm proof that Abdul is the man behind these bio strikes. We have him full figure and full face on videotape in the Pierre TV studio news set just before he made the TV announcement."

"That's good, but it doesn't help us catch him. Where is he headed, did you find out?"

Duncan told him.

"You'll be there faster than we could. Stay on the track. We need him bad. Washington has been flooded with calls from irate citizens. Jammed the White House line and took down the circuits. Half of Washington is blown out by so many calls. People are outraged. We have to stop this man. The number with smallpox at Lost Mine is climbing. It's nearly six hundred already."

"We understand the pilot of the charter changed the flight plan. He told the tower his passengers ordered him not to correct it, but they wanted to go to a different location. He called the tower when the passengers went to sleep. This might be the break we need."

"Stay with them. We're still running down Arab leads here."

They said good-bye and hung up. Duncan checked with the Gulfstream pilot. Minneapolis was only four hundred miles away. Less than an hour. They had left Pierre at 8:30

P.M. They figured the other plane had already landed at Minneapolis, probably before dark.

"The small field at Johnson Air Park has too short a runway for us to land," the pilot said. "I checked with the Minneapolis tower. We'll land at Minneapolis, and then you can rent a car. I'll radio ahead and have a car waiting for you at your parking spot."

It was after ten that evening when Roger and Duncan pulled up to the only building with lights on at Johnson Air Park. It was the manager's office and he was about to close up shop and go home.

"Just glad we don't have landing lights or I'd be here all night," the man said. The man in his fifties introduced himself as Wing Charlie. "Yeah, I used to do some wing walking at the air shows. Legs got too beat up and I don't do it anymore. What can I do for you two boys?"

They asked about the charter that had come in just before dark.

"Yeah, I remember. Don't get many charters. Pilot said he was going into town to a motel."

"You see his passengers?"

"Sure, three Arab gentlemen. Didn't talk much. Asked me to call them a cab. Did. Red Top taxi from here in town. No cab stand out here."

"You have the number of the cab company?" Roger asked. "Like to give them a call." Roger showed the manager his FBI ID and the manager grinned.

"Arabs. FBI. Hey, understand some Arabs killed all those folks out west there with smallpox, that right?"

"No announcement has been made yet about those responsible," Duncan said.

The cab company cooperated. Five minutes after talking with them, Duncan and Roger were on their way to the Citadel, biggest hotel in downtown Minneapolis, where the cab company had taken the three Arabs. The manager gave them directions. Duncan couldn't wait to get there. He tried to make the car go faster, but it didn't help. This was a real shot at nailing these guys and ending this nightmare once and for all. At least for this particular terrorist. He flexed his hands, tightened them into fists, then relaxed them. It didn't help the car go any faster, but it helped to bring his surging blood pressure back under control.

At the hotel the night manager was impressed by the FBI cards.

"Sure, I remember them. We don't get many Arabs here. Three of them, and they took two rooms on the eleventh floor."

"I'd like the room number and a passkey," Duncan said.

"Can give you a passkey, but I'd rather go up with you and open the door for you if they don't want to," the manager said.

"Let's go," Roger said.

On the eleventh floor, Duncan shooed three people out of the hall and they approached the first of the two rooms rented to the Arabs. Duncan knocked. There was no answer. Roger pushed the manager away from the door. Duncan stood to one side and tried the key. It unlocked the door but the dead bolt was thrown inside and the door wouldn't open.

"Open up or I'll kick the door down," Duncan bellowed. A moment later three shots blasted through the door, missing Duncan by a foot. A second after another round thundered past and hit the far hall wall, Roger ran toward the door, jumped, and kicked out, both feet hitting the door on the lock side with his 215 pounds. The inside of the doorframe splintered and the door blasted open. Roger dropped to the floor on hands and knees.

Before Roger could move, Duncan rolled a flash-bang grenade into the room. Two seconds later someone in the room threw the nonlethal noise grenade back into the hall, where it exploded at once.

The surprise move kept Duncan and Roger from pushing their hands over their ears before the grenade went off. The five pulsing explosions and the six strobe lights deafened and blinded the Specialists and the hotel manager for a few moments.

The three Arabs stormed out of the room. They jumped over the two Specialists and charged down the hall to the steps and vanished.

Duncan came out of his blindness first. He still couldn't hear a thing. The manager lay on the hall carpet, moaning and holding his ears.

Duncan shook Roger, who came up blinking. Duncan pointed down the hall. The two Specialists ran that way, then took the elevator down. In the lobby they looked around but saw no Arabs. By that time they could hear a little. They charged out to the street and looked both ways. Duncan ran one way down the sidewalk, and Roger ran the other way. Duncan pounded the walkway, sprinting for a block. He could see no group of three men rushing along. They would be in a hurry. He slowed and checked all the people he could see ahead of him. He hadn't seen the men come out due to the flash-bang, so he didn't have any clothing to look for. He walked a half block, then ran again. He thought of commandeering a car, but he didn't know which way to drive. He circled the block at a jog, checking every pedestrian in sight. None even looked like an Arab. After twenty minutes of futile running and walking, Duncan went back to the hotel.

He found Roger catching his breath in the lobby. He had just called the local FBI office and a team would be over quickly.

Duncan looked up. "Let's search their room." They went back to the eleventh floor. The manager was still sitting on the floor near the terrorists' room. Two employees were helping him. He waved them away and stared at Duncan.

"Was that a grenade?" the manager asked.

Roger explained it to him, then joined Duncan in the Arabs' room. They went over it carefully. Ten minutes later, the local FBI men hurried into the rooms and took over.

The Specialists found fake IDs, twenty thousand dollars in hundred-dollar bills, clothes, and some disguises, but no smallpox canisters. There were two 9mm pistols and a .357 Magnum along with plenty of rounds. The three Arabs had left in such a rush they didn't even stop to pick up their weapons.

"Where are they keeping the rest of the canisters?"

Duncan asked. "They should have seventeen of them left if they used one in Iran."

"Hoped we'd find a hit list with their next target," Roger said.

The FBI experts lifted prints and went over the room for any other evidence. Duncan and Roger sat on the floor outside the room. The manager had opened the second room for the FBI men but there wasn't much in that one either.

The manager pointed to the splintered door. "Can I put in a claim for damages?"

Duncan said he could, but took out his wallet and gave the manager two one-hundred-dollar bills of Mister Marshall's money. "This should cover the damages. If not, send the FBI a bill for the rest of the costs." Duncan grinned. "How did you like our flash-bang grenade?"

"Just as soon not be near any more when they go off," the manager said.

"Not one in a thousand," Roger said. "Never had a flash-bang thrown back at me before. It had to be just right. The grenade must have bounced right into the guy's hand for him to get it back outside that fast."

"Yeah, ninety-nine out of ninety-nine we would have had them down and out and cuffed," Duncan said.

"So, what now?" Roger asked.

"FBI locals put out an APB on the three Arabs. Chances are they'll drive out or fly individually. Driving would be safest for them until they get away from this area. My bet is we won't see them again. I'll check with Wade. My guess is we head the Gulfstream back to La Guardia."

A few minutes later, Duncan put away his digital phone. "My guess was wrong. We stay here for the night and fly back in the morning. Bet we can get a room right here at the hotel." He called the airport and told Roy the pilot that they would be staying overnight. Roy said he'd be ready anytime they were in the morning.

Staying in Minneapolis didn't please Roger. He figured they could be more help back in New York. There was nothing more they could do there. The terrorists had either rented a car and raced out of town, or they had holed up in a hotel somewhere. Not a chance in a million to find the bastards. He still didn't see how those guys had caught the flash-bang and thrown it back. It had a four-and-two-tenth-second fuse. Not long enough to think about it. He shook his head, took a long hot shower, and dived into bed.

The next morning they looked at the local newspaper with surprise. Somebody in the FBI or local police had leaked the story to the newspaper.

ARAB KILLERS IN MINNEAPOLIS!!

The story went on to detail what had happened with the three Arabs who were suspected of being those who dropped the smallpox virus on the two small towns. The mayor of Minneapolis called for the nation to ship four hundred thousand doses of vaccine to Minneapolis-St. Paul at once. "We need to inoculate every person in the metropolitan area," the mayor said. "Those mass murderers were in town. They could have dumped the smallpox virus into our airspace or into our water system. We need the protection now, not when we start coming down with the disease."

The story was complete, including the flash-bang grenade at the hotel and the escape of the three Arabs. They watched the early-morning local news and saw two Arab-run stores that were smashed and looted. Signs of "Arabs Go Home" and "Kill All Arabs" were posted outside the trashed stores. Local authorities were looking for suspects, the anchor said.

Duncan and Roger had breakfast, checked with the pilot, and told him they would be ready to fly out in an hour. They talked with the local FBI, who had no reports of the three Arabs.

"Nothing more here," Roger said. "Let's get back to New York."

They flew out an hour later.

Right after the flash-bang grenade went off, Abdul and his two countrymen rushed out of the hotel, then walked so they wouldn't attract attention. They agreed to meet at another hotel in the city, then each took separate cabs to the hotel, where they registered individually and paid for one night.

In the hotel they all gathered in one room and did as they had agreed. If they were ever seen and identified, they would change their appearance. They began by shaving off their mustaches. Then each had haircuts to American "business" style.

Next they bought supplies at a drugstore and all washed their new short hair and lightened it to a soft brown color. The final task was to temper their Arab skin shade. They used makeup and toned down the color to a much lighter shade. Then they put on sunglasses and were ready. They played it safe, rented a car, and drove south out of Minneapolis on Interstate 35.

WASHINGTON, DC

That same day the Specialists flew back from Minneapolis, a package came into the FBI mail room and was duly sorted and put in a special bin for the director. Every package that comes to the FBI headquarters is inspected. This one was about a foot square and eighteen inches long. The handlers remarked that it was light in weight for its size.

First it went to an X-ray machine that showed a cylindrical object inside made of some metal. The operator scowled, shook the box, then passed it on to his supervisor with the curt note. "Looks like a canister of some kind."

The trigger word, canister, prompted the supervisor to rush the package in a bombproof lead box on a forklift to the basement, where it was quickly put in a bombproof and air-sealed vault in which mechanical hands were manipulated to unwrap the package. It didn't explode when unwrapped.

The pointed aluminum cylinder simply lay on the table. A small probe came from one of the mechanical arms and bored a tiny hole in the aluminum, retracted the drill, and sealed the hole. The drill bit was then put in a sealed container and two men received it in a pass-through box.

"Take this to our biological-warfare section and have any residue on it analyzed," the arm operator instructed.

An hour later they knew what was in the canister: smallpox virus. The canister was transported in an airtight container to the biological testing grounds in rural Virginia, where it was gently placed in a sealed, high-temperature incinerator. The temperature inside would rise to over five thousand degrees, and everything inside would be melted, disintegrated, burned, and reburned. It was the only sure way to kill the virus.

The director was told of the incident.

"Sloppy. Abdul is getting sloppy. This should be the start of the end of his killing ways. He's down to sixteen canisters."

★ TWENTY-SEVEN ★

NEW YORK CITY

Kat paced the situation room in the Marshall Specialist building in lower Manhattan like a caged tiger ready to eat her keeper. It had been two days with almost nothing for her to do and she felt so frustrated that she needed to run a marathon.

"There has to be something we can do," she said again. It was midmorning and the other three Specialists watched her, wondering when she would suggest they go back up to the reservoir for a hundred circuits.

"What have we missed? What could we have checked out better or more or longer? What are the buttons we didn't push looking for leads out there? Take it from the top. Kuwait was where we started the hot trail and that proved useful. Then Kennedy. What didn't we do there?"

Kat reached for her shoulder purse with her side arm inside and tapped her foot a dozen times. "Yes. There has to be something we missed out at that British Air Freight."

"What?" Wade asked.

"I don't know. Something. They were there. They were on the ground. We should have more than we picked up."

Kat turned to Wade. "Let's go back out there and nose around. What can it hurt? We're not doing any good here."

Wade took a deep breath and stared at her. "You're serious."

"Damn serious. What good are we sitting around here?"

"We're on call," Ichi said.

"Yeah on call for what, dinner? Come on, Wade. You come with me and you'll know I'm not cruising for a sailor."

"Right now?" Wade asked.

"When sooner?"

The big Lincoln Town Car steamed into Kennedy nearly an hour later and parked outside British Air Freight. They went inside and told the manager they were back. They wanted to look over the loading dock and talk with the men there again.

"Thought we'd helped you all we could," the manager said. Then he shrugged. "Help yourself."

On the loading dock it looked the way it had last time.

One of the men there had been on duty when the casket was picked up and had talked to them before.

"Hey, the spooks are back," he said.

Kat wagged a finger at him. "Not so, Geronimo. Spooks are CIA. We're FBI."

"Oh, yeah, the good guys. Catch those Arabs yet?"

"Not so you could notice," Wade said. He stared around at the setup, walked through what must have taken place the day the pickup backed into the dock and they let the casket down into the body of the rig with a forklift.

The handler who had been there before watched them. He had a baseball cap that said "Bill" on it. He was about thirty, not more than five-eight, and to Wade looked strong, tough, and wiry.

"You Bill or did you kill Bill and steal his cap?" Wade asked the handler.

He grinned. "I should have. Bill is my brother and, yeah, I stole his cap. He had two so we share." He watched Wade a minute. "Still bugs me, those guys not showing any emotion when they picked up the casket. Me, I've loaded dozens of caskets out of here. Most of the time it's into a funeral-home hearse. Sometimes there are loved ones along and they cry and wail and scream. Yeah. Put a few into pickups but not many. Loading dock ain't made for them. Too high."

The handler shook his head. "These damn guys were like sticks. I mean they didn't even bat an eyelash when they saw the casket or when we finally got it loaded and tied on. Business. It seemed like it was business to them."

Wade kept looking around the place. Kat came up and scowled at him.

"Where is it, Wade? There has to be something here. I know it."

Wade pointed to the far side of the loading area. "Let's change sides. I'll do the far side and you do this side."

"Can't hurt."

Wade prowled the area, visualized the pickup backing in, the men waiting with the casket on a forklift. Then the rig moving the casket down to the edge of the loading dock.

Nothing.

Wade took another deep breath and looked up at the high ceiling in the dock area. Twenty feet up there. Lots of space for tall cargo. Something moved. What? He looked again.

Yes.

"Kat, come over here."

She moved his way. "What is that up there on that beam that keeps swinging back and forth in a slow arc?"

"A closed-circuit surveillance camera," she said. "Where is the manager?"

It was almost twenty minutes later that they found the video from camera two that was shot on the day they needed. Halfway through the scratchy tape played out on a thirty-inch TV screen, they spotted a pickup backing into the dock.

"Nope, wrong one," Bill said. "That one has New York plates and it's black."

Five minutes later Bill waved. "Yep. That's the one. Freeze that frame. Oh, yeah, Jersey plates, what did I tell you? My eyes ain't that good, can you read the plate?"

Nobody could. They let the tape move ahead slowly as the pickup backed closer to the dock. Just before the plate vanished below the lip of the dock, they froze the tape again.

"Yes, I have it," Kat shrilled. She read off what she had written down in her small notebook and Wade agreed.

"Why couldn't we see the two Arab men?" Wade asked. "They had to be in the camera's view."

"They were there," Kat said. "But I could never get a good look at their faces. They could have been anybody."

"At least we have the license on the pickup," Wade said. "Now, how do we get in touch with the New Jersey Motor Vehicles group or whatever they call themselves?"

Bill said one of the handlers lived in New Jersey. He'd know. He did. They phoned for information for the number and soon Kat talked to the motor-vehicle people.

"I'm Kat Killinger, an FBI agent, and we need to get the address on a pickup license plate."

"How do I know you're FBI? You might be somebody trying to get even for a cutoff on the highway."

"I'll give you the number of the New York office and you can call them and confirm. This is important. You want the New York number?"

"No, I guess not. What's the license-plate number?"

It took them over an hour and a half to beat their way through afternoon traffic and get to Manhattan, then another hour across the island and through the tunnel into New Jersey. It was almost four that afternoon when they found the street the New Jersey motor-vehicle man had given them as the registered name and address of the pickup owner. It was in Union City, right across from the Lincoln Tunnel.

"Looking for 4315," Kat reminded the driver. A block later he pulled up.

"This is 4325. Should be two or three houses down," Harry, their driver today, told them.

"Guy's name is Joe Ali Akbar," Kat said. "Let's go see what he has to say."

The man who answered the door looked like an Arab.

"Ali Akbar?" Wade asked.

"Yes." He stood at the open door looking through an aluminum screen door.

"You own an eighty-nine Ford pickup?" Wade asked.

"Yes. I loaned it to a friend. Was he in an accident?"

"Not that we know of; do you have the pickup here?"

"It's in the side yard."

"Could we see it?" Kat asked.

"Are you policemen?"

Wade showed him his FBI card.

"Oh, FBI? Never met one of you people before. The truck, right back here." He came out the screen door and went to the side of the house.

The Ford pickup was in a driveway beside the house. It had the same license tag as the one in the video.

"Who did you loan the rig to?" Kat asked.

"A guy I know, Larry Hoseini."

"Is he an Arab?"

"Yes, from Syria. Why? What did he do with my truck?"

"You don't need to know that, Mr. Ali Akbar. We may send some people out tomorrow to look it over. Will it be here?"

"Usually I drive it to work."

"Leave it here tomorrow."

"Are you looking for an Arab?"

"Yes."

"I know several who live in this area. We have an Arab-American Friendship club. Would you like to go there?"

"We've been to several in this area. Is this one different?"

"I don't know. We gather, talk about home, help each other get jobs, a kind of club."

"We'd like to go," Kat said. "Will there be people there now?"

"Oh yes. Let me get my hat."

They arrived at the New Jersey Arab-American Friendship League. It was in an unused store that had been cleaned up and adapted.

Twenty men stood around in groups, or sampled the punch. It looked like any other community group. This one was made up of all Arab men. Some of the men came and shook hands with Kat and Wade. Then Wade was asked to talk to three men at the far side of the room. He walked over there. Twice he looked back at Kat. She was talking with the man they came with. Then one of the Arab men began recounting the wrongs the United States had done against Syria and Iraq.

Wade waited his chance to reply.

At the other end of the hall, Kat had just answered a question that Ali Akbar asked her when she sensed someone close behind her. Then in an instant she was grabbed and a cloth forced over her nose and mouth. Her arms were pinned to her sides. She couldn't scream. She couldn't get to her weapon. She knew the smell of chloroform. She couldn't get away from it. She struggled, then she had to breathe. She knew she shouldn't. At last she gulped in air and chloroform. Then the lights dimmed and she collapsed in the man's arms.

Wade had just defended the U.S. for two or three minutes. When he looked back, Kat wasn't in the room. He hurried to where she had been. He didn't see the man they came with.

"Where is the woman I came here with?" he demanded loudly. All talk quieted. One man shook his head.

"Ain't never no women in here. This is men's place."

"What the hell you mean? You all saw me come in here with Kat. Now what have you done with her?" He grabbed the man who spoke and slammed him against the wall, his fist full of shirt and holding the Arab fast.

"Where is she?"

"Don't know what you mean," the man said in Arabic.

"The hell you don't know," Wade shot back at him in Arabic. Then he pushed the man away and charged around the hall. There was only one other door. He slammed through it but found nothing there but a table and chairs.

Wade stormed back into the main room. He picked up

a chair and smashed it into the floor, breaking off three of the legs. He held one of the broken legs and waved it at the men.

"You'll tell me where she is or half of you are going to be picking your brains up off the floor."

Half the men darted out the door and escaped. Two eased that way. Wade charged the last four, but they evaded him. He really wasn't trying to hit them, just scare them. One of the men held up his hand.

"Stop that right now, or I'll call the police."

Wade snorted. "Good, call them, be sure they get here before I brain the rest of you."

The man stared at Wade, then produced a cell phone and dialed a number. Wade ignored him and searched the rest of the building. There was no place they could be hiding Kat. She simply wasn't there.

He went back to the man with the phone. "You look like the leader of this riffraff. What have you done with Kat? It's kidnapping, you know. I'll charge all of you still here with kidnapping."

Three of the last four men faded out the door. Wade stared hard at the remaining man. Before he could demand to see the man's identification, a Union City police officer walked in the door.

"What seems to be the trouble here?" he asked.

Wade showed him his FBI credentials.

"This man just kidnapped an FBI Special Agent. He won't tell me where they have taken her." He explained the situation quickly.

The cop grinned. "I've never had a kidnapping before."

"I need your help. I want you to cuff this man and arrest him on a charge of kidnapping a federal officer. Hold him until one of our people can come collect him."

"Yes, I can do that."

The Arab man screamed in fury. "This man is a liar. This is a man's club. No women are permitted."

The cop shrugged. He handcuffed the Arab and led him

out the door. "You can tell your story to a judge. If you ever see one."

Wade scoured the building again, then walked out and left the lights on. He wasn't going to go far away until he found Kat Killinger. Where could she be? Where had they taken her?

⋆ TWENTY-EIGHT ⋆

UNION CITY, NEW JERSEY

The whole world was a black hole.

The black hole had a roaring headache.

How can a black hole have a headache?

One eye slid open reluctantly. The view was still black but now with shades of gray. The other eye popped open.

Kat moaned and felt her face against the cold wooden floor.

What the hell?

Slowly it came back to her. The Arab-American Friendship League meeting hall. The sudden grab from behind, the cloth over her mouth and nose. A struggle not to breathe.

"Oh damn," Kat said. She pushed hard to sit up. Her hands were tied in front of her. She worked at them. Sloppy job. They must figure she'd be unconscious longer. Wooden floor. No purse, no weapon, no penlight. A thin shaft of pale night light oozed in a shadeless window.

Empty. The room she had been left in was bare except for one old wooden chair. An apartment? Where? Kat kept working on the thin rope around her wrists. She bent and pulled at the loops with her teeth. Yes, better, one strand was loose. She worked at it more, got another loop loosened, then pulled the second end free. A moment later she had her wrists untied. The necktie wrapped around her ankles came loose quickly. Then Kat tried to stand, got to her knees, and almost passed out. Damned chloroform. Dizzy. She sat down and waited a minute, then tried again. This time she pushed up to her knees and onto her feet.

At least she was still dressed. She held her hands in front of her for balance and direction and moved slowly toward the window. Yes. Better. The window looked out on an alley. Three floors down. No help there.

The headache drilled a pattern of agony through her skull.

Damn chloroform.

Now her eyes widened to take in all the light possible. She could make out the far wall and a door. Locked? She walked toward it and found she was moving better. Not a hundred percent, but better.

She tried the knob. It was locked. The door was a hollow-core kind, flimsy if you hit it right. She looked at the chair. Kat picked up the chair and slammed the two back legs down hard on the floor. One broke off. It was two inches square and two feet long. She picked it up and hefted it. Yes. She went to the door and began pounding at the thin panel of wood over the doorframe opposite the door lock. It took twenty blows and her hands ached before she shattered the thin wood. Then she worked on the outside panel. It broke off much easier. Gingerly she reached through and found the door handle. Yes, a turn-and-lock type. She turned it gently and heard the lock snick open. The door swung outward.

The hallway angled away from her door. At the far end she could see an opening where steps must go down. A small night-light bulb glowed at the head of the stairs. Convenient. Where was her guard? They wouldn't just trust to some cord and a locked door.

Kat peered down the hall again. Any guard on this level would have heard her pounding on the door. So, maybe downstairs. She moved down the hall without a sound. She still carried her trusty chair leg.

Kat moved into the hall, walking, looking into each empty room that she passed. Evidently it was a vacant apartment house. Probably due for destruction. She tested the steps. No reaction. Gently she moved down the stairs to the second, then the first floor. The front door stood open two inches. Why? Light came from a streetlamp outside the windows. It was a small lobby. Kat studied the faintly lit lobby. At first she saw no one, then on the far side, in a chair leaned back against the wall, she saw a figure. A man who looked asleep. She watched him for three minutes. He didn't move. No book, no radio . . . He was sleeping. She stepped across the floor soundlessly on the ancient carpet. He was sleeping. She lifted the chair leg and slammed it against the top of his head hard enough to knock him out.

The man half lifted off the chair, he tried to say something, then he collapsed on the chair and tumbled off to the floor. She frisked him quickly. No gun. She went to the half-open outside door and checked the scene she could see.

A car sat at the curb directly in front of the building. She thought she saw two men inside. The dome light was on. The near window was down. One man sat there reading a book. The other one was sleeping. She edged the door open an inch at a time. The reader in the driver's seat would have to turn his head to see her.

Kat slid through the door and stepped softly, angling to the rear of the car. Once there, she took a deep breath and hefted the chair leg. It would have to do.

Inch by inch she moved along the car's side until she was almost even with the front door's open window. She had been squatting, to stay below the window level. Now she lifted up, holding the chair leg in both hands over her left shoulder.

The reader sensed her presence and turned to look out the window. She swung the club. It smashed hard into his forehead and drove him back against the seat. He shook his head once, then it lolled to the left against the seat back as he passed out. The sleeper went right on snoring softly. She went around to the passenger's side door. The window was down. She leaned in and checked the sleeping man's pockets. No pistol. She jolted the chair leg into the sleeper's throat and held it there with both hands as he woke up.

"What the hell?"

"True, where you're headed if you try to move. You do what I tell you, or I'll ram this wood against your throat, crushing your larynx. You'll be dead in two minutes."

The Arab nodded slowly.

"First, where are we? Is this still Union City?"

"Yes."

"Do you know where Ali Akbar lives?"

"Yes."

"Move down and sit on the floor, cross your arms behind you, and lean back on them."

"Sit on the floor?"

"Yes, unless you want to test out a new throat and voice box." The man moved slowly. She pulled the club away from his throat and held it over his head, ready to strike with it. He whined as he slid to the floor and put his arms behind him.

"Stay that way, or I'll rattle your brains with this chair leg." Kat ran around the car quickly, jerked open the driver's door, and pulled out the still-unconscious driver and dumped him on the street. The man on the floor hadn't moved. She got in the car and saw the keys were in the ignition.

"Tell me how to drive to Ali Akbar or you're a dead man."

Ten minutes later she pulled the car to a stop in front of the house they had been at before, where Ali Akbar lived.

"Don't move," she told the man on the passenger's side floor. "I'm coming around the car."

The moment she stepped out of the driver's side, the man on the floor surged up, opened the passenger's side door, leaped out of the car, and ran like his shoes were on fire and he was heading for a river.

Kat paused beside the car and watched him fade into the darkness. She looked at the house and began working on a plan how to get inside and what she would do when she found Ali Akbar. He must have come home after they kidnapped her. He would be sleeping, sure she was dead.

Kat walked to the sidewalk and started toward the back

door when she heard a car coming. She froze against the side of the house. The car stopped in front of the house and the lights shut off. Kat looked around the corner and saw a familiar figure in the dim light running toward her.

"Wade, over here," Kat said softly.

The runner heard her and hurried to the side of the house.

"Thank God, you're all right," Wade said.

"I'll tell you about it later. When I got free I figured Ali baby here knows a lot more than he told us."

"Me too. I figured he'd know where they had taken you. Now we can have a chat with him about Abdul." They walked to the back of the house. Wade worked on the simple rear-door lock a moment and had it open.

They found Ali in the bedroom on the first floor. Wade clamped his hand over the man's mouth and dragged him from the bed without waking the woman beside him. Wade carried him into the kitchen and on outside to the back of the yard. Ali Akbar wore only boxer shorts.

Wade put him down and slapped his face gently on both sides.

"Ali, we're going to have a long talk. How much fun it will be for you depends how well you answer my questions. Do you understand?"

"Yeah, sure."

Wade put all of his weight behind the sudden right fist that slammed into the Arab's jaw. It knocked him down. He sat on the ground wailing. Wade went to his knees in front of the weeping man.

"Look, asshole. This Abdul character you're protecting has killed over three hundred Americans. At least two hundred more will die from what he did out in Wyoming."

"I didn't know."

Wade hit him again; this time Wade heard his jawbone crack. Ali Akbar screeched in pain and passed out. Wade brought him back to consciousness by gently shaking him. When he came to he screamed. Wade held his hand over the man's mouth.

"Listen to me, killer of women and children. You're as

bad as he is. You revel in it. Now comes the question and no lie. Tell me his next target for the smallpox virus."

Wade let his hand off the Arab's mouth. "No. He'd kill me if I told."

"He'd have to find you first. We have you. What do you think we'll do with you right here, right now, if you don't tell us? We'll slit your throat and let you bleed out. You want that?"

Ali Akbar shook his head.

"Then talk. The next target."

"I don't know."

Wade picked up the Arab's right arm and holding wrist and elbow, smashed it down across his raised knee, shattering both arm bones. Ali screamed for a moment before he passed out.

It was ten minutes before the Arab came back to the conscious world. He moaned and babbled. He held his right arm with his left hand, his eyes pleading with them.

"Yes. I know the three towns. Clear Lake, Iowa, Columbus, Nebraska, and Broomfield, Colorado. Now get my jaw and my arm fixed. Take me to a hospital."

Wade helped him stand and walked him to the Marshall Lincoln they had come in. Kat helped get the man in the backseat, then Wade used his phone and called Mister Marshall. He glanced at his watch. Three-fifteen in the morning.

"Marshall here."

"Mister Marshall, Wade. We have news. Tracked the pickup and found a guy who knows a lot. Bringing him in. He knows the next three targets for the smallpox." Wade repeated them to Mister Marshall.

"Maybe we can stop him this time. I'll get the FBI and the Air Force on this one right away. You better get back to the HQ here and get some rest. We'll have a lock room for our guest. Will we need a doctor?"

"Yes, some plaster casts will be needed and maybe some pins for some jaw work."

"We'll be ready. Your ETA?"

"Harry says about forty-five minutes this time of morning. See you soon."

By the time Wade and Kat and their guest arrived at the downtown Specialists' HQ, the company wheels were turning. The same doctor they had seen before met them at the medical room, where they put their patient on a hospital bed and handcuffed both legs to the iron rails.

"This guy fell down the stairs," Wade said. The young doctor scowled at him and went to work.

Upstairs in the situation room, Mister Marshall was up, dressed, and talking on the phone. He hung up and smiled.

"Progress. The CSG is working. The FAA will ban all civilian flights at and around the three small towns. They have talked the Air Force into putting an AWACS planes over each of the towns in a 'coordinated exercise' to watch for any incursions. Atlanta will have thousands of doses of vaccines flown into each town by daylight today. Mass inoculations have been ordered.

"In connection with the Air Force exercise, they will also have rotating CAP fighters flying over the three towns. They will be F-18s with full combat loads of rockets and 20mm rounds. Oh, also a DEST team has been assigned to each town and will be in place by noon today."

Wade grinned. "When you get your dander up, things get done out there," Wade said.

Mister Marshall shook his head and sat down. "Afraid it wasn't me. I just lit the fuse. All of this is from the FBI and the CSG operation. Just shows you that big government can get into action fast when it has to."

Kat and Wade were too jazzed up by that time to go to bed. They had cups of hot chocolate and dozed on the two couches. Mister Marshall went to sleep with his head on his arms sitting at his desk.

Wade came awake when the traffic sounds and the hum of city hit him about six. He had coffee and met Roger and

Ichi, who were the early risers in the group. Wade filled them in on the developments overnight.

Kat came back to reality a half hour later. She vanished to her room for a quick shower and change of clothes and a hair comb. She came back looking ready for business.

By eight the whole crew was on hand, and Mister Marshall was looking better. He tightened his tie, combed his gray hair, and checked out the fax machine and the Internet. He had no mail. When the rest of the team members were briefed, they turned on the TV set to see what CNN had to say.

They knew about the ban on flying in or around the three towns, and that there would be some Air Force "exercises" nearby, but they didn't know what they would be. The announcer took some leaps of logic and came close.

"We have asked our experts and they say that this is a function of the federal government through a group known as the Coordinating Sub Group. It comes from the deputy secretaries of all the departments and important agencies. It coordinates operations on emergencies by all government agencies."

"Abdul should back off on these three," Wade said. "He must listen to the news and knows that his secrecy is blown this time. No way he'll try for any of those towns."

A half hour later, word came in from the FBI that the AWACS plane over Columbus, Nebraska, had tracked a small light plane that was by then within twenty miles of Columbus.

The FBI Director Vincent talked with Mister Marshall. "We sent in the two F-18 fighters and they did flybys so close it almost made the Piper Cub stall out. Then they fired the twenty mike-mike across the prop of the little plane and it turned around and rushed out of the area heading east. We had given explicit instructions not to shoot down any plane that tried to break in. Didn't want to scatter any virus that might be on board."

"So, did the AWACS plane keep on tracking the intruder?"

"Oh, yes, and the F-18s found it just as it landed at a little dirt strip south of Omaha. Trouble is, we had no people in that area. By the time we contacted the local sheriff and he got men out to the landing strip, the Arab from the plane had hauled ass out of there and we never did find the car he used."

"So we scared him but he's still on the loose."

"Yes, but we hit the jackpot on the rented plane. Inside we found a batch of papers in Arabic we're going to translate, and three of the canisters with dynamite and detonators attached. We've had them defanged and sealed in airtight containers, waiting instructions from the DEST people."

"I'd say we won one there, Vincent."

"More like a draw. At least we nailed down three of the canisters."

"But where is the bastard going to strike next? That's our main problem now."

The FBI director was silent for a moment. "Just a minute, I'm getting something from that airstrip. Some of our guys are on-site now. Yeah, go ahead."

"Mr. Director. Looks like we might have a break. The guy who rented the plane to the Arab, said he had light brown hair now, cut short, and with a paler skin than most Arabs. He also said when the guy left so fast without even checking the plane in, the operator took down the license plate on the guy's car. We have it solid. Checking now with the Nebraska state auto people. Our guess is that the car came out of Omaha. This could be our big break. Most car-rental agencies are nuts about a firm, real home address for the renter. Most make them prove it at least two ways. Be hard for him to fake that. He might have used some actual home-base address. Will let you know soonest."

"So, Marshall, maybe a break. I'll keep you in touch."

Mister Marshall said good-bye and hung up. He dialed again. "Willard. Get the jet checked out and do your preflight. We could be going on a trip this afternoon."

★ TWENTY-NINE ★

Ichi looked around the table. "Shouldn't we be getting ready to travel?"

Wade shook his head. "From right here, we're three hours from Omaha. The FBI has an office there, men on the turf. If they get a hot address from that rental car, they will be all over the place like fleas on an old coon dog. It will go down before we could get out there. This is the FBI's baby."

"Let's hope they nail Abdul, the rest of his men, and the last of the canisters," Kat said.

Roger looked up. "Hey, Kat. Hear you've been playing footsie with the Arabs again."

"For a while. When things get dull I'll tell you about it."

"Couldn't be much duller than right now," Duncan said.

Kat told them about her kidnapping and eventual escape.

"At least we found the pickup and saved those three small towns a smallpox-virus bath," Kat said.

It was a half hour before the phone rang. Mister Marshall put it on the speaker.

"Marshall here."

"Marshall, good. Vincent. Our men did get a good address from that Omaha car-rental agency. We have two teams moving in now backed up with Omaha PD. It's a small house out in the suburbs a ways, a little isolated. We won't shoot unless absolutely necessary. We don't want to punch holes in any canisters if they are in the house."

"Good thinking, Vincent. Wish we could help you, but we're too far away. I hope your men close this out right there today."

"We hope so, too. The one thing worries me is that this jasper has had about a three-hour jump on us. He could be into the wilderness now and the damn house vacant."

"On the other hand you might nail him with the rest of the canisters and close this one up tight. Good luck." They signed off.

"So?" Roger said.

"So we sit and wait, or we go chat with our little Arab friend from New Jersey," Kat said. "I bet he knows more than he told us."

"Can we use the needle?" Wade asked.

Mister Marshall rubbed his face with his right hand. "We never have. Is this the time we start? Is it worth it?"

"If Abdul gets away, I'd say we give the needle a try," Duncan said. "It isn't all that bad. My other employer used it a lot."

"So did we at the CIA," Mister Marshall said. "I've always held the practice in disfavor."

"At least we can think about it," Hershel said. "I've been on more than a dozen question-and-answer sessions with the juice."

The phone rang and Anne from the front desk asked if they wanted to order lunch. Two did, the rest didn't.

A half hour later the phone rang again.

"Marshall here."

"Yes, this is Vincent."

He put it on the speaker. "How did it go?"

"Wrapping it up. We collared three men. Abdul had been gone a half hour by the time we sealed off the place. He's in a car somewhere and we don't know the plates. It wasn't much of a shoot-out. Only one of their men fired. He took four rounds to the chest and expired. The other three threw out their weapons and marched out quiet as little lambs.

"We found ten canisters still in their airtight envelopes.

You told us he started with twenty from Odessa. By our count, that leaves only three outstanding. The bastard must have them with him. This was his home base. We've got maps and cash and passports. We found no clue where he might go or where he might hit next."

"We have one of the Arabs from Abdul's local support group in our medical unit," Mister Marshall said. "He gave us the information on the three cities. Do you want him?"

"Absolutely."

"Will you use the needle on those three you caught?"

"Absolutely. It's now under way. We need everything we can get any way we can get it."

"Do you want to give the drug to the Arab we have here at our place?"

"I'll tell our men to use the truth serum on him over there."

They hung up.

"It's out of our hands," Mister Marshall said.

The large-screen TV set in the room had been tuned to CNN but with the sound off. Duncan let out a yelp and made a lunge for the set and turned on the sound.

"Be damned," Ichi said.

The sound came up and they saw Abdul, this time with large sunglasses, a fake beard, and mustache.

" . . . so I repeat what I said before. The Great Evil will suffer greatly and will scream and moan but will know the pain of a million deaths all because your government cheated our nations, lied to our leaders, and stole billions of dollars of oil from us without even a thank-you.

"Now is the time for retribution. Now is the time for payback. The Sword of Allah will swing again, and the mighty shall be brought to their knees. The Great Evil will suffer even as the Arab states have suffered at your hands.

"Yes, smallpox. Three of your large cities will be visited tonight. My people will drop the smallpox virus on them, and there is nothing you can do to stop us. What cities? There is no time to get ready. Anytime after dark these cities will be baptized with the deadly smallpox virus.

Those places are Baltimore, Las Vegas, and Portland, Oregon. Get ready, your fate is sealed. It is now almost noon. You have little time left to flee."

The picture cut off. The sound continued with screaming and yelling, two gunshots could be heard before the feed to the networks was cut off.

Moments later an anchor-type-looking man came on the air.

"This is Charles Monnet, from KEXO in Littlesburg, Iowa. That was the real thing you just heard. One of our station guards was wounded in the shooting. The two gunmen got away. Our guard is not seriously wounded. The tape you just saw was made only minutes before it was broadcast. That means the perpetrators have had about a half hour head start on the Littlesburg police. We are located about forty miles from the Iowa/Nebraska border just off Interstate 80. We return you now to your regularly scheduled programming."

"Bluff?" Mister Marshall asked after he snapped off the TV.

"Absolutely," Wade said. "But it's going to create panic in the streets of those three cities. It's a bluff nobody wants to call. If you're wrong, thousands will die."

"But we know he has only three canisters left," Kat said. "He doesn't have that many people to be in those cities."

"We know that, and the FBI can broadcast denials that the cities will be hit, but it won't do much good," Hershel said. "I'd bet the FBI is working on some television time right now."

Wade looked at his watch. "One-fifteen. It won't be dark in those cities for hours yet. I'd bet the panic has started and the roads and highways out of town will be clogged with traffic within two hours."

"What can we do?" Kat asked.

"Not a damn thing," Roger said. "We're too far away; and what could we do if we were there?"

"No, I mean what can we do here?"

"We could talk to Ali Akbar before the FBI come to give him the needle," Wade said.

They all stood at once and headed out the door.

Ali Akbar sat up in the hospital bed in the medic room. His feet were still handcuffed to the iron bed rail. One arm sported a white-plaster cast. His face showed several bandages. He could talk but not plainly.

"Get him away," Ali Akbar whimpered when he saw Wade.

Kat took the lead. "Ali, that man is the most gentle and easygoing person in our group. You should see the others when they really get angry."

He frowned past the bandages, his black eyes staring at Kat.

"Don't let him hurt me."

"Ali, why would he hurt you? You told us part of what you know. Now we want the rest of it."

"Nothing more. They didn't trust me."

"He threatened on a TV broadcast to dump smallpox on Portland, Oregon, Baltimore, and Las Vegas. That's a bluff, isn't it?"

"He didn't tell me."

Wade took a step toward the injured man. Ali surged away from him to the other side of the bed, crying out from the pain as he hit his arm on the bed rail.

"I talk only to the woman," Ali Akbar said.

Kat looked at the others and nodded. They left the room. Wade was last one out. "You hurt this lady, I'll come back and kill you."

The Arab glared at Wade.

"Some men are coming with long needles. Do you know what barbiturate thiopental sodium is?"

"I call it sodium pentathol, truth serum."

"Those men from the head FBI office here in New York are coming to work on you. Save yourself some pain by telling me, now."

"Tell what?"

"What is Abdul's real objective? What big city does he want to hit? Washington, DC, or New York City?"

Ali Akbar watched her, then looked away, his mouth a tight, thin line.

Kat walked up to the bed and touched his left arm.

"Looks like you have one arm ready for Wade to give a treatment. Shall I call him in?"

"No," Ali Akbar said, sweat edging down from his forehead into his face bandage.

"Is it Washington, DC?"

"I . . . I . . . I just don't know. Abdul never told me. He didn't trust me."

"Wade, could you come in here, please?" Kat called toward the door. Wade pushed through the door and stood watching the Arab.

"We might jog Ali's memory if his arms were evened up. His left one makes him unbalanced. What do you think?"

Wade smiled and moved toward the bed.

"I still don't know. He didn't tell me."

Kat held up her hand and Wade stopped. "I can hypnotize you, and you'll remember everything from the time you were three."

"No one has ever been able to hypnotize me. Many have tried."

"I haven't tried," Kat said.

The door opened and Mister Marshall stepped inside. "The FBI men are here," he said.

Shortly four men entered the room. One was short wearing a white medical lab coat and holding a black bag. Two of the men in suits were over six feet four inches.

"This the one?" the doctor asked.

"He's all yours," Kat said. "Oh, the cast and bandages. He fell down some stairs. His jaw is broken so he talks a little strange."

"We're in no rush," the doctor said.

"May I stay?" Kat asked.

"We have no secrets," the doctor said. "Do you know how to use a syringe?"

"Not really."

The doctor put his bag on a chair, opened it, and took out a tray with six syringes on it and a pair of small vials. The middle-sized man of the team stepped up to Kat and held out his hand.

"I'm Mizolara. I'll be doing the talking. Thanks for finding this one for us."

Mister Marshall left along with Wade and they took the rest of the Specialists back to the situation room. Wade snapped on the TV set tuned for CNN.

". . . that's the situation in Baltimore. Las Vegas looks like a laid-back place, but feelings are running high there. Schools have been let out early. It is a little after 10:30 A.M. here, Pacific Time. Churches will remain open. Two of the huge casinos have closed down and sent the gamblers, show people, employees, and guards all home. Traffic in Las Vegas has already reached the 'rush hour' level and authorities here say it will be gridlock within two hours.

"All local, county, and state police have been ordered to traffic duty to try to keep the cars and buses moving. It's still morning here, well before the threatened bombing, but residents are worried and close to the panic stage. Thousands of people have been seen walking along highways and streets leading out of town. They are moving mainly to the west, since any wind drift of the virus would be to the east with prevailing winds."

PORTLAND, OREGON

It was a little after 11:30 A.M. and already traffic heading out of Portland was like a parking lot. Traffic crawled, but a police officer standing beside his patrol car knew that the situation could only get worse. He bellowed at a motorist who was heading the wrong way down a one-way street. The man gave him the finger and kept going. Traffic was at a standstill heading in the other direction a block over.

Up the street half a block three teenagers with long hair and double layers of hand-me-down clothes eyed a jewelry-store window. One slid a brick inside his loose-fitting shirt. The other one had a small hammer, and the third a fist-sized rock. They walked slowly toward the entrance, then went inside.

Without a word the three ran to different glass display

cases and smashed the glass tops. An alarm went off. Tear gas flooded from two vents in the ceiling, filling the small store with a cloud of the thick, white smokelike gas.

The three teens grabbed what watches and jewelry they could see, and bolted out the door, eyes smarting and running. They sprinted down the block while the owner and employees hurried out of the store to escape the tear gas. The owner locked the front door and rubbed his eyes.

Half a block the other direction six Mexican youths watched a small computer store. Then they all sauntered in, bellowed at the clerks to drop to the floor. Then the six grabbed expensive computers and rushed out the door, two with plug-in cords trailing along behind.

The clerks ran out after them but lost them in a wave of people who had just been released from work and were rushing toward parking areas and garages.

By three o'clock the Burnside Bridge was clogged with cars going each way but none of them moving. All the bridges over the Willamette River, which splits Portland in half, had been closed down by police. Traffic along the freeways out of town was still moving, but on-ramps were crowded and the speed on the freeways slowed to twenty miles an hour.

An AWACS plane that had been on duty over Omaha had been diverted to station over Portland.

National Guard fighter aircraft took off from the joint civilian-military Portland Municipal Airport and patrolled the skies over Portland. Small planes heading toward Portland were warned by the tower to find alternate landing fields. No local small aircraft were permitted to take off.

Portland's mayor went on local TV stations at 4 P.M. and tried to calm the public. But Portland was on the move, by any means possible. By five that afternoon, traffic out of Portland in any direction was hopeless. Police estimated that more than two hundred thousand cars were hopelessly jammed in the Portland streets, highways, and freeways. Nothing could be done about it. Police guessed that at least 20 percent of those cars had been abandoned, as the owners and passengers decided to see how far they could walk before the bomb fell.

NEW YORK CITY

The Specialists watched the TV set as CNN brought word on the third threatened city, Baltimore. Baltimore, in the Eastern Time Zone, did not react with panic the way the other two towns did. The highways were busy going out of town, but it looked like a holiday weekend. Few cars were abandoned. Looting in two small areas was short-lived when one looter was shot and killed by police and word traveled fast in the poor neighborhoods. The mayor went on TV congratulating the town and assuring everyone that this was nothing more than an empty threat by a criminal terrorist who was quickly running out of options and would soon be caught.

"The FBI has told us that AWACS planes will be over each of the threatened cities well before dark, and that all civilian aircraft will be banned from the area around and over the three cities. They said the Air Force will conduct exercises over the cities on practice alerts."

Hershel frowned and rubbed his chin. "What's so different about Baltimore?"

Before anyone could answer, Mister Marshall took a phone call on the intercom line. He smiled with grim resignation. "The CIA doctor with his needles is through with his work. One of the FBI men is coming up to talk with us. He knows what Abdul's big-city target is."

⋆ THIRTY ⋆

NEW YORK CITY

The Specialists stared at each other, listened to the CNN report of rioting in Portland, and waited. Ichi lit a cigarette and quickly put it out. He was trying to stop smoking without much success.

Wade walked to the situation-room door and opened it. Almost at once Agent Mizolara hurried in. He was the shorter of the three agents and the one who handled the questioning.

"Well, we know. The man said Abdul talked about nothing but New York City in his tirades. He said Abdul would take the best target he could get here. He listed a sports stadium packed with fans, the subway system where victims would be trapped, or the Empire State Building."

"Did he say which one he liked the best?" Kat asked.

"We'll have more data from the three men in Omaha. I've called, but haven't had their information yet. From what this man said, Abdul wanted the place where he could have the largest possible number of people."

"That should rule out the subway," Wade said. "Even Times Square doesn't involve huge numbers of people at any one time."

"Yankee Stadium filled with fans is something like fifty-seven thousand," Roger said. "Would he try for an airburst from a plane?"

"How many people work in the Empire State

Building?" Duncan asked. "Probably at least twenty thousand. If not that many, they are all trapped in there with no way to get out. That's a closed-atmosphere building, right? No windows open. The whole thing is heated and cooled by fans from the basement somewhere."

"If he got to the air-conditioning system . . ." Hershel said.

"Yeah, the air-inlet ducts . . ." Ichi said.

A cell phone buzzed.

"Mine," Mizolara said. He took out his small phone and raised the antenna. He listened for a moment, then said something the others didn't hear and turned back.

"The three captives in Omaha were questioned separately. One of them listed Yankee Stadium as one of Abdul's targets. The other two said he was most interested in the Empire State Building."

"I've phoned our agent in charge here. He knows the three potential targets. He told me that he appreciates your aid, and that you can pick the target you want to help protect. He's working out his strategy now."

"Did the other men say if Abdul had a time schedule for the targets?" Mister Marshall asked.

"None of the four mentioned any timing. By now we must have upset any timetable he had. My boss says we start protecting those targets as soon as we can. The subway will come first since it's a target at almost any time, but morning rush hour would be the most populated time."

"There's a Yankee game tomorrow night against the Red Sox," Roger said.

"Empire State Building would be a target anytime during the workday," Kat said. "Midmorning, or midafternoon when the most workers would be there, would be the prime time for a hit."

The Specialists looked at each other.

"Let's work at the Empire State Building," Hershel said.

The rest of them chimed in with their agreement.

Mizolara started for the door. "I'll be in touch or someone will. I'll tell our agent in charge your preference. I'd guess we'll start covering the big terminals of the subway as early as rush hour this afternoon. Times Square at least. I better get moving." He waved and hurried out the door.

"So," Mister Marshall said, "we shouldn't have any assignment until tomorrow morning when we get into the tall building and check out any possible air-intake systems for their air-conditioning systems. There must be several sections."

"We'll find out," Wade said.

"Weapons?" Ichi asked.

"Side arms and MP-5s," Wade said. "Give us the best results in that restricted area. Now, let's get ready in case we have an early call."

RIDGEFIELD, NEW JERSEY

Abdul and Hashemi rented a car in Ridgefield and headed for Manhattan. They crossed the George Washington Bridge and drove south on the Henry Hudson Parkway, then over to Broadway and found a subway entrance. They parked and walked down the steps to the entrance stanchions and looked around.

"Where are all the people?" Abdul asked.

"Maybe this is the slow time of day," Hashemi said.

"But even if the station was crowded, there could only be a few hundred people."

"We could ride it and watch for a larger station," Hashemi said.

Abdul agreed. Hashemi was one of the smartest of his men. He had been with him for three years now. They were like brothers. He wondered why he hadn't heard from any of his men in Omaha. He had called them three or four times on the digital phone, but nobody answered.

Abdul pointed toward the ticket booth where they bought tokens and discovered they needed only one in the slot to get through. They took what Abdul saw was a downtown train.

For an hour they rode up and down the Broadway line. At Times Square station they got off and looked around.

"Lots of people here at rush hour," Hashemi said.

"Yes, but no more than two or three thousand. We need more. Where is this Yankee Stadium?"

They asked three people before they found two who gave them the same directions. They had to go back uptown on the subway to 145th Street, take the bus across the Harlem River into the Bronx to Grand Street. They couldn't miss it.

They got off the subway where they began their journey and found their rented car. From there it was easy to drive to 145th and across it into the area they called the Bronx. They found Yankee Stadium. They drove around it and stopped in the parking lot and tried to get a guided tour, but the ticket seller said there was no tour today, but the gates would open at five-fifteen for the seven-thirty game with the Red Sox.

Pictures on the wall outside showed the seating arrangements and where your ticket would let you sit. Abdul stared at the charts for several minutes. He was looking at the aisles, the tunnels, and walkways to exit the stadium. It was far too small for a good soccer game. It said it seated 57,545. Stadiums in Europe would seat over a hundred thousand. Still, 57,545 would make the Great Evil swallow a deadly pill.

They walked around the ticket-selling area, then saw a gate with a guard out front.

"Sure would like to get a look at the field," Abdul said.

"Sorry, no one allowed. Not long before the gates will open."

"How about a small favor for some tourists. We might not be able to get back for the game. Sure wish we could get in."

Abdul took a hundred-dollar bill from his pocket and folded it four times. He held out his hand, holding

the bill with his thumb. "Could we at least shake?" he
asked the guard. The man looked around, saw no one
watching, and shook Abdul's hand. The hundred-dollar
bill vanished into the guard's pocket. He turned and
opened the gate.

"Go in and take a look around, but don't go anywhere
near the players' area. You have ten minutes. Remember
where this gate is. You got to be back here in ten or I could
get fired."

"Oh, we'll be back," Abdul said.

They slipped through the narrow opening of the door and
hurried down a corridor to where they could see the seats and
the field. It looked huge, with thousands of seats. But the exit
flow of people would be terrible. Any small panic and nobody would get out. That would be good.

"How can we detonate the canisters in here and get the
coverage we need?" Hashemi asked.

"A problem, I'm working on it."

They walked one way, then the other, and Abdul looked
at his watch.

"We better run for that exit." They knocked once on
the door and it slid open and they squirmed through, then
it shut at once. The guard lifted his brows and wiped
sweat off his forehead.

"Damn, didn't think you would make it. Cutting it kind
of close for me. Now get out of here."

As they walked back toward their car, both men
thought over the stadium layout.

"Too small and too hard to get away," Hashemi
said. "How could we get an airburst to hit all of the
people?"

"Couldn't," Abdul decided. "Let's try the other target."

They drove back to the subway, found a parking spot
and left the car. This time they took the two suitcases that
had been locked in the trunk. The subway ride downtown
seemed faster the second time. More people were moving
each way. Times Square station was jammed with people.
They got off at Thirty-fourth Street and walked over to
the Empire State Building. The guided-tour desk was

closed. So was the elevator ride to the observation platform.

They wandered around the lobby until a uniformed guard asked them if he could help.

"Observation ride?" Abdul asked.

"Closed for some minor repairs," the guard said.

They thanked him and walked outside. They moved down one side of the large building and found what looked like a maintenance entrance. Yes. Men in coveralls with all sorts of names on their backs went in and out.

"We have our entrance," Hashemi said. "I just wish we knew exactly where we were going."

"No time," Abdul said. "If we spent two days researching the place, finding drawings and taking a tour of the underground area, someone would get curious. It's got to be tomorrow morning. We'll bluff our way through. We're air-conditioning experts. They will show us where to go."

The two men did not look like Arabs. Both now had short haircuts, hair lightened to a brown, no beards or mustaches, and hands and face lightened with creams. They found a small hotel toward the Hudson side of Manhattan and ate and then slept. They had to be at their best in the morning.

The next morning, the Arabs walked to the side workman's entrance of the tall building. Both wore coveralls with stitching on the back that said they were "Best Air Conditioning." Both carried black bags such as workers carried that usually would contain the man's tools. Abdul slowed as they approached the workmen's door. Then he stopped and let three men go ahead of them. He speeded up and joined the other three heading in the door all in a group. Once inside they asked a guard where the broken air-conditioning system was.

"Don't know of any breakdowns," the guard said.

"That's what we're here to find. Where are the main units?" Abdul asked.

"Fourth level down, that would be D level," the guard

said. He grinned. "Oh, yeah, you take the freight elevator right over there."

He pointed to an elevator with the doors closed. The two Arabs went to it and waited. Two security men rushed past them and down the hallway.

The car came and they got on. There were three other men already on the car.

"What level?" one asked.

"Four," Abdul said, putting down his case. The car stopped at each level and men got on and off. When they came to level four, the two Arabs were the only ones left. The door opened and they stepped out.

They were in a semifinished corridor that looked like a forest of pipes and many ducts and tubes overhead and on both sides. They saw no one. They walked down one way in the tunnel-like passage until they saw a door leading to the left marked MAIN ELECTRICAL. Farther on there were two more doors. One of them opened into a side tunnel that was totally unfinished. Raw rock and dirt made up the ceiling and sides. In the middle stood a huge concrete pillar eight feet in diameter going down into the ground and upward through the rock of the ceiling.

"Support column," Abdul said, and they went back to the main corridor. Fifty feet on down the tunnel-like passage they came to three men working on a junction box on the wall. Abdul walked right past as if he knew where he was heading.

"We could have asked directions," Hashemi said.

"Sure and have somebody remember us?"

"Won't matter if they're all down with the pox," Hashemi said in a soft rebuttal.

They kept walking until they came to where all of the pipes and tubes turned upward and vanished through the top of the tunnel. They had seen four or five other workers, but passed them by. Now they headed back the way they had come. Halfway to where Abdul figured the elevator was, they came to the same three men working on the open electrical box on the wall.

"You guys lost?" the tallest asked.

"Told us the main air-conditioning units were down here on fourth level," Abdul said.

The three laughed.

"Yeah, the guard up there gets his jollies sending new guys on wild-goose chases. What part of the air-con you looking for?"

"The intake elements. Something is wrong with them."

"He sent you on one, all right. Most of them units are up on underground one, which we call level one. Damned intakes have to be open to the ambient air, wouldn't you guess?"

"Yes, of course. Level one."

"Right and all the way to the other side of the building. They really got you messed up."

Abdul led Hashemi back to the elevator. They had to wait for it.

"Don't worry, we have time. I built in time. If we can't do it by midmorning, we wait until three o'clock. Then we let loose all three canisters and rush out of here as fast as we can."

"We use the half stick of dynamite same as usual?"

"No, for this one we only need the timer detonators. They are as powerful as a dynamite fuse. Blow that aluminum all to pieces."

"We set the fuses for a half hour?"

"At least. Who's going to find them? Nobody will be looking."

"What about those security guards we saw?"

"They have them all over the building. How could anyone know we would come here? Not even the FBI could guess that good. They have a whole huge country to protect. Not a chance they know this building is our target."

"We dump the canisters, walk out like we belonged here, and then what?" Hashemi asked.

"We take off the coveralls, throw them in a trash bin, catch the subway back to our rented car, drive to the airport in Newark, New Jersey, and take a flight home. Nothing to it. Now let's get out on the first level and find those intake ducts. They must be huge. All we need is one of them we can get to. We look over the situation, find a place to hide, then wait until it's the right time. Let's move it. This is the payoff time, the day that I've been waiting for, for most of my life."

★ THIRTY-ONE ★

The Specialists went on duty at 5 A.M. There had been a meeting before that of the various agencies involved. The FBI was the lead and control unit. They called the shots. CIA had an observer on hand to help identify the suspects. The FBI and the Specialists were the front-line troops.

In close backup was the team of bioweapon experts from DEST, an action group from FEMA, the Federal Emergency Management Agency, the Environmental Protection Agency, and the Department of Health and Human Services. Each had a big job to do if the front-line troops didn't stop the smallpox bomber.

Kat and Ichi drew the assignment of watching a door on the side where employees and maintenance people came into the building. There was a guard there, but he didn't check IDs of visiting maintenance or repair teams.

"We're watching for one or two men who look like Arabs and who are carrying large toolboxes or equipment bags," Wade told the pair. "Just a general look over. Don't be obvious. Stand well back from the door, but if you see anyone who is the slightest bit suspicious, pull them out and check their gear. It's tough because we don't know for sure what they will look like when they come. We're not even positive that this is the target, but we think so."

Kat twisted her mouth the way she did sometimes when she was miffed. "I wanted inside where the action will be," she said.

Ichi chuckled. "You always want the hottest action. Hey, if we stop them right here, there won't be anything going down inside. Let's look alive, the workingmen are starting to arrive."

Just after six-thirty, Kat came away from the wall where she had been leaning. "Check the third guy back. An Arab for sure."

"True, Kat, but he isn't carrying anything, not even a lunch pail. He couldn't be our man. He looks too much Arab with his mustache and beard. We know that old Abdul has changed his appearance for this outing. Light brown hair and no beard."

They let the Arab pass.

Inside, the FBI had been shown the air intakes for the big air-conditioning system. There were several stations where fresh air was pulled in, filtered, and then processed through the air-cooling system.

Most of the air intakes were on the ground floor, but some had been installed on the twentieth floor. Those on the ground floor were at the side and back of the building where they could do their job with the least noise and not ruin the architectural beauty of the structure.

Wade and Roger settled into hiding spots near the number-one fresh-air intake on the side of the building. They were in a room and near a screen of air ducts that fed the two-story intake area. One major intake had a ten-square-foot mouth that sucked air into the maw of the gluttonous air-conditioning system. Wade could see the front of the intake where it had at least two mesh grills over it to prevent anything larger than a quarter of an inch wide from going into the air system. The smallpox vaccine would fly through with no trouble at all.

Duncan and Hershel had positions on a similar intake system farther along toward the back of the building and also on the ground floor. The FBI covered the three other inlet areas and had more than thirty other plainclothesmen roaming the ground floor, some posing as guards, others as tour guides.

Everyone was in place by 6:15 A.M. The Specialists all had on their Motorola radios and the communication was good even through the steel and concrete of the huge structure. The FBI men had their own radio net. All the FBI men carried 9mm Ingram submachine guns under their suit coats. They hung on a cord around their necks and were hard to see. Most people wouldn't know there was a weapon there.

Wade stared at the giant intake screens and tried to figure how he would do the job if he were Abdul. There was no good place to hide in this room. The sound of the fans was hypnotic and the noise considerable. It made talking in a normal tone impossible.

What could Abdul do except walk by, run in, and throw the canister into the mesh and let it shatter? There was no sump, no holding place for the air, so no place to drop the canister in with a timed explosive on it. Any explosive would be minimal, Wade figured. Abdul wouldn't want to attract attention to it or to damage the regular air-conditioning equipment.

Were they on a wild-goose chase themselves? Was this the one place in all of New York City where the terrorist would strike? Were they simply wasting their time?

If Abdul came into this room, he would be carrying something. Therefore, anyone entering the room carrying something as large or larger than the canisters would be suspect.

The door to the room opened. Wade tensed, fitting his finger into the MP-5's trigger. A uniformed man came in. Wade recognized the maintenance uniform of the building. He carried a clipboard and looked at some gauges and readouts on the intake equipment, made some notes on his clipboard, and left.

"False alarm here," Wade said on the net. "Just an inspector with a clipboard."

"Nothing doing out here," Kat said. "Saw one Arab-looking man go in, but he carried nothing. He looked too much like an Arab to be our boy."

"While we're doing the net, all is quiet at air intake number six," Hershel said. "*Nada, nada.*"

Abdul and Hashemi left the elevator on the first level, one down from the ground floor. "We'll walk up the stairs and see what the lay of the land is up there," Abdul said.

At the landing on the ground level, Abdul opened the door an inch cautiously and peered out the crack. There were many more people here than on the floors below. He saw two men in suits he was sure were FBI. They looked stiff and out of place. Down the hall twenty feet he saw a men's rest room.

"We go out one at a time and into the men's bathroom down there. Give us a place to lie low for a while. We're early anyway. I'll go first."

Abdul walked halfway there before he saw a man staring at him. He was one of those out-of-sync guys. Abdul waved at the guy and went into the men's room. Once there he headed for the stalls, went in one, and closed the door. He breathed easier. He hadn't counted on so many people being around. Only one man was in the bathroom and he left. Abdul heard someone come in and looked out.

Hashemi. He motioned him over into the stall next door. Quickly, Abdul took a clipboard and a pen out of his bag, then pushed his black bag with the two bombs in it under the partition.

"Watch this. I think the bags are what are attracting attention. I'll go out and survey the place, find the right spot to place the canisters, and be back."

"Yeah, good idea."

With the clipboard and pen, Abdul drew no special notice. He walked most of the hallway on this side of the building and found two doors marked, AIR-CONDITIONING. He went back to the one nearest the washroom he had been in. He opened the door to the air-conditioning room and walked in. For just a second he was puzzled, then he strode deliberately to a set of dials and gauges on the side of the huge air intake. He read dials, put down readings, checked around the side and back of the device. Yes. Press the canisters against the screens and they would be pinned there by the flow of air.

Then he saw the foot-wide grills a foot from the back of the intake that were built into the outside wall. Huge fans somewhere sucked in air like a small tornado. He nodded, then made another note on his clipboard and left the room. For just a moment in there he had the feeling that someone was watching him. He shook his head. Impossible. There wasn't much of a place for a man to hide.

He walked back to the men's room and went into the second stall from the end where Hashemi should be.

"Found it, the perfect spot. About fifty feet down this hallway. A separate room with an air intake open to the outside. We move in, set the timer for fifteen minutes, ease the canisters against the intake screen where they will be held fast by the strong incoming airflow. Then we walk out on our way to New Jersey and home."

"When?" Hashemi asked.

"Precisely at ten-thirty. That will be in about a half hour."

"I'm getting tired of sitting on this damn stool."

"So stand up a while."

Wade twisted slightly in the cramped space and shrugged his shoulders high, then let them down to relieve the tension. He had the patience but not the practice for this stay in one place for ten hours without moving job. He pushed the Motorola send button.

"Net check," he said into the lip mike.

"Kat watching."

"Ichi out front."

"Duncan cramped and waiting."

"Hershel ready to collapse."

"Roger rarin' to go."

"Hold tight, we're coming up on midmorning. Prime terrorist time. Hang in there."

Five minutes later, Wade looked up as two men came into his room. They both carried black tool kit soft bags. Both wore coveralls with the name of an air-conditioning firm lettered on the back. He started to relax. One of them was the same man he'd seen with a clipboard less than a half hour ago. He brought up his MP-5. He couldn't risk a radio transmission.

Roger coughed where he was hidden on the other side of the room. Both men with the black bags froze. Then one ran for the screen in front of the air intake. He opened the bag and took out an aluminum cylinder. Four pistol shots slashed into the closed room, exploding like grenades in the restricted area. Wade had his MP-5 tracking the man with the canister. Head-shot, he told himself, to protect the canister.

The MP-5 chattered off three rounds. The runner stumbled and fell, the canister rolling away from him after a soft landing on the floor.

The other man turned and fired at Wade's position. He had no target, but he blasted six shots into the area where Wade hid. Two rounds nipped at his sleeve, one slammed past his head. Wade ducked and turned. By the time he came up where he could shoot, the man had bolted out the door and was gone.

Wade hit the Motorola switch. "Mayday. We've been hit. Intake room number one. One of his men is down. One canister intact. Second man running with black bag. Wearing coveralls with an air-conditioning firm name printed on the back. Close in on air intake room one."

Wade pushed out of the camouflage and rushed to the door. Outside he saw only people who should be there. He spotted an FBI man walking slowly. "You see a guy with a black bag come out of the air-intake room?"

"Nobody like that passed me."

Wade ran in the other direction. The elevator was near

and the stairs. Two FBI men rushed up. "You see a guy with a big black bag run down that way?"

The FBI men shook their heads. "Not past us."

That left the stairs. No time to get on the elevator. He had to go down the stairs. Wade rushed through the stairway door as he used the radio. "Somebody check on Roger in room one. He was fired at. May have been hit. I'm at the stairs chasing the other one down."

Two FBI men and Hershel and Duncan rushed to the air-intake room one and found Roger on the floor crawling toward the door. He had two slugs in him. The FBI called for an ambulance.

Hershel sat beside Roger on the floor. "Take it easy, big guy. The medics are on their way. You caught one in the thigh and another one up just under your shoulder. I've got the bleeding stopped. You'll make it to fight another day."

An FBI man pointed to the canister that lay three feet from the Arab. "That's the smallpox canister?"

Duncan nodded. "Yeah, get some of the DEST people in here with an airtight container, right now."

The FBI man used his radio. Duncan checked the Arab. Two slugs in his head and one in his neck. "This one is dead," Duncan said. The FBI man waved and went on talking on his small radio.

Wade took the steps slowly, pausing often to listen. He could hear shoes hitting the concrete steps. He moved faster. He went past the second level down, then the third and on to the fourth. The steps went down one more level. A sign on the door there read:

DANGER, THIS SECTOR ONLY FOR SPECIALISTS IN INDUSTRIAL POWER AND DISTRIBUTION.

The door was unlocked. Wade jerked it open, standing to one side behind the wall. Four shots blasted through the opening, but Wade wasn't there.

That was eight rounds. Would he have more magazines? Probably. Wade dropped to the floor and looked around the doorjamb. He saw a maze of pipes, ducts, tubes, wires, and what looked like a thousand other units for moving power, water, air, and steam. The tunnel had not been finished and raw rock showed in many places. It extended twenty yards straight ahead, then made a left turn. He could see no one in the area. Faint bulbs far apart gave off weak lighting in the tunnel.

"Give it up, Abdul. You're through. The games are over. That smallpox virus won't hurt anyone down here."

Two shots exploded from the front, the rounds echoing like thunder through the closed tube. Ten rounds. Wade held his fire. He didn't know what tube or pipe he might puncture down there. He didn't need a jet of scalding steam spraying into the area.

Something moved to the right not ten feet away. Then it moved again. A huge sewer rat more than a foot long stared at Wade, then scurried back under some tubing and out of sight.

Wade heard movement down the tube.

"Give it up, Abdul."

There were no answering shots this time. Wade spotted a place thirty feet down the tunnel where he would be protected from the front. He surged to his feet and sprinted for the cover. No shots came his way. Behind the pipes, he paused and listened.

He heard angry Arabic from the front. Some swear words Wade didn't understand. Was Abdul in trouble?

Wade picked out another spot of cover. The tunnel lights continued but were farther apart now. They had come on when the door opened. They were safety lights. Wade jolted through the void, heard two shots, and slid into the dirt floor behind a concrete support beam as two rounds skipped past him through the dust. Abdul had used twelve shots.

Ahead Wade could see the last lightbulb; beyond that was only darkness. Here and there a set of tubes and pipes turned and went upward through holes drilled in the rock roof to serve some purpose above.

He heard movement ahead, then more cursing in Arabic.

"This is a dead end, Abdul. You'll never get out of here.

You'll be dancing with Allah before time for evening prayers."

No shots answered him.

Wade stared into the soft light and the darkness. Once Abdul got back in there, the odds evened up. There was no way to stop him if he chose to go there. Wade had no flash-bang grenades. He heard someone behind him.

"FBI, if that's you back there by the door, hold your place. Don't shoot this way. Wade Thorne of the Specialists. Abdul is boxed in back here. Nowhere to go."

That brought a pair of shots from deep in the darkness. The rounds slanted off steel pipes and ricocheted down the tunnel. Fourteen shots. Most of the new 9mm pistols held fourteen rounds. Abdul might be out of ammo.

"We'll hold here," a voice said from near the doorway behind Wade.

He looked ahead again. No more cover. Abdul might be out of rounds.

Risk it.

Wade spotted a shadowy blackness twenty feet ahead just past the last lightbulb. He did a zigzag run in the narrow tunnel and dived for the cover. No rounds greeted him. A rat screeched its anger and scampered out of the shadow Wade had rolled into. It brayed its fury and ran into the darkness.

Two rats in the same hole, Wade decided. He stared into the dark. The pipes must continue, they had to feed this whole side of the huge building all the way to the top. Wade looked into the black void ahead of him, wondering what to do next.

Thirty-five feet from where Wade lay in the shadows, Abdul crouched behind a pair of upright steel tubes a foot in diameter that turned sharply from the floor and went straight up to the rocky ceiling.

He slammed in a fresh magazine. Now he had fourteen more rounds.

At first he decided to bring just one magazine for his pistol. More would be too heavy. Early on he had convinced himself there would be no shooting at all, so one magazine with fourteen rounds would be plenty. He had changed his mind and brought a second magazine.

They were waiting for me. How did the bastards know I was coming for the tall building? One of my men must have been captured and talked. Did they take down Omaha? Shit. They must have. Enough of this. How in hell do I get out of here? Only one way out, over the corpse of that FBI man in back of me. A tight spot but I've been in them many times and always come out a winner. Like recently when those fighter aircraft blew up my torpedo boat in the gulf. Only now I don't have a hundred miles of ocean to hide in.

Hide? Yes, I'll hide and let them come past me, then slip out the door and up the steps. It could work.

Something brushed past his leg in the darkness. What? Then he remembered spotting a big rat running into the darkness. He hated rats. He shivered. He felt a sudden sweat on his forehead and his hand trembled. Ridiculous to be afraid of a rat. It would be more afraid of him than he was of it.

Where to hide?

In the dimness he could see the pipes and tubes. At this point the tunnel was twice as wide. In places there were spaces between the pipes and the rocky wall. Yes. He moved slowly that way, not making a sound. He was sure the FBI was listening for him to move. Not a sound.

He wiped sweat off his forehead. Why was he sweating? It was slightly chilly in the rocky tunnel, not warm. He moved ahead, found his niche, and crawled over one large pipe that could be air-conditioning and past two smaller ones. Steam, maybe, or electrical conduit, even water.

He found the opening large enough. He couldn't move much, but they couldn't see him from the main part of the tunnel, even with strong flashlights. Yes, a good spot.

For a moment he felt dizzy. Why? He shook his head. It had to be the thrill, the rush of the chase and his chance to place the virus to kill a hundred thousand Americans. It would pass. But it didn't. The sweating came back and he frowned. Then he remembered the early symptoms of smallpox. A chill darted through him. He felt his forehead. No it couldn't be. It was. He had a fever and it was getting higher by the minute. How could it happen? How could he get smallpox? The headache hit him like an anvil and he shuddered. He began to ache all over. He was in the early stages of smallpox. One of the canisters must have had a minute hole in it or a flaw in a seam. He shivered again with a chill.

Abdul tried to settle down. He would get out of here and beat the disease. He could do it. The best doctors. For now he wouldn't make a sound, not until the FBI men were far past him down the dark tunnel. Some of them would have flashlights, or get them and explore the cavern all the way to the other side of the building. Then he would slip by them, take his two canisters, and plan another hit. It would happen. His spirits rose.

Something brushed his bare leg where his pants had slipped up. Then sharp teeth bit viciously into his leg.

Abdul screamed. He kicked his leg as much as he could. He felt blood flowing down his leg, into his shoe. The damn rat. Abdul screamed again, flailing with both legs. The rat slithered away.

He was panting; the scream seemed to unleash new heat in his system. Sweat poured down his face, stung his eyes. His breath came in gasps. One hand reached down to his wounded leg. He felt the blood, then a gouge where there was flesh missing. He bellowed another scream of terror and agony.

He waited for the FBI to move forward.

Instead something touched his outstretched arm. He jerked it back. The creature came forward and he could hear it sniffing the air, then it brushed his arm again. Abdul screamed three times and turned and fired four rounds from his automatic at the rat. The sound deafened him. He couldn't hear anything. Then the rat at his right leg moved in and bit him again. He heard something. It began slowly at first, then a hissing sound like an old-fashioned locomotive engine.

A jet of blistering hot steam blasted out of the ruptured

pipe where his second shot had punctured it. The steam hit his left leg first, tearing away cloth, roasting his leg in a fraction of a second. The pain seared through his brain, ravaged his whole nervous system. Three rats that had come to the feast clawed in fright, getting away from the deadly flow. The hiss of the steam drowned out his screams, which lasted only a few more seconds.

The rupture grew from the small bullet hole as the pressure ripped at the steel tube. Soon the tear was three inches long and the steam bathed Abdul from head to foot.

He died before the steam tore at his cheeks and cooked the flesh off his torso.

Wade heard the first scream, then the shots, and the hiss of the deadly steam. He frowned for a moment, then bellowed at the FBI men behind him.

"Get some maintenance men down here fast to fix a ruptured steam pipe," he shouted.

"Steam pipe?" a voice came back.

"Yes, don't question it. Use your radio and get some experts down here to turn off this scalding, killing steam. Do it right fucking now!"

Wade waited, wondering if Abdul had the last two canisters of virus with him in the black tool bag. He must.

It was ten minutes before Wade sensed the steam flow slow. The hiss turned into a softer sound, then stopped completely.

"Bring up a flashlight," Wade called to the FBI men behind him. One did and Wade used it as they walked with careful steps toward where the steam had erupted.

They saw a dead sewer rat first. It had been scorched by the steam and half its skin peeled off. It had crawled away from the vent before it died. Against the far wall they saw where the steam had left a trickle of water coming down the rock wall behind some foot-wide pipes. Wade shined the light there and they saw what was left of a black-leather bag. It had been ripped in half and blown three feet away from the pipes.

Wade rushed to it and examined what was left. In each half he found a canister.

He used his radio, hoping it would carry. "Specialists, i

you can hear me, get the DEST people down here double time with airtight bags for the last two canisters. Make them move it."

"Hear you, Wade," Kat said. "I'm at the head of the stairs. We've got lots of power around here. Hold tight."

Two minutes later, as Wade and the FBI man watched the canisters, Wade's radio came on.

"DEST bio team is on the way. Just passed me running down the steps. A minute at the most. What's with Abdul?"

"Not sure. We haven't reached him yet. I think the leaking steam parboiled him. Haven't heard a sound from him since his screams cut off suddenly in the middle of the steam bath."

The DEST men ran up, checked the canisters, and sealed them in airtight triple-secure plastic bags. They put those in separate heavy canvas bags and carried them gingerly back down the tunnel.

"Our man?" the FBI man asked.

Wade shined the flashlight on the wall and the two worked toward it past the slow seep of water. Wade ducked under one of the pipes.

"Careful, that steel is still hot," he warned the man behind him.

Wade found Abdul crumpled behind the pipes against the rough rock wall. His face was gone, half his clothes had been blasted away. Two dead rats lay under his body. One large section of his left leg had been chewed to the bone.

Wade jumped back and kicked at a prowling rat, sending it scuttering away.

"Kat, we need a coroner and an ambulance. I just found Abdul. He's no more now than a footnote in history, a terrorist who died by his own stupidity. His hatred has at last turned on him, and dealt with him harshly."

★ THIRTY-TWO ★

The Specialists met in their New York headquarters far downtown and took stock.

"The FBI agrees with us that the death of Abdul puts to an end this bio-strike operation," Mister Marshall said in the situation room. "He may have one or two associates in the area we haven't accounted for yet, but they will be quiet and be gone quickly. Abdul was the driving force behind the Sword of Allah."

"Is there anything else that is urgent that we need to look into?" Wade asked.

"I haven't checked with London today, but there have been no red-flag messages. I'd say we're clear for the moment. Which brings up the point of some free time. Usually you get a week's option time after an operation. Would that be acceptable?"

Kat smiled and put down her coffee. "The Ironman is coming up in three days in Hawaii. I'd like to give it one more try."

Wade put down the *New York Times*. "There's a conference on Egyptology over the next three days here in town. I'd really like to attend."

Roger Johnson was back from the emergency room. He had a bandage on his left leg and one around his right shoulder. He said he wanted to visit some relatives in Brooklyn. "Then I'd like to drop in on the SEALs in San Diego and see if I still know anyone there."

Duncan Bancroft wanted to get back to England and take out his sailboat for a week's tour.

Hershel Levine had some fences to mend back home in Israel. Ichi wanted to stay in New York and visit some of his friends from the FBI.

Mister Marshall nodded as each one outlined plans. "Good, because I have a particularly tough merger to take care of here at the uptown office. You'll all get expense and travel money, and we'll see you back at the castle in ten days.

"Oh, there is one small item you might be thinking about. I've had reports that Osama bin Laden is in a major bid to take over the cocaine trafficking in Mexico. My sources say he already has control of one of the Mexican syndicates that accounts for over half of the cocaine and marijuana shipped into the U.S. and is working on the other syndicate. With his link to so many terrorist activities, he may be looking for new sources of cash."

"Bin Laden in Mexico?" Wade asked. "Now that is something to consider."

Mister Marshall stood. "Don't let it spoil your small vacation. You've earned it. I understand that the death toll in Wyoming is not as serious as they first thought it might be. The government flooded them with vaccine and all sorts of medical help and doctors. We were lucky on that one.

"Take care and we'll see you back at the castle."

Kat looked at Hershel. "Bin Laden, now he would be a challenge even for us."

ABOUT THE AUTHOR

CHET CUNNINGHAM, an army veteran of the Korean War, experienced combat firsthand as an 81mm mortar gunner and squad leader. He has been a store clerk, farm worker, photographer, audiovisual writer, and newspaper reporter. A former freelance writer, he has published 295 books—mostly action, historical, and western novels. He was born in Nebraska, grew up in Oregon, worked in Michigan, went to college in New York City, and now lives with his wife in San Diego.